ALSO BY SHARON BIGGS WALLER

A Mad, Wicked Folly

THE
FORBIDDEN
ORCHID

Sharon Biggs Waller

VIKING

VIKING
An imprint of Penguin Random House LLC
375 Hudson Street
New York, New York 10014

First published in the United States of America by Viking,
an imprint of Penguin Random House LLC, 2016

LIBRARY OF CONGRESS CATALOGING-IN-PUBLICATION DATA IS AVAILABLE
ISBN: 978-0-451-47411-7

Printed in U.S.A.   Set in Latienne   Design by Kate Renner

1   3   5   7   9   10   8   6   4   2

FOR my little sister Carrie Biggs
And for my niece Patricia Noelle XinLan Biggs
You are both my heart and soul

THE
FORBIDDEN
ORCHID

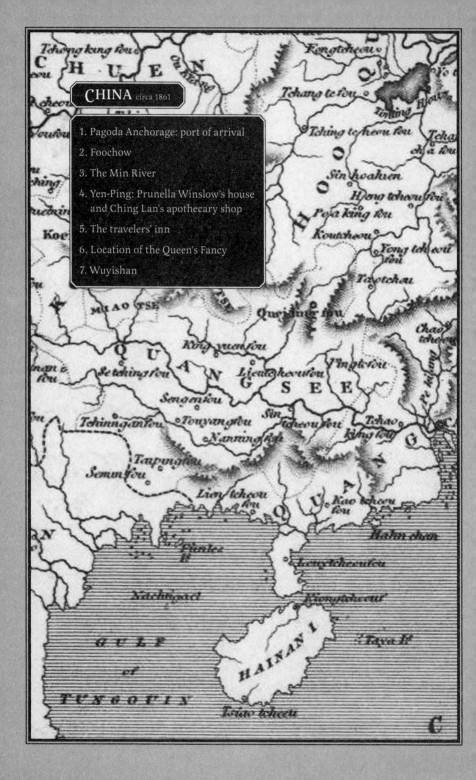

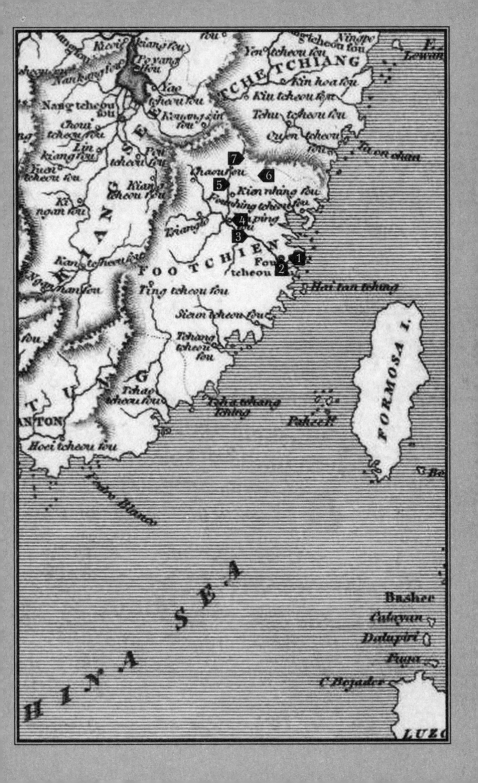

*"It broke one's heart to think of man,
the civilizer, wasting treasures in a few years
to which savages and animals
had done no harm for centuries."*

—Marianne North (1830–1890),
Victorian traveler and botanical painter
of tropical plant species in their natural habitat

PART ONE

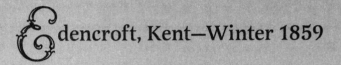

Edencroft, Kent—Winter 1859

ONE

y father was a plant hunter—an adventurer—and I saw little of him my first fourteen years, even less the next two, but after I turned seventeen he became my whole world.

He returned home once a year or so, as was his promise to our mother, venturing to our house in Kent each Christmas bearing strange gifts, such as a cachepot filled with prickly cacti, a geode—a large rock that split open to reveal a crystal treasure within—a brass ship's compass, and once a hessian sack of foul-smelling compost, which my father called bat guano. All things a boy might love, but certainly not a girl, my mother said. And we were a house filled with girls, each of us named after a flower. There were nine sisters, all born around the same time, begotten during my father's annual visit home. I came to regard Christmas as a herald, trumpeting the arrival of yet another sibling in late summer, most likely a girl. One more flower to add to a bouquet already bristling with un-wanted blooms.

One would think my father would be happy in a house surrounded by females named after flowers, but women and flowers are not the same. No matter how much rose attar eau de toilette or lavender powder we wore, we could not compete with the real thing. Flowers lured my father to faraway lands filled with savages, barbarian princes, exotic ladies in silk saris, and even marauding cannibals. My father wrote to us of his time tramping up and down hill and dale, canoeing rushing rivers and climbing rocky mountain passes in search of an elusive bloom heard of but never seen by a Westerner. His plant hunting continued through my childhood until September of 1860 when my father met his misfortune. Not through the poison-tipped arrow of a pygmy warrior, but by his own miscalculation. His headstrong behavior had come home to claim its due. Or so my mother said. My father said nothing.

The last time I saw him was in 1859 when he came to Christmas toting a large, mysterious box wrapped in brown paper. The year the youngest, Dahlia, was conceived. And the year I was sixteen.

Mamma always looked forward to Papa's visit, growing more and more excited as the date drew near. Instead of visiting the church every day, as was her habit, she spent those hours at her sewing basket, updating her wardrobe in the latest style. When the day approached, she sat near the window peering out at the street, waiting for Papa to arrive. He had always walked from the train station before, but this year he arrived in the back of a delivery cart, his long legs dangling down, his arm across the reason for the cart: the package wrapped in brown paper and tied with rough twine. Although Papa dressed in an elegant tartan waistcoat and a black coat, his bushy beard, befitting his status as an explorer, always gave him a raffish look.

Mamma rushed outside and threw herself in Papa's arms. And as usual, after a cursory hello to us, he whisked Mamma off, and we did not see them again until lunchtime.

"That shan't last long," Violetta said, her face grim. "If this rapprochement continues to Boxing Day, I shall be surprised."

"Violetta," I chided. But she didn't respond. Instead she plonked herself down at the piano and began playing Brahms's Piano Sonata no. 3, crashing her hands down on the keys a little harder than Mr. Brahms required for the somber piece.

Although Violetta was a devotee of gothic novels, she didn't often have fits of melodrama. But over the years she had stopped believing that our parents' affection toward one another would endure. Their love balanced on a knife-edge, and it took little to make it topple to the ground. I suppose Violetta remained cynical because it was too painful to wish for something that could never be.

Two days later, on Christmas morning, Papa presented the mysterious package.

He stood, his strong hands clasped behind his back, his eyes shining, as he watched my little sisters strip the brown butcher paper away to reveal a domed box made of glass, filled with miniature plants, dainty furniture, and tiny handmade twig dolls. There were ferns, mosses, and jumbles of strange-looking plants, including a clump of tangled roots that perched atop a little carved statue's head like a wig. Peony, Lily, and Delphine stared at the box, unable to make either head nor tail of it.

"Well now," Papa said. "How do you like that, my girls?"

"What is it, Papa?" six-year-old Lily asked.

Papa looked taken aback. "Isn't it obvious?" he said in a booming voice. "It's a dollhouse. I made it from a Wardian case! An absolute miracle of an invention. Plants can travel across oceans in Mr. Ward's cases remaining as fresh as the day they were collected. They are the very reason why your papa is the success he is."

Lily's eyes filled with tears. The other two hid behind my mother's skirts. Two-year-old Fleur didn't care one way or the other. She remained on the floor, happily banging blocks together.

My mother frowned at the little glasshouse. "Reginald," she said. "Is this the . . . *dollhouse*?" I could hear dismay prickling through her voice. I knew she had written Papa a letter asking him to purchase a dollhouse at Hamley's toy shop in London for the little ones.

"I thought the girls would prefer this, my dear," he said. I could see the doubt in his eyes. My heart cracked a little to think of his hands, so deft when handling delicate blooms, clumsily dressing the twig dolls in little scraps of material, gluing acorn caps to sticks, all in the hope of pleasing his daughters. He had no inkling that the contents of such a dollhouse would be torn to bits under my sisters' eager hands. Their fingers, sticky with jam, would smear the glass, and the little dolls would be lost amongst their jumble of toys in the nursery.

"It's a little fairy garden, Lily." I knelt next to her and put my arm around her thin shoulders. She shoved her fingers in her mouth and looked at me, her chin quivering. "Can you not see the little fairies Papa has caught for you?" She pulled her fingers from her mouth and reached out a curious finger to touch the glass. I folded it back down. "Mustn't touch, darling. Mustn't disturb the fairies."

"Fairies," she repeated. Her breath fogged the glass. "Where are the fairies?"

"Just there, darling." I pointed at the sticks. "Can you not see them hiding?" Lily leaned closer. Peony and Delphine crept out from behind my mother and joined her, staring into the tiny jungle.

"I thought little girls would like such a thing, Elodie," Papa said to me later.

"It's lovely, Papa. They are only young and don't understand how to look after such a treasure."

It was a kind gift, made from my father's heart, but I was sure I was the only one who saw it as such. My mother, constantly disappointed by my father, saw everything he did as a slight. But I didn't blame her. Papa could be a difficult man.

Mamma had married my father when he was a student at Oxford, studying to become a priest. She was a bishop's daughter, and for her the church was everything. But Papa, like many men of the church, studied the natural world as a fancy. Inspired by the writings of Mr. Charles Darwin, he went on a voyage to the Canary Islands of Spain, where he collected cacti. He was so good at acquiring plants that he was hired by wealthy men to gather plants for them to display in their fashionable glasshouses. Papa turned away from the church and from God and to a life of plant hunting. The year he turned away from the church, Mamma lost her firstborn, a son. Since then she has only given birth to girls, and Mamma believes this is God's way of punishing Papa.

Later on Christmas evening, Mamma and Papa had a horrible row. It was over the simplest thing: Mamma's choice of wallpaper. Mamma had recently papered the youngest children's room in a brilliant and beautiful shade of green, like the brightest emerald. Mamma had been proud of the room, but Papa was incensed. As soon as he laid eyes on the walls he tore the paper down, exclaiming and shouting. Mamma followed behind him, shrieking and grabbing at his hands.

"Poison, this is poison, don't you understand?" Papa said, tearing a long strip of paper down, exposing the whitewashed wall behind it. Some of the paper clung stubbornly to the walls, as though taking my mother's side.

"How can you say such a thing?" Mamma said, sinking onto Lily's bed in a flood of tears. "It's beautiful. Why do you ruin everything that's beautiful?"

Papa stared at her, stricken. He started to speak and then saw me standing in the doorway. He straightened up. "Elodie. My dear. Do you understand why I took the paper down? Do you know what makes this paper green?"

I stepped inside the room and looked at my mother. Her eyes were red from crying. "I . . . from the green dye, I expect, Papa," I replied hesitantly.

"This brilliant green can only be gotten from copper arsenite," he said. "As I have told your mother repeatedly." He cast an angry look at her.

"Arsenite?" I repeated.

"Arsenic. Poison. The paper puts off vapors that can cause constriction of the throat. And then death." Papa shook the clump of paper. "This . . . this prevalent color, most likely papering acres and miles of British walls, will kill people. Mark my words. I told your mother no when she wrote to me with her request to paper the room, but she's only gone behind my back . . ." Papa's words trailed off, and he looked down at the crumpled paper in his hands.

"No one believes that is true," Mamma said through sobs. "The paper man said he'd eat a pound of it himself."

Papa's face turned red with rage. "If the blaggard were here, I'd cram a pound of it down his throat!" he shouted. "And how can you take his word but not mine?"

I stood there, a few feet inside the room, unable to speak, almost in a trance, viewing the tableau as someone else would see it. Mamma sitting on Lily's bed, her bell-shaped skirts flowing over the tiny mattress, staring down at her slippers in despair. Papa, standing with one hand braced against the wall, a wad of green paper in the other, and an expression of anger mixed with confusion on his face. My parents were both beautiful: Mamma with hair light as a sunbeam, Papa's dark as a raven's wing. Mamma lovely and delicate, Papa handsome and strong. I used to think my parents were Staffordshire porcelain dolls come to life, stepping down off the mantelpiece, hand in hand, to become human. But now I think there was a mistake. The dolls were mismatched, created in different workshops but yet placed inside the same box.

I knew then that they really weren't arguing over wallpaper; I knew they were arguing over something that was far deeper and far more destructive.

Mamma went to her room and shut the door behind her. Papa closed himself in the children's room and finished stripping off the paper. My sister Violetta and I took all the children, frightened by the shouting, into our bedroom and made them beds on the floor and read them stories until they fell asleep.

Unable to sleep myself, I went to the kitchen and made a pot of tea. I'd forgotten my slippers upstairs with the children, and so my feet were bare on the cold tiles. I sat on the chair and tucked my feet under my nightgown, cupping the mug in my hands.

"Father is beastly," Violetta said. She stood in the doorway holding my slippers in her hands, her long dark hair hanging in a braid over one shoulder. "Is there any tea left?"

I pushed the pot toward her. She handed me my slippers and then went to fetch a cup from the scullery. Presently she returned, and I poured her tea.

"Papa isn't beastly, Violetta," I said. "He feels the wallpaper is poison, and I'm inclined to agree with him. But I do think he was wrong to rip it down like that. He should have been more tactful."

Violetta snorted. "Tactful? May as well ask a monkey to be tactful." She blew on her tea and took a cautious sip.

"That's unkind. Papa thought the children were in danger. Mamma saw her beautiful paper in ruins. The two had their own views on the matter, and they are both very passionate people. It was inevitable that they should become overly emotional."

Violetta eyed me over the cup and then sighed. She set her teacup down and dragged her shawl around her shoulders. "How can a color become poison? It's absurd!"

"How can water become poison? How can gas become poison?" I said. "There are many things we don't understand. Papa is a man of science, and he loves beauty, despite what Mamma says, so he'd be the last person to destroy something if he didn't think it important to do so."

"He did it to hurt Mamma," Violetta said, unwilling to see

any other side in the matter. She picked her cup up. "And I shan't forgive him. I hope he never comes back."

"Violetta!" I chided, but she turned her face away.

My heart ached over the division of our home. I tried to make it better, but the cracks were too wide, too difficult to bridge. But I knew myself. I knew I would not stop trying.

PAPA LEFT THE FOLLOWING MORNING, SAYING NOTHING TO MY mother and only a cursory good-bye to us. The little ones' eyes grew wide when Papa approached to kiss them, so he let them be. Violetta bobbed a curtsy and kissed his cheek, but her face was stone. I alone saw him out.

He held his hat in his hand, an old felt homburg that looked as though it had been sat on once too often. "You understand me, don't you, my dear?" Uncertainty skittered over his face. "You understand why the paper had to go?"

"I do, Papa." I hadn't the heart to tell him he should have been gentler and kinder when tearing the paper down. I knew that worry and fear can make people act in ways they wouldn't ordinarily.

He smiled, and it was the saddest smile I had ever seen. He put his battered hat on his head and fumbled in his satchel, pulling out a book. He handed it to me. "I meant to give this to you on Christmas morning, but I wasn't sure your mother would approve."

The book Papa handed me was called *On the Origin of Species by Means of Natural Selection, or the Preservation of Favoured Races in the Struggle for Life* by Charles Darwin.

"Have you heard of this book, Elodie?" Papa asked, his face eager. "Mr. Darwin published it in November. Quite extraordinary. I went round to the bookshop and secured a copy, and I'm quite glad that I did. The book sold out immediately." He took the book back and flipped through a few pages until he found the one he wanted and turned the book to face me. "Here Darwin makes a case for transmutation of species through natural selection. He says that every plant is shaped perfectly for its own pollinator, the two evolving side by side. That everything on the earth evolves according to its needs."

I took the book from him, glancing at the page he had sought. I had heard of this book. The deacon of our church, Bernard Wainwright, had preached a sermon against it recently, claiming that Mr. Darwin was trying kill God. I should have handed it straight back to Papa, but I wanted to read it. I wanted to read it very much, if only to see what all the fuss was about. I had been taught that God had created the world and all the creatures within it. But I also knew that people had discovered ancient creatures not mentioned in the Bible, in rocks throughout the world, even in our own England. These creatures no longer existed, and no one could explain them. Many people, even those in the church, were saying this proved stories in the Bible were meant to be parables and not to be taken literally.

My father had met Mr. Darwin many times. His home, Down House, was not far from our own, and both he and Papa belonged to the Geological Society. Like my father, Mr. Darwin had once been very devout, and a clerical student. But after he'd made his voyage on HMS *Beagle*, he became critical of the Bible and thought all religions might be valid, not just Christianity.

I hugged the book to my chest. Papa had always been very free about sharing his books with us, encouraging us to explore his library. Our parish school taught us girls the very basics, with an emphasis on religion and housewifery, and only until we turned thirteen. Papa hated that our education was so sparse, so he had a standing order with a London bookseller who sent us several books each month. I alone received them to unwrap the brown paper and twine and to shelve them by category, carefully writing down the titles in Papa's library journal. Violetta availed herself of the novels, but I loved the books on geography and natural history. My favorite book was an enormous leather-bound atlas that sat perched on a stand near Papa's desk. I spent hours turning the pages and then locating the countries on his globe, spinning it round slowly, reciting the names of the countries—exotic names like Ceylon, Malaya, and Zanzibar—wishing that I might someday see them for myself. "Thank you, Papa. I would love to read it," I said.

He tapped my nose with his forefinger, smiling. "Perhaps do so when you're on your own. Your mother is angry enough with me as it is. I don't think she'd like you to have such a controversial book." He kissed my cheek, put his hat on, and climbed into the waiting carriage. The horses stamped their hooves and chewed their bits, eager to be off. The carriage driver spoke gently to them, waiting for my father's command. Papa let down the window and leaned out. "Look after your mother and sisters for me, Elodie. I'm leaving for China next week to collect plants."

"Isn't China quite dangerous right now?" I asked. The Second China War, sparked by China's seizure of a British merchant ship, had been ongoing for several years, and although

China was a large country and Britain was prevailing, I worried that Papa might be swept up in the violence.

Papa waved his hand. "Oh, no. I'll be moving through the interior, well away from the action. The China War is not a conflict of the common man but rather one between the emperor and the West. Some of the villagers won't even know there is a war ongoing. I'll be perfectly safe."

"How long will you be away, Papa?" I asked, dreading the answer.

"I plan to return in October."

"Perhaps you will be home in time for my birthday."

"Your birthday?" Papa furrowed his brow. "Yes, of course, your birthday is in October, is it not? The twenty-seventh, I believe?"

"The first," I replied.

"Yes, yes of course. The first." He thought again. "I'm not sure, but I will try. I will write to you all, but remember it may take months for the letters to reach you. I don't want for you to worry, but if anything goes awry, you can write to Sir William Jackson Hooker at Kew, and he will assist you in my stead."

"Are you collecting for Kew now?" I asked, thrilled at the thought of Papa working for such a venerable institution.

"I have collected for Kew for the past several years." He smiled. "Only don't tell my employer. I don't think he'd like to know he's not my only priority."

The Royal Botanic Gardens, Kew, held the largest collection of plants in the world. Plant hunters traveled to the far reaches of the earth to discover new wonders for the garden. The most exotic of these lived in a marvel of glass and iron engineering called the Palm House, which resembled an upside-down ship. Inside, massive palm trees from faraway lands towered over delicate flowering plants below. Visitors stepped over the threshold, leaving cold, rainy England behind, and into a warm, steamy rainforest, the mist gentle on their faces and the scent of the jackfruit trees and flowering vines filling their senses.

Or so I'd read. I'd never been to Kew, which lay in Richmond upon Thames, an hour's train journey away. Indeed, I'd never left Kent in the whole of my life. Edencroft was my life and always would be. I would have loved nothing more than to see Kew for myself. *Dash it*, I wanted to go farther than Kew. I wanted to feel a real rainforest's mist on my face and smell the jackfruit trees in their native land and not in a glasshouse, no matter how marvelously built.

"I long to go with you, Papa," I blurted out.

"Oh, my dear," Papa said, his voice wistful. "If you were a boy, I'd take you with me directly you asked." He smiled. "The things I would show you! But alas, such adventures are not for you. Besides, I need you here to look after Mamma and the girls. You are my eyes and ears whilst I'm away, and I depend on you to remain my steadfast and dependable Elodie."

I felt ridiculous for showing Papa my heart and for making him voice what I loathed to hear: Because I was a girl, I would always fall short in father's eyes. I would never be able to make up for the loss of my brother. I would never be able to walk by his side. The only way I could make him proud was to remain home, locked like a fairy doll inside of a glass Wardian case, looking after the other fairy dolls. I looked down the road that led to the train station, unable to meet his eyes. "I know, Papa."

"Please tell your mother . . ." He hesitated and glanced at her bedroom windows, where the drapes remained closed. "Never mind. Good-bye, my dear." He tapped the roof of the carriage with his walking stick, and the driver clucked to his horses.

"Good-bye, Papa." I stood on the gravel drive and watched until the carriage had crested the hill and disappeared down the other side.

The weather was threatening snow, the sky grim and foreboding. I went inside and up to Violetta's and my bedroom. I tucked Mr. Darwin's book on top of my wardrobe, behind the ornate carving where no one would look, to read later. Then I went in search of the little glass dollhouse, finally finding it in the scullery. Our maid had placed it on a high shelf next to a stack of saucepans and copper bowls. I stood on a stool and fetched it down, trying not to jostle it and upset the plants. I carried it to my bedroom, where I placed it on my dressing table. I looked at the little dolls, the wee twig figures with the faces drawn on and little dresses made from scraps of hessian, and I couldn't help it. A great sadness overtook me, and I cried. I cried for my father's kind gesture, so misunderstood, and for my mother's broken heart, but most of all I cried for myself, because I wanted my papa.

I wouldn't see or hear from my father again until April of 1861, when the bailiffs came to take our possessions away.

TWO

y sisters had no interest in my father's gift, so I alone cared for the little glasshouse, which I kept on a shelf in our bedroom. But I didn't mind. The house and its contents stirred a fancy for plants I'd long harbored. A small conservatory attached to the back of our house had lain neglected for years, storing broken furniture, chipped crockery, and piles of old newspaper. In early February of 1860 I decided to return it to its former use as a greenhouse. I carried out all the rubbish and burned it on a bonfire, and washed the grime and soot off the windows, letting in a flood of sunshine. On my hands and knees, I scrubbed years of dirt off the flagstone tile floor until the former pattern shone through—a handsome red-and-gold diamond pattern inlaid with a twining green vine.

An old dilapidated fountain sat in the middle of the room. It was fed and powered by a small stream outside, and I wanted to see it moving again. I had no idea how to fix such a thing, but I had nothing to lose in trying. So I took it apart, drawing a diagram of where everything went so I could reassemble it. I cleaned all the bits and pieces with a small wire brush and put it back together. While the little children and Violetta waited inside, watching the fountain for signs of life, I removed my shoes and stockings, tucked up my skirts, and waded into the cold stream to locate the pipe that led into the conservatory. It was blocked with leaves and a dead frog, and so I pulled these out, wincing just a little when my fingers brushed against the frog's slimy skin. The water rushed into the pipe, and I heard the cries of delight from the children and the flowing of the water as it fell from the tiers of the fountain

I consulted my father's books about plants in his study to learn about botanical collection and cultivation. Bit by bit, I filled the room with pots of ferns, fuchsias, and primroses. The conservatory was my refuge, and when I was in it, I felt closer to Papa. Some of the plants, I found on my walks through the nearby woods. As I dug them up, I pretended to be plant hunting with Papa, discovering a new fern and exclaiming over it. It was a silly game, I knew that, but it comforted me.

Summer came and went, and Papa failed to acknowledge Dahlia's birth in mid-September, but that was not so unusual. It took at least three months for mail to reach us from the Orient. That, coupled with Papa's remote locations, meant we knew we'd hear from him rarely. We had already received the usual wodge of letters, all at once, when they arrived on a homebound China clipper in late spring, but we'd had nothing since then.

Mamma had a difficult time giving birth to the baby, laboring long and suffering more than she ever had before. Her stoicism and practicality had grown with every pregnancy and delivery, but there was something different about this one. She wanted Papa by her side, and nothing Violetta or I could say or do would comfort her. The village physician, Dr. Thumpston, visited her late in the day, hours after her waters broke, and dosed her with some sort of medicine, which calmed her for several hours but did nothing to bring the baby forward.

Late in the night, in her delirium, she called out to Papa time and time again, waking the children. Violetta and our maid tried to keep the little ones occupied in their nursery while I tended to Mamma, but her cries were so loud that the girls became frightened.

In the early morning I put my cloak on and hurried out to fetch Dr. Thumpston, who was not pleased to be drawn away from his breakfast table.

"She's been laboring harder than ever, Dr. Thumpston," I said as we walked back to our house. "Calling out for my father."

"Of course," he replied, huffing to keep up with me. "Of course she would. Any woman who has been abandoned by her husband would do so. She is suffering from melancholy. If she would only try to turn her attention to her baby, she would be delivered of it immediately."

I stopped walking. "I apologize, Dr. Thumpston, but did I hear you quite correctly? Did you say my father abandoned my mother? How did you come of this knowledge?"

The doctor took advantage of our pause to set his bag onto a nearby stone wall and lean over to catch his breath. Our village doctor was an elderly man, and not given much to smiling. He was as stout as he was tall, and Violetta had remarked on several occasions that his dour countenance coupled with his penchant for dark brown suits gave him the appearance and personality of a block of wood.

He cleared his throat several times before answering. "I have no direct knowledge of this, but anyone possessed of sense could see that your family has been abandoned. Is your father currently present? From what I understand, he has not been home for some time."

"My father is in China, sir," I replied. "His occupation bids him to be away from home for a goodly length of time. He has not abandoned my mother any more than a naval captain or soldier has abandoned his."

"Is your father a naval captain or soldier?"

"No, he—"

The doctor interrupted my reply with a glare, and the words stuck in my throat. "I have not the time nor the inclination to debate this with you." He stood upright, collected his bag. "Now, do you wish me to deliver your mother of this child, or shall I return to my home and finish my breakfast?"

I shook my head. "I do apologize. Of course, let us proceed."

As we walked along, the doctor puffing at my side, I couldn't get the word the doctor had used out of my head—*abandoned*.

❧❀❧❀

WITH THE USE OF FORCEPS AND CHLOROFORM, DR. THUMPSTON coaxed forth our new sister. After my mother had a cursory look at the child and named her Dahlia, Dr. Thumpston dosed her with another cup of medicine, and she fell into a sleep that did not abate for days.

When Mamma had failed to rise from childbed after the customary fortnight, Dr. Thumpston prescribed Collis Browne's Chlorodyne to help her exhausted nervous system recover, but she seemed drained of all life. She wanted to lie abed, rousing only to attend church, and even then she was in a daze, mumbling into her folded hands during prayer and staring round her with wide eyes during the lesson.

Because Mamma was unable to look after herself, much less an infant, Violetta and I minded the rest of the children while a nurse hired from the village saw to Dahlia. The doctor, snapping his bag shut and handing over another bottle of Collis Browne's Chlorodyne, said she would recover soon and that we shouldn't worry, but as the days drew on, I began to feel as though my mother and father were both gone. And never coming back.

When my seventeenth birthday arrived in October, Mamma was too ill to assist me in changing my wardrobe, so on my own I lengthened and widened my skirts by sewing on a wide flounce and donning one of my mother's cage crinolines. It took me a little while to get used to my new silhouette, and indeed I had to move many of my plants up to a higher shelf so I wouldn't turn them over while I worked. The first morning I wore my new clothing down to breakfast, Violetta jumped up from her place and hugged me hard.

"I forgot it was your birthday. You should have said something, Elodie," she said. "I could have baked something special for tea."

"Never mind, Violetta," I said, stepping back from her embrace and taking my seat at the table. At seventeen I was now an adult, and fripperies and birthday sweets were for children.

"I could have at least helped you with your skirts."

It was sweet of her to say so, and I could have asked her to help me, if only to have someone to talk to while I sewed. But more and more I was learning that I preferred to do things on my own, and I found that I liked my own company more than anyone else's, which worried me. I wasn't sure why I felt this way, but even with my sister, my dearest friend, I felt somehow wrong and awkward in her presence.

I used to have a friend from school. Her name was Cordelia Brooks, and we had shared everything together, but just before Dahlia was born I started to draw away. She stopped believing me when I told her I had to go home, had to see to the children. Her feelings were hurt, and soon she stopped handing me sweets from her father's confectionary shop after church, stopped asking me to visit, stopped speaking to me. It was as though we had never known each other at all. It was my fault, and I knew it. So now, at church, our gaze would meet for a brief moment before she looked away, pretending she didn't see me.

I felt no one could understand me because I didn't understand myself, and I didn't know how to explain it. So I chose to be alone than confront this new truth.

My days continued on, one sliding into the next, their very sameness blurring them together. Rise, wash, help our maid, Mary, start the fires, see the little ones dressed, the middle ones off to school, sit with Mamma, fetch the children home from school, help Mary prepare tea, feed the children, wash the children, put them to bed, sit with Mamma. And again and again. In between all of this I managed to snatch time in my conservatory or an hour outside the village searching for new plants. If I hadn't had those little respites, I would have run mad.

October drew on, and Papa hadn't returned to England. Nor had we received answers to our letters or word of his whereabouts. Mamma grew more and more despondent as her letters went unanswered and no word came from him. She stopped asking after the mail, and with each day's passing she seemed to get a little worse. I couldn't help but think Papa's presence would help her greatly. In early November I wrote to Sir William at Kew, who replied that he had not heard from my father, either, nor had he returned on the ship he'd booked passage on, which had returned to England in late September. But Sir William noted that the China War had clogged correspondence coming out of several treaty ports in that country, and that my father might be on his way home as he wrote. I shouldn't worry, he'd written.

But he might as well have told me to stop breathing. This was the longest we'd ever gone without hearing from Papa, and the fact that he hadn't gotten on the steamship alarmed me. I knew in my heart that something was wrong.

Mamma's illness and my father's disappearance had become the talk of the village. It seemed that we were either the family to pity—ten females on their own without a man to help them— or the family to scorn: what moral misstep had Mamma made that had caused my father to abandon her without a word? Why had she not made a home of perfect peace to encourage Mr. Buchanan to stay with his family?

It was impossible to walk to the village without being stared at or tutted over. Our situation made Violetta so angry that her repeated slamming of our bedroom door caused the plaster over the lintel to fall away and reveal the lath beneath.

"He's missing," I told Violetta, insisting she listen. "He's not abandoned us. I'm sure he remains in China. Somewhere."

"Then why hasn't he written? Why hasn't he sent word of his whereabouts?" Violetta was sitting in the window seat on the upstairs landing, her knees tucked up under her skirt and a book facedown on the embroidered cushion.

"Perhaps he cannot," I said. "Perhaps he is in a very remote area."

"Do you know what one of the Thatcher girls said to me today?" Violetta turned away from the window, her face rigid with anger. "Suzette—the one with the blonde ringlets and front teeth as large as headstones. She said she'd heard that Papa had the bailiffs at his heels, and that is why he remains abroad. She asked me if that was the truth. I said nothing. I snubbed her and left her standing there with her ridiculous mouth gaping like a trout's."

I sat down next to her. "You should take no heed of such gossip. Who cares what they say or think? It doesn't make it true."

"But what if it *is* true?"

"Dearest, there is no proof to this. We have money aplenty and nothing to worry about on that score."

Violetta scowled out the window toward town as though she could hear what the people were saying that very moment. As for me, I went on enduring the unwanted attention of the villagers and hoping desperately that Mamma heard none of it.

Christmas was a grim affair.

With Papa still in China and Mamma still unwell, Violetta and I did what we could to make the holiday merry for the children. But even little Delphine knew something terrible had taken hold of our parents. All the girls, save Fleur, Chrysantha, and Dahlia, who were too young to understand, played with their Christmas dollies quietly, declining to pull their crackers and picking at their plum pudding. The pantomime at the church hall on Boxing Day was the only thing that made them laugh, apart from nine-year-old Calla who was terrified of Clown, and shrank down in her seat and hid her face in my shoulder whenever he appeared, finally giving way to tears when Pantaloon and Clown began chasing Harlequin and Columbine. I took her home at the interval, leaving Violetta and Mary to mind our remaining sisters.

When I arrived home with Calla, the afternoon post had been. On the hall table amongst the jumble of dolls' clothes and frayed ribbons sat a letter addressed in copperplate and affixed with a wax seal stamped with the word KEW. It was addressed to Mamma, but I knew it could only have come from Sir William Hooker, the director of the Royal Botanic Gardens, Kew, whom Papa had left as his proxy.

I sent Calla up to the nursery to play with her doll and then turned the letter over in my hand, considering whether to give it to Mamma. If Sir William knew of Papa's whereabouts, I wanted to know it first so I could prepare her if the news was bad.

I took it over to the window, where some light from the afternoon winter sunshine streamed through, and broke the seal.

December 26, 1860

Dear Mrs. Buchanan,

I have received word that Mr. Buchanan had been caught up in some conflict in

September while collecting specimens for Royal Botanic Gardens, Kew, and was taken prisoner along with several other Englishmen. I understand he had been injured, to what extent I am not privy, but I'm told reliably that his healing is ongoing and that he will make a full recovery.

Mr. Buchanan is returning home on a steamship as I write and should be arriving in England in early February. I will keep you apprised of any further news. If there is anything I can do for you or for your family, please do not hesitate to ask.

I remain your humble servant,
Sir William Jackson Hooker

Relief and fear filled me in equal measure. Papa had been injured. How badly? And then a very selfish idea occurred to me, one that made me so ashamed I blushed with the thought of it. If Papa was injured, then he'd be forced to come home, at the very least so we could nurse him back to health, but maybe he would be so happy here that he would remain. Forever.

I folded the letter and went upstairs to Mamma to tell her the news, hoping that she'd be able to comprehend. All the while I chided myself for my wicked thoughts.

I sat on the side of Mamma's bed, where she lay staring up at her canopy. "Mamma," I whispered. "Papa will be home in February. I've had word from Sir William at Kew." I held the letter up. She turned her head, and for the first time in months, smiled.

January of 1861 came and went, and Sir William wrote that Papa's ship would be docking any day. As the first week in February unfolded, Mamma took to sitting in her window, staring down the road, waiting for Papa to arrive.

The second week of February drifted past, as did the third. Finally we heard from Sir William, who told us that Papa had arrived in England, taken a cottage in the grounds of Kew, and had chosen to remain. He was suffering from melancholy and wanted time alone, Sir William wrote, promising that he would keep us apprised of any further news.

"Why don't you go to him?" I asked Mamma. "Convince him to come home, where we can look after him."

"No," she said. "I don't agree with the way your father has lived his life. His headstrong behavior caused his troubles, as ever. I'm weary of trying to convince him to stay home and to stop taking chances, but I can't nail his boots down."

"But Mamma, maybe—"

"No, Elodie. I've always held your father by a gossamer thread. The last we saw one another, on that ill-fated Christmas, I felt that thread begin to sever. Don't you understand, Elodie? He's chosen. He wants to live apart, and I will not give up the little pride I have left by begging him to return."

"I'm so sorry, Mamma." I hugged her close.

She kissed the top of my head. "I tell you, my daughter, do not fall in love with an adventurer. Your heart will never stop breaking."

Mamma left her window, returned to her bed, and refused to rise.

THREE

I don't think this medicine is doing my mother much good," I said to the doctor at the end of February. "She only wants to sleep."

"Forgive me, Miss Buchanan, but sleep is often the best medicine." He smiled tightly and handed me yet another bottle of Chlorodyne.

"How much sleep could she possibly need? It's been months since Dahlia was born. Mama lies in bed constantly, and when she's about, she has the look of a corpse."

"All the more reason to keep to the regimen. These things cannot be rushed, my dear."

"Perhaps this concoction is doing her more harm than good." The medicine's bottle was a very pretty cobalt blue, stopped up with a wide cork. Underneath the medicine's name was a motto that declared: *The Most Valuable Remedy ever Discovered: Assuages pain of every kind, affords a calm, refreshing sleep without headache, and invigorates the nervous system when exhausted.* A list of ingredients in very small print ran round the base of the bottle. I'd never thought to look at them before, but now I held the bottle close to the sunlight coming from the window to read it better. *Morphine Mur., Ext. Cannabis Indica, Nitroglycerin, Oil of peppermint.*

The last ingredient, oil of peppermint, was the only one I recognized, as we used it while making sweets at Christmas. "Perhaps one of these ingredients causes her to sleep."

Dr. Thumpston's tight smile immediately transformed to a tight frown. Violetta was mistaken in her assessment of the man. Dr. Thumpston, with his round, red face, rather looked like a wheel of Dutch cheese. "I don't think a young woman such as yourself would understand if I explained how the tincture works, and what is more, I don't think it's in your best interest to have such knowledge." He cocked his head to the side. "And I'm unsure as to whether I welcome these queries from you. You have not studied the art of medicine, as I have. Has it escaped my notice? Are females now licensed by the Royal College of Physicians?"

"I'm merely asking—"

"And I'm merely telling you such knowledge is not for you." He set his bag down on the floor and took my wrist, turning it over and laying his fingers upon the inside. His hand was cold and his touch grasping. He lifted his pocket watch and consulted this for a few moments, his lips moving as he counted. He nodded to himself and then tucked the watch away. "It's as I thought. Your pulse is elevated, which is quite harmful for a virginal young girl such as yourself. You need to consider your fertility and safeguard yourself against anything that would bring harm to it. I fear you've become overwrought and I dare say bordering on hysteria. Perhaps caring for your mother and your sisters has undone you."

I pulled my hand away. "I disagree, Dr. Thumpston; I feel quite well."

But the doctor went on as though I hadn't spoken. "Do you have relatives that can help you?"

I shook my head. Both sets of grandparents were dead. There was an uncle somewhere in Scotland, but my father never spoke to him, and we didn't know much about him. My mother had a sister who lived in France. I supposed I could write to her, but she had children of her own, and leaving them would be a hardship for her.

"Hmmm," the physician said, looking thoughtful. "I can recommend your mother to an asylum and the younger children to the care of the parish. I'm sure the parson can find a place for you and Miss Violetta as governesses. It might be the best thing for you and for them. We must think sensibly now. Your father is out of the picture. . . ."

I stopped listening to him, because right then I would have dearly loved to shove him into the nearest armchair, put my knee on his chest, and pour the damnable mixture down his own throat, just to see how he would like it. But such an outburst would most likely result in my own committal to an asylum. Calmness was the order of the day.

From the corner of my eye I saw a scrap of pink print cotton swing past the door. Then Violetta peered inside the room and made a face, her nose scrunched up in distaste, but she did not come in.

Coward! I mouthed as the doctor bent down to retrieve his bag. Violetta shrugged.

"I suggest you take fifteen drops of the Chlorodyne yourself," the doctor said. "It will do you no end of good."

I wanted to say something else; to tell him that I was unable to lie about when I had things to do, but nothing I said would do any good. Instead I went to fetch his payment from the box in my father's desk. But at last I was unable to hold my tongue.

"I'm unsure as to how you've made the leap from a simple question to having my family smashed to bits," I said, giving him the money. And then I held my hands behind my back in case he wished to grab them again

"I'm only looking after your well-being, as is my job."

He hesitated, regarding me for a moment as though to make an assessment as to whether I was sane enough for him to leave the house. What he was looking for I do not know, but I stood at my full height and did not slump or shy away. Perhaps he was expecting me to burst into tears under his steady gaze or wring my hands in misery, but I was my father's daughter. And my father would never back down from such a ridiculous man. Finally he sighed, took his hat and coat from our maid, put them on, and left.

Violetta came into the room. "Good riddance to bad rubbish."

I gave her a long look. "Thank you for your help earlier."

She scowled and threw herself into the upholstered chair by the fire, swinging her legs over the arm. "And subject myself to his pinching hands and quackery? No thank you. I believe that doctor hastens people to their death directly they see him. As soon have the Grim Reaper touch them as Dr. Thumpston, I'd say."

"We have no choice. There's no other doctor available unless we take Mamma to the next village, and she's certainly in no fit state to travel." I sat down on the other chair, placing the blue bottle on the little table next to it. "Dr. Thumpston would tell me nothing about this concoction. And he made me feel stupid for questioning him."

"What else did you expect? You're a virginal girl; he's a learned man. You must think about your fertility." Violetta said this in a perfect imitation of his voice—low and pompous.

I laughed. Violetta could always make me laugh. But then I sobered. "Did you hear him talk about placing Mamma in an asylum and the girls in the care of the parish?"

"Those are mere words," Violetta said. "I doubt he could bring about such a thing." Her tone was light, but I could hear the doubt behind it. As females, we had little input in our own decision-making. And with our father absent, our situation was precarious at best.

"He could if he had others on his side, such as the parson."

"Reverend Tuttle would never agree," Violetta said. "I know he wouldn't."

I hadn't the heart to point out that Reverend Tuttle's age and frailty had forced him to give more duties to the new deacon, Bernard Wainwright, who barely knew us. Deacon Wainwright acted as our reverend's assistant and would become ordained and a full priest in a year's time. I doubted that Reverend Tuttle even knew Mamma was unwell. Deacon Wainwright, as a new-comer, had shown himself eager to please, and I was sure he would agree with the doctor's assessment immediately.

"We have to find some way to communicate with Papa," I said, even though I knew exactly how Violetta would react. Lately the near mention of the word *papa* was enough to send my sister in a snit.

Immediately her face hardened, and she swung her legs to the floor and stood up. "Much good may it do you."

"If he knew what condition Mamma was in—"

"He wouldn't give a pin," Violetta said.

"He is unwell, Violetta; you know that."

"He has the ability to come home to his family. He can be melancholic here! Let us put him and Mamma side by side so they may stew in their own sad thoughts together."

"Violetta!"

"And so then, how will we go to see him? We need someone to accompany us. We've never been out of Kent. Do you know where this garden is?"

"Richmond upon Thames," I said. "It's only an hour's train journey away. I'm sure dafter people than us have worked out how to get there."

But Violetta paid my comment no mind. "Do you know how to hire a hansom cab if we need one? I certainly don't. And what if we arrive and Papa refuses to greet us? He won't reply to our letters, so what makes you think he'd see us? It would be a fool's errand."

"Papa would never turn us away—"

"Of course he would! I don't know why you insist on seeing the good in him! In taking his side. Always. He's never shown himself to be anything more than selfish. He put us in this situation. If he were here, we wouldn't have to be pushed about by men like that doctor!"

"I can't give up on him like you can," I said quietly. "He loves us. I know he does."

"Then show me the love, for I cannot see the evidence." Tears pooled in her eyes, and she dashed them away with the back of her hand. "The man you speak of is one created in your own imagination. He doesn't exist!"

"I'm sorry, dearest. I didn't mean to upset you. Please sit down and let us be friends again—"

"When are you going to understand that he'll never love us? Never. We'll never compare with his flowers; he'll never see us over them. And I don't wish to be friends. Not just now!" In a swirl of petticoats, she stomped out of the room.

I didn't go after her. Instead I sat slumped in my chair, staring at that pretty blue bottle that promised to cure everything.

⁂

I DRESSED FOR CHURCH THE FOLLOWING SUNDAY AND DECIDED THAT I would seek out the new deacon about the medicine. Fresh out of university, Deacon Wainwright would likely know what the ingredients on the Chlorodyne bottle were.

At last, the organ wheezed out its final chord, and the service was over. I sent Mamma home with Violetta and then went up to him after the last parishioner had left.

There were several things that put me off of Deacon Wainwright, and so I'd never directly spoken to him before. His sermons were filled with hell and brimstone instead of forgiveness and God's love, as were the topic of our usual vicar's sermons. I'd often left church filled with dread rather than happiness. In truth, I felt God's presence in the forest and while tending my plants more than I did in the deacon's church.

Earnest to the brink of mania, Deacon Wainwright had embraced every aspect of his occupation, which was to look after the weaker members of the parish, namely the poor and the ailing. As to whom these might be, that was up to the deacon's discretion, which caused him to overstep his bounds, as

I had learned last week when he'd scolded Violetta for reading *Wuthering Heights* under the big oak tree on the common. "An unwholesome tome," he'd said, glaring down at her, and suggested she read the Book of Common Prayer instead. I'm not sure what offended Violetta more—that he'd poked his nose into her business, cast aspersions on her favorite novel, or used the word *tome*.

He'd also managed to step on the toes of the local schoolmistress, who taught the six- to thirteen-year-old boys and girls of the parish at our only school, which was patronized by the church. He sorted through her curriculum in front of the children, and then stood chiding and correcting her as she taught. Lily and Calla had come home in high excitement, explaining how the indefatigable Miss June had stood at her desk, her face coloring from pink to red until she looked like she might explode from fury. I often longed for my school days, but that day I was glad I no longer attended.

His care for the weak, however, did not include everyone. He refused to have anything to do with an unmarried mother of a baby boy, called Jane Dunning, who had recently arrived in Edencroft. She lived in a shabby one-room cottage in the shadow of the parish workhouse. Whenever she went abroad, the villagers hissed terrible words at her, such as *harlot* and *whore*. Only the baker would serve her, and that was just because of the little boy. Miss Dunning refused to fall upon the mercy of the parish and enter the workhouse, and so she took in work, unsavory work that no one else would do, such as cleaning up after the village dogs and selling the resulting pure to the tanner, and picking stones from the claggy soil in the nearby farmers' fields. Mamma was furious that no one in the parish would help Miss Dunning, and before she fell ill she often took baskets of food and cast-off clothing to her.

Deacon Wainwright blinked down at the slip of paper where I'd written the Chlorodyne's ingredients, his brow furrowing in concentration. "Of course I know what these ingredients are," he said, tilting his head back to speak to me. Deacon Wainwright wasn't a short man, but I was a tall girl. I'd ignored the advice several women in the village had given me on numerous occasions to slump so as not to intimidate men with my inexplicable and unfeminine height. God had made me tall, and I saw no reason to question his wisdom in doing so. He'd also made me curious, so I saw no shame in seeking out answers. But for some reason or other, certain men found my height and my curiosity exceedingly annoying. Perhaps it was the devil in them that caused them to act so.

Deacon Wainwright frowned and then stepped up onto the pulpit's bottom step to consider me better.

The deacon had lovely eyes, rather the color of a tortoise-shell cat's fur—brown with speckles of gold—and trimmed by very long lashes; they appeared strange coupled with the rest of his face, which was long and unremarkable. He looked as though God had assigned him someone else's eyes.

"The morphine is derived from opium, but unlike opium, its qualities do not create cravings," the deacon went on. "In point of fact, several missionaries I know who work in China are helping opium sots to overcome their taste for the stuff by providing them with morphine tablets. The sots take these, and soon they are back on their feet and returned to work in the rice paddies and tea gardens."

"But Mamma is not back on her feet. If that is the case, then this morphine isn't doing what it's meant to do."

"Perhaps the savage Chinaman has a different constitution from the delicate Englishwoman, such as your mother, Miss Buchanan."

"And the other ingredients?" I asked him.

He broke his gaze. "Ah, for flavoring, I believe. To make the concoction . . . less noxious."

"I understand the peppermint for flavoring, but this cannabis indica?" I turned the paper to him and pointed to the name. "What flavor does that give?"

He turned to two elderly ladies who had toddled up, leaning on one another. "Ah! The Misses Jenkins! And how did you find the lesson today?"

I waited for a moment, hoping Deacon Wainwright would turn back to me, but instead, he stepped down from the pulpit, took each lady by the elbow, and helped them down the stone steps and outside. I had the feeling that Deacon Wainwright didn't know what the ingredients were at all, and this made me question his knowledge of the morphine.

I sighed, and thus dismissed, I went home, only slightly the wiser for my questioning.

At home, Mamma was abed again, having had her dosage of the medicine. I wasn't convinced the Chlorodyne was as harmless as Deacon Wainwright or Dr. Thumpston claimed, and I made sure to keep control of the medicine so that Mamma couldn't have access to it. I was terrified she would go into a sleep so deep she'd slip away into death.

That night, I lay awake in bed, staring at the blue bottle of Chlorodyne perched on my nightstand. Perhaps I had no right to question the doctor; after all, he had my mother's best interest at heart.

I wondered what Mamma felt when she took the medicine. If I knew what Mamma was experiencing when she was under the Chlorodyne's influence, then maybe I could stop worrying.

I pushed the blankets aside and swung my feet onto the rag rug. Fifteen drops in water, the doctor had said. Maybe I should try it. I looked at Violetta on the other side of the bed, fast asleep. Then I took up the bottle, pulled out the cork, and held the bottle over my water glass, carefully counting as each dropped settled, blooming into the water, turning it a murky brown. I stopped the bottle with the cork and set it aside, picked up the glass and took a tentative sniff. The water held a faint smell of peppermint and something else. Something sickly and cloying.

Violetta snorted in her sleep and rolled over, turning her back to me. I took a tiny sip and made a face. Despite the peppermint oil and the other flavorings, the medicine tasted overly sweet; so sweet that it made my teeth ache.

Faint heart never won fair maiden, so I shoved my braid over my shoulder and downed the water in one gulp. I set the glass down and settled back onto my pillows, expecting to be taken by the medicine right away, but I lay awake, staring up at the celling for a while, feeling nothing.

A quarter of an hour later, a tingling lit my body, and I relaxed fully into the mattress, every muscle in my body losing tension. I had stubbed my toe on the iron bedstead in the children's nursery earlier in the day; I could still feel the throbbing, but I no longer cared about it. Followed by this, a sense of euphoria overcame me, as though I were flying in the air like a kite. No. Flying untethered, like a bird, like a hawk. I worried about nothing; I only knew happiness. I was no longer fretting about my parents. Instead, I imagined myself at my father's side, in a foreign land, filled with flowers of every color and size. I could smell them. I could almost reach out and touch them. This reverie went on and on, never ceasing, until, close to dawn, I finally slept.

When the sun had risen, my euphoria was over, and in its place was a sense of despair like I had never known, as though everything had been taken from me. As though the sun would never shine again. Violetta later told me that she could not rouse me, and so she left me. I finally struggled awake, hours after I normally did, feeling wretched. I wanted to cry. I wanted to crawl under my blankets and take more of this capricious elixir that gave life and took it back so easily.

When the clock struck ten, I forced myself to rise, fumbling to dress myself, my fingers slipping on my blouse buttons. I carried the bottle outside and dumped it out under an oak tree. I hurried to the house and refilled the empty Chlorodyne bottle with weak tea and, as we didn't have any peppermint oil, the essence of peppermint I'd extracted from mint leaves and boiling water. I didn't want Mamma to have any more of the Chlorodyne. I didn't care what the doctor said.

I was right to destroy the medicine. Day by day, Mamma returned to herself. At first prone to fits of crying and bouts of nausea, she eventually agreed to walk around the garden with me and Violetta, and then we expanded our wanders to the village and eventually the downs. After a fortnight of this regime, the bloom began to return to her cheeks, and she began to resemble her old self. She was still very quiet and continued to miss our father, but she no longer lay in bed hour after hour.

"Did I not tell you the medicine would work?" Dr. Thumpston said on his next visit as he handed me a fresh bottle, which I swiftly decanted under the oak tree directly he left, replacing it with my own recipe of weak tea and peppermint infusion.

"You did, Doctor, and we are ever so grateful," I said, nearly gagging on the lie, but it would do me no good to tell him what I had done.

"I hope you've learnt your lesson not to question those who know better than you."

"Oh, I have," I told him. "It does me no good to argue." This was, of course, the truth.

FOUR

tried to occupy my mind and hands so as to keep from worrying about my family. I spent as much time in my conservatory as I could. The little children were happy to sit splashing their hands in the fountain or playing quietly amongst the plants, while I worked.

At Christmas, Violetta had wanted the shelf in our bedroom for her new books, so I placed Papa's little glasshouse in the conservatory. And at the end of February, a strange thing occurred. The conservatory was quite cold at night, and this appeared to suit the odd little plant atop the carved statue. I had assumed it was only a jumble of dried roots that Papa had used to make a wig for the statue, as they had lain dormant for over a year. But by and by, the roots began to change, pushing out leaves, and then a single stem, followed by a tightly closed bud. And then in early March, the bud burst into the strangest flower I had ever laid eyes upon. It was tiny, only the size of a twopenny piece, and it was the darkest purple—almost black at certain times of the day. It possessed a large bulbous pouch underneath three curving petals. What use this pouch served I could only guess. I wondered if my little plant had a matching pollinator, as Mr. Darwin claimed, and if the pouch lent itself to this purpose.

I opened the little window on the house and reached in to touch the bloom. The petals felt like the softest skin, not flowerlike at all. And the scent of it, wafting through the open window, was exquisite—the most delicious raspberries topped with a dollop of vanilla cream. The flower captivated me so much that I snatched time away from my duties to lean over the glasshouse's open window, staring at the bloom and inhaling its fragrance. The bloom lasted and lasted, never going over, never fading. It was as though it were touched by magic.

A few days after the flower bloomed Deacon Wainwright and his mother came to call, and since our maid and Violetta had taken the children to a puppet show and Mamma was in bed, I received the pair myself.

After making chitchat, I invited Deacon Wainwright and his mother to see the conservatory. I must admit I made the offer because I had run out of things to say to them, and as I often saw him tending the rectory's small cottage garden, I thought he might find the bloom as captivating as I, and that this might put us on some common ground.

Mrs. Wainwright demurred when I made the invitation, behaving as though I had invited her to view the contents of our rag and bone barrel. "Bernard, are you sure you want to go into such a place?" She bobbed her head as she spoke. She wore a very old-fashioned bonnet that covered her entire head, a peaked tarlatan widow's cap tucked underneath it, with streamers hanging down each side of her face. The whole thing was tied onto her head with a large black velvet bow. She was a widow and had continued wearing mourning for her husband, and her black crape skirts were so voluminous that one couldn't tell the actual size of her. "It must be thick with flies and moths of all sorts. Think of the miasma. Think of your constitution."

"I'll be quite fine, Mamma," Mr. Wainright said, pressing his mouth into a smile. He set his teacup on the side table and stood up. "I'm sure Miss Buchanan is an excellent housekeeper, and I'll wager she banishes all pestilence from her plants."

I would have to make sure to steer Mr. Wainright away from the corner where I stored my earthworm casts and ladybird house.

Mrs. Wainwright reached out a gloved hand. "You know best, Bernard. But I shall remain here by the fire."

Deacon Wainwright squeezed her fingers. "Not to worry, Mamma."

I was filled with annoyance. *Mamma. What man calls his mother Mamma once he is out of the nursery?* My hand itched to reach out and slap him. I could picture it, my arm shooting out, my fingers and palm making contact with his cold cheek, the loud crack it would make, and his unaccountably beautiful eyes widening with surprise, his mother leaping to her feet and bursting into tears.

Shame filled me for even thinking such a thing. What was the matter with me? Mr. Wainright was a kind man, and I was a wicked girl to have such thoughts. Such terrible thoughts.

The dismay must have appeared on my face because Mr.

Wainright looked concerned. "Are you all right, Miss Buchanan?" he asked. "You look quite pale."

"I'm . . . fine, thank you," I stammered. I held my hand toward the conservatory. "Shall we go?"

Inside the cool conservatory, the sunlight beamed through the glass, turning the plants' leaves and fronds a bright green. And with the scent of the soil filling my nose, I couldn't help but feel calm and happy again. I found I was truly pleased to share it with someone new, even if that someone was Deacon Wainwright.

"My word, Miss Buchanan," he said, pausing next to the fountain, and watched the water shoot up into the air and fall into the little pond below where I had planted tiny lily pads. "You say you repaired the fountain yourself? How remarkable."

I showed him all around the conservatory, pointing out plants and naming them for him. He seemed quite enchanted.

"You do know, of course, Miss Buchanan, that plants and nature are very good for the soul's salvation. I'm pleased to see you embracing this very wholesome fancy. I quite approve." He glanced around my conservatory and smiled. I noticed that his mouth never curved up when he smiled. It remained straight across, rather like a mail slot. His deacon's hat must have been too small for him, because it had made a perfectly circular dent into his curly brown hair. His air of solemnness mixed with this comical appearance made him look quite ridiculous and quite stupid. . . .

"Here," I said, quickly reining in my unkind thoughts. "Here is my pride and joy. My favorite thing. My father gave us this little house one Christmas and only recently this flower appeared. It's an odd little plant but quite beautiful, as I'm sure you will agree." I opened the window and stood back. "To get the full effect, you must lean over the window and inhale its scent. The perfume is only present in the day, not the evening. As the sun starts to set, the fragrance goes."

Mr. Wainright smiled his mail-slot smile and stepped forward. He leaned over the house, and I could hear a little whistle coming from his nose as he breathed. He sniffed and sniffed, and remained unmoving for a long while, his expression dreamy, seemingly captivated by the flower's hypnotic charm.

"I'm so pleased you find the bloom as enchanting as I do," I said.

He glanced at me for a moment, a faraway look on his face; and then his gaze drifted back to the flower. He appeared to be fixating on its large pouch. He glanced at me again, his eyes slightly glazed over and his cheeks the color of the postbox itself. Apart from the flushed cheeks, I'd once seen that expression on a ram's face as he was let out into a meadow full of sheep. As I was thinking this, Deacon Wainwright's eyes dropped to my bodice and stayed there. He swallowed, his throat tightening.

I followed his gaze down, expecting to see toast crumbs or compote on my bodice, but then I understood what he had been looking at. He had been ogling my breasts. I crossed my arms over my bodice, embarrassed.

My movement jerked him into awareness. He averted his gaze, pulling himself loose from whatever thrall had overtaken him. He cleared his throat and then placed his fingers over mine, snapping the little window shut so hard that the flower swayed on its perch.

"Miss Buchanan." He lifted his hands to his head and pressed his fingers against his temples. "I'm at a loss as to understand how you came to possess such a flower—"

"As I said, my father—"

He held up a hand. "Please, do not interrupt. This flower is an orchid and most unsuitable for a female to look at, much less own."

"Why?"

His face colored even redder. "It is not for me to say why, but you must get rid of it, immediately."

"Well I won't, unless you tell me why! You appeared enchanted with it, yourself."

"I cannot tell you. It would be . . . unseemly." He clasped his hands in front of his chest, as though to pray.

I shrugged. "Well, I care not, Deacon Wainwright, whether it's unseemly or seemly. I love this flower, and if you can't tell me why such a harmless bloom is forbidden for a female, I'm afraid I will not listen to your advice."

"You are very willful," he said, eyeing me with a haughty look that I found most offensive, and I wanted, once more, to slap him, and this time I did not feel guilty for it. "I blame the bloom for that. It's as they say, orchids raise the heat in a person, and you are a prime example of this."

"Bernard," came a voice from the door of the conservatory. "Dearest, I'm growing quite cold. I believe there is a draft in that sitting room." The brim of Mrs. Wainright's bonnet poked into the room.

Mr. Wainright flicked his fingers toward his mother. "Mamma, I would ask you to come inside and look at this flower. Miss Buchanan does not believe me when I tell her she must rid herself of it."

Mrs. Wainright took a hesitant step into my conservatory, holding her capelette around her as though to keep any moths from fluttering their tiny feet against her. Her wide crinoline nearly turned a table of potted freesias on their heads as she swept down the aisle.

She reached us and lifted her spectacles from a chain around her neck and held them to her face. When she peered into the glasshouse, her eyes, already magnified by the spectacles' lenses, widened even further, and she let out a little shriek. "Oh, my word!" She stepped back, dropped the spectacles and began to fan herself with her hand. "Oh, my word."

"Do you see?" Mr. Wainright asked. "Please forgive me, Mamma, for upsetting you. I was trying to tell Miss Buchanan that the plant is quite unsuitable for females."

"And Mr. Wainright refuses to tell me why!" I wanted the two of them to leave my place immediately. They were ruining it. I regretted inviting Mr. Wainright in.

"I will take my leave, Miss Buchanan, and perhaps Mamma can explain it to you." He left as though chased by a demon, his shoes tapping quickly on the tile floor, *clickity clack*, *clickity clack*.

Mrs. Wainright took my hand, her tulle glove scratchy against my skin.

"My dear Miss Buchanan. An orchid is not appropriate for young ladies," she whispered, as though the plant would hear us. "Its shape, particularly the bottom part, is very like . . ." She paused, groping for the right word. "The . . . uh . . . *male*, and the top part is very like the female."

I stared at her for a long moment. "What," I finally said, "are you talking about?"

She bit her lip, her face coloring. "The bottom half, this . . . pouch"—she was whispering so quietly that I had to lean in to hear her—"resembles a man's . . . parts. And the top of this flower resembles a lady's"—she waved her hand below her waistband—"bits."

"Oh," I said. I looked at the plant, and I could see it, at least I thought I could see it, having never seen the male part myself, but it made sense, it all made sense. Then I couldn't help it. I began to laugh and laugh despite Mrs. Wainright's sputters of indignation.

And I could not stop.

FIVE

 felt very badly for laughing at Mrs. Wainwright, and indeed I wrote to her expressing my apologies, but I refused to rid myself of the orchid, and nothing Mr. Wainright or his mother could say would make me budge.

The orchid looked nothing like our little British bee orchid that I often saw in the hedgerows lining the lanes. Instead of a bulbous pouch below its petals, the British bee orchid had an appendage that resembled a bumblebee, and indeed I had read that this was an adaptation used to trick a male bumblebee into pollination. I could never bear to dig the bee orchids up to add to my collection. They gave me much delight as I passed, and I assumed they would delight other passersby, too.

I wrote to my father about my orchid, hoping that perhaps news of this wondrous flower would cause my father to respond, but he didn't reply. I tried again, this time sending the letter to Sir William, the director of Kew, hoping he might intervene. Sir William wrote me back himself, saying he would do what he could to encourage my father to write.

Toward the end of March, our maid announced a visitor. As Mamma was a-walk with Violetta and some of my sisters, the maid brought him into the conservatory, where I was watering my potted plants. The man was richly dressed in a long black frock coat, a gold watch chain dangling from the pocket of his waistcoat. A pearl pin studded his ascot, and he held a cane walking stick and bowler hat in his hand. He bowed slightly when I saw him.

"Forgive me, Miss Buchanan, for barging in on you like this." He glanced around the conservatory. "My, what a beautiful room. Your father's work, I expect."

"No. My own, but thank you all the same, Mr. . . . ?"

He stepped forward. "Pringle, Erasmus Pringle, at your service." He bowed again and then tucked his bowler under his arm.

I recognized the name. Mr. Pringle was the man who paid my father to go out hunting for plants. He was a well-known collector and a very rich industrialist. He lived on an estate in West Sussex.

"Very impressive that a girl should put together such a pleasing display." He pointed his cane at a display in question, which I had created by stacking fuchsias and begonias on risers so they looked like a vertical garden.

"I'm afraid your visit is wasted, Mr. Pringle, and I do apologize," I said. "My father is not here. He lives at Kew now."

Mr. Pringle waved his walking stick. "No, no, I understand he's ensconced himself at Kew. I've tried to correspond with him, and he's not replied to me. I quite understand he should want some time to himself after what he went through in China.

Terrible business. Terrible. But I've indulged him long enough."

"I'm sorry, sir, but I don't know the details of what befell him. We understand from Sir William that he was in an accident but was unharmed. Perhaps you'd care to enlighten me?" I couldn't help but feel alarmed. I had assumed Papa had fallen or had been robbed, and that the loss of his plants had caused his melancholy. It was upsetting to me that this man knew more about my father than I did. And he behaved as though my father belonged to him and not to us. As though he had more right to him than we did.

Mr. Pringle looked at me for a long moment, saying nothing. He seemed to be wrestling with himself, weighing the words in his head before saying them out loud. Finally he spoke. "I don't think it's my business to say, but his ordeal was written about in the newspapers around Christmas of last year. Perhaps you might contact the *Times* for an answer."

"But if it's public knowledge, then surely you can tell me?"

He smiled and said nothing. Instead he began to walk the aisles of my conservatory. "I want to ask your father if he would go back to China to retrieve more specimens of an orchid called the Queen's Fancy. A beautiful little thing. Quite small, dark purple, and with a scent that matches its color—a berry scent. It's very valuable, and I must say I've made a great deal of money on it."

"The Queen's Fancy?" I glanced toward the glasshouse. My own orchid fit that description perfectly. If it were as valuable as Mr. Pringle said, then perhaps he would demand to take it. I sidled a little closer to the glasshouse, standing in front of it to block his view.

"Yes. Its Latin name is *Paphiopedilum buchananii*, named for your father, as he was the one to discover it. But your father failed to collect for me that last time he went to China. Instead, he chose to travel to the north and collect for Kew. Alas, before he could do the job he was hired to do . . . well . . . there it is. I've sent men out to look for the orchid, but so far no one has been able to find it. I'm afraid these expeditions have cost me a pretty penny and with no return on the investment."

"Can you not grow new orchids from seeds of the ones you have? Or breed it somehow?"

He paused, leaning over one of my aspidistras, touching the leaves with his gloved hand. "Unfortunately not. Orchids are strange creatures, you understand. Devilishly difficult to keep alive, let alone breed. They keep their secrets locked inside. A beguiling flower, but she's most coy with her charms, not unlike many women." He straightened and smiled at me. "And the last Queen's Fancy perished in my stove in November."

"Your stove?"

"Pardon me. I mean my glasshouse. Conservatory, if you will." He gestured around my little room. "But steam-heated by a stove, as the orchids prefer it. Unlike your humble little place here."

"Forgive me, Mr. Pringle, but I don't know how I can help you. My father isn't communicating with us, either."

"Now why do I find that unlikely?" Mr. Pringle said this statement more to himself than to me, and I was becoming more uncomfortable in his presence. I wished the maid would come back in. Mr. Pringle used the tip of his cane to push some fern fronds aside. "Charming," he remarked.

I should have simply let him have the orchid, but I couldn't do it. My father had entrusted it to me, for what reason I didn't know, but I couldn't betray him by letting the man have it. And what was more, I didn't want him to have it.

It was mine.

I leaned back a little, letting my shawl slip from my shoulders and fall over the little house. I hoped it had covered enough of it. I hoped I hadn't draw attention to the glasshouse by doing so. But Mr. Pringle was staring at the fountain and hadn't seen me.

I stepped away and held my hand toward the door. "Perhaps you could come back when my mother is at home."

He sighed. "It's a shame." He tapped his cane on the floor. "I'm afraid I must insist that I speak with your father." He moved toward me. "You see, your father has not fulfilled his obligation to me. And he owes me quite a lot of money for that failed journey. I'm not a man to forgive debts."

"He owes money?" I was taken aback. As far as I knew, my father was paid well. He was not a wealthy man by any means, but we lived gently and were able to afford a few servants and a good-sized home. We did not keep a carriage or have much of a social life, but in rural Kent there weren't many balls.

Mr. Pringle leaned in close to me, closer than was socially acceptable. I could smell the cologne he wore and feel his wine-tinged breath on my face.

I felt the weight of my little billhook pruning knife in my pocket. I kept the curved blade sharp; so sharp that I was able to slice through the toughest plant stem with one effortless snip.

Mr. Pringle lifted the walking stick above my head. I stepped back away and slipped the knife out of my pocket, flicking it open, my arm tensed, ready to strike him. *One slash across the eyes. Just one slash would stop him.*

He tapped the stick against one of the pots on the tiered display and it toppled to the floor, taking its neighbor with it. The terra-cotta pots smashed to bits, tumbling the compost and the fuchsias onto the flagstone floor.

"I am ever so sorry, Miss Buchanan," he said. "I'm quite clumsy at times. It's a terrible thing to lose a plant." He stepped away, treading carelessly on the plants, crushing the delicate pink and white petals under his fine leather sole. "Tell your mother she will hear from me," he said.

"There's nothing more to say, sir," I said. I hid the billhook in the folds of my skirt, stunned to my core that I had responded so readily. It was as though I were taken by something else, something stronger than I was. I knew I could do it again. I could act in that way again, easily, if pushed. And the thought of it frightened and thrilled me at the same time. "It's as I said, we have no contact with my father. Your business is with him, not us."

"Oh, I fear you are mistaken, Miss Buchanan." He put his bowler hat on and touched his brim with his fingers. And then he left.

I waited a few minutes and then hurried to the front door to make sure he'd gone. And then I ran back to the conservatory and pulled my shawl away from the little greenhouse. *Never*, I vowed. *I will never let Mr. Pringle, or anyone, take my orchid. Or threaten me or my family ever again.*

I wrote Papa again about the orchid and the visit from Mr. Pringle, begging him to reply. But this time my letter was returned unopened.

SIX

To the Editor of "The Times"

Edencroft, Kent
April 1, 1861

Dear Sir,

I am desirous of receiving information regarding
an incident that befell my father, Mr. Reginald
Buchanan, toward the end of the Second China War
in that same country. He was collecting plants for
Kew in the summer of 1860 and fell into misfortune.
I understand that his sorry circumstances were
written up in your newspaper around Christmas
of 1860. I'm writing to ask if you can give me any
information in regards to this misfortune.

Yours very truly,

I hesitated, biting the end of my ink pen. If I signed my name, the editor might not be willing to disclose any information he deemed unfit for a female. I couldn't bring myself to be so dishonest as to write a man's name instead of mine, so in the end I used my first initial, letting the editor draw his own conclusions.

E. Buchanan

I blotted the letter, addressed and stamped the envelope, and took it to the post office myself to send straightaway before I had a chance to change my mind. After Mr. Pringle's visit, my billhook remained in my pocket. I felt better when it was within reach.

While I waited for the editor's reply, I kept myself busy. In addition to my father's books about plants, I had quite taken to Mr. Darwin's *The Origin of Species*. A lengthy and absorbing read, it required quite some time to make my way through. I kept stopping to consider each page. My favorite chapter was the one called "Miscellaneous Objections to the Theory of Natural Selection." Here Mr. Darwin considered objections made against his views, and I felt as though I were reading a guidebook to the natural world—God's manual about how he created it all. Even though many religious people had taken offense from the book, I was heartened to hear that some Church of England members had spoken in favor of it, including Reverend F. J. A. Hunt, the venerable scholar who had made a revision of the New Testament.

On the first Saturday in April, Reverend Hunt came to nearby Sevenoaks to lecture, and I, along with several other church members, accompanied by Deacon Wainwright, went to hear him. Reverend Hunt had been Deacon Wainwright's tutor at Oxford, and so he was eager to speak with him at the reception afterward.

"I was interested to read your comment on Mr. Darwin's book," I said to Reverend Hunt. "I was surprised that so many clerics approved of his theories." I didn't look at Deacon Wainwright, knowing that such a direct comment against him would fill him with disapproval, but I refused to change my opinion of Mr. Darwin just to please someone, especially someone who declined to let me have opinions of my own. It was odd, this unspoken row we continued to have with one another. Neither of us acknowledged it, but yet we both knew it was there, lingering, simmering under the surface. Perhaps if we had been able to acknowledge it, we might be able to become friends. But then again . . .

"Yes," the reverend replied. "As I wrote, in my opinion, it was a treat to read such a book."

"Miss Buchanan," Deacon Wainwright put in, "I fear you misunderstood the reverend's comments. He only meant it as an enjoyable read, much as one would enjoy a work of fiction. Mr. Darwin's *theory* is just that. A theory. There's simply not enough proof."

"Proof?" I asked. "Why does Darwin's book have to be iron-clad in its proof and substance and the Bible does not?"

Deacon Wainwright's eyes goggled. "The Bible does not need to be proven. Christianity is based on faith."

"But cannot faith apply to Mr. Darwin's theory, too? I haven't seen the Galápagos finches and tortoises, but I have faith in Mr. Darwin's observations."

"I believe in God rather than man," Deacon Wainwright said.

Sometimes I wondered if Deacon Wainwright was indeed twenty years old. He behaved as though he were much older, as though he were acting an older man in a play, and if you sat in the audience, you'd be convinced he were actually elderly. Only when you saw him up close would you realize that he was young.

"Sir," Reverend Hunt said, "I think you'll find yourself in the minority. Many men have embraced this theory as fact."

"I don't see why Mr. Darwin's theory disproves God's existence," I put in. "Every artist has his process. Perhaps in the fossils in the earth and in the Tree of Life, we are seeing evidence of God's work and how he created the world. What could be more astonishing?"

"Very well said, Miss Buchanan," the reverend said. "What an interesting young lady you are."

Deacon Wainwright did not comment. Instead he took a sip of his tea, looking as though he wanted to bite a chunk out of the teacup instead.

"I've memorized the ending of the book, and I think about it every day," I told him. "*From so simple a beginning endless forms most beautiful and most wonderful have been, and are being evolved*. So well said."

"It echoes Genesis, does it not, Miss Buchanan?" he said. "Deacon Wainwright. I wonder, have you actually read the book in question?"

"No, I have not. I don't need to read it." Deacon Wainwright set his teacup down on a silver tray on the side table with a clatter. "And what is more, sir, and please forgive me for saying so, I don't wish to. I refuse to speculate on the mind of God."

❧ ❧ ❧ ❧

UPON OUR RETURN HOME, I SAW A LETTER ADDRESSED TO ME IN UNfamiliar handwriting on the hall table. I could hear Violetta arguing with Lily in the sitting room, so I snatched the letter and crept upstairs before anyone saw I had returned home. I sat at my desk and slit the envelope open.

April 5, 1861

Dear Mr. Buchanan,

I have made enquiries with regard to the incident that befell your father at the end of the China War. I regret to say that I was unable to locate any article referring to Mr. Reginald Buchanan. The only incident at that time happened in mid-September 1860 and involved a correspondent for this very newspaper, Mr. T. W. Bowlby. After the allies captured Tien-tsin, Mr. Bowlby accompanied Admiral Sir James Hope and several others to Tungchow to arrange peace proceedings. They were set upon by a Tartar general and thrown into prison, where they were terribly mistreated. Only a handful of men lived to tell the tale of their torment. The individuals who lived said that the captors had tied their feet and hands behind their backs as tightly as possible with leather cords, and then tipped water on the bindings to increase the tension as the cords dried. The men were kept in this position until the condition of their hands and wrists became putrid and riddled with vermin.

Twenty-seven men were captured and taken to the Board of Punishments in Peking; of these, 12 died of their suffering, including 4 Englishmen—Mr. Bowlby, Lt. Anderson, Private Phipps, and Mr. DeNormann—and 8 Sikhs. Three Englishmen were released—Harry Parkes, consul at Canton, Henry Loch, and Hugh McGregor—and 11 Sikhs. One, Captain Brabazon of the Royal Artillery, remains missing presumed dead. The remains of the three Englishmen, returned by the mandarins, were all buried in one grave in a Russian cemetery. In retaliation for the men's ill treatment and subsequent deaths, the allies burned the Summer Palace to the ground.

I wish I could have been more helpful to you. Any further information it may be in my power to give is most heartily at your service.

Yours sincerely,
John Thadeus Delane
Editor of "The Times"

I dropped the letter as though it were painted in poison and pushed my chair back from my desk. An image rose in my mind of these men enduring their tortuous bonds, the straps growing tighter and tighter with each moment. I rubbed my own wrists, imagining the pain of it. To die from such a wound must be agony, and I wondered how the survivors had managed to live. As horrible as this story was, I was relieved my father was not part of it. But I had come to an impasse in regards to my father's ordeal in China. The news of his incident was not in the *Times* after all. I couldn't understand Mr. Pringle. Perhaps he had been fibbing to me, but for what reason? I sighed and tucked the letter in my writing case and went to tell Violetta that I was home.

❧ ❦ ❧ ❦

AFTER OUR OUTING, I HOPED THAT DEACON WAINWRIGHT WOULD not visit us for a good long while. But a week later he and his mother came to call. I was walking up the back lane after searching for plants in the wood, swinging my woven basket by the handle when I saw him. He was marching up the lane, leaning forward, as if a stout wind was at his back, his hands clasped at his chest as though in prayer, his black vestments fluttering around his skinny frame as he strode. His mamma accompanied him, clinging to his arm. I hoped they would walk past our house, but no, they turned into our front garden. I hid behind the oak tree waiting for them to go inside. *Dash it all! Why did they have to call and catch me on the hop like this?* My hands were filthy, and mud rimed the hem of my skirt. I was sure there were leaves in my hair, as I had been crawling through a thicket in attempts to reach a little fern that I wanted for my collection.

I hurried into the house, dropping my basket by the hall tree and wiping my hands on my apron, trying the best I could to get most of the dirt off. I bundled the soiled apron into my basket and went to find the visitors in the sitting room. There, Deacon Wainwright and his mamma were perched side by side on the settee, their hands in their laps, staring ahead like two grim puppets. Mamma sat across from them, dressed in her navy silk gown, which accentuated her porcelain skin and the smudges beneath her eyes, giving her the appearance of tragic heroine. Judging from the unladen tea table in front of Mamma, she hadn't expected them to call, either. Mamma would never receive callers without something to greet them with.

"Deacon Wainwright, Mrs. Wainwright, how nice to see you," I said. "I was not expecting you, otherwise I would not be dressed so. If you'll give me a moment, I'll make a pot of tea. I think there might be some scones or something or other," I said vaguely, having no idea what I might offer them. I had charged Violetta with the task of baking early in the day, but last I saw of her, she was squeezed into a corner of the dormer window in the attic nursery reading *The Tenant of Wildfell Hall*.

Mrs. Wainwright demurred. "That's quite all right, my dear. This is not a social visit." She shook her head, the lace on her widow's cap waving, and looked down at the carpet sadly.

"Isn't it?" I asked, unease crawling up my spine. Papa. Could they be here with news of Papa? Perhaps something dreadful had happened, and they were here to bring Mamma and me the news. *Please, God, do not let these two be the ones to deliver news about my father.*

"Do sit down, Elodie," Mamma said quietly. Her lovely brows were pinched together, and she began to massage her temples, the telltale sign of an impending megrim.

I sank down on the little footstool next to her; dread filling every corner of my body. "What is it?" I whispered to her. "Is it Papa?"

"It concerns that vile plant," Mrs. Wainwright said, answering for my mother.

For a moment I was confused, still thinking about my father. "A plant? Which plant? Do you mean one that my father sought?" I blinked. "Forgive me, Mrs. Wainwright. I'm at a loss as to what—"

"I've made enquiries as to returning your orchid to Sir William Jackson Hooker at Kew," Deacon Wainwright said, interrupting me. "As your father lives at Kew, they will know how best to return the bloom to him. If he does not accept it, then Sir William will know what to do with it." He pulled a card from his pocket and peered at it. "I contacted a Mr. Cleghorn in London, who is a collector of such things." He waved the card at me. "I described the bloom to him, and he has told me what you possess is quite valuable." He tucked the card back into his pocket and crossed one leg over the other. His mamma leaned over and plucked a bit of lint off his jacket, smiling demurely at him.

"I'm sorry . . . but . . . who asked you to do such a thing?" The tone of my voice was calm, but just barely. I knew, as sure as the sky was blue, that Deacon Wainwright had found a way to get back at me for playing him up in front of Reverend Hunt. His revenge was to take my orchid away. He'd managed the one thing he longed to do, to wiggle his way into our lives and begin directing things. He and his dear *Mamma*.

I felt my mother's hand on my shoulder. "Quiet, my dear."

"But, Mamma, I don't understand this. How is the orchid his concern?"

"It is every bit my concern," the deacon said, affronted. "As the vicar of this parish, I have your soul in my keeping. I cannot sit by while one of my members places her feet on the wrong path, the one that promises to lead her into a life of debauchery."

"You are not the vicar," I said. "You are only a deacon, yet to take your vows." Although my words were true, they were rude. I didn't care.

The deacon scowled. "You are quite lucky that I take any notice of you whatsoever, Miss Buchanan. You are very fond of your own opinion, and most men would not stand for that. As it is, I let you have your say and try not to cast aspirations upon it."

"I think you mean *aspersions*."

Deacon Wainwright stood up. "It's rude to correct someone, particularly for a woman to correct a man, or has no one ever told you so?"

I stood up, too. "Fine. You may go on saying the wrong things and looking ridiculous for it."

Mrs. Wainwright let out a little squeak of outrage.

"Elodie!" Mamma said.

"I can see you are not yourself right now," the deacon said. "And once more, this is perfect example of how that flower has affected you. Indeed Dr. Thumpston and I discussed this very thing only yesterday when he came to me, concerned about your welfare. I understand you have been pushing at him, questioning him about your mother and the medicine he prescribed, the very one you came to me about, not trusting the good doctor's opinion."

"Am I not allowed to ask questions?" I asked. "How ridiculous." I caught sight of Mrs. Wainwright, who had pressed her lips into a line until they nearly disappeared. Her fingers twitched in her lap as though she, too, longed to scold me—and perhaps to pinch me. Mrs. Wainwright had the look of a pincher.

"I will be back tomorrow morning to crate the orchid up and take it away. And then we shall put all of this behind us. Perhaps then you shall be released from this plant's grip and see sense." He put his too-small hat on, pulling it hard onto his head, his curls poking out around the edge.

"I shan't see sense! For if seeing sense means seeing things your way, then I'd rather be a lunatic." This I addressed to his back as I followed him and his mother through the sitting room and to the hall, where he opened the door and stepped out into the rain, leaving his umbrella behind in the wrought iron stand by the front door. I would not tell him he'd left it. He and his mamma could jolly well get wet.

I returned to the sitting room, where Mamma remained, watching the rain patter against the window. "Can you believe the deacon, Mamma? He thinks I'm going to let him take my orchid!"

Mamma shook her head and pulled her gaze from the window. "Elodie, I am in agreement with him. I had no idea you possessed such a thing. The orchid must go back to your father. As the deacon explained to me before you came in, it's not something a young girl should possess. I don't want you to be the talk of the village. It's bad enough people know your father is gone and we are women on our own."

My face burned with shame. I felt as though my mother had caught me doing something wanton and evil, possessing something unsavory. The thought of the villagers thinking this shamed me even more. And for a moment, just for a moment, I almost gave in, but then I tried another tack. "Papa gave it to us, Mamma. He wouldn't give me something unhealthy. I know he wouldn't."

"My dear, your father has very poor judgment in many things. I understand he also gave you Mr. Darwin's book, even though he knows I would disapprove."

"But Papa said—"

"Your Papa is not here!" Mamma said, her voice cracking with emotion. "He is not. And what is more, I do not believe he'll be coming back. I have to seek counsel from a man I trust, and the church is my solace, as it always has been. The bloom must go back. I cannot go against what the deacon advises."

"He's not yet a vicar!" I said, knowing my orchid was slipping from my grasp.

"As the deacon, he speaks for the vicar, and you know that. Please, Elodie, do not gainsay me. Please." Mamma looked heartbroken, torn between her love of the church and her love of me. I felt ashamed then, and I knew I had to let the flower go for her sake.

I knelt at her feet and hugged her. "I'm sorry, Mamma, please forgive me. I didn't mean to be selfish."

She hugged me back, resting her chin on the top of my head. "Flowers took my husband away, Elodie. I don't want to lose you to them, too."

"That will not happen, Mamma," I said. "I promise."

That night after everyone had gone to sleep, clad in my nightgown and with a candlestick in hand, I visited my orchid to admire it for the last time. As I held the candle close to the glasshouse, the light flickered against the dark bloom, the statue's face serene underneath her elaborate hat. I opened the little window, hoping some of the raspberries and cream scent had lingered, but it had disappeared as soon as the sun had set, as was the flower's wont, and all I smelled was the earthy scent of damp compost.

I reached in and touched the little petals, saying good-bye, knowing I would never see anything of its kind again.

✿❈✿❈

THE NEXT MORNING, DEACON WAINWRIGHT DULY ARRIVED, CARRYING a small wooden crate. I couldn't bear to let him remove it from atop the statue's head, possibly crushing the bloom in his clumsy hands, so I bade him to wait in the sitting room with Mamma and Violetta whilst I packaged the orchid myself.

I vowed this would be the first and only time I would enter my conservatory with an unhappy heart. I stood before the glasshouse with my grim task, set the crate on the floor, and reached out to open the little window. But my hand froze in midair. I stared, disbelieving.

The orchid was not there.

I scanned the bottom of the glasshouse, thinking maybe it had toppled from its perch, but it wasn't there, either. I searched the conservatory, knowing such a hunt was fruitless, because unless the plant had suddenly sprouted legs, I couldn't imagine how it could have moved from the glasshouse to another location all on its own.

Someone had to have taken the orchid, but who? Who would know the plant was valuable apart from Deacon Wainwright and the man he had written to in London? The conservatory door leading out to the back garden didn't have a lock, so it would be nothing for someone to come in and take what they wanted. Everything else in the conservatory was where it belonged, not so much as a pot overturned. My gardening tools were the most valuable things to hand, easy to sell quickly, if some passing vagrant had been the thief. But my trowel, spade, and fork all hung on the pegboard near the door, which is where I placed them after I cleaned them each evening.

I sat down on my stool, disbelieving. Someone had stolen my orchid.

Because I had not returned in the sitting room with the crate, Mamma sent Violetta in to find me.

"If you meant to aggravate Deacon Wainwright by making him wait, your scheme was a success," she said, leaning against the door.

"It isn't here," I said.

"What isn't here?"

I pointed at the glasshouse. "The orchid. It's gone. I saw it last night after everyone had gone to bed, but now it's gone. Someone's taken it."

Violetta leaned close to the glasshouse, peering in. Then she straightened up and looked at me. "It's gone!"

"That's what I'm telling you."

Violetta bit her lip. "Did you take it? Did you hide it from

Deacon Wainwright? I wouldn't blame you if you did. You can tell me, Elodie. I won't be angry."

"No!" I stood up from the stool. "I wouldn't do that to Mamma! She asked me to give Deacon Wainwright the orchid, and I promised her I would. Someone's stolen it, I'm telling you."

"He'll never believe you," Violetta said, shaking her head.

"That thought had occurred to me."

She took a breath and blew it out. "Well, what do we do now?"

It heartened me that Violetta had said *we* and not *you*. Since the quarrel we had had over Papa when the doctor came to visit Mamma we hadn't spoken much. My little sister could hold a grudge longer than anyone I knew.

"I don't know. I suppose we'll just have to tell him."

"Perhaps Mamma took it, with the intention to give it back to you as soon as Deacon Wainwright left."

As much as that suggestion filled me with hope, I knew it couldn't be the reason for the plant's disappearance. I would dearly love for Mamma to produce my orchid, smiling, and telling me everything was going to be all right. Color this fantasy by placing my father at her side, and all my Christmas wishes might come true, too.

"She was adamant, Violetta. She cares naught for the thing. Indeed, I think she sees it as another needless problem father has created. What is worse, now Mamma is going to be upset, and that is something I don't wish her to be. She's only just risen from her sick bed."

"What if . . . what if we tell him the plant died?"

"I'm sure he'd ask to see its carcass. He'd want proof."

"Maybe the maid threw it away?" Violetta was grasping at straws, but I loved her for it.

"We'd have to involve Mary and encourage her to tell a fib. I don't want to do that to her. It wouldn't be right."

A step fell on the tiles. Impatient with waiting, Deacon Wainwright had come to chivvy us along. "Forgive me, ladies," he said, "but if I am to make the morning post for the train to London, I must take the orchid now."

My sister and I exchanged a glance.

"Ladies, please," he said, looked quite irritated.

I would simply have to come out with it and let the chips fall where they may. "The orchid's gone," I said. "Someone has taken it."

"What do you mean?"

"It seems that an intruder has come into Elodie's conservatory and taken her orchid," Violetta said. "We think sometime in the night when we were all asleep."

"What *do* you mean?"

I gestured to the glasshouse. "See for yourself, do. Someone's been in and taken it."

Clearly thinking we were trifling with him, the deacon strode up to the glasshouse and glared at it, as though he'd dearly love to smash it to bits. Then he turned his wrath on me. "Do you take me for a fool, Miss Buchanan? I don't appreciate having my time wasted nor do I appreciate being lied to. Now I will give you the benefit of the doubt because I know you wish to keep the flower, but hiding it like this and trying to pin it on an intruder is such a childish thing to do."

"Can you only address me in anger, sir?" I said. "You claim yourself to be a man of God, but you talk to me as a buffoon and a cad!"

He jerked his head back as though my words had slapped

him directly in the face. "I apologize if you've taken my tone of voice as anger," he said, not sounding sorry in the least and not adjusting his tone at all.

And then Mamma appeared at the door, surrounded by a cloud of my little sisters. It was the nursemaid's morning off, and Mamma looked harried and not a little angry herself. She held a crying Dahlia in her arms; Chrysantha, Lily, and Peony clung onto her skirts. "What is happening? Why is there shouting?"

Violetta hurried over and took Dahlia, patting her back and making shushing noises.

"It seems Miss Buchanan is claiming someone has stolen the orchid," Deacon Wainwright said.

"I didn't take it, Mamma," I said. My anger was beginning to turn to tears. I didn't want Mamma bothered with this business, and here she was, dragged in once more. "I promised I would give it to Deacon Wainwright, and I fully intended to. I don't know what happened."

"I do believe your daughter is telling tales, Mrs. Buchanan."

"I take offense at that suggestion, Deacon Wainwright!" A spark of Mamma's old self sprang to life. She possessed an anger that matched my father's in its intensity. "My daughter does not tell tales. If she claims the flower has been stolen, then I believe her. Shouldn't you be more concerned with whether an intruder has entered the house than whether my daughter is telling tales?"

Deacon Wainwright tugged at the bottom of his jacket, breathing so hard that the whistle in his nose sounded like a teakettle rising to the boil. "Of course, you are correct, but I doubt a thief is the cause of the orchid's disappearance. After all, nothing else has been taken."

"In light of the fact that nothing else has been taken, perhaps the bloom finished and dropped off its perch," Mamma said. "This is a flower we are speaking of, after all, and they do not last forever."

"Overnight?" Deacon Wainwright said, disbelieving. "Without withering beforehand? Who ever heard of such a thing?"

"The plants my husband collects are odd things indeed, Deacon Wainwright," Mamma replied, her voice now soothing. "There is one he told me about, a giant lily that blooms in one night. There is a grass that grows four feet in one day. How can we know this plant's nature as it dies?"

I highly doubted Mamma's explanation was the cause of the orchid's disappearance because there was nothing left of the plant, not a snippet of root, not even a dried petal, but I could see on Mamma's face her desire to see this plant business put behind her. She had the same look on her face as when two of my sisters argued over a dolly and she wished for the ruckus to end.

"Well, I was only trying to help, and I can see that I may have overreacted, Miss Buchanan," he said to me in what was plainly a sorry excuse for an apology.

"I do understand you mean only kindness, Deacon Wainwright," Mamma said, taking Dahlia back from Violetta. "It seems to me that the matter has been settled one way or the other. The flower is gone, out of Elodie's hands, and that's what you were after, isn't it? Now, I think we all need a cup of tea. Let us go into the sitting room, and I'll call for Mary."

The deacon straightened his shoulders, and after sticking me with a cold look, he followed Mamma out of the conservatory. My sisters trailed behind them, leaving Violetta and me alone in the blissful silence.

"Heaven help you when he becomes the new vicar of this parish," Violetta said, folding her arms. "You'll have no peace."

"I shall go off plant hunting with Papa then. A tribe of cannibals would probably be more welcoming."

Violetta's brow furrowed. "Don't even jest about that, Elodie. What a horrible thought." She tapped her fingers against her sleeve.

Violetta and I looked at the glasshouse again, searching for anything else that would lead to the flower's whereabouts. "Here!" Violetta pointed. "What is this?"

I looked closer and saw a faint handprint on one side of the case. My hand fit easily inside the print with room to spare. Whoever had made it had very large hands. I looked on the other side to see if there was a matching print. Maybe someone had thought to lift the entire case to steal it wholesale. There was something there, but it wasn't a handprint. It was a long scratch, as though made by a tool or some such. "Do you see this?"

"Could someone have tried to pry the glass out?" asked Violetta.

"But why, when the door is inches away?"

Violetta shook her head in frustration. "I suppose we will never know. There's nothing for it. We'd better join them for tea or else the deacon will think we are conspiring against him."

My mind was whirling from the events of the morning, and I would have liked nothing better than a cup of tea, but I would rather gulp down a teacup full of arsenic than sit under the basilisk glare of Deacon Wainwright's disapproval.

SEVERAL DAYS PASSED AND THE MYSTERY OF THE MISSING ORCHID still had not been solved. The deacon had come for tea after church on my mother's invitation, but Violetta and I did not want to see him and so we chose to avoid him by hiding in the conservatory, despite my mother's protests.

"We can't stay in here forever," Violetta said.

"I can," I replied.

There was a sudden noise coming from a large potted fern in the corner, a little squeak, as though made by a wee mouse, and we both turned toward it. A scrap of blue pinafore trailing on the ground gave the mouse away: our nine-year-old sister, Calla. Small for her age and very shy, Calla was easily upset and hid often.

Violetta and I exchanged a glance and went to her hiding place.

"Come on out, dearest," Violetta said, holding out her hand. Calla shook her head, her curls bouncing.

I knelt next to the pot, my skirts blooming out over the floor. Calla sat with her back against the wall and her knees tucked up, the fern's long fronds brushing her face. Her chin was trembling, and she clutched her alphabet picture book against her chest. "Please come out, sweeting. You look so lonely behind my plant all on your own, and I'm too big to squeeze in there with you," I said.

Calla looked between Violetta and me, remaining where she was. "Why are men in the house?"

"Only one man, sweeting," Violetta said, peering at her over my shoulder. "Deacon Wainwright. You've seen him here before. He brings his mamma with him. You've seen him at church, too. He's the deacon. No need to be frightened."

"Not him." Tears gathered in her eyes. "Not him. There are men. Big men walking all over, touching our things. I was on the front step, reading my book, and they came in through the gate and walked into the house without knocking, without waiting for Mary to answer the door. They trod on my book." Her lip quivered, and she opened her little book—a large muddied mark of a hobnailed boot covered *A for Apple*.

"Do you know where they went, dearest?" I asked, trying to keep the fear from my voice.

She pointed at the ceiling. And then we heard it—the sound of hobnailed boots stomping over the floor boards, sifting through the raised voices of Deacon Wainwright and Mamma. "In the nursery."

SEVEN

stood and lifted Calla into my arms. She wrapped her arms around my neck and her legs around my waist, clinging on like a barnacle. "Sweeting, I want you to run next door to Mrs. Hardcastle's house and ask her to send for the village constable. Do you think you can do that for me?" She nodded, her brown eyes wide. I set her on her feet and opened the back door of the conservatory. "Quick now, through the garden gate." I watched her run across the garden, her sturdy boots swishing through the long grass, and her pinafore ribbons flying behind her. As she turned through the gate in the hedge and disappeared behind the privy, I heard Mrs. Hardcastle exclaim, her little rough-coated terrier, Albert, barking along with his alarmed mistress. My heart thrumming, I felt my pocket to make sure my billhook was there. I grabbed Violetta's hand, and we ran for the back stairs.

By the time we reached the top of the landing, the men had progressed to my parents' room. We heard them talking.

"There's a good dressing table. Mark that down as worth a guinea," one man said.

The other scoffed. "More like half a crown."

"We ain't here to rob them blind, Mr. Jones. Have a care. A guinea is what I say, and a guinea is what it'll be. Moving on to items on the dressing table. An ivory comb, a silver brush . . ."

I flicked open the billhook, and we entered the room. As little Calla said, the men were huge. There were two of them, burly men dressed in long blue smocks. The one speaking, the larger of the men, held Mamma's porcelain swan-shaped hairpin holder, which Papa had brought her back from China several years ago. The dainty object in his workmanlike hands looked absurd, but he held the object with deference, as though he were used to dealing with such things and knew that it needed to be handled with care.

They looked up briefly when we entered the room and then returned to their assessment. They were not startled or fearful. They looked like they knew they belonged there.

"May I ask who you are?" I said, holding out the little knife. "And why you are in my mother's bedroom?"

Violetta strode into the room and snatched the hairpin holder from the man's hands. Several pins fell from the swan's back and clattered to the floor. "Are you the thieves who stole my sister's orchid?" she said.

The smaller man laughed. "We ain't thieves. And don't know nothing about no orchid." He saw me holding out the knife, and his lip curled. "Bill'ook. Two shillings."

The larger man scowled at him. "Hush it, you." The smaller man shrugged and then opened Mamma's wardrobe and began rifling through her gowns.

"Don't touch those!" Violetta barked. She set the pin holder down and squeezed in front of the man. She slammed the door, leaning against it, her arms spread out. "How dare you!"

"Leave off for a moment, Dawson," the bigger man said, and then he turned to me. "We're here on official business for Mr. Erasmus Pringle, miss. I believe you know him to be your father's employer."

"What would Mr. Pringle want with my mother's hairpins and her gowns?" Violetta asked, her eyes snapping with fury.

"We're assessing the value of the contents of the house to be sold to recoup a debt," the man replied.

"A debt?" I said, lowering the knife. "What do you mean?"

The smaller man sat down on the end of Mamma's bed, bouncing a little, as if to assess the comfort of the mattress and thus its price. "He means your dear old papa never fulfilled his contract, and he owes Mr. Pringle a whole lot of coin, treacle."

"Your father has been warned this would happen. Mr. Pringle has written to him, and he's not replied," the larger man said. "It's within his rights to demand recompense, as your father is personally liable for his business debts, which means his possessions can be sold. We're assessing the value of the house to determine whether that will settle the debt."

I swallowed. "Just the contents of the house? That will discharge the debt?" Saying good-bye to our furniture and belongings would be hard to bear, but we'd still have a roof over our heads.

The man shook his head, suddenly looking very sorry for us. "No, miss. The contents of the house and the house itself."

"But where will we live if the house is sold?" Violetta asked.

"I suppose you'll have to go on the parish." The smaller man stood up from the bed and returned to the wardrobe. Violetta's mouth dropped open. "Now, we got work to do." He took her by the elbows and danced her to one side, Violetta too stunned to resist him. He opened the door and began to shuffle through the contents once more.

"On the parish?" she finally squeaked out. "Do you mean the workhouse?"

The smaller man tapped the side of his nose with one short finger. "You're a clever one," he said.

"Look, miss," the bigger man said to me. "This is only an assessment. If your father fulfills the obligation, then Mr. Pringle is willing to let the matter settle." He reached inside his jacket pocket and pulled out a sheaf of papers and handed them to me.

I opened them and read Mr. Pringle's demands: Either my father return to China to collect three hundred Queen's Fancy orchids and burn the forest behind him or he was to repay Mr. Pringle for the prior failed voyage to China, plus recompense for the three hundred Queen's Fancy orchids. The sum was an astronomical amount that my father could never hope to pay in a lifetime, nor could our house or its contents ever fulfill it. At the bottom of the page was written: *For any amount unfulfilled, the aggrieved party will exercise his rights to have Reginald Buchanan seized by the authorities and placed in debtors' prison until the debt is satisfied.*

EIGHT

eacon Wainwright was still in the house drinking tea when Calla came back, clutching our neighbor's hand. I told Mamma about the men in the house, and then Mrs. Hardcastle informed our astonished mother that the constable refused to come because they were within their right to assess the house.

"What do you mean?" she said. "What are you saying?" Overwrought and frightened, Mamma stood up and fainted, striking her head on the tea table and necessitating a call from Dr. Thumpston, who dosed her with Chlorodyne and stitched the cut on her forehead.

There was only one solution left to us, whether Violetta liked it or not: we had to travel to Kew and appeal to my father.

"I will go and speak with your father at Kew," Deacon Wainwright said after the doctor had left. Our neighbor and Mary had taken the children upstairs and fed them bread and jam. Violetta, the deacon, and I sat in the sitting room surrounded by empty teacups and a plate full of crumbs.

"I do appreciate that, Deacon Wainwright," I said quietly, knowing that Papa would not take kindly to him. "But I don't think such a visit will be fruitful."

"What do you suggest, then?" he said, reaching absently for the cake plate, and then, finding only crumbs, drawing his hand back and pretending to search for his handkerchief inside his pocket instead.

"Mamma is not well enough to travel, so I suggest Violetta and I go." I would have to find someone to travel with us. Perhaps my neighbor's husband would agree to go.

"All we'll find is Papa going on about his business, uncaring," Violetta said, her voice made faint by despair. "He won't do anything. He won't." Violetta sat close to the fire, staring into it, her shawl tight around her. "Our house will be taken. All our lovely things and our books. We'll be forced to live in the workhouse and made to dress in hessian sacks and pick oakum, even the little children."

I made no move to comfort her and tell her she was imagining the worst, because for once Violetta wasn't being dramatic or relating some plot from one of her gothic novels. The workhouse was a very real possibility for all of us. Our parish's imposing workhouse lay at the edge of the village, more like a prison than a place of respite, its high stone walls hiding the inmates from view. Workhouses were meant to shame the poor rather than help them, and shame them they did. Very few people who entered the workhouse ever left it, and those who did were unable to remove its stigma. We would never see the young children again, as little ones were separated from the able-bodied. Dahlia would stay with Mamma until she turned two, but if Mamma slipped back into Dr. Thumpston's cure, she would be sent to an asylum, to lie possibly chained to her bed.

But I did correct her on one thing. "Papa is not uncaring, Violetta. He loves us and won't see us fall like this."

Violetta didn't even try to disabuse me. She kept gazing into the fire as though the answer were marked there on the flames.

The deacon sat forward and took the summons from my hands and read it. "Hmmm," he said. "It seems this Mr. Pringle will pay for your father's return to China, but the cost will be added to the amount owed if he fails in his mission. He has your father tightly bound, make no mistake." He handed me back the contract. "You cannot presume to travel to Kew unchaperoned," Deacon Wainwright went on, his voice gentle and calming, as a man of the cloth should be, showing me that perhaps the deacon wasn't as unsuited to his chosen profession as I thought he was. "I will go with you."

"Thank you," I said. And I meant it. We did need Deacon Wainwright to accompany us. We so rarely left Kent, and I was a little terrified of traveling on the train and finding our way to Kew. I was mentally and physically exhausted, and I wasn't sure I could deal with this new situation without assistance. "I would appreciate that very much."

"Elodie . . . I . . . Miss Buchanan," Deacon Wainwright said. "I hope you will forgive me for acting the cad. You were quite right when you said I was not acting as a man of the cloth. I've been told from time to time that I'm too ardent, and that I let my emotions get the better of me. I fear you paid the price." He held his hand to his heart. "If any of my doings caused you distress, I humbly apologize." He reached out and laid his hand over mine. "You look quite unhappy. I hope that I can help take some of the burden off."

I looked down at his hand over mine, the skin almost translucent, his signet ring on his third finger a somber black. I slid my hand out from under his. "Thank you," I said.

Lying in bed next to Violetta that night, I knew she was as awake as I. Terrified by the way she'd looked earlier that evening, I felt my closest ally and confidant slipping away from me. If I lost my sister, I would run mad, truly.

"Please, Violetta," I said. "We have to remain hopeful that Papa will help us."

She remained quiet for so long I thought she'd fallen asleep. "What if he has another family?" she finally said. "What if that is the reason he's turned away from us?"

Violetta had expressed the thought I hadn't dared to speak myself. There had been whispers to this end in the village. I'd heard one of the Jenkins sisters speaking of it outside of church only last Sunday. She'd stopped gossiping directly she saw me, but I'd heard her.

My imagination painted a picture of Papa turning down a lane and into a thatched cottage, children tumbling out of the open door and into his arms, followed by a smiling woman, her face filled with love, not knowing that his heart had once lain elsewhere.

And why not have a new family? Why couldn't this be the case? As Violetta had pointed out so many times, we didn't really know our father well. The man in my mind was perhaps a figment of my imagination. Perhaps the attributes I had given him were ones I'd hoped he possessed. Mamma said he had poor judgment, and she knew him better than any of us. They quarreled so much when he was at home, maybe . . . just maybe Violetta was right.

It wasn't an uncommon thing, to be sure. Divorce was difficult to obtain, so many men simply severed emotional ties with their first family and began a second one anew, usually in another city or town under an assumed name.

Adventurers had recently lit the imagination of the public, and even women were turning up at lectures by such notable men as Dr. David Livingston and John Hanning Speke to hear of their travels. Perhaps Papa had such a following as well. Maybe he wasn't melancholic; maybe he'd fallen in love with an admirer.

I shuffled my legs under the blankets, suddenly feeling restless. I heard Violetta hiccup, and then a little sob broke forth. I turned toward her, and we clung to each other, crying together as quietly as we could, keeping our grief to ourselves, because we both knew if everyone in the house heard us, we'd all be lost.

Deacon Wainwright dealt with everything, and I was indeed grateful. There were many details to traveling that I found confounding, from purchasing the tickets, to stepping on the correct train, to looking for the proper station to disembark. This terrified me the most, as I might have ridden the train to its terminus, possibly to the end of Britain, for all I knew. The deacon seemed full of self-confidence doing these things, as though they were second nature to him. I wish I possessed such ease and worldliness. I studied him carefully at every little task to learn for myself how to do it. I watched as he handed our tickets to the conductor without fumbling, how he opened the door of the train when it came to a full stop and escorted us over the little gap on the platform. When we left the station at Richmond, I noted how he hailed a hansom cab by stepping into the street and holding up an arm. At Kew, he located Sir William Jackson Hooker as though he knew exactly where to find him.

Papa's little thatched-roofed house sat on the outskirts of the garden, at the end of the arboretum. It was beautiful, filled with trees I'd never seen before, and it made me sad that the memory of my first visit to the garden would be marred by angst and trepidation. Violetta clung to my hand as we approached the cottage, both of us terrified of what we'd find. But there were no children playing outside, no woman who had replaced Mamma in our father's affection. Violetta loosened her grip on my hand, and I heard her breathe out in relief.

The windows were shut, and the curtains drawn over. It looked as though no one was home. And indeed, no one answered when Sir William knocked, and so, after a few moments, he opened the door and we went in.

The cottage was tiny, with only one room, which was divided in half by a large bookshelf crammed with bottles, plants, and various tools of the botanist's trade. The rest of the room was sparsely furnished. Two chairs sat near a small hearth: an upholstered armchair with the stuffing poking out of various holes, and a ladder-back chair with a frayed cushion that looked as though mice had been nibbling at it. A steep staircase at the back of the room led to another floor or maybe an attic.

"Buchanan?" Sir William called. "Are you about?"

A man stepped out in the cottage's dim light from behind the shelves, wiping his hands on a towel. He was most likely expecting to see only Sir William, and his eyes widened when he saw the four of us standing there. He spun about and stepped back behind the shelves.

I looked at Sir William, uncertain as to why he had taken us to this man's cottage and not to my father's.

Indeed, Violetta thought the same. "Where is our father, Sir William? Is this not his cottage?"

"Mr. Buchanan?" Sir William said, and I looked around to see from where in such a tiny room my father might appear. "It's all right, my good man. It's only your daughters come to see you."

"I . . . I'm not able to see you today, my dears. I'm indisposed, you see. I don't wish to make you ill." It was my father's voice that had spoken. Perhaps the other man was his assistant.

Sir William gestured for us to wait and disappeared behind the shelves. There was a quick murmur of voices, and then Sir William stepped back out, his face sorrowful. "I'm terribly sorry, Miss Buchanan, Miss Violetta," he said. "He's adamant. Perhaps give him a little time and come back again. There's a tea shop not far from here. I suggest you go there and then come back in an hour or two, and we'll see where we are."

"Really, this is ridiculous." Deacon Wainwright huffed. "We've come all this way, Sir William. Surely the girls can speak with their father for five minutes. It's of the utmost importance." Deacon Wainwright raised his voice. "Mr. Buchanan. This is the deacon of Edencroft Parish speaking. I've escorted your daughters here to talk to you. We're not leaving until you show yourself."

"Papa!" Violetta said. Her voice cracked, and then she burst into sobs so loud that I could see by her face that she was surprised. I knew she would be embarrassed, for my little sister hated for anyone to see her as weak. She put her hands to her mouth as though to push back the escaped sobs. I was moving to go to her side, when the man stepped out from behind the shelves again and into a shaft of sunlight that fell from a small, uncurtained window. I was able to get a better look at him, and I was shocked to my core.

That shabby waif of a man was my father.

He was thin. My father had always been slender, but now he possessed the frail figure of an invalid. His skin was pale, and his eyes, normally so full of life, looked dull and depressed. The bridge of his nose had a lump in it, as though it had been broken. My father had always worn a colorful waistcoat, usually some sort of tartan, as befitted his Scottish background. But now he wore a shapeless workman's smock that was too big for him—the sleeves hung well over his hands, almost touching his fingertips.

What distressed me the most was his beard. That was gone. He was as clean-shaven as a soldier, with only a small moustache. I'd never seen Papa's face without a beard before. He looked like a different adaptation of himself.

A sadder, broken adaptation.

At the sight of him, Violetta cried harder. She crossed the room and did something I'd never seen my sister do. She put her arms around him and hugged him close. Papa did nothing for a moment, but then his hand rose up and he patted her once on her back. "There, my dear," he said. "There now. No need to weep."

"I must take my leave, Miss Buchanan, Miss Violetta," Sir William said, tactfully making no mention of Violetta's emotional outburst. "But if you need me, I'll be in the Palm House for the rest of the afternoon."

Sir William left, and the room fell quiet as a tomb. I didn't know how to begin, or what to say. Papa stepped back away from my sister and looked at me warily, his shoulders tense.

I stepped up to him to kiss his cheek, but he flinched and moved away, grasping his hands behind his back, as though he were restraining himself. I tried not to feel hurt by his snub, tried so hard not to cry. Papa's desperate appearance and his cold manner confounded me. While it was true that we had only ever seen him once a year, he was always affectionate toward us. But now he looked as though he'd be happier if we went away.

"We've missed you, Papa," I said.

He turned his face from mine, as though the sight of me was too much of a burden.

"Will you not take my hand?" Violetta said. "Will you not allow us to kiss your cheek? Why will you not look at us?"

"You've not replied to our letters," I said, trying a different approach. "Or to your employer's letters. He came to see me to enquire about you. Did you know that? He said he wrote to you."

"I received his letters," father said, his voice sounding weary with despair, "but I've nothing to say to the man, so I returned them to him unopened." This he addressed to one of the potted plants on the shelf.

"Yes, I know, that's why he came to our house. He was very angry."

"I'm sure he was. That is his nature when he does not get his way. In time he will find another plant hunter to do his deeds for him. I'm no longer under his employ, and I made that quite clear to him. He should not have pestered you."

"There's more to it than that, Papa. He wants you to return

to China to search for the little orchid; he says his last one perished recently, and he—"

"I'll not go back to China!" he said, his voice rising in anger.
"I've vowed never to go back." He held his hand out to the door.
"I'm sorry, my dear girls, but as I said before I'm indisposed.
Perhaps we can visit on another occasion."

Papa was dismissing us, as though we were door-to-door
knife grinders looking for work and not his own flesh and
blood. Violetta had gained control of her tears, and now her
face was grim, her mouth pressed into a line. That was her
expression when she was biting back words. I knew my little
sister would never show disrespect to either of our parents,
but I also knew that holding her tongue was agony to her, and
at that moment, she quite resembled a pot of custard about to
boil over. She was very like Papa in her temperament, although
she'd scratch my eyes out for saying so.

"Enough of this, Mr. Buchanan," Deacon Wainwright said.
"You must brace yourself for news you do not want to hear.
Your employer demands that you fulfill your contract. You
must return at once to China or else this Mr. Pringle will have
you sent to debtor's prison and your family to the workhouse!"

Papa looked as though he had been punched. His face
grew even paler, and he sank down in the overstuffed chair.
"Workhouse? My family?" he whispered. "No, he . . . he would
never do such a thing."

I glared at Deacon Wainwright. "Deacon Wainwright. If you
please . . ."

"Well, he has done it. The bailiffs have already assessed your
family's belongings. I was there and saw them with my own
eyes."

"They went through our things and frightened the life out of everyone," Violetta said, her words falling out in a jumble, a mixture of fear and reproach. "Mamma fell and struck her head, and the doctor had to be called. Calla was so afraid, and they trod on her book."

"Your mother?" Papa's face paled. "Was she badly injured?"

"No," I said at the same time Violetta blurted out "yes." I glared at her.

"Doctor Thumpston has the care of her, sir," the deacon said. "We must deal with the business at hand."

"I will buy my contract out in time." Papa nodded. "Yes, I am in Kew's employ now, and I can arrange payments."

"You'll have to work all the hours that God gives, sir, to repay him," Deacon Wainwright replied. "He's demanding a sum that no one, save the wealthiest man in the land, could possibly pay."

"How much?" Papa asked.

Deacon Wainwright named the colossal figure, and my father flinched. "He arrived at that figure by working out the cost of each orchid and how many you stated you could retrieve," the deacon added. "This is what the contract says. You signed the document; it's legal and binding. No court would come down on your side."

My father looked quite sick. He held a hand to his mouth, and I could see his throat bobbing as he swallowed. I knelt at his side. "Papa, are you well?" Up close his eyes were sunken into hollows, but what was worse was the haunted look they held. My father was not well enough to go back to China. Anyone could see that. "Perhaps we can try to reason with Mr. Pringle. Perhaps you know someone else you can send in your stead?"

He shook his head slowly.

"I'm sure it's quite safe for you to return to China, sir, if that's what's frightening you," Deacon Wainwright said, going on as though I hadn't spoken. He sat down on a ladder-back chair next to him. "What befell you is in the past. Our country has brought those godless and wanton people to heel now. Now they know how to behave in a modern world. Now they know they cannot harm a British subject. We have God on our side, and I do think you are afraid of nothing. Come now, man. Pull yourself up." Deacon Wainwright smiled, seemingly pleased with himself.

From the set of Papa's jaw, I knew what usually followed such a comment, but I wasn't sure if this new Papa would rise the same way. I needn't have worried. My old Papa was still there. "Oh, yes," he said, his tone friendly, but I could hear the rage lying just beneath the surface. "We have brought the Chinese *to heel*, as you say. Just like a master would his dog. But a master can only beat his dog for so long before it turns on him. And that is what happened. We subjugated China and treated her badly, very badly indeed over the years. I don't hold China responsible for what *befell* me. As for God, well, I can tell you that God is on nobody's side. And why would he be? How could he be when we persist on destroying one another—for what? For the ability to sell opium to those poor people, make them addicted and weakened so we can swan in and take our fill?"

Deacon Wainwright waved his hand, as though dashing the words away. "That's as may be, and we must agree to differ. But think about it, how much trouble can such a journey be?" Deacon Wainwright stood up. "Book yourself a passage on a steamer, collect the flowers for this man Pringle, and return home to your family. I'm sure it isn't difficult. I'm certain the fresh air on the sea and in the Oriental mountains is just what you need to shake yourself out of this gloom." Deacon Wainwright loomed over Papa, a beatific look on his face, as though my father were a little boy he was trying to coax into giving up his toys.

"Deacon Wainwright . . ." I tried to interject, to prevent the blast of fury that I expected would be forthcoming from Papa. I knew that the deacon's attitude would not endear him to my father, but it was too late. That anger of my father's, which I knew so well, bubbled to the surface.

Papa stood up. He was head and shoulders taller than the deacon, and even though he was nothing like his former self, Papa still had a touch of his old presence about him. He held himself in a manner that meant he would not be trifled with. "That's all there is to it?" he said, a low warning to his voice. "Is that what you think, sir? Picking flowers in the countryside?"

Only a fool would answer yes to those questions.

"Well . . . yes," Deacon Wainwright said, the smile fading from his face. He glanced around him, as though perusing the room for the nearest way out.

"How difficult can that be?" My father's bare cheeks pickled with rage. "How difficult can that be?" He took a step closer to Deacon Wainwright, who backed up, alarmed.

"I . . . I . . ." Deacon Wainwright stuttered.

"Let me disabuse you of that opinion," Papa said. "Shall I tell you the horrors that await the plant hunter? Storms, sinking ships, headhunters, quicksand, wild animals that would eat a man as soon as look at him. And then there are the insects that burrow under one's skin and cause such a terrible burning pain that death would be a blessing." Father took another step closer to the deacon. "A mist that is never-ending and rots the skin on one's feet. And then there is kidnapping and murder from tribesmen and rival orchid hunters. There is, in point of fact, one particular orchid hunter who has a hook for a hand and has made it his life's mission to slit my throat with said hook at the very next opportunity."

Deacon Wainwright, backing away from my father in alarm, fetched up against the shelves, causing several pots to teeter. Papa shot out his arm, and Deacon Wainwright threw his hands up, cowering, turning his face away from the anticipated blow.

But the punch never fell. Instead, Papa reached over the deacon's shoulder and righted one of the teetering pots before it tumbled to the floor. As he did this, his sleeve fell back from his wrist. Violetta was looking away. But I saw it. I only glimpsed it for a moment, because Papa immediately dropped his arm, but a moment was enough. Because, from the base of his wrist to several inches back, the skin was marred by several terrible dents, as though someone or something had gouged out his flesh, leaving behind scars so horrific that my father chose to hide them with smock sleeves.

Chose to hide them from his own family.

The rest of the conversation between Deacon Wainwright and Papa was reduced to babbling, because I no longer heard them. My thoughts were only for Papa now and his well-being. Something horrible and desperate had been done to him. He had been subjected to a torture that I could only guess at, and my willful imagination conjured up all sorts of scenarios. Perhaps it was the same torment that the *Times* editor had told me about. Perhaps someone had bound Papa or beat him or left him for dead in some noisome Chinese prison. And for what? What had my father done to deserve such treatment?

"You're mad, sir," Deacon Wainwright whispered, fear sparking in his eyes. "Mad."

Papa bowed. "You've finally spoken sense, Deacon Wainwright. Because you are correct. I am indeed, as you say, mad." Without looking at Violetta or me, he left the cottage, pulling the door behind him with a bang.

We sat for several long minutes, waiting for Papa to return. When it was clear he wasn't going to come back, Deacon Wainwright placed his curate's hat on his head. "Well now," was all he said. Then he took me by the elbow and marched me out of the house before I had a chance to say anything. Violetta hurried behind.

Deacon Wainwright stomped down the Kew Road as though the devil were at his heels, tugging me along, his hand squeezing my elbow tightly. I pried his fingers off my elbow and moved away from him. He had no right to talk to my father in that way. Now he'd ruined everything. Instead of explaining things in a way Papa would understand, Deacon Wainwright had sallied forth with his remarks, as though he were addressing little children at a church picnic. It was clear to anyone with eyes that my father was not well.

The welcoming sign of the aforementioned tea shop loomed ahead: THE MAIDS OF HONOUR.

"There's the tea shop Sir William mentioned before," I said. "A cup of tea would do us all some good." *Would do you some good, if you choked on it*, I thought. And for once I didn't feel guilty about my unkind thoughts toward the deacon.

Deacon Wainwright brightened slightly. "You're right. A sensible idea, Miss Buchanan."

He held the door open for us, and as Violetta and I entered the tea shop I felt her take my hand. "What now?" she whispered, her voice marked with dismay. "What do we do now?"

I squeezed her hand. "We'll sort something out," I said, but I had no idea what that might be.

⚜ ❧ ⚜

INSIDE THE SHOP IT WAS WARM AND SMELLED OF JAM AND BAKING pies, but the sweet smell did nothing to quell the panic inside of me. Did nothing to assuage the anger I felt toward Deacon Wainwright and the worry I felt for my father and the rest of my family.

We sat in silence while the tea table was rolled out. I waited until Deacon Wainwright had drunk his first cup, and then I poured him another. The tea seemed to calm him a little bit. His breath wasn't coming out in such short gasps anymore.

"Your father is impossible, quite impossible," Deacon Wainwright said.

"He's truly ill," I said. "You don't know what he looked like before, Deacon Wainwright. He's a different man."

"He is," Violetta owned. My poor sister looked exhausted. Her face held that same desperate expression she had when the bailiffs had come.

"I believe he was only telling the truth," I put in.

"And what rot, banging on about cannibals and the like?" The deacon waved his hand, but I could see little beads of sweat pop out on his forehead, and his throat bob as he swallowed. He set his teacup down and pulled at his neckcloth.

"Even still, with all those dangers, I think it would be worth the strife just to see an entire forest full of orchids," I said, attempting to steer the conversation well away from my father. "All those colors. And the smell would be heavenly. I can see how a man would jump at the chance to experience such delights, and experience such adventures. It's so romantic." I was only speaking in general, trying to change the timbre of the conversation to something more pleasant, but my words enraged the deacon.

"Don't be ridiculous!" Deacon Wainwright snapped. "What do you know of it?"

I gaped at him, openmouthed. Deacon Wainwright's extension of an olive branch did not last long. "I beg your pardon?"

He leaned forward in his chair. "What would you know of it?" He reached into his coat and pulled out his money pouch.

Desperately trying to smooth things over, I said, "I'm simply saying—"

Deacon Wainwright paused from counting the coins and looked up. "Well, don't. Don't say. Don't speak of things you have no mind for."

He was the second man in the space of a few weeks who had told me not to speak of things, and I'd had just about enough of it.

I stood up. "How dare you speak to me so!"

"I'm trying to help you, and you persist in hindering me at every turn! Do you know what the villagers say about you and your family? And I defend you, tell them you are ladies under dire circumstances and require our pity, not our reproach."

Violetta let out a little *eep*.

"Why yes, I do know what the villagers say. And they are free to think what they want to think. We do not need your help to change their minds! Nor do we need anyone's pity."

"Perhaps I was wrong about you. I think you are very like your father." He straightened in his chair. "I do believe if given the chance, you'd accompany your father to China."

"Oh, how correct you are! I am like my father, and given half a chance, I would get on a ship with my father and sail away. Sail far, far away from here. And from you and your meddlesome ways!"

I turned, followed swiftly by Violetta, and wove my way through the tables, past the astonished patrons who had heard the entire exchange. I pushed the door open and headed down the Kew Road, away from the deacon and back toward my father's cottage.

hen we returned to the cottage, the deacon following glumly behind me, my father had come back and was sitting in a chair reading a book. I marched straight up to him, not giving him a chance to speak his mind. "Papa, I'm going to remain here with you while we sort out what to do. Deacon Wainwright will escort Violetta back to Kent." Both Violetta and Deacon Wainwright stared at me as though I had suddenly sprouted wings. "I think it's best that I speak to Papa alone." Violetta looked relieved, but Deacon Wainwright looked taken aback.

"How will you return to Kent on your own?" the deacon said. "I hardly think you are capable—"

"My daughter is right, sir," Papa said, not lifting his eyes off the book. "I think it best that you escort Miss Violetta back to Kent. I will take Elodie home on the train."

The surprise and relief on Violetta's face must have matched my own. Papa would see Mamma, which would surely help her recover.

"Well, that's . . . that's . . ." For once Deacon Wainwright found himself at a loss for words. So he placed his hat upon his head and told Violetta to come along. "Mustn't miss the train. I will explain to your mother what is afoot."

"No need," Violetta said. "I'm sure I can explain it myself, Deacon Wainwright."

The deacon's mouth pressed into a smile. "Very well, then."

"Violetta," I said. "I will return as soon as I am able."

"I will look after your plants, no need to worry." Violetta looked at Papa, and then she darted forward and kissed his cheek. I saw a flicker of affection cross Papa's face, and then he held her elbow and kissed her back.

The two took their leave, and Papa slammed his book shut. "The man is a booby."

"Papa, don't be unkind," I said, turning away to hide my smile. Papa had summed him up perfectly. And I was happy to hear him sound more like himself, even if it were Deacon Wainwright that raised his ire.

"I hope you don't plan on marrying him. He's not for you. You need someone with more gumption, more . . . intelligence."

I turned around. "Of course I don't plan on marrying him. Whatever gave you that idea?" Indeed, I had reconciled myself to never getting married. With Papa constantly traveling, Mamma needed my help with the children. When Dahlia turned seventeen, I would be into my thirties, an old maid and well past marriage. And besides, I didn't know if I wanted a man telling me what I could or could not do. Best to be practical about these things.

"Why else would he come all the way down to London to sort me out?"

"To help. He's the deacon, and it's his prerogative to help with these sorts of matters. Mamma's hands are full with the children, and so he offered to chaperone us to you."

Papa held the book upright against his thigh, his fingers tapping lightly on the cover as he regarded me. "That's as may be, but the man has his eye on you, make no mistake. He has you pegged as a vicar's wife, and you'd better make it clear as to whether you welcome his attentions. These things can get quite awkward if one person gets ahold of the wrong idea."

"He has taken an inordinate interest in my life," I admitted, my heart sinking. *There was that look he gave you, too*, a small accusing voice inside me chided. *And the time he placed his hand over yours.*

"There you have it. You see?" Papa said. "He does have his eye on you."

"He hates me, I'm sure of it," I said, hoping that was the truth. "He finds me wanting on every turn, and I'm sure his mother does, too."

"Well, I don't know about that, but perhaps he's hoping to mold you into someone more to his liking."

"He hasn't been successful and nor will he be."

He stood up. "I'm glad to hear you don't harbor affection for him." He shelved the book and scanned the offerings for another. "Say the word, and I'll put a stop to his courtship. I only need write a letter and put him in the picture."

"Oh, so now you're willing to write a letter?" I said, suddenly feeling quite angry with him. "Do you know how horrible it has been, not hearing from you? Mamma has been so ill, and now we may lose our home, and you've done nothing."

Papa's hand paused over the books. "Your mother has been ill? From that fall?"

"No. After Dahlia was born, Dr. Thumpston had her on a horrible concoction that caused her to sleep night and day. Collis Browne's Chlorodyne it was called."

A shadow crossed my father's face. "Chlorodyne, did you say?"

"Yes, and the doctor would not tell me what it was or what it could do. I tried it myself and it was perfectly awful, so I poured it out. Mamma is better now, but the shock of maybe losing the house caused her to fall and strike her head. Dr. Thumpston dosed her with the medicine once again."

"You were right to pour it out, my girl. Chlorodyne is wicked stuff. The morphine causes horrible cravings. Some say it doesn't, but I have seen otherwise." He muttered something about Dr. Thumpston under his breath that sounded like the word *quack*.

"We need you, Papa. It's been so awful. Won't you come home for a bit?"

He remained quiet for a little while, and then he finally spoke. "Everything is my fault, and I know that. I will sort Mr. Pringle and the bailiffs out, no need to fear. But I can't see your mother, not just now. It's for the best, my dear."

"How can that be so? We need you. I know you had some things happen while you were in China, if you're ashamed—"

"The less you know about what befell me, the better, Elodie. Please do not ask me about it, for I don't wish to speak of it. Not now and not ever."

I wanted to ask him straight out about those scars on his

wrist. I truly did, but I was afraid that if I behaved like Deacon Wainwright, pushing and pushing, I'd lose any ground I'd gained with Papa. So I let it go, saying nothing, and instead I perused his library with him, letting him tell me about the book he was currently reading. And I listened, happy to be in my father's presence.

⁂

IT WAS LATER, DURING A SUPPER OF TINNED BEEF ON TOAST, WHEN I told him about the flower.

"A bloom? What kind of bloom?"

"The orchid. You one you gave us."

He turned his head sideways. "I never gave you an orchid." He laughed a little. "The very idea! Why would I do that?"

"Oh," I said, feeling taken aback.

"But go on, what do you mean? A plant that bloomed in the garden?"

"No. The flower in the little dollhouse you gave the girls. I put the case in the conservatory at the back of the house. I cleared the conservatory out, and I've been filling it with plants. I think the cold pleased the plant, and so it bloomed. It sits on the top of the statue's head. Very tiny. Nearly black—"

He sat up and dropped his knife and fork with a clatter. "A scent similar to raspberries and cream?" His expression was eager. "Elodie, my dear! But this is wonderful. This plant you describe *is* the Queen's Fancy. I've not been able to get it to re-bloom ever. No one has. You say the cold made it bloom? That makes very good sense to me, as the flower is found high in the mountains, where it's cooler. My word, when I gave the girls the Wardian case I used the last of the plants as simple decoration, never imagining it would bloom."

Papa went on prattling about the orchid, but I barely heard him. His words kept clanging around in my head: *I never gave you an orchid, the very idea.* My face burned with the shame of it. I had completely misunderstood Papa's meaning behind the dollhouse. And how could I have assumed he meant for me to have the orchid? The gift was not for me, after all. It was a curio, a decoration to delight little children.

He stood up and disappeared behind the shelves, returning at once with a leather-bound notebook and a stub of a pencil. "You must tell me everything you know about the plant, when it produced leaves, a spike, when it flowered. What does it look like now?" He opened the notebook and flipped to an empty page. "This will solve all of our problems in one fell swoop. I've been working on propagation techniques in orchids. I think I've cracked the secret of getting the seeds to sprout. You see, orchid seeds require fungi to germinate and if I can get the plant to produce a seedpod, there's no need for me to return to China. I can grow as many Queen's Fancies as Mr. Pringle wants." Papa laughed. "As anyone wants!"

"Papa!" I shouted, near tears. "Stop!"

He looked at me, startled, holding the pencil aloft.

"I don't have the orchid any longer. It was taken."

"When Mr. Pringle's men came?"

I shook my head. "No. It was stolen after I showed the bloom to Deacon Wainwright. He took it upon himself to enquire about posting the plant back to you at Kew. He . . . he said it would undo my constitution. That it was unseemly for a girl to look at it." I expected Papa to nod in agreement, but he surprised me.

"Not that old twaddle. Men seem to think women will lose their minds from looking at an orchid, but the male species is the one driven mad over this plant, as I can attest myself."

"Deacon Wainwright had arranged for the orchid to be returned to you. He'd written to an orchid enthusiast his tutor at Oxford knows, a Mr. Cleghorn."

The pencil dropped from Papa's hand and clattered onto the floor. "Granville Cleghorn?" he whispered. "Oh. Tell me it's not him."

"Yes, that's his name. Why?"

"Cleghorn is Pringle's nemesis. They both despise each other and think nothing of setting their plant hunters against one another like soldiers. It's my best guess that Cleghorn sent someone to steal the orchid. It's not beyond him to do so."

"The only evidence the thief left behind was a large handprint on one side of the glasshouse," I said. "But the other side bore a scratch on the glass, as though someone had tried to use a tool."

Papa looked grim. "And so now I know who the thief was. Cleghorn's man—his plant hunter, Luther Duffey. There was no matching handprint because he has only one hand. The other is an iron hook. That explains the scratch. Duffey is the man I mentioned to Wainwright, the one who would be pleased to slit my throat."

"I don't understand. Why would he take the orchid?" I crossed my fork and knife on my plate, having lost my appetite.

"Mr. Cleghorn has desired the Queen's Fancy ever since I found it four years ago, but his hunters have been unable to locate it, and I have been very careful to keep its whereabouts unknown." He stood up and pulled a leather-bound sketchbook down from the shelf and opened it to a page, turning it toward me. On it was painted a map of some sort, but instead of words, there were line drawings of mountains, rocks, trees, and cliffs. The drawings were beautiful and highly detailed. "My maps are never labeled with destinations. You must know where to start to follow this map." He ran his finger over the route. "Here you begin at Foochow, up the Min river, and then into the mountains toward Wuyishan."

"Like a treasure map?" I asked.

"Exactly so." Papa closed the book and shelved it. "Pringle refused to sell Cleghorn a Queen's Fancy at any price; that is how much he despises him. But now Wainwright, that ass, has delivered the very thing into Cleghorn's hands. I'm sure Cleghorn has wasted no time in writing to Pringle to crow over his *finding.* No wonder Mr. Pringle will not be placated. No wonder he demands that I return to China."

"Can't Mr. Cleghorn coax the stolen Queen's Fancy into a seedpod and sell the resulting plants? I can't imagine Mr. Pringle wanting a plant that everyone has."

Papa shook his head. "I've kept the technique a very great secret. Cleghorn's men know very little about science, and he's no friend to Kew, so I doubt he possesses such knowledge." He sat quietly for a moment, pondering. "Well, if we no longer have the orchid, then to China I must return." This he murmured, more to himself than to me.

"I'll help you, Papa. Whatever you need," I said. "I shall help you."

That evening we looked over Mr. Pringle's demands together. He specified that each flower must be in spike, bud, or bloom. Any plant not in this state would be rejected. The usual blooming season for the Queen's Fancy orchid in its natural habitat was late summer. It was already April, and it took at least a hundred days to reach China, so Papa had very little time to waste. He would need to leave for China as soon as he had brought me home.

Papa carefully considered how he would travel. A steamship was most expedient, but it would be too easy for Mr. Cleghorn's men to follow him. They needed only to make an enquiry at the ticketing agent to find out which ship Papa traveled. They could purchase a ticket and bunk in the same room with my father if they pleased.

Instead, Papa decided to seek passage aboard a tea clipper. Tea clippers, built for speed and cargo, traveled with a small crew and rarely took passengers, but Papa had a few contacts in the Merchant Navy who might be able to help him find a place on a China-bound clipper. Tea clippers often kept their destinations secret so as to stop other ships from beating them to the port and purchasing the best tea from underneath them. So Papa would be able to travel as secretly as possible.

I wrote to Mr. Pringle, telling him that Papa would embark on the journey and that he agreed to the contract. I also wrote to Mamma and told her that I would remain with my father and help him organize his journey. I fibbed a bit over his condition, saying that he appeared rejuvenated by the idea of traveling again. The lie stabbed at me like a thorn in my finger, and I had to write the letter over three times until I'd got it right.

Papa gave me his bed upstairs under the eaves and set up a pallet on the sitting room floor. That night I lay in bed thinking about Papa returning to China and the orchid. As dangerous as the journey would be, I wasn't lying when I told Deacon Wainwright that I longed to go with him. The thought of returning to Kent, to my staid and simple life, filled me with sadness. I longed to see for myself where the orchids grew, the magic of such a place. I wished with all my heart that I could accompany my father. But I couldn't. I knew that. Girls didn't travel to such places. And even if they did, Mamma needed me.

A NOISE WOKE ME IN THE NIGHT, AND I SAT UP, MY HEART THRUMMING hard. What was it? I clutched the blanket in my fists and listened. There it was again—a sound similar to the call of an owl or maybe a loose shutter a-swing on a rusty hinge. I pushed the blanket back and swung my feet to the floor, waiting, listening. Perhaps I'd imagined it, but no, there it was again. I stood up and went to the top of the stairs.

My mind couldn't comprehend what my heart already knew. My father was weeping. They weren't tears of sadness; his sobs were marked with pain and fear.

I wanted to go to him, to comfort him, but I didn't know if he would welcome that, or if he'd rather keep his emotions to himself. I took a hesitant step forward, unsure of what to do. The wooden floorboards squeaked under my feet, and the sobbing stopped abruptly.

I waited for a moment. If he called out to me, I would go. But I heard nothing.

I crept back to bed and buried my face in the pillow, choking back my own tears. For the first time I wished with all my heart that I'd never put the dollhouse into my conservatory, that I'd never shown the orchid to Deacon Wainwright, that I'd never lain eyes on the Queen's Fancy orchid. If the orchid had remained a jumble of roots upon the little statue's head, Mr. Pringle would not have driven my father back to China. After all, Papa had never meant for the roots to produce anything. I had forced them to life.

It was all my fault.

TEN

he following morning Papa and I made our way
to the East India Docks on the north bank of
the Thames. Papa had refused the breakfast of
eggs and bread I'd made. Instead he sat drink-
ing tea, his brow furrowed and his jaw set. After he took each
sip, he clapped the pottery mug onto the table, fingers clenched
tight around the handle, as though the cup were struggling to
fly away.

I couldn't think of a single thing to say to him that wasn't
an apology. I wanted to beg his forgiveness for everything, but I
was terrified to say the words because I didn't want to hear Papa
give voice to what I already knew. That it was my fault he had to
return to China. Instead I kept quiet, putting myself to use—
tidying up the house, helping him find his boots, and writing a
note to Sir William, putting him in the picture. All I could do to
make up for my folly was to help Papa as much as I could.

As we grew closer to leaving, Papa's face broke out in a flush,
and a gloss of sweat marked his forehead. The long journey to

the docks seemed to calm him a little, but he'd spent the entire journey writing in his notebook, only looking up twice when the growler stopped abruptly.

To distract myself, I stared out the carriage window, watching the London scenery go by as though I were watching a magic lantern show. I'd never seen so many people in one place in my life, and they all appeared to be working earnestly. Sellers crammed the street's gutters hawking their wares of reach-me-down clothes, pots and pans, chairs, bouquets of violets, newspapers, song sheets, and penny dreadfuls. Costermongers pushed barrows of fruit and vegetables past knife grinders treading their whetstones with their hobnailed boots. A boy shouted out goods available in his master's cart: "onions, potatoes, lettuce, and cress!"

The noise from the wheels of the cabs and carriages and people talking created a din that was so loud I could barely hear myself breathe. It was exciting and new and I wanted to press it all into my memory lest I forget. I would never have cause to return here, after all.

As we drew near the docks, a line of wagons and cabs blocked the entrance, and the hansom cab Papa hired couldn't make its way through the traffic. We alighted in the street.

"It's the tea races causin' all this commotion," the cabdriver explained. He set his whip in its socket and took the coin Papa handed him. "The clippers from China were sighted in the Channel early this morning, and the race is on. The people are watching to see who docks first."

The driver gestured to several men standing on the side of the road who were holding slates and marking numbers on them in chalk. "People are wagering on the ships." He cast a longing look at the boards. "I've a mind to put a shilling down on the *Osprey* meself. Now that's a fast ship."

"The *Osprey* is in?" Papa asked.

"Do you know the ship?" I asked him.

He nodded. "I know the captain well. He won't stay at the docks for long. I'm sure he plans to return to China as soon as the ship is ready to go. All the shipping companies will be after the *Osprey*. The captain has never lost a cargo, and he brings the freight in on schedule. Not many captains can lay that claim. And if he wins this race today, he can be guaranteed an outbound cargo. He'll be returning to Foochow to collect more tea, so I may be able to obtain passage on the ship." Papa appeared relieved by the news of the ship, and indeed I was gladsome that he could be traveling with peers who might be able to calm him should he grow anxious.

"That's me decided, then," the driver said. "I'll make a wager on the *Osprey*." He waved his arm at the bookmakers, and a small boy scuttled over to collect the driver's wager.

We left the driver to his business and made our way through the crowd. Instead of lingering at the back, Papa made his way to the front. I held on to his arm, trying hard not to tread on anyone's toes as he pushed through the crowds and to the riverbank. When we reached the dock, a loud cheer rose from the crowd that made my ears ring.

"There they are, Elodie," Papa said, pointing upriver. "The tea clippers."

I was glad of my height because I could see over the people leaning against the railing in front of me. And oh, what a majestic sight it was. I had never seen the like. Chubby paddlewheel tugboats towed two tall ships, their sails furled, masts raking the cloudless blue skies, through the river's brown water. Men on the ships' decks rushed to and fro, attending to their duties. The ship the cabbie mentioned, the *Osprey*, was closest to our side of the river and was in the lead by two ships' length.

The *Osprey*'s tugboat chugged ever nearer until finally it reached the entrance to the docks. As the wheel churned through the river, water plumed over the paddles. Black smoke curled away from the tug's steam pipes, and when the captain inside his little wheelhouse pulled a chain, a high-pitched whistle peeled out.

The tug swept by, and the *Osprey*, tethered to it on a long length of rope, was so close I could almost reach out and touch her figurehead's cheek. And what a beautiful figurehead she was—a mermaid holding a seabird in her upturned palm as though offering it to the waves purling around the ship's graceful bow. The clipper rose and fell through the river, splashing water over the spectators. I felt the droplets fall, cool against my cheeks. I did not wipe them away.

A young dark-haired man appeared on the *Osprey*'s deck, a square crate stamped with bright red Chinese lettering balanced on his shoulder. A little black-and-white dog, no bigger than a cat, ran around him, barking. The sleeves of the young man's checked shirt were rolled to his elbow, and the collar was open, the neck handkerchief knotted loosely around his neck. He made his way toward the front of the ship, then stopped at the railing and braced one foot against it.

The young man's expression was intent, but a broad smile crossed his face, as though the race was nothing but a larkabout. Another sailor nearby called out to him, and the young man lifted his free hand and laughed. The little dog leapt into the air as its master spoke, its tiny folded ears and pointed snout disappearing and reappearing over the rail as it jumped.

"What is that sailor doing?" I asked Papa, nearly breathless with the thrill of the race. "What is that he's holding?"

"It's a tea crate. As soon as the dock is close enough, he'll throw it over the ship's gunwales. The other sailor stands ready as well." He pointed to the second ship, which had now reached the entrance to the dock, where a man stood holding a similar crate. "The first crate that lands on the dock marks the winner. These ships have been racing for three months. They'll have left the Chinese port together. It's quite the battle, and there's much prestige for the winning ship. Its captain will be hired before any other. Sometimes ships have to wait for weeks in China before they find a tea cargo. But not a fast ship, not a winning ship. They are snapped up quickly." Papa smiled. "Are you enjoying the sight?"

"It's beautiful! I've never seen the like of it."

"Tall ships are indeed a grand sight." He looked at me curiously, as though seeing me for the first time. "But do you not find the wind and sea smell and bustling crowd an annoyance?"

"No," I replied. "I find it exhilarating."

"Well, well, well," he said, more to himself than to me. "Upon my soul."

The second ship's tugboat put on a burst of speed, and the vessel began to close the gap, but it wasn't enough. Several people, who had most likely placed their wagers on the other ship and were already anticipating the *Osprey*'s win, began to make their way out of the dockyards.

The man standing in front of me tore up a ticket and pitched the pieces into the water. His friend clapped him on the shoulder. "I warned you not to wager against the *Osprey*," he said gleefully. The man grumbled something in response, his face a scowl. "Come on, then," his friend replied. "Let's drown your sorrows at the alehouse."

The two men departed, and I stepped into their place. I leaned over the iron balustrade, over the river as far as I dared. I pushed my bonnet back, letting it dangle by its ribbons around my neck, as I used to do when I was a little girl. The wind whipped my hair, pulling strands of it from my bun. I climbed the bottom of the railing and leaned out even farther, gripping the top railing with my hands and imagining I was on the deck of the clipper. I could almost feel the sway of the ship's deck under my feet, the crate on my own shoulder, the wooden boards rough against my hand, the edge biting into my shoulder. I swore I could smell the woodsy scent of the tea over the brackish odor of the river.

The *Osprey* reached the docks, and I saw the young man quite clearly. I noticed the sweat streaking down his face, despite the chill of the day, and his eyes snapping with excitement. I couldn't help but smile. He looked in my direction, and I imagined he saw me. Imagined the nod that followed was for me. His grin grew even wider, and then with a shout and a heave of his arms, he tossed the crate overboard. It crashed onto the dock, and the sides split open, pouring its contents out. A breeze swirled over the curled tea leaves, picking them up and tossing them like confetti over the crowd. A boy about ten years old, dressed in knickerbockers and a flat cap, dashed forward and scooped a pile of the leaves into a hessian sack and ran into the trading house. The tugboat continued on, pulling the *Osprey* toward the docking yards.

Moments later a bell rang out and the boy reappeared.

"The *Osprey* wins!" he shouted.

The crowd erupted into cheers. The sailors on the *Osprey* gathered around the young man, clapping him on the shoulders.

"Come along, Elodie," Papa said. "Let us find a coffeehouse. We'll come back once the crowd has dispersed." Reluctantly I left the railing and followed Papa down the docks. I glanced at the ship one last time, and I saw the young man had left his celebrating comrades and moved to the back of the ship. He was looking toward the spot where I stood.

❇ ❇ ❇ ❇

PAPA AND I WERE GONE ONLY AN HOUR AT THE COFFEEHOUSE, BUT AT the East India Docks the stevedores had sprung into action. When we arrived, towering stacks of tea, ten crates high, stood on the quayside while men barrowed them into the warehouse with handcarts. Crates were winched out of the *Osprey* with ropes and swung over the docks, replacing the boxes on the stack as fast as the stevedores could barrow them off.

"They are already unloading?" I asked Papa.

"Oh, yes," he said. "Buyers have been waiting since the ships left China. The porcelain packed alongside the tea is worth a fair bit, too. As soon as the ship gets unloaded and reloaded with wool and cotton to sell in China, they will be off again. No rest for them, I fear."

We went into the Merchant Navy office at the side of the warehouse, and while I remained in the vestibule Papa went off to find a clerk and make his enquiries for passage aboard a clipper. I waited in the windowless room for a quarter of an hour, but the lure of the action on the docks was too much for me to resist, and so I stepped outside to watch the ships unload, sheltering from the sun under the eaves of the building. The Merchant Navy office was at the end of the quay, and the action unfolded in front of me as though I were watching a Christmas pantomime. The men shouted in various accents, some regional to England and some foreign. It seemed that several countries had converged on this one dock with the same purpose.

I thought about the many hands that had gone into transporting that tea, and the hands that had held the leaves that filled my teapot each day at home. My thoughts drifted to the mountains of China, where the tea grew high up in the clouds. Who were the people who set out that season to pick the tea? Did they wonder about the person who would drink the cup of tea made from the handful of leaves they plucked that morning? I wondered what the air smelled of in that mysterious world, and if the flavor of the tea carried the land's very essence. I could not fathom a place where tea and orchids grew together. What a mystical place it must be. I didn't think I would look at tea the same way again.

A commotion beyond the warehouse drew me out of my reverie. Angry voices shouted, and footsteps pounded the boards of the wharf.

Sprinting down the dock was the little black-and-white dog I'd seen on the *Osprey* earlier, a chicken leg clenched in its dainty mouth. The dog was running so fast that its front legs stretched straight out. Every few strides the dog bounded through the air, as though attempting to fly. A man in pursuit, a napkin tied around his neck, most likely the erstwhile owner of the chicken leg, brandished his fists.

"Stop, you little thief!" he shouted.

Hard on his heels was the young man on the *Osprey* who had tossed the tea crate onto the dock. He was yelling, too, but it wasn't in English.

The little dog dodged around the men unloading tea. It dashed in front of a stevedore pushing a cart piled high with tea crates. Startled, the stevedore jerked the handles of his barrow, tipping it sideways and dumping the contents onto the quay. Another stevedore, carrying smaller boxes, tripped over one of the fallen crates and crashed to the ground, his booted feet flying up in the air. Another skidded to a halt just in time before he tripped over the prone stevedore. The dog dashed behind one of the towers of tea crates and, wisely, did not reappear.

The man pursuing the dog stopped and glanced around. The stevedore who had lost his cargo rumbled the dog's whereabouts, gesturing angrily at the tower.

The man jerked his head toward the dog's hiding place. "I have you now, you whelp!" He lunged behind the tower, and the dog left its hiding place, popping out right in front of me. But there was no more dock left, and the dog had nowhere to escape to. It would have to jump into the water or turn back right into the path of the angry man. The dog skidded to a halt, the tiny claws digging into the wooden boards and a whine leaving its throat. The little animal turned its head and looked at me. Its eyes were the sweetest chocolate brown color. It lifted one ear, those brown eyes pleading.

I took a step forward, picked up my skirt, and dropped it over the dog.

ELEVEN

he man appeared from behind the crates, staring around him, his face red with rage. He was very short and portly, but muscles bulged beneath the sleeves of his canvas shirt. I imagined that once he'd gotten hold of a person—or a little dog—he'd never let go.

"Where is that wee beast?" he shouted. "Did ye see it?"

I shook my head. "I saw nothing. Perhaps it's gone into the warehouse."

He glared. "I saw it come this way."

I shrugged. "I'm very sorry. I . . . I didn't see a dog come this way."

Safely underneath my cage crinoline, the dog dropped the chicken leg on my boot and sniffed my ankle. I could feel the wet of its nose seeping through my cotton stocking. Its whiskers tickled, and I bit my lip to keep from laughing. Delighted with its new hiding place, the little dog began to dart around the perimeter.

The young sailor stepped out from behind the crates, and his face blanched when he saw the end of the dock. When he glanced at me, I flicked my fingers toward my skirt, and the young man's eyes widened, comprehending the dog's hiding place.

"That beast of your'n has taken my dinner!" The sailor rounded on the young man. He poked him in the chest with a stubby finger, the nail thick with grime. "What are you going to do about it?"

The young man looked bewildered and replied to the sailor with a slew of words, shaking his head and holding his hands up. The language had a melodic tone, rather like a song than a sentence.

The sailor narrowed his eyes. "Hey? What's that yer saying, eh?"

"I don't believe he speaks English," I said to the sailor. "I don't think he understands you." Underneath my skirt, the dog ceased its lark-about and sat down on my foot, leaning against my leg.

"How's about I make him understand me?" The sailor cracked his hairy knuckles and then grabbed a handful of the young man's shirt. "How about that?"

"There's no call for that!" I said. "Let him go!"

The young man shouted something in his native tongue again, and the dog growled, its throat rumbling against my leg.

The door to the Merchant Navy office swung open, and Papa stepped out. He put his hat on and looked around, his eyes searching. I waved to catch his attention. "There's my father. He speaks several languages, so perhaps he knows what the sailor is saying." I dearly hoped he knew the young man's particular language.

"There's been a bit of a disturbance," I said to Papa after he'd made his way over. "It seems a little dog has stolen this man's dinner, and he is claiming this other man as the owner."

"Where is the dog in question?" Papa asked, looking around.

"No one seems to know where it went," I said.

"The bloke is speaking gibberish," the sailor said, releasing the young man's shirt. "A load of nonsense."

The young man flew forth with another string of words.

Papa listened, nodding, and then he turned to the sailor. "I believe that *gibberish*, as you say, is Russian. Allow me to translate." Papa said something to the young man who then replied. "He says he has no idea who owns the dog," Papa translated.

The sailor scowled. "Oh, is that right? Why was he hollering at the dog and running after it, then, heh?"

Papa bowed politely. "I will ask him." The two spoke again and Papa replied, "He says he was shouting at the dog because he took some food from him, too." The young man said something else to Papa. "He says if he finds the dog, he'll wring its neck."

The sailor poked the young man in the chest again. "Well, see that you do!"

Papa put his hand in his pocket and drew out a shilling. "May I be so bold as to offer to replace your dinner? Perhaps that will settle the matter."

The sailor squinted at the coin and then snatched it out of Papa's fingers. "That settles the matter for now, but I'll be on the lookout for that scamp. If I see it around here, I'll stuff it in a sack and drown it. Mark my words." Glaring at the young man once more, the sailor left.

The young man blew out his breath and grinned. He held

out his hand to my father. "*Spasibo*. Many thanks to you, sir," he said in perfect English, marked with a slight accent.

Papa shook his hand. "Hello, Alex. Good to see you again. I'm happy to be of service to you."

"That was a sailor on the ship we raced. He's very angry at losing. No bonus for them. That chicken leg was probably the first bite of meat he's enjoyed since he left Foochow. She's naughty, Kukla; she should not be poking around the public houses like a starved waif. I didn't know she'd left the ship until I saw her and that oaf thundering past while I was helping to unload the ship."

"Where is the little dog in question?" Papa asked.

"Well, it seems your daughter came to her rescue," Alex replied. "And I'm quite glad she did."

At the sound of her master's voice, the little dog poked her nose under the edge of my skirt. "I dropped my skirt over her to hide her," I said. The dog pulled her nose in, returned to my boot and retrieved her chicken leg. This firmly in her jaw, she popped out from my skirt and ran to Alex, her whole body wagging in delight.

He knelt on the dock and pried the chicken leg out of her mouth, tossing it into the water. "You are a naughty girl, Kukla, and I cannot let you have your pirate's booty." He scratched the dog's ruff affectionately. He looked up at me. "Thank you for hiding her, miss."

"Elodie, this is Alexander Balashov, second mate aboard the *Osprey* and the adopted son of the captain, a very good friend of mine," Papa said.

"*Spasibo*, Elodie. Thank you," Mr. Balashov said. "Please call me Alex."

"It's my pleasure," I said.

A man came around the stack of tea crates then, a worried look on his face, which faded when he spied Alex.

"Alex," he said. "There you are."

Alex turned around, a dismayed expression on his face. Whoever this man was, Alex must have disobeyed him in some way. I hoped he wasn't in too much trouble.

"Just the person I wanted to see." Papa stepped forward and shook the hand of the man who had spoken. "It's good to see you, Horatio. Elodie, this is Captain Everett of the *Osprey.*"

The captain appeared to be about my father's age, but his face was lined with wrinkles, his cheeks red and chapped, which I imagined was because he'd been exposed to sun and sea for many years. He looked exhausted and not a little fed up. I was sure bringing in such a ship, and racing it across the oceans to be the first to England, must take its toll on a person. "Good to see you again, Hugh," the captain said, addressing my father. "I trust you are well now? I was very concerned when I heard—"

Papa cleared his throat interrupting the captain. "I'm very well," he said quickly. "Captain, this is my daughter, Elodie."

"Your daughter? Oh, I see. Please forgive me . . ." His voice trailed off.

Hugh? Why had he called my father Hugh?

"What are you doing off the ship, Alex?" Captain Everett asked. "I've been looking everywhere for you."

Alex stood up, holding Kukla in his arms. "I'm sorry, Father. Kukla ran off, and I left the ship to find her."

The captain frowned. "That matters not. You need to tell me where you are going and what you are doing. You promised you'd do that, remember?"

Alex's expression tightened. "I was not doing anything wrong. I was not looking for trouble." He flicked his gaze toward me, and I saw he was embarrassed. I felt very bad for him. I wouldn't like to be chided so in front of other people. Alex's good day seemed to be traveling a downward path very quickly.

"I know you weren't." The captain laid his hand on Alex's shoulder. "I'm just concerned."

"Please don't be." Alex said this quietly and then looked out over the water, his shoulder tense under his father's hand.

"Forgive me for interrupting," I said, longing to break the tension for Alex, who looked for all the world as though he'd love to be anywhere else but there. "But we have to decide what we can do about the little dog. I don't know how long you'll be here at the docks, Captain, but if that man sees Kukla again, I don't think Alex can save her. He was very angry."

"You'll have to tie her up in the 'tween decks until we embark for China," the captain said.

Alex's arms stiffened around his dog. "She'll never stay there," he said. "She'll find a way out." I could almost feel the horror and panic wafting off Alex. I didn't blame him. If that sailor saw Kukla again, no telling what he would do to her.

"I see no other solution," the captain said, his face grave. I was beginning to think that Captain Horatio Everett was incapable of smiling, but I suspected that the running of such a vessel as the *Osprey* probably left little time for gaiety.

"I wonder, Captain," my father said. "Might I have a word with you? Just a few minutes of your time is all I need."

"Oh, yes, yes of course," the captain replied. "Alex, would you mind looking after Hugh's daughter for a few moments? Can you escort her to the ship in a quarter of an hour?" The captain stood for a moment, looking unsure, and then, apparently deciding Alex didn't have mischief in mind, departed.

"I knew Kukla's food thievery would bring her grief one day," Alex said. "I've tried to break her of it, but she lived off her own cunning in the streets for too long, and it's impossible for her to understand that she no longer needs to fear an empty belly."

"Is it just a matter of hiding her from the sailor she stole from?"

He nodded. "We hope to sail in a fortnight. We have to return for a cargo of the early season's tea, the gunpowder tea, which is most valuable. We have some repairs to make to the *Osprey*'s mast and spars. Once we set sail, Kukla will be out of the sailor's way."

"How about if I take her home with me to Kent and then return her the morning you're ready to sail?" I found I wanted to help the sailor more than anything. The idea of doing something kind for someone else made the shame I felt about the orchid a little more bearable. "I'm sure it would do her a world of good to run in the meadows near our home. I'll make sure she never leaves my side. I promise you that, Alex."

Relief filled the young man's face. His shoulders relaxed, and his fingers unclenched from the dog's fur. "You would not mind? She's very good company."

It would be nothing for me to give Kukla a home. In truth, I would love to have the little dog, and my sisters would find her a delightful diversion, I was sure.

"Then it's settled," I said. "We'll have to hide her as we walk back. I don't think the stevedores who lost their cargo will be happy to see her." I tugged my shawl from around my shoulders. "Will she let me hold her like a baby, do you think, Alex? I can wrap her in my shawl."

Alex laughed. "She would adore such a thing. She's always acting the sad one in hopes someone will hold her." He handed her to me, placing her in my arms like a newborn baby and drawing the edge of the shawl over her face and tucking her long fox's tail in. Kukla immediately assumed a doleful expression. Then she snuggled against my bodice and made a little sigh.

"Poor little thing," I crooned.

Alex snorted with laughter. "Spoiled little thing, more like."

We made our way back through the stevedores, making sure to skirt well around a good bit of the action. As happy as Kukla was for me to hold her, Alex wasn't at all sure she'd remain that way should a cat leap onto the dock or someone push a fish-filled barrow by. But in my arms she remained.

"Is there some reason you and the captain call my father Hugh?" I asked.

Alex looked puzzled. "But that is his name, is it not? Hugh McGregor?"

"No. His name is Reginald Buchanan." *Hugh McGregor* sounded familiar to me. I'd heard it before in the not so distant past. Where, I couldn't recall.

"Why would he not want us to know his name?"

I shrugged. "He must travel under a different name," I said, and left it at that, adding this information to the pile of secrets my father kept. It was as though he conducted a completely separate life away from us.

"What brings you both to the dockyards? Did you come to see the race?"

I shook my head. "My father has to return to China to fulfill his contract with his employer. His mission to find orchids was a failure the last time he was there. His employer is insistent."

Alex looked taken aback. "I'm surprised to hear this. It's very brave of him to return after what happened to him."

"Were you able to assist my father after he was wounded?" I asked.

"No. We knew so little at the time," Alex said. "It's very sad that the emperor's Summer Palace was destroyed in retaliation for the men's capture; it was a beautiful place, I'm told. But I suppose one barbaric act deserves another. Your father looks better than he did when the Chinese released him. I saw him before he was sent home and he appeared a walking skeleton. . . ." My face must have registered the horror I felt because Alex stopped talking. "I'm sorry. I've said too much. The details no longer matter. Your father is on the mend, and that's good."

Papa appeared on deck with Captain Everett. He had secured passage on board the *Osprey*, which would depart as soon as repairs were made and a new cargo secured. With Kukla done up like a baby in my shawl once more, Papa and I returned to Kew.

Alex's report about Papa kept turning around and around in my head. Papa looked content after speaking with Captain Everett, and indeed he looked brighter and more himself, but I couldn't help wondering what were we doing sending him back to China. What if the men who had hurt him wanted to do him harm again? What if his name was linked with this Summer Palace destruction forever?

But he had no choice. No choice at all. And there was nothing I could do but pray for his safety.

I TOOK ON ALL THE TASKS REQUIRED TO SEND PAPA TO CHINA. ALL OF his supplies had been lost in China, and he'd left the country with the clothes he stood up in. I sat down with Papa, with Alex's Kukla at my feet, and wrote a list of things needing replacement. I turned his wardrobe out, inspecting the clothing he had to hand and packing what he needed in his traveling trunk. I wrote to Thomas Burberry, ordering a new waterproof coat, and to Harrods for expedition equipment: a tent, compass, several gas lanterns, cases of tinned and dried food, a medical kit, and a folding bath, chair, and bed. And finally, I wrote to James Purdey & Sons for a rifle, revolver, and ammunition. This last purchase only served to remind me of how harrowing Papa's journey truly would be.

At night, I fell into an uneasy sleep, waking several times to listen for Papa's sobs, but I never heard him cry again, and I hoped this was a sign that he was on the mend.

Several days later, Papa returned to Kent with me. I tried to chat with him on the train journey about this and that, but he seemed diverted and only answered when I repeated my questions, always fading off before he finished his thoughts. He sat across from me in the train carriage, staring down at his hat, turning the brim round and round in his hands. He'd left off the smock and was wearing a coat with overly long sleeves, and by now I knew this was to hide the scars on his wrists. I wondered how he would explain the wounds to Mamma. I had assumed they would have their usual reconciliation as soon as Papa appeared. It would do Mamma a lot of good to see Papa again, even for just a little while. And even for the villagers to see them together. Perhaps that would stop their wagging tongues.

After the train arrived at the station, Papa helped me alight from the train, and we set off on foot for home. When we reached the common, Papa stopped.

"Do you need to rest, Papa?"

"No, my dear. I'm not going any farther," Papa said. "I'll say my good-byes here. There is an evening train back to London in an hour, and I mean to be on it. There's much to do to prepare for my journey. I have glass Wardian cases to consign and other bits and pieces . . ." His voice trailed off, and he looked toward the train station.

"What do you mean? I'm sure Mamma wants to see you. And the children, as well." Kukla, tired of waiting, lay down in the grass. Her gaze switched from me to my father.

He shook his head, a sorrowful look on his face. "I don't think so."

"Well, you are quite wrong! Papa! How can you come home and not see them? That's cruel!"

"You don't understand—"

"You are quite right! I don't understand. I don't understand you at all. Mamma has been so ill, and it would be nothing for you to go inside and greet her. And for the villagers to see you doing so. People have been gossiping, and it affects Mamma's health."

"Elodie, stop!" Papa said, sounding angry and a little desperate. "All the more reason for Mamma not to see me. Now please do not argue with me. It's better this way. I know it is, and you must not quarrel."

"Please, Papa, don't make me go in there alone and tell Mamma and the girls you refuse to see them." I tugged on his arm, trying to force him to come with me, but he stood solid as a stone.

"I can't. Elodie, you saw the way Violetta reacted when she saw me. I won't have your mother distressed. We only argue when I'm home, and if she sees . . . if she knows of certain events, well, things will grow worse between us."

"What do you mean?"

"This is between your mother and me."

"How can you think her so coldhearted that she wouldn't welcome you?"

"There are certain things you don't understand, Elodie. Things your mother and I have decided. People already look on you as different. A father who is gone a great deal of the time is not usual, and people judge. I know this. I wish I could change things. But, Elodie, God help me, I cannot be any different. I travel under an assumed name because I don't want my deeds to affect your mother, you, or your sisters, ever. To the villagers here I'm simply a man who finds plants and nothing more."

And then, just like that, I recalled where I'd heard the name Hugh McGregor. This name was amongst the few survivors released from China's Board of Punishments. Hugh McGregor had survived while the others had perished of their injuries. I remembered what the newspaper editor had written: *The captors had tied their feet and hands behind their backs as tightly as possible with leather cords, and then tipped water on the bindings to increase the tension as the cords dried. The men were kept in this position until the condition of their hands and wrists became putrid and riddled with vermin.*

Hugh McGregor was my father.

"Papa. I know what happened to you. I saw your scars. I know that a Hugh McGregor was captured during the war. That's you, isn't it? Papa, how could you think what had happened to you would change how we regarded you? You were a victim, not a villain."

He stared at me, and then he started to laugh—a joyless, cynical laugh. "Oh, my dear, you don't know half of the story. If you did, it would most certainly change how you *regarded* me."

His words chilled me so much that I shivered.

And then he kissed my cheek and left. I let him return to the train station without saying another word to him.

What had my dashing and adventurous father done?

Scenarios filled my mind. Had my father killed someone? Had he been the cause of someone else's downfall? Had he stolen?

It was Kukla's whining that snapped me out of my trance. In a daze I took her up in my arms and went home. I didn't know what else to do.

TWELVE

hen I walked in my front door, I was very grateful for Kukla's presence. The little girls fell on her the moment her paws touched the tiled hall.

"Puppy!" Peony shouted, rushing toward her with outstretched arms. My other sisters followed swiftly. Kukla sat in the middle of their circle, thumping her bushy tail on the floor and looking at each of my sisters in turn, eyes snapping with glee, thrilled by their attention and admiration.

"A dog?" Violetta said, humor in her voice. "Wherever did you find a dog?"

"I'm only minding her for a fortnight or so," I said. "I'll tell you where I found her later. Girls, why don't you take Kukla out into the garden to play?" I watched my giggling sisters run off, Kukla dashing alongside them, her claws scrabbling for purchase on the wooden floorboards. "Where's Mamma?"

She looked resigned. "In bed. Dr. Thumpston insisted. He said arising from her sickbed too soon caused her accident. He's blaming you, as it happens. I think he suspects you did something to her medicine. He wasn't amused when he saw the empty Chlorodyne bottle on Mamma's bedside table doing duty as a sweet pea vase."

"Well, he can think what he likes. Papa agrees with me. The Chlorodyne is bad for her. Don't give her any more."

"Now that you're home you can take the responsibility of it," Violetta said, her voice petulant. "I don't want anything more to do with Dr. Thumpston."

I rubbed my forehead where a headache was beginning to form. I didn't want to snap at Violetta, but honestly, I was getting exhausted with looking after every last detail. At times of self-pity, such as this one, I wished that someone would look after me every now and again. My shoulders were beginning to ache with all the burdens I carried. I was only seventeen. I should be going to dances and meeting young men and reading novels. What I wouldn't give to sit under the oak trees on the common and read, as Violetta did constantly. Or have time to while away alone, with no children present, in my conservatory.

"Where is Papa?"

"He's returned to Kew," I said shortly, having not the energy or the desire to moderate my words, as I did usually, so that Violetta wouldn't become cross. I cared not how harsh my words sounded or how she'd react to them. "He won't come in, and I'll thank you not to throw a tantrum over it."

Instead of her usual grim retort when it came to my father's actions, Violetta simply nodded. "I don't think it would be wise for Mamma to see him right now. She's too poorly."

My irritation with Violetta drained away with those words. If Violetta had grown angry, I could not have borne it; I would have burst into tears. "Do you think so?" I said. "Papa said the very same thing. And now I feel that I'm inclined to agree with you."

"The look of him, Elodie!"

"I know." I glanced up the staircase, wanting to hold back telling Mamma that Papa had returned to London without seeing her for as long as I could. "I'll have to tell her something. I'm sure she's expecting to see him. What shall I say?"

Violetta considered for a moment. "Tell her he didn't come back with you. That he has much to do to prepare for his voyage. She'll understand that."

And indeed that's what I told Mamma, but I'm not sure she understood me; so deep she was, once again, in the thrall of Collis Browne's Chlorodyne.

Later that day, I showed Violetta the editor's letter.

"Putrid with vermin?" she said, looking up from the letter. "Are you quite sure one of these men he is describing was Papa?"

"The captain and his son called Papa Hugh. Hugh McGregor." I took the letter from her and ran my finger under the name. "There it is. And that is why Papa wears those oversized smocks, to hide the scars."

Violetta looked doubtful. "Papa had nothing to do with this government mission. He's not a soldier, and he's never been one. The name is common enough. Perhaps there's another Hugh McGregor."

"I wish that were true, but Papa didn't deny it. And the captain's son, Alex, told me a little bit about Papa's ordeal and mentioned the burning of a palace. And I saw the scars on Papa's wrist myself. Violetta, it was horrible. You can't imagine how horrible."

"If it is true . . ." Violetta whispered. And then she voiced the worry that I had held in my mind. "Then what are we doing making him return to China?"

THE CHILDREN WERE SO TIRED AFTER PLAYING WITH THE DOG THAT they went off to bed with no complaints, even Lily, who tended toward tantrums as her bedtime approached. Once the children were safe asleep, Violetta and I lay in our own bed, Kukla at our feet.

"So go on, tell me how you came to have this dog."

I told her about Alex and how I had hidden the dog under my crinoline, in between Violetta's peals of laughter.

"I'm sure the boy was most grateful." She turned on her side, her eyes snapping with interest. "Is he handsome?"

I nodded. "Yes. Very." I recalled Alex's warm eyes and the few inches of skin between his wrists and elbows where he had rolled up his sleeves. And how noble his profile looked. And how sweet his expression was when he looked at his little dog.

"How much?"

"Oh, I don't know, Violetta. How does one quantify handsomeness?"

She flopped over on her back and played with the end of her braid, considering. "Is he handsome like Heathcliff or handsome like Mr. Darcy?"

"I don't know. If I have to choose I'll say Heathcliff, but he does not share his black temperament."

She sucked in her breath. "Tragically handsome, then."

I laughed. "I suppose so. If there is such a thing." Suddenly

I felt a waft of happiness and love toward my little sister. Her charming imagination was sometimes so adorable I wanted to hug her. Kukla, perhaps feeling left out of our conversation, rose on her little paws and moved to lie down between us, resting her head on Violetta's shoulder.

"You're lucky," she said, stroking the dog's little triangle-shaped ear. "The offerings are very thin on the ground here. No tragically handsome boys to be found." She turned on her side again, resting her chin on the dog's head. "Do you fancy him?"

I didn't want to think about whether I fancied Alex Balashov or not. Certainly I didn't want to admit it to my little sister, who wouldn't let such a thing pass. "No, I don't," I said. "Not a bit."

"Hmmm," she said. "Your face is telling me differently. You do fancy this boy."

I threw her a sour look. "Yes, and I'm going to run away with him and marry him and live a life sailing the seven seas with him. And while we're at it, fairies will fly us to a land filled with boiled sweets and chocolates that grow on trees."

"Sometimes I don't believe you have a romantic bone in your body, Elodie. Sometimes I think you'll end up married to some dull boy and live the dullest life imaginable."

"Go to sleep, Violetta," I said.

She harrumphed and turned over. Before I blew out the candle I looked at the little dog, whose brown eyes regarded me so intently. I wished she could speak, because I wanted to ask her all about her tragically handsome master.

KUKLA SLOTTED PERFECTLY INTO OUR FAMILY. SHE LOVED TO SLEEP in a basket by the fire that was two sizes too small for her, but she always insisted on squashing herself inside of it, her tail and head balancing on the rim. She adored the little girls and didn't mind if one of them pulled her tail or stepped on her paw accidently. Calla, in particular, took to her, reading to the little dog from her picture books. I found them together one morning, Calla's cheek resting on Kukla's furry back like a pillow. I had to remind the girls that Kukla was only a guest, and that she would be returning to Alex any day now. But I had a thought in my mind to find the girls a dog. One with a jovial temperament like Kukla's who would return a merry atmosphere to our home.

If my family was happy to have me back home, Deacon Wainwright certainly was not. Church had become almost unbearable with his blank stares. He treated me coldly, behaving as though he were a jilted beau rather than my deacon. I was beginning to think that Papa was correct, and that Deacon Wainwright did want me to become his wife, and the thought of it filled me with dread, especially when I started to consider the more intimate aspects of married life. I wasn't completely in the dark about what went on between a husband and wife. My mother had made sure to sit me down before my monthlies first arrived to tell me what lay in store. She herself had been left ignorant when she was a young woman and she was terrified when her body began to change. A kind chambermaid had seen her blood-soaked cloths, took pity on her, and told her about how babies were started.

Unbidden, my imagination conjured up a pantomime of our

wedding night. I saw the Deacon, waiting outside our bedroom while I changed out of my wedding gown. After knocking and waiting for my invitation, he entered the room, wearing a long nightshirt that exposed his nobbley knees and skinny calves. A nightcap to keep away drafts sat perched upon his head. After one perfunctory kiss, he did his marital duty quickly, his head politely to one side, our nightdresses rucked up, exposing only what was necessary.

I couldn't think of anything worse.

I stared at Deacon Wainwright railing away about something or another in his pulpit, feeling a flush creep up my neck, unable to stop myself from thinking of the deacon in any other way now.

Violetta, catching me in the middle of this hideous daydream, elbowed me in the side and hissed in my ear. "What's come over you? You look as though you've seen a ghost. We're meant to be singing a hymn. Stand up!"

I stood hastily, staring down at Violetta's hymnal, mortified. I spent the rest of the service with my face buried in my Bible, unable to look in Deacon Wainwright's direction for fear of my imagination posting yet another marital encounter between the two of us.

At the end of April, a letter arrived from Papa telling me that the ship was ready to depart and I was to meet him at Richmond with Kukla the next day. I was glad to leave Kent, gladder than I thought possible, and this made me feel immensely guilty. But it hurt me that Papa hadn't offered to fetch me himself.

So I made the journey to Richmond on my own. I was glad I had watched Deacon Wainwright so carefully on the first journey to Richmond. Kukla, unhappy with the lead I had fashioned from a bit of clothesline, had been a nightmare, refusing to settle at my feet. Instead she spent her time whimpering and testing the limits of her tether and my patience. In the end I held her on my lap so she could peer out of the window at the scenery, and this seemed to settle her.

I disembarked at Richmond Station, my valise in one hand and Kukla's lead in the other. The station was quite busy with people bustling all around, and since Madame Kukla refused to walk on her lead, I picked her up and tucked her under my arm. I glanced around the arrival hall and saw Papa waiting by the clock.

Kukla wriggled frantically in my arms as I made my way through the crowds. *Little beast!* "I cannot wait to deliver you back to your master," I told her. She pressed her cold nose against my cheek and wagged her tail.

Papa did not appear gladsome to see me. His face was pinched with strain, and he tugged repeatedly at the cuffs of his jacket.

"Good morning, Papa." I set Kukla on the floor and leaned forward to kiss his cheek, but Papa recoiled at my touch and stepped away from my embrace.

"What is it, Papa? Are you quite well?"

"I'm sorry, my dear, but I'm a little out of sorts this morning." He was acting strangely, staring at the face of each person who passed by, peering intently at each one.

"Are you looking for someone?"

"Did anyone follow you from Edencroft?" he asked, not taking his eyes off the crowd. "Did you see anyone looking at you on the train?"

"Looking at me? What do you mean?"

"The question is a simple one. Did anyone see you? Did their eyes lie upon your personage? I don't know how I can make the question clearer."

"Only the conductor when he clipped my ticket."

"There were no passengers in your car? I find that difficult to believe," he barked.

"Of course there were passengers," I said, feeling hurt by his tone of voice and line of questioning. I felt as though he was trying to pin some sort of blame upon me. "But they were minding to their own affairs. Why are you asking me this?"

"Because someone has seen fit to burgle my cottage. While I was out walking this morning."

"Burgle?" I was astonished. Burglaries were common enough in cities, but Papa's cottage was well inside the garden. A thief would have to know the cottage was there to make it worth his while. And Papa didn't seem to own or keep anything in the cottage worth stealing.

"That's what I said!"

"What did they take, Papa?"

"I haven't had a chance to look, have I? I've had to come here to greet you so you can take that dog back to where it came."

"But Papa . . ." Kukla, wound up by the crowds of people pressing around her, began to tug at her tether. "Kukla!" I chided.

"Control that damnable dog, will you!" he said.

"It's hardly her fault. She's not used to such crowds, I expect. She's only a dog, and she doesn't understand." I leaned down to pick Kukla up, but she slipped from my grasp. She gamboled around my father as though on a merry chase and then raced back to me, dragging the clothesline around his ankles as she did.

The change in my father was immediate. He punched his fists in the air. "Leave off!" he shouted, his voice high and trembling. "Leave off! Leave off!" Papa's face was wild with fear, his face white as milk. Kukla, terrified by my father's shouting, jumped away, snugging the rope around his ankles.

I dropped to my knees, uncaring of the people stopping to stare, and untangled the rope. I scooped Kukla into my arms. "It was only the dog, Papa," I said. "See? She didn't mean any harm; it was the crowd that frightened her and she tugged her lead around you."

I might have been addressing a statue. Papa stood unblinking, staring at nothing. Tears pooled in his eyes, and he began to shake all over. I took his arm. "Papa, please! It was only the dog."

"Man's round the bend," I heard someone say to his companion as he walked passed us. "Belongs in an asylum and not out amongst decent people."

"Papa?" I touched his arm, but it was almost like stone. I didn't know what to do. No one stopped to help. Passersby left a wide berth around us, as though Papa's fit might rub up against them. We stood there for what seemed like ages. I soothed my father as best as I could, hoping he would snap out of his catatonic state, when a man in a bowler hat and wire-rimmed spectacles stopped.

"May I help at all?" he asked, his voice soft-spoken and gentle.

"My father has taken a turn," I said. "Could you help me settle him into a cab, perhaps?"

"Yes, yes of course!" The man waved for a porter and handed him a coin. "Will you find a cab for us and take the young lady's dog and valise?" The boy nodded, took Kukla's lead and my bag, knuckled his forehead, and headed outside, half dragging the reluctant dog behind him.

"Now then, my good man. Let's see what we're about, shall we?" The man took Papa by one arm and I took the other, and little by little, my heart breaking with every step, we shuffled my stricken father out of the station and onto Kew Road, where a cab stood waiting. Papa gave us little resistance as we settled him into the cab.

"Take him home, miss," the man said, his hands resting on the cab's door, "and have a doctor look after him."

I opened my reticule. "I wish to pay you for your help and for the porter," I said.

He waved his hand. "Not at all, miss. It was my pleasure to assist you." He touched the brim of his hat. "Best of luck to you both."

Papa had recovered a little of his wits on the short ride to his cottage, but the fit had exhausted him. He remained quiet, refusing to look at me. Instead he sat staring out the window.

I was never more grateful to see Papa's little cottage nestled on the edge of Kew's arboretum. It looked a paradise after the horrors of that morning, and I could understand why he had chosen to seek sanctuary here. Papa alighted from the cab, shrugging off my attempts to help him. He staggered to his door, as though sleepwalking, fumbled in his pocket, and took out a large brass key. The key rattled against the escutcheon as he tried over and over to fit it into the lock. Wanting to spare him further humiliation, I stepped back, pretending to be distracted by Kukla, who was wagging her tail and staring off into the trees.

Finally the key slid into its mark, and the door swung open.

I followed Papa in, expecting to be met with neat shelves lined with books, his plants and papers organized just so. But that was not the scene that met us.

The cottage hadn't simply been burgled; it had been ransacked. Every book had been pulled out of his bookcase, shaken out and then flung onto the floor. The pots had been smashed—the shattered clay pots and compost dumped all over the room, and the little plants lay forsaken on the tile, their leaves shriveling and their blooms crushed under an unknown foot. Papa's desk drawers had been pulled out and overturned, and the contents of his traveling trunk had been scattered across the room.

I stood in the middle of this, staring, my mouth open. Papa hesitated, scanning the mess, and then shook his head. He shuffled through the shambles, climbed the stairs to the loft, and left me alone.

My father's journals. His treasure map that led to the Queen's Fancy. I searched the shelf where Papa kept them, looked through the mess on the floor. But they were not there.

They were gone.

❧ ❦ ❧ ❦

THE ONLY PERSON I KNEW AT KEW WAS SIR WILLIAM HOOKER. I shut Kukla into the little shed out back and went to seek him out. I found him after one of the garden workers directed me to the herbarium. He stood at a bench near one of the iron spiral staircases, leaning on his elbows, examining a pressed specimen.

"Come to see your father depart?" he said, his face kindly. After I told him what had befallen my father he stood up, abandoning his task, and returned to the cottage with me immediately.

"You say the dog set your father off?" he asked.

"It was its lead. It wrapped round Papa's legs."

Sir William glanced at me, his expression worried.

"He was already upset when I met him at the station. When we returned home, I found the reason why. His cottage had been ransacked. I'm sure these two incidents caused the turn."

"I'm very sorry to hear this. Very sorry indeed."

"Has this happened before?" I asked. Sir William seemed reluctant to speak. "I know what befell him in China. You don't have to keep his secret, because I've seen his wrists. I've seen the scars."

Sir William stopped walking. "Does he know you possess this knowledge?"

"Yes, but he says we don't know all of it."

Sir William let out a sigh. "I don't know what to say to put you at ease. Mr. Buchanan has not taken me into his confidence about everything."

"But we are his family," I replied, frustrated. "Why does he insist on hiding anything from us?"

"I can tell you this—the trauma he suffered was truly wretched, and he does not wish to burden his family with such knowledge. The fit you witnessed is not a one-off. He's had them many times, many times since he returned from China. It's quite startling, as you now understand. He refused to return home until his health improved because he didn't want his family to see the state of him. It's a terrible thing for a man to be seen as weak, especially in the eyes of his family. And as much as it pains me, I have to respect his wishes. I suggest you do the same. Don't press him. Don't force him to confide in you. He'll come to tell you of it in his own time. If he chooses to."

We continued through the garden in silence, past the ship-like glass Palm House and the massive cedar and oak trees, whose boughs had stretched ever skyward for hundreds of years. The beauty of Kew felt utterly at odds with the horror my father had experienced. The trees, palms, and orchids of Kew had continued to thrive, while my father, the very person who had discovered many of these delights, was tortured. While people in a faraway land saw fit to torment him so unspeakably that he would remain in a prison of his own mind, perhaps forever.

AT THE COTTAGE, WE FOUND PAPA RESTORING ORDER TO THE ROOM. He stood surrounded by chaos, carefully slotting books back into place.

Sir William stopped short when he saw the mess.

"Ah, Sir William," Papa said, looking up briefly from his task. "I do apologize for the clutter, but it appears that I've been burgled."

"When did this happen?" Sir William asked.

"I went out for a walk in the morning, and when I returned, I found this."

"This looks very bad, very bad indeed," Sir William said. "Have you sent for constables yet?"

"Dear me, no. No need. I expect this is the work of street urchins up to mischief. Nothing stolen that I can make out."

"But, Papa," I said. "Surely this vandalism cannot go unreported." I searched through the mess. "What about your journal, your map of China? I couldn't find it earlier. Perhaps this is the work of the man who stole my orchid."

Papa shelved the book he was holding and then knelt down next to the pile of books he'd gathered, shuffling through them so quickly that the pile collapsed. "It's in here, I'm sure I saw it."

I knelt down next to him to help him search, but he shot me a look so fierce that I stood up. I had never been afraid of my father before, but if I were honest, I was wary of him now.

"Are you feeling quite well, Buchanan?" Sir William grasped his hands behind his back and leaned forward a little, gazing at father intently.

"I'm very well." He discarded another book. "Only a small headache. I'm afraid my daughter overreacted. I'm sorry she took you away from your work."

Papa would not look at Sir William or me. He kept on at his task, squinting at the spine of each book. And then he threw up his hands. "The journal must be here!" He was growing ever more frantic.

"Papa, we have to face the truth that the journal was stolen. Can you paint it again from memory?"

"Maybe," he replied. "I don't know." He went to the couch and lifted up the cushions, throwing them onto the floor. The pot shards crunched under his feet as he moved.

"Papa, let me fetch a brush and pan to clean the shards. You'll cut yourself."

I knew this was a mistake as soon as I said it. Papa's shoulders stiffened.

"Shall we have a spot of lunch? I'm sure a hot meal and a pot of tea will do your headache some good," Sir William asked.

"An excellent notion, Sir William, but I'm not hungry," Papa said. "Elodie may go with you if she wishes." Papa addressed this remark to another pile of books.

"I believe I'll cry off, too, Sir William," I said. "But thank you all the same."

Sir William hesitated; glancing at Papa and then me, as though loathe to leave us in the room together. "Well then. I'll leave you to it, Buchanan."

Papa nodded and studied another book. "Good day to you, sir."

I followed Sir William outside. "I think this was the work of the same man who stole my orchid. The man with the hook. Do you know of him?"

Sir William inclined his head. "Yes, I know of him. Luther Duffey. He's dangerous, no one to trifle with. Because no one other than your father has been able to locate the Queen's Fancy, it's known as a lost orchid, and therefore worth a fortune. Your father keeps the locations of all of his plants secret, and he is well-known for doing so. His secrecy has made him very successful but at the same time susceptible to attack from men like Luther Duffey. If he is able to read your father's map, then he holds the key to a veritable treasure chest."

The cold spring wind blew around me, sending the fringes of my shawl flapping.

"The map doesn't say where he's traveling to. Surely China is a large country."

Sir William nodded. "This is true. Duffey would have to have knowledge of the port your father was headed to. Before the China Wars there were only a few ports open to foreigners, but now with China's loss there are many more. As long as his destination remains a secret, your father has nothing to fear."

"Will the people he hires in China look after him well? Will they be good to him?"

"I'm afraid he insists on traveling alone this time, with only a few servants known as coolies. He doesn't want to imperil anyone else. He told me he wishes to travel as unnoticed as possible."

"Will the coolies look after him? Should something go wrong?"

Sir William hesitated.

"Please tell me the truth, Sir William. I'm not a child."

He sighed. "Very well. The answer to that question is no. And not because the Chinese are heartless or hate Westerners, although some of them are and many of them do. It's because of their culture. If a Chinese person cares for an ill person and he dies, the Chinaman is liable for the dead man's funeral expenses, and that can be quite a hardship for a coolie, who barely earns enough to afford rice and a roof over his head."

"If no one will help, will he be able to manage on his own?" In actuality, I was asking Sir William if my father would survive the journey. I felt dread rise in me, and my eyes prickled with tears again. What if something happened to him on the journey? We'd never know what befell him. What if he became injured and died in the wilderness all alone, with no one to comfort him, no one to bury his remains? Mamma would go mad with not knowing.

Uncertainty glimmered in Sir William's expression, but then he smiled. "I'm quite sure, Miss Buchanan. I'm quite sure all will be well." He touched his hat and took his leave.

I waited until Sir William disappeared into the landscape of Kew before I stepped into the cottage to fetch a brush and pan, to help Papa in any way I could, even though that help was unwanted.

�֍ ❀ ❧ ❦

THAT NIGHT I WAS AWAKENED BY THE SOUND OF PAPA SCREAMING—A terrifying high-pitched wail that echoed through the cottage. I rushed down the stairs to his side, but he had fallen back to sleep. He had thrown the blanket off, and sweat beaded on his forehead. I sat in the battered rump-sprung chair for the rest of the night, my knees tucked up under my nightdress, watching over Papa as he slept in his pallet.

I returned to my bed before he awoke. I knew then that it was impossible. If Papa went alone to China, he'd never return to us alive.

THIRTEEN

hen we arrived at the *Osprey* the next morning, Papa bade me to wait on the dock with Kukla and went aboard to find Alex and his father.

I watched the sailors at work, climbing the masts, shouting orders, and running to and fro. My curiosity got the better of me. I wanted to stand on that ship's deck, to feel its boards under my feet, and to see the world from its vantage point, if only for a moment. The *Osprey* could be boarded by a small bridge-type apparatus that spanned the water from the dock to the ship, and so I stepped aboard the little bridge, taking care to hold tight to the hemp ropes on either side, Kukla following behind me, and in seconds I was onboard the *Osprey*. Everything was tidy and neat as a pin. Ropes lay coiled up like springs, and perfectly spaced and tied lines held the canvas sails to the masts. Even though the ship had fulfilled its mission, there appeared much work to do still. Several boys knelt in a line on the deck, each one slowly scraping a stone against the boards. Their actions likely accounted for the stark white boards underfoot. Another group of older boys knelt in a circle pushing oakum into cracks on the boards. The term *ship-shape and Bristol fashion* suddenly made a great deal of sense. Kukla, happy to be home, ran off in the direction of the cabin.

A bearded man appeared from below and stood for a moment scowling at the boys. He was dressed in canvas trousers and a patterned jersey, a blue cloth knotted around his neck. He held a long narrow strap in his hand, and this he flicked against his leg as he watched the boys toil. After a moment he made his way toward the first group of boys and said something to the smallest, a thin boy with dark, stick-straight hair that hung in sheets around his face. The boy replied, but clearly his answer was not to the man's liking, and his scowl deepened. He crossed his arms over his chest, the strap dangling from his hand, and asked something else. This time the boy shook his head and stared at the deck, stilling the stone in his hand. The man looked away for a moment and then shouted, pulling his arm back as though to strike the boy with the strap. The boy shrank away, mouth open in fear.

The man did not bring the strap down; the boy's cowering seemed enough to please him, and so he dropped his arm and backed away. The boy knelt closer to the deck, so close he was almost doubled in half, and returned to the task of scrubbing with his stone, this time, picking up the pace. The man grinned and said something to a red-haired lad next to his victim, who laughed and punched the boy on the arm.

The man looked up and saw me watching him. His jovial expression left his face only to be replaced by that same scowl he had directed at the boy. In a trice, he crossed the deck.

"What is your name, miss?" he asked when he reached me.

His accent was foreign. I guessed he was Scandinavian or from one of the Low Countries. He wore his long blond hair clubbed at the nape of his neck. His face was very rugged and browned by the sun, brown as a biscuit. So tan was his skin that his dark blue eyes seemed quite piercing. He was very handsome in a fierce way. A dangerous way.

"Elodie Buchanan," I replied.

"Egon Holst at your service." He bowed his head briefly, a small illusion of manners, because the look on Mr. Holst's face was anything but polite. "Well, Miss Buchanan, are you lost?"

"Not at all," I replied. I looked around, hoping that Alex was close by.

"Have you business on this ship?"

"Yes, I brought Kukla back to Alex. And I'm waiting for my father."

"I suggest you wait for him on the dock," he said flatly.

"I apologize, sir. I had no idea I was in the way. Perhaps I'll wait over there." I gestured toward the end of the ship, unwilling to yield to him and show him he had intimidated me as he had intimidated the boy. He was not my master, after all.

"You are not in the way. You are unwelcome." Up close, I could see the strap was a kind of riding whip. It was even more menacing up close—a folded piece of black leather about a foot long, held together with a brass tack and finished with a braided handle. It was decorated along the edges with an interlinking star design. The black color had worn to silver on the ends—perhaps from the whip being wielded often.

"I beg your pardon?" I was humiliated by the man's unfriendly words and not a little offended by his holding the whip in my presence. Across the deck I could see the boys were still hard at work, but their toil was less ardent, their eyes directed toward us.

"Women have no place aboard this or any other working vessel." The whip twitched in his hand, and I had the feeling he would dearly love to employ it on me. "Females are bad luck, very bad luck. The only woman allowed aboard is the figure-head, and unless you are carved from wood, I'll thank you to take your leave."

Unwilling to continue engaging with such a man, and knowing I would never be the winner of the field, I turned to depart the ship, planning to wait for my father on the quayside, when Alex came across the deck. He spied the man standing next to me, and stopped short.

"Leave her be, Holst," he called.

"A woman shouldn't set foot on this ship, Balashov, and you know that well." Holst's tone was cordial, but I could sense the ghosts of past arguments and disagreements between them lying just under the surface.

"She's a guest of the captain's."

Holst's eyes raked my figure from top to toe and then back up again. "She's a bit young for the captain's taste."

"Exactly what are you implying, sir?" I said, outraged.

Alex came over and stood in front of me so that Holst could no longer stare at me. The two men were tall and faced one another evenly. Neither one looked willing to back down. "Have a care, Mr. Holst," Alex said quietly.

"I do beg your pardon for my bad manners, miss," Holst finally said. "We sailors have little use for swaying about and hoity-toity nonsense. We have work to do."

"Manners cost nothing, sir," I said. "It takes as much time to be rude as it does to be polite."

He barked out a short laugh and then touched two fingers to his forehead. "I'll take my rude self away, then." Holst went off, tapping his whip against his leg. As he passed by the boys stuffing oakum, he swung the leather and let it fall against a boy's back with a heavy slap.

Alex muttered something in Russian and then turned to me. "I'm sorry about Holst. He's a very superstitious man. Many sailors believe women on board a ship are bad luck, and he is the worst of them."

"He looks like a bully."

"Nothing makes him happier than to see people cower. My father steps lightly around him because he's the best carpenter to be found and can repair nearly anything while out at sea, and he knows how to navigate, as well. Holst's status has given him a sense of his own importance, and he thinks he can do as he wishes."

"I didn't mean to create trouble for you or your father. I didn't know there was a rule about women. I should have waited on the quayside."

"You are not making a problem. You are as welcome as anyone. Your father is supervising the loading of his cargo and asked me to keep you company." He looked over toward Holst. "But I think we'd better leave the ship for now."

I looked around the ship once more and reluctantly followed Alex over the little bridge.

"Thank you for looking after her," Alex said as we walked along the quay at the East India Docks the next afternoon. Alex said that the angry sailor's ship had left the day before, so little Kukla could once again walk freely alongside Alex. She ran ahead to chase some seagulls, and then she came bounding back to her master to trot alongside him, head cocked, her eyes always on him, as though to make sure he wasn't going away. "I'm sure she had a good holiday with you, but I did miss her. I'm so used to her being by my side that I kept looking around for her."

"She did enjoy it." My conversation with Violetta left me feeling self-conscious around him. I felt a little tongue-tied in his presence, unsure of what to say to him. I found myself worrying about how my hair looked and if my bonnet ribbons were tied neatly. Ridiculous, really. What did it matter? I was sure Alex didn't notice a thing about me.

"What will you do now?"

"Return to Kent. Help Mamma with the children. Work in my little conservatory." I shrugged. "It doesn't sound an exciting life compared to yours, I'm sure."

Alex shook his head. "It sounds a fine life to me. My life has not always been so pleasant."

I felt suddenly ungrateful for saying what I did. "Of course. Forgive me. I forgot you . . ." *You are a dolt, Elodie*, I thought.

He stopped walking. "You forgot I was once an orphan. You can say it. I don't mind. In England it's a humiliation to be without parents and a family. But I don't see it as others do. Sometimes bad things happen in order to lead us to good things. And good people."

"How did you come to be on the *Osprey*? If you don't mind my asking, that is."

"I don't." He shrugged. "I was born in Russia but we lived in Sevastopol during the Crimean war. My parents were killed early on in the war, when I was twelve."

"I'm so sorry, Alex." I tried to picture Alex as a little boy on his own, forced to make his way after his parents died in that terrible war that claimed so many lives.

"I found work on a British naval vessel and ended up in China. When I turned fourteen, I was without a job and living in the streets of Foochow. I was desperate to leave China, so I smuggled myself and Kukla aboard the *Osprey*, and we became stowaways. I hid in the hold amidst the cargo for a week before I showed myself. The captain saw something in me and made me his ward. It's one of the reasons why Holst hates me so much."

Something behind me caught his attention, and I thought I saw a flicker of resignation cross his face. When he returned his gaze to me, it held a sorrowful expression. "The captain has run up the blue peter. We must all make our way back. We sail in the morning, as soon as the tide is high. I must bid you farewell now."

I turned to look at what Alex was talking about. A square blue flag inset with a white square was inching its way up the mast, and Papa was coming toward us.

"Will you . . . will you keep an eye on Papa for me?" I asked Alex. "While he's on the ship, I mean. I worry about him so. You yourself said he looked a walking skeleton when he was released from that prison. I'm afraid he's not going to make it home to us. I wish I could travel with him. . . ." My voice trailed off because I couldn't say any more. I felt sick inside, and a mounting feeling of dread began to take hold of me. My mind flashed to Papa lying in a jungle, in a catatonic state as he was in the train station, perhaps brigands robbing him of everything he owned. Stuck in the wilderness, perhaps lost and bewildered. I could feel my bodice grow damp with perspiration. If Alex tried to jolly me along by assuring me that Papa would be fine, I would scream.

Mercifully, Alex did nothing of the kind. Instead he took my hand in his. "I understand what it's like to worry about your family, Elodie. Of course, I shall assist him in any way I can."

"There are things he does at nighttime," I said. "He has these terrors where he cries out. I leave him alone when he does so, and he seems to prefer this. Perhaps you can put the captain in the picture and any of those who might have contact with him?"

"Of this you have my promise." He squeezed my fingers and dropped my hand.

Kukla chose that moment to come flying back down the dock and leap up between us, into Alex's open arms. And I was glad she did, because I suddenly couldn't see for the tears misting my eyes.

A moment later, Papa reached us. "Your father has need of you, my boy," he said. "I'll see Elodie settled and then I'll return to the ship."

Alex nodded and set the dog on the dock. He put his hand on my shoulder. "I owe you much for looking after Kukla. I'm forever in your debt. Farewell, Elodie. *Do svidaniya*."

"Take care of yourself," I replied.

Alex walked away, and I wondered if I should ever see him again. He paused and leaned down to scratch a tabby cat under the chin. The cat rolled over and waved its paws in the air. Kukla licked the cat's face and barked. Alex laughed and continued down the dock, the little black-and-white dog leaping at his side.

Papa looked at me curiously. "He's cut from fine cloth, that boy."

"He is," I said, turning away a little so that Papa could not see my tears.

I put my hand up to where Alex had touched my shoulder. I could still catch his scent in the air—he smelled of wool and wood and of the wind.

⚘⚘⚘⚘

PAPA SAW ME INTO A CAB TO TAKE ME TO VICTORIA STATION FOR THE train home. He kissed my cheek and departed as though I'd see him again the next day, with no good-bye or message to Mamma or the children.

It was an interminable, dismal ride to the station, and I stared out the window at the shifting light from the afternoon sun, feeling numb with worry and aching for my father. My hand dipped down several times to touch Kukla's head, and my heart wrenched when my fingers fell on nothing but air. I missed her cheeky presence, but I also missed her master. Silly of me. I barely knew him. Yet I felt he would never judge me for my father's absence, as others had. I felt he would understand possibly more than anyone, and this was a rare thing indeed.

I wished I could return to Kew to walk the grounds one last time. I still hadn't been inside the Palm House, and I would probably never get another chance. I found I wanted to go there bady, if only to feel the warm mist on my face and the brush of the palm fronds in my hands. It was probably the only chance I would have to experience a rainforest. And somehow, I felt this would bring me closer to Papa. I knocked on the roof of the carriage and the cabbie slid open the hatch. "Can you take me to Kew instead?"

He nodded and touched the brim of his cap.

VICTORIA GATE, THE ENTRANCE TO KEW, HOVE INTO VIEW, AND I gathered my valise and reticule and departed the cab. I was making my way down the pavement when I heard a voice call out from behind me.

I turned to see a blonde-haired woman dressed in a bright yellow gown festooned with many ribbons and gewgaws. A tiny green bonnet sat perched in front of a round braided hairpiece. She looked rather like a sunflower advancing down the road. She inched along, taking tiny careful steps and holding a handful of her skirt. "I do beg your pardon, miss," she said, "but aren't you Hugh McGregor's daughter?"

"Who is asking?" I replied, unsure of who this woman was and what she wanted from my father. For a dizzying moment, my mind gnawed on my old worry, and I was afraid she was going to claim Papa as her love.

She held out a lace-gloved hand. "I'm Eugenia Pringle, Erasmus Pringle's wife. He sent me here to find your father, as I was staying in London with some . . ." She looked around as though searching for an answer. "Friends." She had a strange accent. At times she sounded quite eloquent and well-spoken but then I could hear the patter of an East Ender slipping through.

I shook her proffered hand briefly. Her fingers were thin and cold under the lace. "I don't understand," I said. "What would Mr. Pringle want? Papa is on the ship to China this moment. Mr. Pringle knows that. There's nothing more we can do to appease him."

"I have a letter for him from my husband. I understand your father lives at Kew, so I was just about to go there. Could you point the way to his cottage?"

"How did you know I'm his daughter?"

"Mr. Pringle described you perfectly. Quite perfectly. Not many girls are as tall as you. Why, upon my soul, Miss Buchanan, I believe I could have picked you out in a crowd! And your ginger hair shines like a new penny." She reached out a hand and touched the hair in front of my bonnet. "So straight and so fine. How I wish I possessed such locks. Yellow ringlets such as mine are so old-fashioned—"

"My father is not at his cottage. He's already on the *Osprey*," I said, interrupting her patter. "The tea clipper. Mr. Pringle knows this. I wrote to him myself with all his details. Why didn't he send the letter to the ship?"

Mrs. Pringle let out a little titter. "I'm such a flibbertigibbet. I do recall now. The *Osprey*. Headed to Canton. Of course, of course." Mrs. Pringle looked around again, frowning, and then turned her attention back to me.

"No," I said. "Not Canton."

"My mistake. Foochow, then?" she said, more of a question than a comment.

"Of course," I said. "I'm sorry to be hasty, but I do have a train to catch. Can I ask what the letter says? He departs early in the morning. You've not much time to contact him."

"I do beg your pardon!" She tittered and rested her hand

on my arm as though we were the dearest of friends. "My husband's other plant hunter found the orchid, and he has no need of Mr. McGregor."

"How? By my understanding the orchid is quite difficult to find."

She waved her hand. "Dumb luck, I'm guessing."

"But the debt?" I said. "What of that?"

"The debt?" Her brow furrowed.

"What Papa owes to your husband? We have no way of paying it if Papa doesn't fetch the orchids."

"Oh, the debt!" She waved her hand. "My husband has discharged it."

What a peculiar and capricious man Mr. Pringle was. First, all threats and aggression, now he showed this benevolence. But it mattered not. I was so relieved that Papa could depart the ship that my knees nearly buckled with it. I needed to return to the East India Docks and get Papa off the *Osprey*. I would insist he leave Kew and come home, and that we draw a line through this terrible ordeal. "I'm very glad of this. I must say it's quite a relief for me, as I know it will be for my father."

She glanced over my shoulder again, and I turned to see what was distracting her. A man leaning against the brick wall a little ways ahead stepped back into the shadows. Something flashed in the sunlight as he moved, and I saw it clearly, as though he'd held it up for me to see.

Instead of a right hand, he possessed an iron hook.

There is, in point of fact, one particular orchid hunter who has a hook for a hand and has made it his life's mission to slit my throat with said hook at the very next opportunity. My father's words came flooding back, and fear shot through my veins like quicksilver.

There, on the Kew Road, was my orchid thief.

And I had told his accomplice where Papa was going. I should have known she was an imposter as soon as she called Papa Mr. McGregor. Mr. Pringle knew Papa's real name, knew that he traveled under an assumed name.

"It's a lovely orchid, is it not, Mrs. Pringle?" I said, trying valiantly to keep my voice from shaking. "Mr. Pringle told me how much you adored it. Why, the color matches the very yellow of your gown."

"Oh, yes. It is my favorite bloom, that orchid. A stunner."

"And a scent to match. Almost lemon."

"Very much so. Such a treat." Again, her gaze flitted over my shoulder.

I did not know who this woman was, but she was certainly not Mrs. Pringle.

I stepped back from her.

"The orchid is most assuredly not yellow."

"A mistake! I confused it with . . . with another orchid of my husband's." A mark of apprehension flickered in Mrs. Pringle's eyes for a moment.

"Then tell me the color of the Queen's Fancy, if you say you know it."

She hesitated. "I don't know it," she finally said, her voice petulant. "I cannot be expected to know the colors of all the blooms."

I held out my hand. "May I see the letter?"

"It's not for you, it's for your father." She held her reticule to her chest as though I would snatch it. "Besides, what would that matter? You won't know me 'usband's fist." This she delivered in a broad East End accent, dropping any pretense of an upper-class accent.

"I would recognize his handwriting, as I have seen it myself."

The woman bit her lip, her eyes shifting again.

I spied an empty hansom cab waiting across the street, the cabby sitting high atop his perch waiting for a fare. I could not visit the Palm House, nor could I return to Kent. I had to warn my father. I had given away the ship's name and its destination, and now the treasure map would make sense. It would be nothing for them to follow him now. A simple trap. How could I be so stupid?

I picked up my skirts and dashed over the road. I had to get away. I had no idea what the orchid thief would do to me, but I knew one thing: they would not take lightly to me rushing to warn Papa.

"Curse it!" the woman shouted. "She's rumbled us, Duff!" I heard her little heels clacking on the pavement behind me. "Thief!" the woman shouted. "Stop her! She's stolen my bag."

I reached the cab and opened the door, flinging my valise and reticule inside. The cabby stared down at me. "Steady on, there! I ain't taking fare from a robber. Be off with you!" He flicked his whip at me.

"I'm not a thief," I told him. "Please—"

Someone grabbed the sash of my gown and jerked me away from the cab. I twisted about and found myself in the grip of the orchid thief.

"Let me go!" I stamped on his foot, hard.

He grunted. "You little hellcat!"

I stumbled away from him, tumbling into the gritty road, landing on my elbows in front of the wheel of the cab.

The horse shied, rearing and leaping forward in his traces. I pushed myself out of the way of the rolling carriage, my cage crinoline spinning around my legs.

The man loomed over me, grabbed a handful of my blouse, and pulled me toward him. "You stupid, stupid girl," he said, his breath hot and fetid. His cap had been knocked off in our tussle, and he grinned like a jack-o'-lantern, showing two front teeth made of gold. "You ain't going anywhere." His voice was low and menacing. "You ain't telling your Pa nothing. And he won't be getting none of them flowers, neither. Much obliged to you for telling me where he's headed. I'll be there before he will. You can count on that."

I felt my billhook, heavy in my pocket, and fumbled for it.

He didn't expect it, and he didn't bother to defend himself.

I struck out. I felt the blade rip into his flesh, flaying his cheek open. I saw the blood spill from the wound.

The man screamed—an unlikely piercing screech for such a big man—filled with pain and horror. He let go of me and grabbed at his face, blood dripping gruesomely though the iron hook.

I struggled to my feet and scrambled into the cab. "Go!" I shouted at the driver. The doors swung wildly as the cabbie plied his whip and the horse leapt forward.

Out the window, I saw the orchid thief lying in the street. The sunflower woman knelt next to him, staring, open-mouthed, at my fleeing cab.

We'd put a good distance between my attackers and us before the driver pulled his horse over. "I'm sorry, miss, but this is as far as I'm willin' to take you," he said, addressing me through the little hatch through the carriage roof. "Seeing as you're a young lady and all, I didn't want you to get hurt. But I don't want to get mixed up in no bad business."

I couldn't risk getting out of the cab and looking for another. Every single minute counted if I was to reach the *Osprey* ahead of the orchid thief. "No, please, don't turn me out!" I said. "I'm not a robber and I'm not up to any scheme," I said. "I don't have time to explain, but I'm begging you. I need to go to the East India Docks. Please take me?"

His gaze dropped to my hands. I hadn't noticed that I still held the knife, the orchid thief's blood drying on the blade. "Pardon me for saying so, but a young lady wouldn't be carrying an evil-looking flick about like that, much less using it, if she wasn't up to mischief. Not that I'm saying the man didn't deserve what he got."

If altruism would not touch his heart, then perhaps avarice would. "I'll pay you double your fare."

He hesitated. "All right, then. Double. But you'll have to pay me now." He named the colossal fee, and I swallowed.

I counted out the money from my little purse. All I was left with was a few shillings, but it couldn't be helped. Papa would give me more money when I saw him. I handed the coins up. The driver took them, shut the door on the little hatch, and the horse set off.

I fumbled for my handkerchief and wiped the blood from the billhook's blade. I wanted to vomit. Once an innocent implement used to care for living things, my billhook had been turned into a tool of savagery. I would never again pick it up to take a plant cutting without feeling the blade sinking into the man's skin, seeing the gash open on his face. Maybe he would carry the mark of my knife on his face forever. Maybe he would remember me each time he looked into a mirror. I was part of the orchid thief's life as surely as he was now a part of mine.

Was this how soldiers felt on the battlefield? Did they always feel this way or did they reconcile themselves to violence? How much of their humanity slipped away when they drew their weapons to maim and kill?

I shoved the billhook inside my reticle and pulled the drawstring tight. I hoped I would never have to hurt someone again. I wasn't sure that my soul could survive it.

I had the intention of telling Papa about the orchid thief and then returning home. But with every turn of the cab's wheels, I felt a certainty grow inside of me—that warning him was not enough. Now that I'd experienced for myself Luther Duffey's ruthlessness, I couldn't let Papa search for the orchid alone. I had to find a way to go with him. I could help him, I knew I could. I could help him find shelter if he should become catatonic. I could cook and clean for him and keep him focused on the tasks of the day.

Papa wouldn't allow me on board the ship, that much was clear. Maybe I could appeal to the captain? But I then remembered how much Holst hated women on board. The tea clipper wasn't a passenger ship, and the captain had nothing to gain by putting my request over his men's superstitions.

I fumbled with the strings of my reticule, tying and untying them, frustrated beyond measure. If I were a boy, I wouldn't be dithering like this. I'd be at my father's side right now. If I were a boy, the captain would welcome me on board, and I could make myself useful stuffing oakum or scrubbing the deck. If I were a boy . . .

The cab stopped for traffic, and I happened to look to the left at that moment and I saw a street seller whose stall was hung with clothing. Boys' clothing.

My pulse began to quicken. I thought about what Alex told me a few hours ago. How he had stowed himself away in the hold, hiding amidst the cargo.

I *could* be a boy. At least for a little while. I could get onto the boat disguised as one of the apprentices, and then stow away, just as Alex had. I could wait for the ship to sail far enough away from England that it wouldn't be worth turning back, and then I would reveal myself. Papa would have to take me with him then.

If Alex could do such a thing at age fourteen, then I could at age seventeen. It had turned out well for Alex; perhaps it would turn out well for me, too.

But this sensible thought failed to stop my heart's hammering.

What about Mamma and my sisters? They needed me.

But who needed me more? Neither of my parents was possessed of their full faculties, and so I was the only person who could make any rational decision about anything. At home, Mamma had the help of Violetta and our maid and even, dare I say it, Deacon Wainwright and his mother. I knew we had enough money put by to care for household expenses for many months—unless and until Mr. Pringle took it all away, of course. Violetta would have to rise to the challenge, as I had, and help Mamma.

But who could help Papa? No one. Everything I had done to help him prepare for the trip was tantamount to equipping an ill person with an umbrella and shoving him out into the wind and sleet to take his chances. Papa would be angry with me, but I'd rather him angry than dead or shut away in a debtor's prison, which for him might as well be death.

I took my writing case from my valise and wrote Violetta and Mamma a letter telling them that Papa had asked me to accompany him to China and I had agreed. My penmanship was messy and the paper dotted with blobs of ink from the cab's jouncing, but it would have to do. I blew on the ink to dry it, folded the letter into an envelope and affixed a stamp.

I knocked on the roof of the cab and asked the cabbie to let me out near the street sellers. I handed the letter up, which he agreed to post for me. I got out of the cab and went back to the stall I saw earlier, where I had enough money to purchase a large hessian sack and two sets of boy's clothing—trousers, a rope belt, striped shirts, a heavy wool jacket, a neck handkerchief, and a knitted hat.

I searched for a privy where I could change my clothes, and found one in a weed-choked garden down a lane off the busy street. The smell inside was almost overwhelming. I held my breath as best as I could, and teetering in the small space, I removed my skirt, bodice, and petticoats. As careful as I was, one of my gloves went down the necessary, disappearing into its dark, foul reaches, to be discovered by the night soil men, who would probably clean it and sell it on.

I wanted to leave my corset on for modesty's sake, but my chemise underneath it was too long to tuck into the trousers, and without a shift, the corset would chafe my skin to red welts in no time. I ripped my petticoat into strips and tied them around my breasts, flattening them as best I could. I hoped it would do. My breasts were small enough and the shirt voluminous enough that they wouldn't show. I took the rest of my clothing off, apart from my pantaloons, and donned the boy's clothing. My bonnet went into the sack along with everything else, and when I pulled the cap down over my head, the knit was thick enough to hide my bun. My boots were workmanlike enough to pass for a man's, although they were probably finer than the usual hobnailed boots of a sailor.

I pressed my crinoline flat, and left it standing on its side against the wall. Perhaps the privy's owner could sell it. It'd be worth a bit of money.

I imagined I looked a very feminine boy, but there were boys like that about, who had not yet begun a beard. For the first time I was grateful that I didn't have fashionable round curves. I was glad for my narrow hips and long limbs, as I would pass for a boy more easily.

Despite the noisome atmosphere of the outhouse, I was hesitant to leave it in my new garb. The Bible forbade a woman to dress as a man, but men in biblical times wore long, dresslike robes, so who knew what God had meant exactly? My hesitation lay in my own timorousness. No man had ever seen my legs before, and when I was clad in breeches, everything would be visible—the shape of my calves, the roundness of my buttocks, and the joining of my legs.

I gathered up my courage and left the privy. With the rest of my coin and by trading my empty valise, I purchased two jugs of ginger beer, a loaf of bread, and a large wheel of cheese coated in red wax, enough provisions for at least a week if I were careful. I had no idea when I'd have another hot meal again, so I bought a hot pie from another seller and ate it where I stood.

A woman selling cockles and whelks from a tray called out to me, "Fancy some cockles, boy?"

I shook my head. Heartened that my disguise had fooled the woman, I slung my sack over my shoulder and walked the rest of the way to the docks.

The sun had long set by the time I arrived. The docks were busy, far busier than in the day. Women wearing shoddy gowns stood outside the noisy taverns that lined the quay, calling to the many sailors passing by. A preacher in black robes stood on a nearby soapbox, looming over the women and warning them of eternal damnation. They paid him little heed, but one seemed to delight in marching up and down in front of him, lifting her skirt to expose her ankles as she did. A bearded, peg-legged man played a concertina and sang a sea chanty, an upturned hat on the ground. His voice was plaintive and beautiful.

> Come me own one, come me fair one, come now
>   unto me.
> Could you fancy a poor sailor lad who has just
>   come from sea?

I ducked my head and wove my way through this crush to the *Osprey*. I hurried as fast as I could, wanting to leave the scene far behind me. I should be home by now, having supper with Violetta and Mamma in the warmth and safety of our house. How worried they must be. They expected me on the last train. I wished my letter could reach them instantaneously.

The crowd thinned as I made my way down the dock, as there were no taverns or businesses here. The *Osprey* hove into view, floating at its berth in the dark, as though asleep, readying herself for her long journey. Everything was still and quiet. No one appeared to be about. The gangplank was up, and I stood, unsure of what to do next. My heart sank, remembering that the captain had called everyone aboard. It was cold, and the wind was kicking up.

My scheme wouldn't work. How could I possibly get on the ship?

I wanted to cry.

I wanted to go home.

Stop it, baby, I told myself, dashing tears from my eyes. *Crying will not help you—*

I swallowed my fear and went to the other side of the ship to look for another way of getting on board, but there was nothing. I decided to wait to see if any of the sailors in the tavern belonged to the *Osprey*. Perhaps I could join them when they returned. I'd been to enough country fetes to know how men were touched after quaffing beer and the like. I could fall in with them and pretend I belonged on the ship. If they were drunk enough, they might not notice me. I set my bag on the dock and wrapped my arms around me.

The great ship's hull cast a long shadow on the pier, and I

hoped it would be enough to hide me. The wind shifted, carrying the peg-leg man's song down the quay. The cold sea air bit
through the fine leather of my boots, and I stamped my feet to
warm them.

The ship's bell rang seven chimes, then eight. My elbows
throbbed where I had fallen, and I was growing ever more despondent. Finally, when I had nearly given up hope, two sailors
appeared, weaving and hanging on to one another, singing a
sea chanty. One of them whistled, and a man appeared and let
the gangplank down.

The men trundled up the plank, and I fell in behind them,
pulling my cap low over my face, hunching my shoulders and
keeping my eyes down. If someone questioned me, I would
lower my voice and claim that I'd only just been hired. If he
didn't believe me, I would reveal my identity, and Papa would
be called. Perhaps he'd change his mind and let me go with
him. If not, I would go home, but at least I would have tried,
and that would quash my fear for Papa a little bit.

But no one questioned me.

When the men went off to the right, I went to the left, and
in the light of the moon I saw the door to the decks below was
open. The door Alex had appeared from when I first saw him.
That must be the storage space.

I darted across the deck and crept down a steep flight of
stairs. In the murky light through a dusty porthole I saw bales
of cotton with only a few pathways between long stacks. The
sound of water lapping against the boat's hull was louder than
it was above, the temperature cooler. There was very little room
to stand up, and the air was fuggy with mildew and dust, like

a dank cellar. Toward the back of the deck sat a line of barrels lashed together. I peered behind them and found enough room to hide. I squeezed behind the barrels and lay down, using my sack as a pillow and my jacket as a blanket.

And I waited.

PART TWO

At Sea—Spring 1861

FOURTEEN

didn't count on having seasickness.

I wanted off the ship. If I could have flown from it like an albatross, I would have done. I had never felt so unwell in the whole of my life. It was a never-ending nausea accompanied by a spinning ache in my head—a torturous illness that I could not shake off. An empty bucket I'd planned to use as my necessary had become my constant companion, and I employed it liberally. I had found a source of water in a barrel at the back of the hold, but its stale taste only made my illness increase.

To make things worse, a storm had broken a day or two after sailing, and the boat pitched and rolled to and fro, and I'd had to brace my boots against the barrels to keep from sliding down the deck floor. I was terrified. In the storm there was much creaking, clanging, and banging as the ship tossed about. From the way the sailors shouted, I thought the vessel was on its way to capsizing and sinking to the bottom of the ocean.

Atop all of this, I was so lonely. I missed Violetta most of all. I longed to wake up to see her lying next to me, her hands bunched under her chin, her knees tucked up under her night-dress, sleeping like a little dormouse, as she always did. I missed our bedroom with its four-poster bed hung with drapes and set with a night table on each side—Violetta's table heaving with novels and mine piled high with books about the natu-ral world. I felt forsaken, as though I might never see another human being again.

I passed the time praying for my mother and father, but it did little to abate my worries and fears. I thought of Jesus in the wilderness for forty days and forty nights and Jonah in the body of a whale. Surely I could manage a few days?

At night, perhaps because of my illness, I dreamed the strangest dreams, the most horrible dreams. In one, my father danced the hornpipe with Alex while the Scandinavian ship's carpenter played the violin. I knelt in the middle of the *Osprey's* deck, my hands tightly bound, begging them to release me, but they only laughed and danced on.

I was on board the ship for a week before I woke one morn-ing to calm seas, both outward and inward. The worst of the nausea had left me along with the storm. I stood. The con-tents of the hold appeared to whirl round me like fluttering maple seeds caught on the wind. I choked back the gathering sickness, praying desperately that I wouldn't be sick again. I slumped back to the floor and lay there until the world stopped its heartless spinning and my nausea abated.

I lay on the floor for another quarter of an hour trying to gather up my courage to leave the hold, rehearsing what I would say to my father. I assumed he and the captain would be in the cabin toward the back of the ship. I pictured myself going there, opening the door, and announcing my presence to my father, making my confession.

The hatch opened and a tunnel of air rushed in, smelling of the briny sea.

I sat up. "Hello? Who is there?" I called out.

No one answered.

I stood up and called out again. "Is anyone there?"

Instead of an answer, I heard the sound of claws skidding on the wooden floorboards. And then a blur of black came hurtling out from behind the bales of cotton and flung itself against me.

I shrieked and buried my face in my hands. The thing threw itself at me again and again, its claws scrabbling against my back.

There was a shout; the beast was pulled away from me. I opened my eyes. The little creature, now panting with delight, was Kukla.

"*Chort!* Elodie?" Alex stared at me in disbelief. "What are you doing in the 'tween deck?"

"I stowed away," I said.

And then I burst into tears.

ALEX PUT HIS ARMS AROUND ME, HESITANTLY AT FIRST, BUT THEN HE held me tight against him. I could hear him breathing, feel the rise and fall of his chest, and the coarse fabric of his shirt under my cheek. He whispered Russian into my ear, melodious words that calmed me. He patted my back as though I were a frightened animal. "Hush, *myshka*. Hush."

After a bit, I stopped crying and stepped out of Alex's embrace. I dried my tears with the cuffs of my jacket. "I'm sorry," I said, embarrassed. "I didn't mean to do that."

He smiled, his expression sheepish. "Ah. Pay no mind. When I stowed away, I had a good sob myself before I left my hiding place." He sat down on a bale of cotton and leaned his elbows on his thighs. "I suppose my story put you in mind to stow yourself away?" His eyes searched mine, waiting; his expression neither judgmental nor angry.

"I had to, Alex. My father won't live through this journey if I'm not with him. I know he won't. He needs help. My help." My voice caught. "No one else would know how to care for him."

"I understand. You wouldn't be the first woman to stow away, and I expect you won't be the last. When you told me your father wished to return to China, I was taken by surprise. I don't think he's fit to travel on his own, either." He looked at me. "You don't look well yourself. Have you been seasick?"

"No," I said stubbornly, embarrassed to admit the truth.

I saw his eyes slide to the bucket, which was wafting noisome smells as we spoke. Thankfully Alex did not comment upon its presence. "You have. I've been a seaman long enough to know the look of a seasick sailor. It's nothing to be ashamed of. You sit, and I'll fetch you something to settle your stomach. And then we'll sort this mess through, all right?" He patted the bale. "Sit down."

I did as he bade. He snapped his fingers, and Kukla jumped up next to me.

"Stay with Elodie, Kukla."

Alex left the hold and returned a few minutes later with a jug of ale and a round biscuit.

"Easy now," he said, watching me down the jug's contents.

182

"That's ale, not water. Drink slower, or else you'll be sick."

The ale's bitterness was bracing, but I found the strength of it calming. My thirst slaked, I broke a bit off a piece of the biscuit. It was hard and very plain, but Alex was right, it did settle my stomach.

"How long have we been out to sea?" I asked through bites of the biscuit, so hungry that I cared nothing for manners. "By my reckoning it's a week."

"Yes, a week," Alex said.

"I'll go to my father and show him I'm aboard. He'll be angry, I know he will, but in time he'll see sense."

The lantern light flickered on Alex's face, and his face was tense. What he said next caused the biscuit to stick in my throat.

"Elodie, I'm afraid the captain will not allow you to remain. Holst, for one, will insist you depart. Madeira is only a day's travel away. It would be nothing to sail into Funchal and put you off. Likely your father will go, too. I can't imagine he'd stay onboard and leave you to find your way home on your own."

I set the biscuit down, the crust suddenly dry and unmanageable. "Then I'll have to stay here in the hold. All the way to China. If Papa doesn't find the orchids by midsummer, then he must forfeit a great deal of money that he does not possess. He will go to debtors' prison and the rest of us to the workhouse. I have to remain. There's no other choice." The idea of remaining hidden for three months did not appeal to me at all. But there was no other alternative. However, my meager rations were only meant for a week, and not three months. "Please help me stay hidden, Alex." I squeezed his hand. "I'm begging you."

He looked unsure but didn't shake me loose, and he didn't

leave. "You can't stay here in the 'tween deck all the time, not for three months. It's too cramped, and the air isn't fit. You'll be crippled when we reach China and probably consumptive. You'll be no good to your father if you're unwell."

"I'm quite robust," I said, hoping to convince him. "I'm sure I'll be fine."

He was quiet for a little while, considering, and I felt my chances of convincing him slipping away by the second.

"No." He shook his head. "You'll come up to my cabin at nightfall," he said. "You'll stay there. More men will be asleep or attending to duties in their quarters, and you're less likely to be discovered. But you'll have to return here in the morning. There are too many people around the officers' cabins during the day, and someone will surely hear you moving about."

"But where will you sleep?"

"I'll have to remain in the cabin with you. I cannot sleep elsewhere, or the men will wonder why I'm not in my own quarters."

I was too embarrassed to reply. The thought of remaining in the same room as Alex at night filled me with anxiety. If we were caught, my fate would be that of Jane Dunning. I would not be able to wed. I would have to remain at home, forever a spinster, and whenever I went about, people would shun me and refuse to have anything to do with me. And worse, my family would be painted with the same tarry brush, and my sisters would have a difficult time finding husbands.

As relieved as I was to have Alex's help, I wondered why he had agreed to help me. I had helped him with his dog, but honestly, minding a dog for a fortnight was nothing compared to aiding a stowaway and letting her share a bed.

But maybe the punishment for smuggling a woman into your room was nothing for a man. Indeed, I believed that Jane Dunning's paramour was most likely living his life happily, with no smirch against his name at all. Maybe Alex simply wanted to help a fellow stowaway. His own scheme had worked out well; perhaps he thought mine would, too.

The ship creaked, and I heard the footsteps of men above scurrying to their duties and someone shouting: "Keep her full and by, lads!"

"And we must make sure no one finds you," he said, giving voice to what I feared. "If they do, and they know we've been there together, they will talk as soon as we return to England. It takes no time for gossiping tongues to wag, and then I fear your life will be a sorry one. I do not want that to happen to you."

I thought about the alternative. To live for three months in this cramped space, all the while worrying about my family back home and my father on the ship, would be tormenting. But three months of misery was nothing compared to a lifetime of misery back home if I was discovered in Alex's cabin.

Between the two evils, was it better for my family to suffer the shame of harboring a ruined girl or to suffer the shame of the workhouse?

We sat in silence for a few moments. Kukla jumped up into my lap and licked my face. I held the little dog against me, hugging her tightly, burying my face in her sweet-smelling fur. She nuzzled her cold nose against my cheek, licked away my tears.

"I'm sorry, Alex," I said quietly.

He patted my arm awkwardly. "All will be well. When we arrive in China, I'll smuggle you off on one of the sampans, and you can reunite with your father in Foochow. No one else will know you were on the ship. No time will be lost for our ship or your father's expedition."

Alex didn't even try to hide the doubt in his voice. It seemed utterly unlikely that our ruse would work, but it was the only choice I had. If I made it all the way to Foochow, my father would have to take me on his journey. And then I could do my best to protect him—his steadfast and dependable Elodie.

FIFTEEN

lex returned to his duties, promising to retrieve me in an hour's time, when the sun had gone down. Many scenarios went through my head, and I knew there was a good chance that I would be seen, at least in passing. I had to make sure to pass for a boy for three months, and although the knit cap concealed my bun, my hair would give me away in an instant if anyone looked closely. I let my hair down, combing through it with my fingers. It hung to the base of my spine, and although some of the sailors had lengthy hair, perhaps to their collars, mine was far too long. I tried plaiting it, doubling the braid up to shorten it, but it still touched the middle of my back. I held the braid in my hand, considering.

I found the billhook in my reticule and flicked it open.

It was only hair. It would grow back.

Before I could change my mind, I sliced the braid off, added the plait to the canvas bag along with my bodice and skirt, and shoved the bag behind the bales.

My head felt so very odd without the weight of my long hair. I kept putting my hand up to the back of my neck to feel the bunch of hair left. I could almost feel a phantom braid swishing over my shoulder.

Alex returned to fetch me a few hours later. He stopped when he saw me, his eyes traveling to my hair. He nodded grimly, understanding, and said nothing.

It was a very dark night with clouds shifting over the moon, the ocean still and calm. The fresh air on my face felt like a balm after so long in the fusty 'tween deck. I wanted to pause, close my eyes and let the gentle breeze flow over me. But we had to move quickly. Alex's quarters were in the back of the ship, inside of a large cabin he called the Liverpool House. Everyone was abed, save the sailors on watch, and no one took any notice of us.

I thought I would simply sleep on the floor of Alex's cabin, curled up in a blanket. But the room was wee, with barely enough space to move about. The small bed took up most of the space. There were maybe six inches of floor left. Enough for Kukla, but not for me.

"I'm sorry, *myshka*. We'll have to share," Alex whispered.

I looked around the small space and nodded.

"The captain is the only one who has large quarters," he said. "A clipper ship is built for speed and cargo and thus we must make use of every inch of space." Alex gestured to an earthenware jug and bowl that sat on a small table near the bed. A small cake of soap and a folded towel sat beside it. "I've brought up some fresh water for you. I expect you want to wash. There is an extra nightshirt of mine there, as well."

The thought of a wash filled me with gladness. Just being clean would go a little way toward making me feel normal again.

Alex made to leave.

"Wait," I whispered.

He turned, his hand on the door's latch.

"You should stay here in case someone hears me moving about," I said. "They will think it's you."

Alex's face colored. "I . . . oh . . ."

"If you turn around and face the wall, perhaps . . . ?"

"Uh, of course." He turned around. Kukla leapt up onto the foot of the bed, turning round and round before settling down.

I disrobed, washed quickly, and put on the nightshirt, which was frayed and much mended. It hung past my knees, but my calves and ankles were exposed. I climbed into the bed, moving close to the wall, and slid my feet under the blanket, which I pulled up to my chin. "You can turn around now."

Alex sat on the side of the bed and untied his boots, tucking them under the bunk. I closed my eyes so as to give Alex some privacy as he undressed. I heard splashing as he washed at the bowl.

A few moments later, Kukla, hearing something, leapt to her feet and let out a high, shrill bark. Startled, my eyes popped open, and I saw Alex. He'd blown out the lantern, but the moonlight streaming in the little window lit up the room. He stood at the foot of the bed with his back to me, completely naked. It was only for an instant as he slid his nightshirt over his head, but I saw enough of him to sear the memory into my mind's eye: the curve of his buttocks and the muscles that ran down his back. He was beautiful.

I squeezed my eyes shut.

I'd never in my life seen a naked boy before. That small glimpse I'd had was enough to send my mind spinning. My fin-

189

gers tingled, longing to touch him, to know what those muscles felt like under my fingertips. This thought was swiftly followed by one of embarrassment. Alex was my friend, not someone to ogle, as Deacon Wainwright had done to me. I felt as though I should apologize to him, but the idea of explaining why filled me with such humiliation that I wanted to grind my teeth.

Alex climbed into the bed beside me. I turned toward the wall so he would have enough room, pulling my shoulders up tight to my ears and crossing my arms across my chest, trying to make myself as small as possible.

Perhaps I should return to the hold and take my chances there. I wasn't sure I could withstand this nightly humiliation, this inability to rein in my own thoughts, for three months. And I wasn't at all sure I could fall asleep next to Alex.

Alex had to lie on his side too, and this he did, facing away from me. Kukla, making things worse, stood up and draped herself over our legs, stretching her entire length across the bottom of the bunk.

Alex said something to the dog in Russian, nudging her farther down the bed with his foot, and as he did so I felt his buttocks press against mine. The picture of what those looked like flashed into my mind again. I inched away from him until my nose was touching the wall. But still it was not enough room. If I could have crawled inside the wall and slept there, I would have done.

I never imagined what it would feel like to lie next to a boy, and indeed my imagination could never have conjured up this sensation. It was the most intimate thing I had ever done in my life. I could hear every breath Alex took and feel the bed and blanket shift every time he moved. I could smell him, too. He smelled like the old wood of the ship, and tar and Kukla's fur and something else. Something masculine that made me want to turn over and rest my head on his chest, tuck my head under his chin and tell him every fear and worry that I had. Tell him about how happy I was to be with him. Because if I were honest with myself, despite the fear over my family and how I would survive the next few months at sea, at that moment, I didn't want to be anywhere else but on that ship, experiencing something I had only ever dreamed of, and with Alex.

I lay there, willing myself to sleep, but sleep would not come.

And then he spoke, his voice sounding clear and calm, "I think we will have three months of no sleep if we don't relax ourselves to each other."

"I must own you are correct," I whispered. "But what do you suggest?"

"I suggest you should stop staring at the wall, for one thing. And I think we should stop holding ourselves still like statues. I will touch you a little bit and then you can touch me. That way it will feel right when we accidently touch in our sleeps."

I laughed.

"What is funny?"

"Sleeps."

"Is that not the correct saying? There are two of us, so it must be sleeps, no?"

"No," I said. "Just sleep."

"All right, then. Sleep." He turned toward me and set his hand gently on my shoulder. His hand was heavy and warm and comforting. My shoulders relaxed and I dared to let myself melt against him.

"*Horosho*?"

"I'm sorry?"

"It means good."

"What does *myshka* mean? You called me that before."

I could sense him smiling. "It means little mouse."

I snorted. "That's hardly complimentary."

He laughed. "I only call you *myshka* because Kukla wanted to hunt for mice and instead she found you. In Russian it's a term of affection. But I will stop."

"No," I said. "I like it." I loved it, in actual fact. I loved the way Alex said it, *mish-ka*, drawing the first part of the word out like a whisper.

Down at our feet, Kukla kicked her paws and made a noise that sounded like a muffled bark.

"She's dreaming," Alex said. "Probably dreaming right now of running and chasing a *myshka*."

"Or stealing food." I smiled into the darkness.

Alex moved his head on our shared pillow. "She is a naughty dog, but I love her still."

"How did you come by her?"

There was a long silence before Alex answered, and I was worried that perhaps I had overstepped the mark, although it felt to me that we could say anything to one another, lying here together as we were. But perhaps it was not the same to Alex. I was about to apologize when he spoke, "She came to me when I was living in Canton. She was a street dog, and she helped me find food. The only time she's been away from me was when she was with you."

"You lived in China?"

"Yes, for a few years."

"Do you speak Chinese?"

"Yes." I felt his arm move as he reached up to brush my hair away from his face.

"Why did you stow away?" I asked.

Alex cleared his throat and took his hand off my shoulder. I thought he was angry with me for asking, but then I felt his hand return, this time to my hip. "That is a story for another day. It is sad, and I'm thinking we should be trying to have our sleeps. Sleep," he corrected himself. "My mother used to tell me it's bad luck to have sad thoughts when you close your eyes at night. Here. Lean back. Pretend I am your own bed at home and think about happy thoughts. We must rise in a few hours to take you to the 'tween deck. Close your eyes."

I did as Alex bade me. I closed my eyes and let my body settle against his. I thought about happy things. I tried to think of home, of my sisters and my mother and my conservatory, but instead I thought about a jungle full of orchids, mountains of tea, and a Russian boy named Alex. And I slept.

SIXTEEN

s the days went by, Alex and I took to whispering long into the night. I knew that I was keeping Alex from his "sleeps," but he seemed happy to talk, often starting up a new conversation long after I thought he'd fallen asleep. We talked about his life on the ship and what China was like and my plants at home. And Alex brought back reports on my father, who, Alex said, spent his days writing in his journals or reading, rarely leaving his cabin or the saloon to walk on the deck.

Always we talked while holding hands or leaning against one another as though I were his bolster and he were mine. In the morning, we'd always awaken in a tangle of arms and legs, Kukla having given up and moved onto the floor or under the bunk in the night. My embarrassment waned as the days went on until I couldn't see what was wrong or shameful about being alone with Alex. His bunk had turned into a world of our own making, one that existed only for us and only at night. I knew that if anyone had any knowledge of what we were doing, that world would shatter, and us along with it.

Every morning, before the sun rose, Alex would steal me back to the 'tween deck, and I would sit wedged between the bolts of cotton and wool, longing for night to fall.

I felt as though I held my breath all day, desperate for the sun to go down so I could return to Alex's tiny bunk and lie next to him. I didn't know if it was a fear that caused me to yearn for Alex or because I was lonely, or something more— something I wasn't sure I could admit to myself.

Perhaps it was because I had so much time on my own that I thought about too many things. My worries about my family were more intense in the 'tween deck. I worried about my family and what Papa would say when he saw me in China. Alex had given me a book to read by the light of a porthole to keep my mind occupied, *The Mill on the Floss*. I had read it before, but I found the familiar story of Maggie Tulliver comforting.

Sometimes Kukla would come with me, and holding her and stroking her soft fur made my fear abate just a little. Once she left, the dread and uncertainty would return once more.

Just when I thought I couldn't take another minute, I would hear Alex's step on the stairs, and his face would appear around the staircase, his smile wide, his hand outstretched, reaching for mine.

As the days wore on, the weather grew hotter and hotter until it was almost unbearable in the 'tween deck. Alex made sure to leave plenty of water for me, and he revisited me during the day to make sure I hadn't fallen ill.

One of the evenings, I'd had to go to Alex's quarters on my own, as he'd been assigned the first watch, which was from eight to midnight. I waited until it was fully dark before I went up. I carried a heavy loop of rope over my shoulder in case someone should see me. Alex had told me to look busy and carry something workmanlike, and few would question me.

When I approached the deck, I paused on the steps and looked left and right. I saw no one, so I started making my way. Alex had taught me about the ship. There were fifty men on the *Osprey*. The officers were Captain Everett; Mr. Ravensdale, the first mate; and Alex, the second mate. Two stewards looked after the officers who lived in the Liverpool House, the cabin in the ship's stern. Mr. Holst filled two roles as carpenter and boatswain. There was a cook and two sailmakers. The rest were able seamen who worked at the helm and hoisted the sails; ordinary seamen who did all the dogsbody work such as cleaning and maintenance; and the young apprentices training for careers in the Merchant Navy. If I encountered an officer, I'd have to stop to knuckle my forehead in salute. Alex had made me practice this until he was satisfied.

The starboard, or right side of the ship, was cast in shadow, and so I headed that way, with the intention to circle round to the stern, remaining in the dark as I did.

A lantern shone from the heads located behind the figurehead at the bow. The light sat at the feet of someone on the "seat of easement," which was a kind of crude necessary made from a square box with a hole cut in the top. I knew, from Alex's comments, that a queue tended to form at the heads, and since it was after supper, many of the line's attendants would have imbibed several sippers of rum.

When I turned, I saw four men waiting, all dressed in ordinary seaman garb, so I was not required to knuckle my forehead. Two of the men at the back were arguing, so they paid me no heed, but the men in front saw me.

The first man carried a lantern, and he stared at me with a quizzical expression. I tried not to return his gaze. No one had questioned my disguise yet, *please God do not let it be now*, I thought.

I could feel the man's eyes boring into my back. I tried to walk tall and with a swagger, but soon I heard a call:

"You there! Oi! Nancy boy! Whatcha doin' on this ship? You should be back with your mamma knitting stockings. . . ."

I tried not to respond, but unable to help myself I snuck a look over my shoulder. It wasn't the man in the queue who had spoken. It was the man who had been on the seat of easement. He was staggering up from the heads now, the lantern left behind. He gripped a jug, his trousers sliding down around his knees. I jerked my gaze forward and pretended I hadn't seen him.

"Oi! I'm talkin' to you, mummy's boy! I wonder if you feel as soft as you look?"

In a trice he was upon me, and I felt a hand grab at my bottom and pinch hard. And God help me, I did it again. I lashed out.

I turned and swung the heavy rope off my shoulder and into his belly.

Oof! The breath left him with a grunt, and hobbled by his trousers, he fell facedown onto the deck.

I hefted the rope back onto my shoulder as best as I could because my hands shaking, and continued on my way, leaving the men laughing at their friend lying prone on the deck.

I wasn't sure whom I had struck, or what his position

on the ship was, but I hoped he was drunk enough not to remember me.

"We'll be crossing the equator tomorrow," Alex told me after we'd been at sea a few weeks. "They will be conducting the initiation ceremony for anyone crossing the line for the first time. So if you hear yelling and running about, don't fret. We won't have been boarded by pirates."

"Will your father be taking part?" I was lying on my side against him, as usual. It was so hot that we had left the blanket off. Kukla had taken to sleeping on the small space of floor, where it was cooler.

"No. I hate it, as does my father. It's a terrible ritual, but it means a great deal to the men, so my father allows it. He despises it so much that he remains in his cabin and lets Holst arrange it. I feel very sorry for the new sailors. The others have been taunting them since we left London, creating fear in them."

"Did you have to go through it?"

"I did. I wasn't harmed because the captain is my father, but one ordinary seaman, whom the others disliked, did not fare so well. They tied him to a rope and threw him overboard, dragging him alongside the ship. He very nearly drowned."

"I used to think life as a boy was much easier, but now I'm not so sure," I said.

"We have more freedom than girls, but we can never show we are afraid. Any sign of weakness can ruin a life."

"Alex?"

"*Da?*"

I turned to face him. "You are very wise." Alex's face was bathed in moonlight spilling in from the little window above the bed. I saw he was smiling. The ship's bell rang out the hour, and two men out on the deck called to one another.

"I don't know about that," he said.

⁂

THE FOLLOWING DAY I WAITED IN THE 'TWEEN DECK, AS USUAL. I hadn't slept much the night before because Alex and I had stayed awake too long whispering in the dark. I was stretched out on a bolt of cotton trying to fall asleep in the heat when the door was flung open.

"In! Get in, you foul griffins!" a burly voice shouted. "Be quick about it!"

Footsteps thundered down the wooden stairs. I sat up, swinging my legs to the floor. I stood up with the intent to hide amongst the bales but it was too late, for coming toward me, blocking my escape, was a line of the young apprentices, shuffling along, stooping so as not to hit their heads on the low ceiling.

The man who had been chasing them wore a mask made of buckram painted green. A wig made of long strips of hessian sat atop his head. Another man, dressed in a similar fashion, appeared behind him and shoved a couple of the boys over bolts of wool, tumbling them onto the tight spaces between them.

"On your knees!" he shouted, his voice muffled by the mask. "And pay homage to Neptune's constables!" Soon, everyone was kneeling in any bare space they could find. There was a stack of cotton bales just to the side; I made to slide between them, but my movement caught the eye of the first constable. "You!" he shouted. "Avast and on your knees! Curse you for a coward!" He climbed over several bales after me, his mask menacing and terrifying. "King Neptune will hear about this, upon my word." He reached me, and before I had a chance to kneel he kicked my legs out from under me.

"All right, you slimy pollywogs!" his mate said. "You'll stay here until King Neptune calls you to the weather deck. Prepare yourselves!"

I looked for a bare space of deck next to another boy. I could make it through this. I could. If these boys could, then I could, too. Whatever they heaped upon me, I would do it. But in truth I was terrified. The stories Alex had told me made my mouth go dry and my heart hammer.

I recognized the boy next to me as the one Holst had threatened when I first set foot on the *Osprey*. "I've forgotten your name," I whispered.

"Tewkes," he said. "Robin Tewkes." His chin trembled, and there was something about him that reminded me of Calla.

"Let's not show these men how afraid we are. We'll stick together and help each other out. And when this is over, we'll be just as good as them, fully initiated. How old are you?"

"Fourteen," Robin said, his voice sounded surer, with less of a tremble. "I . . . I never saw you on the ship before, but I've only just joined."

"I've seen you before," I said. "I'm steward to the second mate, Alex Balashov."

"Oh!" his eyes were wide when I mentioned Alex's name. "That's why I haven't seen you. He's a good man, is Mr. Balashov.

He helped me out a time or two." I recognized hero worship in Robin's voice. "You're that lucky to work with him. I'm having to be under Mr. Holst." He hunched his shoulders as if recalling the sting of Holst's whip.

One of the boys shushed us, and we fell silent. None of us dared move from our knees, not even to lean back on our heels. We all remained, still as statues on their plinths, waiting and waiting. The anticipation of the thing was quite agonizing, and I knew this to be part of the torment, part of the way to break the spirits of the boys in the initiation. I could understand how the constables were so cruel. It was their turn now to mete out the punishment, and this was their time to get revenge for their own mistreatment when they were the initiated. I would have to go along with it and hope that I could melt away in the crowd after and hide myself in Alex's quarters.

After an hour or so, the door creaked open, letting in a blast of fresh ocean air, and the two original constables thundered down the steps. They bade us to come forward, one by one, and tightened a cloth around our eyes. When we were thus blinded, unseen hands pulled us up the stairs. We waited in pairs, our hands resting on the boy's shoulder in front. There was a shout, and we set off, shuffling forward in a long crocodile. Robin walked behind me, gripping my shoulder so hard I could feel his nails biting into my skin.

The first test came with no warning. Freezing cold water bucketed over us again and again, accompanied by jeers and howls of the men, as we were marched round the ship. Even though the day was hot, the blast of cold water against my heated skin was astonishing, and I wanted to buckle under every torrent. I never knew where or when the next deluge would come, but each time

I had a chance to draw in a breath, another bucketful of water would come hurtling out of nowhere. Soon, my hair was running wet and my clothes clung to me. Seawater dripped down my face, and I couldn't help but run my tongue over my lips, absorbing the briny taste of salt into my mouth. My mouth puckered, and I spat to rid myself of the taste.

Blessedly, we were stopped, and men yanked our blindfolds off. A creature dressed in a robe and wearing a blue buckram mask sat on a chair. He held a trident in his hand, and this, I would find out later, he used to choose each victim. Several sailors stood on the sides of the ship, watching the festivities, hooting and calling out. I looked around for Alex, but he was not there. None of the officers were.

One of the constables dragged four of us forward, one by one—Robin and me, plus another young man and an older sailor. "Neptune wishes you to race." He pointed at the mast where ropes formed a cat's cradle that hung a hundred feet or more from the topmast to the deck. "Climb! First one to reach the masthead and ring the bell will win Neptune's favor; the rest of you will win his wrath!"

I eyed the rope contraption and felt my limbs go weak. I was not terrified of heights, and indeed as a child I was fond of climbing trees and settling into the forks of branches to read. But trees did not pitch back and forth as a rule, and I had never climbed a tree as high as that mast. I had no idea how to attempt it until I made out some smaller vertical ropes crisscrossing the larger ropes, which I assumed were meant as footholds.

When the constable shouted, we all ran forward and began to climb. I reached up high to grasp each line, my damp booted feet struggling for purchase.

The ropes twisted underneath us as we climbed, swinging us from side to side and making it even more difficult to ascend. My fingers trembled with each new step, and although I didn't look down, I could sense how far off the deck we were, and I couldn't help but picture myself falling and the horrible thud I would make as I struck the deck. Would I die instantly or would I linger in a horrible death until I finally succumbed to my injuries?

I hung there for a moment, terrified, unable to go forward or back, the ropes biting into my hands. The others had gone ahead and had made it to the masthead and were working their way back down. For a moment, for one single moment, I thought about giving up, telling the men who I was, and calling for my father. But I had come so far; I couldn't give up now. I was sure there were other terrified people than had made it up the rigging and back. If they could do it, so could I.

Newly emboldened, I reached for the next line and resumed climbing, every fiber in my body humming with terror, but I forced myself to climb on. My long limbs held me in good stead, and I was able to reach higher and make my way quickly.

Finally, finally, the masthead was in sight, and I reached out to touch it, the wooden planks smooth under my fingers. I grasped the string on the bell's clapper and swung it to and fro.

Slowly, I worked my way back down the lines to the deck. I wanted to kneel down and kiss the wooden boards, I was so happy to make it down safely. But a part of me wanted to climb the rigging again, wanted to see how fast I could make it up and back. I was grinning, and I turned around, expecting to be congratulated, but instead I was seized and thrust back into the group with the other boys—the older man had won. The race went on, and those who had not won joined those waiting to receive Neptune's wrath. Those who had won Neptune's favor sat in a knot against the mast, no longer victims, but now jeering spectators.

One of the constables walked the line of remaining boys, glaring at us in turn. "Now! Who needs a good shave, eh?" he called out, shoving his face close to each of us. Some of the boys stared down at the deck, but I refused to cower and I kept my expression blank, my eyes straight ahead. The constable grabbed the boy in front of me and dragged him to a long wooden board leaning on one end against a large wooden tub of water. One constable helped strap him to the board with long leather thongs, and then another stepped up, taking up a bucket and a brush and began to paint his face with some sort of black paint. He followed this treatment by scraping down the boy's face with a piece of rusty barrel stave. The boy cried out as the sailors ruthlessly applied his tool, and then, with no warning, he stepped back, and two constables shoved the board backward, dunking the boy under the water, and leaving him there for what I thought to be a good long while.

The men seemed to know how long to hold him under without killing him, because when I thought the boy must surely be dead, the constables pushed down on the bottom of the board and brought him up, gasping and coughing, his face still painted black. They released him and dragged him to one side and dropped him, where he collapsed on his hands and knees.

"Who is next?" the constable shouted. He looked at Neptune, who pointed his trident at his next victim, who was given the same treatment. Several boys went through until Neptune's trident pointed at me.

The constable made to grab me, but I shrugged him off and walked to the board before he could take hold of me. Fear filled me anew, and it was far worse than what I felt climbing the rigging. I was terrified, so terrified that my legs shook and my arms felt weak. I was most afraid of the water. I had no idea how to swim or how to hold my breath underwater. Indeed I had a terror of water closing over my head, of it going up my nose. *Weak-kneed little child*, I chided myself. *Pull yourself together!* The torment appeared to last only for five minutes, and I could endure anything for five minutes.

From what I could tell watching the first victims, all I had to do was to take a gulp of air before the board slid back and hold it for as long as I could. Most of all I couldn't panic.

The men grasped my arms and strapped me onto the board. The ocean breeze flitted cool and sweet against my face, so hot and flushed from the climb up the rigging, but that sensation lasted only a moment.

The constable leaned over me and slopped the paintbrush over my face with little heed to where its contents landed. I recognized the smell as pine tar, an unbelievably sticky stuff nearly impossible to remove. I squeezed my eyes shut and closed my mouth tightly, not wanted to repeat the folly of the seawater.

Another constable approached, and without hesitation, he gripped my chin and began to scrape my face with the barrel stave. "Ha!" he said. "This one has yet to shave at all. Maybe the tar will bring in his whiskers."

"Or mayhap stop them from coming in altogether!" someone shouted from the onlookers.

The board tilted back and the sky rose above me, azure blue with puffy white clouds. The beauty of the sky above clashed with the ugly torment on the ship below. I took a few deep breaths to ready my lungs for the water.

"Wait!" Neptune called out. "Let me have a look at this pollywog!"

The board paused in its descent, and Neptune's masked face floated into my view. Those eyes that met mine were piercing blue.

There was no mistaking them. The man who regarded me from behind Neptune's disguise was Egon Holst, the Scandinavian carpenter, who had accosted me the day I came aboard the *Osprey*.

I waited for the expression in his eyes to change from icy indifference to confusion and then to recognition—to hear him exclaim that he knew who I was. But his eyes didn't change; he said nothing. He merely laughed and then shouted: "Dunk him!"

I forgot to inhale. I forgot to hold my breath.

The board dropped back, and water rushed around me, filling my nose and my mouth. The water burbled in my ears, muffling the men's laughter and casting it in an eerie, devilish sound. Very quickly, I became desperate for air. My face burned with the pain of the water, my lungs fought with the need to breathe. Panic like I have never felt before ran through my body like a lightning bolt. There was no fighting, there was no praying; there was only pure fear. I could only thrash my head from side to side, desperate for the agony to end.

If I died, it would be an accident, and no one would be to blame.

I grew tired, so tired that I stopped my thrashing. Black spots appeared in my eyes and spread and spread until they had blotted out everything.

It was over for me.

SEVENTEEN

I felt hands turn me on my side and slap me between my shoulder blades. I vomited up water, again and again, gasping for air in between each spasm, my knees drawing up to my chest of their own accord.

The gentle hands turned me onto my back, and I opened my eyes, staring, blinking at Alex kneeling over me. His shirt was sodden with seawater, his neck handkerchief askew, and his hat and jacket cast off. "Are you all right?" he said. It was deathly quiet, and I could see the ceremony had halted; the other sailors stood back at a distance.

I coughed again, my lungs still burned from the water I had inhaled. "Yes," I said.

He took my hand and helped me to sit up.

Holst stood leaning against the mast, watching us, his Neptune mask dangling from one hand. "I've never seen this boy before, Mr. Balashov. You appear to know him."

"Oh, I'm sure he's simply escaped your attention, Mr. Holst."

Alex stood up and picked up his hat and coat. "He works as my steward." His fingers tightened around the brim of his hat.

Everyone else stood in a huddle at the edge of the ship, standing so still and quiet that they looked like painted scenery on a stage.

"I've the running of the crew as acting bos'n, sir," Holst replied. "And I say again, I have no knowledge of this *steward* nor have I seen him about the ship."

"What are you implying, Holst?" Alex said. His face was calm, but a red flush was creeping up from his collar, and his jaw was tight.

Holst ignored him. He looked over the crowd. "Have any of you lot laid eyes upon him?"

"I've seen the lad, Mr. Holst." The man who had spoken was neither constable nor griffin. He stepped out from the crowd of spectators lining the sides of the ship. "I've laid eyes on him," he continued. "The first time I saw him on deck near the heads, and then I saw him again a few times leaving Mr. Balashov's cabin when I had the early-morning doggy. I thought him to be one of your'n, an apprentice, seeing he's so young looking an' all, but now I see I got it wrong."

I knew the sailor who had spoken. I recognized that gravelly voice—he was the pinching drunkard I had struck with the coil of rope. Fear took hold of me then, cold and hard.

He hadn't forgotten me in his drunken haze. He remembered.

"Of course you would have seen me leave his cabin, sir," I replied, careful to pitch my voice low. "It's my job to look after him."

"I'm the captain's steward, and I've never seen you turn in with the rest of us. Never seen you in our cabin, in the galley, or anyplace a steward should be." The man crossed his arms and stared at me, his words falling onto the deck like grape-shot; the effect of his statement was just as disastrous as those miniature cannonballs that could blow a man's life to bits in a snap of a finger.

Dropping his mask on the deck, Holst came over to me, grasped my forearm, and hauled me to my feet. "What are you to Balashov?" he said. "Quickly now. Tell me and don't look to him."

I knew that I couldn't resist his questioning. That I should behave in a subordinate way. When I was a boy, in my disguise, he was my superior, and I could not resist his questioning. All I could do was continue my lies and hope he accepted them. Stubbornly, I shook my head. "Nothing. I'm only his steward," I said.

"The devil take you as a liar!" the captain's steward spat out. "The bloody hell you are! Ask him, Mr. Holst, what a steward's duties are, ask him why he hasn't been seen by any of the other stewards!"

"Easy now, Mr. Jakes," Holst said calmly, not taking his gaze off me. "I'll do the questioning. What is your name?"

"Eddie," I said.

"Eddie. No surname?"

I shook my head.

"Ah, so you are a bastard, then. Born in the stews of the East End, I assume. Well then, Eddie with no surname, since you don't want to speak the truth, I'll tell you what I think is the truth."

"Go on," Alex said. "Speak plain. I have no patience for this *fignya*."

"What did you say? I have no ear for Russian."

Alex simply watched him, saying nothing, only waiting.

"I'm implying that he's not your steward, that he's something *other*. No one has ever seen him before apart from your good self, so I'm assuming he's of some importance to you. I believe you smuggled him aboard in the guise of your steward, and the two of you are engaged in the vile act of sodomy."

"What?" I jerked my head up. "No! You're wrong!"

Alex stepped forward, his hands clenched into fists.

"Do you know what happens to sodomites aboard a merchant vessel?" Holst asked me, his fingers biting into my arm. "You and Balashov will be confined in irons below, and once we reach China you'll be tried by fellow merchant navy captains. If you're both proved guilty, you'll be hanged by the neck until you die."

Several apprentices shot fearful looks my way. A few stared down at their feet. Water dripped in a steady stream down their shoulders.

Alex should have left me to drown because I was as good as dead—my life was over.

"If that isn't the truth, tell me what is. Who are you to Balashov?"

I had to tell them who I was. *What* I was, and face the consequences.

"Have you had carnal knowledge of each other?" Holst asked, his voice low and careful, but filled with warning. The tone suggested that this was my last chance. If I didn't speak the truth, his own truth would stand.

"I . . ." My confession was nearly out of my mouth when Alex stepped forward.

"Stop this," he said. And then he nodded. "It's true. What you say is true."

EIGHTEEN

here was a brief silence after Alex's confession. "So you admit it, then, Mr. Balashov?" Holst looked as though he couldn't quite believe it. As though he'd expected Alex to try to find a way out.

As for me, I could only stand there, riveted to the deck, surprised beyond reason. It was the last thing I ever thought Alex would say, and it took every ounce of wit I had to prevent my face from showing the stunned expression that threatened.

"Of course I do," Alex replied. "But you have it wrong. He's not my steward, nor is he a lad. Despite appearances, she's a girl. And she's my wife." Alex took my hand and pulled me from Holst's grip. "And I'll thank you to let her go."

Startled by Alex's revelation, Holst stared at him for a moment, and then with anger simmering in his eyes, he turned and glared at the young sailors accusingly, as though they knew this news before him. He set his gaze on me, next, examining my face with such intensity that I could almost feel his gaze raking against my skin. I waited for recognition to dawn on him, and indeed it didn't take long. "I know who you are!" he said a moment later. "You're that girl who came aboard the ship in London—the plant hunter's daughter. It's you, is it not?"

Alex interrupted before I could reply. "She doesn't have to answer any of your questions. We married. I brought her onto the ship, and she's under my protection. You have no right to question her."

"What does the captain say about this?"

"I wasn't aware that I had to inform you about what my father knows and doesn't know."

"Your father." Holst sneered. "What a jest that is." He looked me up and down. "Why is she dressed as a sailor, then?"

"Because *she* had to," I said, before Alex could reply. I took a step forward, my shoulders square. I heard one of the older sailors laugh. "Perhaps if you weren't so superstitious, I might take my place along my husband's side dressed as a woman should be. As you can see, I've been aboard the ship since we departed, and no harm has come to us. So your bias against females is unfounded."

I hadn't noticed that Mr. Jakes, the captain's steward, had left the proceedings, but now I saw him coming out of the Liverpool House. He held the door open, and the captain appeared in the doorway. He caught sight of us all standing round, and made his way toward us with a thunderous expression.

"What is all of this?" he shouted. "Mr. Holst, Mr. Balashov! If the initiation is over, then put these men back to work."

Holst knuckled his forehead in salute. "Aye, sir," he replied, and then he turned to the crowd. "All right, you men. What are you gawking at? Get this deck cleaned up!"

The men set to their work, and Holst turned back to the

waiting captain. "Mr. Balashov and his *wife* can tell you the tale, sir." And then he touched his forehead again and left.

The captain looked sidelong at me and then at Alex. "Your wife, Alex?"

Alex nodded.

The captain sighed. "In my cabin, Alex. Now."

"Trust me, Elodie," Alex whispered in my ear, his breath raising goose bumps on my neck. He placed his hand on my shoulder. "I promise you. There's nothing to fear."

✤ ✤ ✤ ✤

I WAITED IN ALEX'S CABIN, PACING ITS SHORT LENGTH BACK AND forth, six strides each way, gnawing at my nails. Kukla watched me from her perch on the bunk, her chin resting atop her paws. Marriage was the only way my reputation, and indeed my safety on board the ship, could be secured. An elopement was scandalous, but it was far better than being caught in a boy's bed with no promise of marriage. But married to Alex?

My imagination leapt to our wedding night. And it was a completely different picture from my nuptials with Deacon Wainwright. There would be no night clothing. No gentle knock on the door seeking my invitation. After so many weeks of lying chaste, side by side, Alex and I would be hungry to touch one another.

The door opened and I whirled around, my face burning. Alex stepped in the room. The captain remained at the door, his cap in his hands.

"Best to see your father now, lass," the captain said. He didn't appear to be angry; instead sadness and grief marked his weathered features. Alex held out his hand and gave me a reassuring smile. I put mine in his; he squeezed my fingers and we went off to face my father together.

We found Papa sitting in the saloon reading. He had gained a little weight since I'd seen him last, and his beard was growing in. He had lost the look of an invalid, and there was color once again in his face. He looked up from his book when we came in. Seeing the captain and Alex accompanied by a bedraggled sailor, he most likely assumed the business didn't involve him, so he returned his attention to his studies.

He didn't recognize me. And indeed, he didn't lift his head again until I spoke.

"Papa," I said.

Hearing my voice, he looked up, confusion clouding his eyes. His finger stilled, marking his place on the page.

"It's Elodie."

Papa stood up, his chair screeching on the wooden floor. "Elodie? What the devil . . . ?"

"I found your daughter dressed as a sailor," the captain said. "She was taking part in the initiation ceremonies."

He cocked his head, incredulous. "Did I hear you correctly, sir?"

"She and Alex say they are married. He smuggled her aboard the ship. He says they plan to make a life together."

Papa stared at me. I had never seen him at a loss for words. His mind could not comprehend the situation, and I did not blame him. Here I was, in the middle of the ocean, tossed up upon his ship, weeks after it left England, like a mermaid from the deeps, taking the altered form of his daughter, and claiming marriage to a boy she hardly knew. It must have felt a dream to him. This situation was indeed dreamlike to me. More of a waking nightmare, truth be told.

"Did you say married?" I saw my father's telltale sign of frustration, his fingers clenching and unclenching into fists at his side.

I was embarrassed, humiliated to be standing in front of my father so, to be the cause of tension and strife to him. Of course I knew this reckoning day would come soon enough; I simply wasn't prepared for it to happen at this time, and in this fashion. I certainly hadn't planned on standing in front of my father wearing trousers and with pitch smeared on my face. I had hoped to meet him on the dock in China and explain what had happened, calmly and clearly.

"How did you find a priest or a justice of the peace to do so?" Papa asked, his face tight with anger. "A fleet marriage is no longer possible; this is not the eighteenth century where an imprisoned minister will marry you for a few pennies."

"We pledged ourselves to one another," Alex said. "There was no time—"

Papa stared at him, agog. "So you *aren't* married? It just grows worse and worse."

"Alex and I are married in our hearts to each other, Papa," I said.

"You are not married!" Papa shouted, and I flinched and stepped back, bumping into the captain. "Do you hear me? You are not some working-class girl from the slums of London who can claim marriage without anyone caring to know the truth! You are not twenty-one, and I do not give my permission."

"Papa!" I said, but his held his hand up, interrupting me.

"You will remain apart until we return to England. You will

stay with missionaries in Foochow until I return from the expedition, and then we will go back to England. I will not let this folly stand if I can help it. Alex, you will cease your attention to my daughter. You'll let my daughter have your quarters. You can sleep in the masthead for all I care."

Mercifully, the captain spoke up; he was the voice of reason amidst this hotbed of emotion. I could see why he had become a captain, as he seemed quite skilled at keeping his head in terrible situations. "If you make them stay apart now, Hugh, the men will talk all the more," the captain said. "They will say they are not truly married, that your daughter is merely Alex's plaything. The two must remain together, for your daughter's sake."

"What is wrong with your men, Captain?" Papa roared. "Can you not control them? Are they like biddies at washday?"

"You forget, sir, that I must make note of this in my captain's log, as well. I have no choice. It is the law that I do so. What do you wish me to write? That your daughter was found in a boy's bed or that Alex secreted his wife aboard?"

"Wife!" My father spat. He began to stomp around the saloon. "I can't believe you would do such a thing, Elodie," he bellowed. "To lie with a man you're not bound to. How could you do this? How could you?"

The captain raised his hands. "Come, sir, quiet yourself. We need not give the men more stories to chew over."

Papa rounded on Alex, grabbed his jacket in his fists and backed him against the wall. Kukla barked and threw herself against my father, gripping his pant leg in her teeth, growling, and pulling it this way and that. I dragged the little dog away, gathered her into my arms, but she continued to lunge at my father, her hackles raised, snarling and snapping.

"Have you gotten my daughter in the family way?" Papa roared. "Is this why she's here on the ship? Tell me true and it will go better for you! What false promises did you make to her?" He shook Alex. "Well, what do you have to say for yourself?"

Alex let my father hold him against the wall, let him release his wrath on him, all the while saying nothing, merely looking at him as though waiting for him to spend his anger. Finally Alex spoke, "There is no child. We love one another, and we've pledged to be together."

"Love? You love each other? If you loved her, then you wouldn't have let her on board this ship! You knew what peril she faced, and yet you allowed it. You let her get swept up in that barbarous line-crossing farce. Look at her! Tar on her face, her hair cut like a man's. If you had affection for her, she would not stand before me in this state." Papa grabbed another handful of Alex's jacket and banged him against the wall once more. "Do not speak to me of love, you *pup*, you *orphan*, because you have no knowledge of it."

The captain stood up. "Sir, I beg you," he said. "Hugh, this is not the way. It is not the boy's fault he is without family."

I couldn't stand by and let Alex take the blame. It wasn't fair. "Papa, stop!" I said. "Let him go! None of this is true. We didn't pledge ourselves. We aren't married. Alex said we were married to protect me from the men." I set Kukla down and she slunk away, terrified by all the shouting.

Papa let go of Alex's jacket. "Then what are you doing on the ship?" He glared at me. "And tell me true, Elodie. No more lies."

I started to say that Papa needed help, but I glanced at the captain. I didn't want him to know of Papa's weakness. Papa would have hated me for that. And indeed, he would be angry to know that I thought he was weak. "I didn't want you to travel alone. So I stowed away, and then Alex found me . . . and he helped me." I went on, telling Papa of the false Mrs. Pringle, the orchid thief with the hook for a hand, how Alex had found me in the hold. Papa's face was turning to stone as he listened, his eyes like chips of marble. I began to babble, stuttering out the remaining details of the story.

He turned to Alex. "Mr. Balashov, I take umbrage with your morals. That you could agree to this detestable scheme makes you very suspect. Very suspect, indeed."

"Elodie knows her own mind, sir," Alex said. "I would not dare to show her disrespect by imposing my own decisions upon her."

Papa shot a glance at Alex as though daring him to contradict him. "But it was all right to ruin her by allowing her into your bed?"

"You are right, sir," Alex said. "I am to blame and I will stand by Elodie. No need to say more." He grabbed my hand, and we left the saloon, Kukla trailing behind us. We made a sorry little family.

As Alex shut the saloon door behind him, we could see, up ahead, the cook and Jakes the steward standing in the doorway of the galley eavesdropping, possibly hearing every word that was said. The steward Jakes was grinning, like the cat that had gotten the canary.

Too stunned and heartbroken to speak, I let Alex lead me past them and into his room. I was suddenly shy of Alex.

"I'll leave you to dress." His voice sounded formal, not like the Alex I knew at all. "I'll be back in a little while with something to remove the tar from your face."

He left, pulling the door behind him.

I had never seen my father so angry. Even when he was stripping the green wallpaper from the walls that one sorry Christmas, his anger had not matched this. I doubted he would ever forgive me.

NINETEEN

n hour later, Alex returned carrying a bottle and some rags. I sat on the edge of the bunk dressed in my own clothing. My sturdy tartan gown was only slightly crumpled from its time in the canvas bag, and bedecked with a few spots of mildew. I'd done the best I could with my hair, bundling what was left of it into a bun at the nape of my neck and securing it with the few hairpins I had.

Alex held the bottle up and smiled. "Oil of turpentine. It will remove the tar from your face."

"The captain appeared very upset before," I said.

"The captain worries about me; worries that he's my only family, so I think he's relieved I have a wife, however ill-gotten. He wanted to know why I didn't come to him immediately to tell him about you. I told him you feared the wrath of your father. And that we didn't think it all through."

He sat beside me and began applying the bottle's contents to my face. His touch was gentle as he passed the rag over my cheeks. "These scratches from the barrel stave will heal soon, *myshka*. The same was done to me when I was a griffin. They don't last. I was in the saloon with the captain and your father and I forgot that sometimes they put the griffins in the 'tween deck. Of course I was too late. I'm so sorry. I should have let you stay in my quarters." He shook his head.

I closed my fingers on Alex's hand. "Alex, you don't have to do any of this," I said. "You don't have to marry me."

For a moment I thought I saw a flash of emotion in his eyes—hurt maybe, or something more. Disappointment? He looked away a moment, and then when he glanced back that emotion had gone. Or had I only imagined it?

"Elodie, I have no family. The captain and Kukla are all I have. Kukla means everything to me, and what you did was the greatest kindness. My name is not much, but it's enough to save you, and I'll do this to help you. I won't . . . press you for more, I promise. We can be married in Foochow, and I'll return on the *Osprey*. People understand that sailors are at sea a good deal of the time, so they will not wonder where your husband is. I'm sure your father will see sense and allow you to accompany him."

"But—"

"You're my friend, *myshka*. And there are worse things than being married to your friend." He returned to removing the tar from my cheeks.

Friend. Alex wanted to be my friend. I was embarrassed by my wedding night fancies. *Stupid girl, now you're acting like Violetta sighing over one of her books.* What did I think? That Alex would say he wanted to marry me because he could not live without me? He wanted to marry me because he owed me a favor and wanted to repay it. Nothing would change. He would return to the *Osprey* and carry on. I might never see him again.

Alex must have sensed the kind of girl I was—steady Elodie who handled each day with responsibility and practicality. There was no place in my life for either love nor romance, and the sooner I grasped that the better.

"Thank you," I said, as though I were accepting a gift from an uncle. "I do appreciate your kindness."

❧ ❦ ❧ ❦

THAT EVENING I WALKED THE DECK BEFORE DINNER, BONNET KNOT-ted under my chin, my dress sweeping the deck. It felt strange to wear a skirt once more. My legs felt both free and encumbered. I had to teach myself to walk again, kicking the skirt slightly away from me so as not to tread on the front. My torso felt strange in the corset. I was used to slumping in my sailor's shirt instead of remaining upright all the time, but in truth I was glad of the corset once more, glad of its ability to help me stand straight and tall, and I needed to stand tall as I passed through a gauntlet made from the sailors' scrutiny.

Most of the men had behaved respectfully toward me, knuckling their foreheads and wishing me a good evening. But some of them smirked or muttered under their breaths as I passed. The apprentices didn't dare to look at me, but kept their eyes on their work, pretending I didn't exist. Only Robin raised a hand in greeting, but then he returned to his task of coiling rope.

I had been most afraid of Mr. Holst's reaction and had hoped he'd be elsewhere when I walked the deck. He had been stand-ing over two apprentices as they worked, the handle of his whip tucked into his belt. He said nothing to me, but I felt his accusing eyes following me around the deck as I strode.

The captain, the officers, and my father ate their evening meal in the saloon as befitted their station, and I joined them, as I would for the remainder of the voyage.

The men stood when I came in. All of the officers, including Alex, were there.

Alex held out the chair next to him, and I sat down. There was much scraping of chairs and clearing of throats as everyone sat down, focusing their gaze on the plates in front of them. No one spoke a word. No one dared to look at my father or me.

The door opened, and the captain's steward arrived bearing before him a tray topped with a large pottery bowl. I could see steam rising away from it and smell the enticing scent of onions and gravy. When the lobscouse was ladled before me, I nearly fell on it. I hadn't tasted anything hot or substantial for weeks. Alex could only bring me ship's biscuit, tinned tongue or corned beef—which I keyed open and ate cold from the can—cheese, and the odd apple or slice of cabbage. Hot food was certainly out of the question, as heating it in the galley would have raised impossible-to-answer questions. I had to force myself to attend to the stew and eat small bites when what I really wanted to do was to pick up the dish and eat from it like a wild woman, tear the fresh bread and sop up the gravy, shovel it all into my mouth and ask for more.

Papa picked at his meal, refusing to look at me.

After dinner, I found a place on the ship where I could sit by myself and watch the sun go down. The freedom to gaze out at the sea after so long in hiding felt heavenly. I must have sat there for an hour or so when I sensed someone behind me.

"Am I disturbing you?" It was Alex.

"No." I moved over to make a place for him.

Alex sat down and stared out into the water, saying nothing for a long while. When I could stand our awkward silence no longer, Alex spoke: "Holst is demanding I be punished for smuggling you on board."

"What? But your father knows I stowed away."

"Yes, but the men don't. And it's against the maritime laws to smuggle someone aboard a ship. My father cannot overlook it or make an exemption for me; the men would lose respect for him, they would begin to do what they want. So I have to be punished."

"Will he let Holst whip you with that thing he carries?" All of the sudden I felt very cold, even though the night was hot. I bent forward and crossed my arms over myself, not wanting to hear the answer.

Alex let out a low laugh. "His quirt? Hardly. Holst doesn't use that for punishment; that's what the cat o' nine tails is for. He uses the quirt to start the apprentices to their work. A blow makes them get to work when they are daydreaming, and so they learn to never do it again."

"What is a cat o' nine tails? It sounds gruesome."

"It's a flogger, a whip, made of string with small knots on the end."

"Is it painful?"

Alex snorted. "Yes, it is. I know it is. Holst used it on me about a year after I joined the ship. I suppose I deserved it. I was being cocky, daring an apprentice to a race up the rigging, like boys would do, only the apprentice slipped and fell, broke his wrist. Two lashes is what I got, but two was enough." He rolled his shoulder as though remembering the pain. "But no, the punishment is nothing that simple." He cast an uncertain look at me. "I agreed to leave the ship."

My breath caught. I felt as though I were dropped back into that pool of water again. My chest clenched, and a whirl of emotions tangled inside me. No matter what I did, or how much I tried to help or to put things right, I only succeeded in hurting people. How could that be? I meant no harm. I only wanted to help, and yet people *were* hurt, time and again. I felt so ashamed. I added Alex's punishment to the burden I already carried. Perhaps Papa was right. I should have stayed in Kent. "I'm so sorry, Alex."

"For what?" he asked.

I lifted my hands. "Everything. Where do I begin?"

"*Myshka*, what I did was my choice. I didn't have to help you. I wanted to. We do what we can to help one another, and sometimes it doesn't always work. But we try anyway." He looked grieved. He took my shoulders. "Please don't be unhappy."

"How long will you have to stay away?"

He shrugged. "Until my father calls me back. The ship will return in early spring next year. Possibly then."

"What will you do until then? Will you be able to join another ship?" The thought of Alex unable to sail hurt me. I remembered his face, how happy he looked the day I first saw him with Kukla leaping alongside him, his eyes snapping with joy.

"My father says he'll try to find a position for me on another ship, but I'd have to start as an able seamen. Second mate positions on tea clippers aren't easy to find." Alex looked bereft.

I stood up. "Wait. Alex, why don't you go with Papa on his expedition!"

"What do you mean?"

I laughed. "The expedition to find the Queen's Fancy! You'll be along to help him if he needs it. Oh, Alex, it's perfect. Please say you will. And perhaps I could go with you! If I'm there as your wife, Papa can't refuse me. And then you can return to England afterward and wait for your father there."

I watched Alex as he thought. For a moment I thought he might refuse; he looked unsure, apprehensive. But then he smiled. "Yes," he finally said. "Why not?"

I felt as though the doors to a new world were creaking open. I would set my feet on the path I had only dreamed of. I would help Papa, and I would see those orchids blooming in the forest.

❧ ❦ ❧ ❦

ALEX WENT OFF TO HIS DUTIES, AND I MADE MY WAY TO OUR CABIN. From behind the mast a shadow stepped in front of me. Holst crossed his arms and leaned against the rail, and as he caught sight of me, a smile sketched over his face.

"Good evening, *Mrs. Balashov*." He said the name with a great sense of amusement, followed by a little snort, as though he found the idea of marriage to Alex to be the bravest sport.

"Yes, it is. What do you want?" I eyed him warily.

"No need to fear me; I mean you no harm. I only want a word with you, if you'll so oblige me."

"You are a cruel man, Mr. Holst. Your apprentices are ill-used by you."

"I feel that tidbit of information was wrongly reported to you. Did your *husband* tell you so?"

"I've seen you go about your bullying with my own eyes. That whip you wield."

"Let me disabuse you of your opinion. On a ship we all depend upon one another to do our work in a timely and efficient manner. A slap reminds them that laziness is not to be tolerated. A ship can be sunk for lack of a ha'p'orth of tar. There are bo'suns much crueler than I. Bo'suns who masthead their charges, sending them to sit in the crow's nest for hours in rough seas. Whippings with the cat for tiny infractions. But you may carry on believing I'm a cruel man if you must. Your opinion of me bothers me not."

"Your opinion of me bothers me greatly," I said. "I know how you feel about women aboard a ship. You told me so yourself. I must admit that I am wary of you."

Holst shrugged.

"Nothing terrible has happened since I've been aboard. Surely that must change your opinion of females and ships."

"Yes, it has. And that's what I wanted to say to you. For now I believe that women are good luck."

I was suspicious of him. "How so?"

He dipped his head down, speaking softly, but I heard him clearly. "You are good luck because you're taking that Jonah off the ship. That swine Balashov will finally be out of my life forever, and maybe the captain will begin to see sense, finally."

"Why do you hate Alex so much? What did he ever do to you?"

"It's not what he did to me. It's who he is, what he's made of. And it's not for me to tell another man's secrets. That's for him to share with his wife when it suits him." Holst tipped his hat and then turned.

I WOKE UP WHEN ALEX LEFT FOR HIS DOGWATCH. I TRIED TO RETURN to sleep, but I couldn't. I was filled with trepidation. I told myself that Holst's warning was meant only to frighten me. Alex was nothing but a kind and generous person. Yes, he'd stowed away, but the captain was a wise man, and I couldn't imagine him taking Alex as his ward if he wasn't kind. For Holst, it was sour grapes, that was all. Holst was jealous.

I turned over and stared at the ceiling. So many things were whirling round my mind that I could not calm myself down. I was excited to see China, hopeful that Papa would take me along, and a little thrilled to be marrying Alex.

I turned over again. My heart was a dolt. It heard the word *marriage* and leapt to all sorts of conclusions. *Friends, we were only friends.*

Finally, when the sun was beginning to break, I rose and began to dress. I was searching for hairpins when I found, at the bottom of the hessian bag, my plait. I ran the long silky plait through my fingers. I couldn't imagine ever being the girl who wore it again. I didn't want to be staid Elodie anymore. I wanted her gone. The Elodie I wanted to be craved adventure and a life filled with the pursuit of knowledge.

I stepped outside as the sun was beginning to rise over the figurehead. I held the railing tightly and watched the water purling under the sides of the ship, the wind snapping the sails.

I cast the braid over the railing and into the sea.

PART THREE

China—Summer 1861

TWENTY

e reached China on the tenth of August, mooring the ship on a spit of land called Pagoda Anchorage, a few miles outside of Foochow. From there, Alex told me, Chinese stevedores on sampans would off-load the bales of cotton and wool from the *Osprey* and replace them with tea chests laden with leaves from the Wuyi Mountains.

Alex had decided that Kukla would be safer back in England for the time being. A shard of pain rent my heart as I watched Alex hug his dog close and then hand her to Robin, who had promised to take her to my family in Kent as soon as the *Osprey* docked in London. Poor Kukla whined and cried and tried to leap out of Robin's arms to follow Alex down the ladder and onto the sampan.

Then Alex, Papa, and I boarded a small boat on which we were to be rowed down the Min River to Foochow by coolies.

The captain stood in the bow of the ship, gripping the railing with both hands and watching Alex, his face filled with sorrow.

"You'll see your father again, too, I'm sure," I said to Alex as the pigtailed coolies rowed the boat away from the *Osprey*. A ghost of a smile crossed Alex's face, but he said nothing. He didn't take his eyes off the captain until the ship was out of sight.

China unfolded before me in a kaleidoscope of color. My eyes skipped from one sight to the next, gobbling the scene up, committing it to memory, for I had never seen such things in my life. Such beautiful and incredible things. Papa sat gripping the sides of the boat, staring at the shore, responding to my questions with a grunt or not at all. I recognized the signs of one of his spells beginning: the avoiding of questions, the silence, and the visible tension in his body.

The bay was filled with graceful fishing boats, each one's bow painted with a black-and-white eye. Alex told me the Chinese believed the painted eye helped the boats see their way through the water. Foochow, ahead of us, was beautiful, with a long bridge stretching out into the water. There were two pagodas towering over the walls of the city, one black and one white, each level stacked on top of the next like a wedding cake. The striking hills beyond tumbled off into the distance to mysterious places unknown. I felt an eager tug, yearning to explore them. I hoped my exploration of China would not begin and end in Foochow. Alex and I had decided not to tell Papa about our plan to travel with him until we were on land. Then we would present our idea as a fait accompli. And hope he would accept it.

As our boat drew farther away from the ship I saw ravages of the recent war marking the beauty of the land. The sampan rounded Pagoda Anchorage, and I saw the many graves of the dead, the earth still freshly mounded on top. They lay in the shadow of the destroyed fortresses, blown to bits by Western cannon. Beggars dressed in rags, their limbs covered with suppurating wounds, gathered at the end of the bridge, crying out to us, their hands outstretched, as the sampan passed.

When we arrived on the shore, a band of coolies rushed to our boat, grabbing at our luggage and arguing with one another in Chinese. Papa jumped out of the boat and away from the men, not noticing or caring that he was standing in water.

I shaded my eyes from the sun. "Are you all right, Papa?"

"Of course I am," he said, fixing me with a glare. "Why wouldn't I be?"

"You're in the water."

He ignored me and waded to shore.

Alex sorted everything out, giving the job of carrying our luggage to the first coolies who had arrived, and then caught me by the waist and swung me out onto the shore.

Two men ran off to find us transport, which arrived in the form of three sedan chairs. The sedan was an odd conveyance where the traveler sat in a little windowed box suspended from two poles, which were then borne aloft on the shoulders of two coolies.

"I can walk," I insisted. "I don't wish for these men to bear me. They are not mules!"

"It's considered poor form to walk," Papa said, his tone short and dismissive. "If you walk, you're saying you can't afford coolies, and we'll have trouble dealing with people. Saving face is very important to the Chinese. You're in a new land, Elodie, and you must try to follow its customs."

Reluctantly I climbed into the odd conveyance and gripped the armrests, my shoulders tense. I sucked in my breath as the chair rose up. It felt exceedingly odd to be hefted into the air in that fashion, and I didn't care for it one bit.

Papa's chair bearers set off in front of me, and Alex's behind me.

Apprehensive about how Papa would react to our decision to join him, I tried to distract myself with the scene passing by my little window. I didn't know what I expected Foochow itself to look like. I suppose I expected it to be similar to England, but with an Eastern bent. I couldn't have been more wrong. It was old, so old as to be medieval. There was little planning to the city, and most of the buildings were thrown up higgledy-piggledy. Some leaned against their neighbors, giving the impression that they only stood upright by the grace of the other buildings. If the first building in the line was struck down, the rest of the buildings would probably collapse like a line of dominoes. The smell coming from the houses was oppressive, particularly in the heat of the day. They smelled of rubbish and outhouses and spoiled fish.

Narrow cobbled alleyways snaked through the town in a confusing labyrinth. The roofing of the houses jutted out over the narrow path so that only a chink of sunlight streamed through. I could imagine that rain tunneled through in a sheet of water, soaking everyone who tried to make his way through the street during a rainstorm.

The inhabitants of the houses on these alleys were using the space to hang their washing, pen their pigs, and send their children and dogs out to play. Two little boys dressed in blue pajamas ran up to my chair and touched it, obviously on a dare.

When I smiled down at them, the younger of the two screamed and ran away as though he had seen the devil himself. The second boy lasted a few moments longer before he too dashed off, crying. "Don't be afraid," I called out through the window, hoping they would come back so I could get a better look at them, but they of course didn't understand what I was saying, and disappeared into one of the huts.

The only female children I saw playing were very young, maybe three or four years old. As the chair made a turn around a curve I saw the reason why older girls were not running. A knot of them, about eight years old or so, perched on the curbstones. They sat with their legs stretched in front of them, their feet covered in dirty bandages, their cheeks streaked with tears. They looked up dully as we passed, pain evident in their faces.

I had read about the ancient practice of foot binding in China, but I hadn't quite believed it. But here it was before me. The girls' feet had been broken purposely, the foot folded under the sole and bound tightly with bandages until they were only inches long. The girls would never run and play again. The rest of their lives would be spent hobbling in pain. I thought of Calla and Lily running on their sturdy little feet, skipping and laughing, their pinafores twirling around as they spun about, falling dizzy with joy into the spring grass. My toes curled in my boots. I leaned out of the window as far as I dared, keeping the girls in my sight until the sedan chair turned and the macabre scene vanished behind us.

Ahead, men with long pigtails and shaved heads loitered in the alley space, and every one of their eyes followed us as we passed by. They were so thin, walking skeletons, with sunken eyes and chests and skin that looked like leather. One of them spat on the ground. *"Fanqui,"* he shouted, the word bursting from his mouth like a curse. I leaned back from the window and tugged the curtain closed.

A half hour later, we'd left the town behind us and climbed a steep hill. It was as if we'd entered a different country. Here there were more Western faces than Chinese, and the houses were larger, with tidy gardens enclosed within ominous iron fencing. From the Chinese men's hostile reaction to us, I wondered if the fencing was meant to keep the Westerners in or the Chinese out.

Our sedan chairs stopped at a three-storied building set behind a gilded gate. Two male servants ran forward to open it and see to our baggage.

We went up the cobblestone path to the inn's front door. Walking on land left me with a curious sensation and caused me to stagger from one side to the other. "Still have your sea legs, *myshka*?" Alex said. "Don't fret. A few days will see you right. It takes a little while until the earth stops tilting." He held out his elbow. "Here, take my arm."

I slid my hand around his elbow, relieved to hear his good cheer after his sadness at leaving his father. He sounded like the old Alex.

The inn was light and airy with tall ceilings and glass windows draped with tartan curtains. The hall was decorated with a mix of British and Chinese furnishings. An oaken credenza stood next to a dainty lacquered cabinet dressed with red tassels. A still life painting of a brown-and-white hunting spaniel with a pheasant clenched in his jaws hung amongst porcelain plates painted with blue temples.

The innkeeper stood behind a black lacquered reception

counter that bisected the room. He was a tiny wizened Englishman, so short he had to stand on an upturned soapbox to see us. Behind him, a clutch of pigeonholes held room keys and letters for the residents. Beyond the hall lay a little sitting room furnished with cushioned divans made of rattan. There was only one guest in the room, and he sat reading a newspaper, a glass of sherry at his elbow. He was around Papa's age and had the look of a stork—gangly and thin. His face was bedecked with a bushy moustache that overhung his top lip, and his hair was smarmed down to one side with oil. At our approach, he flicked the paper down and eyed us over the top. "Hugh McGregor!" he barked. He dropped the paper and unfolded his long legs, struggling to his feet with the aid of a walking stick.

Papa noticed him approaching and swore under his breath. "Good god, the day only grows worse."

"Who is he, Papa?" I asked, but Papa didn't reply. He braced his shoulders and gripped the edge of the counter.

The man smirked as he approached, his long mustache bristling. "As I live and breathe. I believe we've ventured into the theater of the absurd! I never expected to see your carcass back in old Foochow."

Papa ignored him and spoke to the innkeeper. "Have you two rooms available?"

"Yes, sir," the innkeeper replied. He opened a book and set it before him, along with a dip pen and a pot of ink. "How long will you be staying with us, sir?"

"A night or two," Papa said, taking up the pen.

"Name's Howell," the man said to Alex, ignoring me altogether, as though I were part of the wallpaper. "Cornelius

Howell. From London's *Daily Sketch*. Mr. McGregor and I are old acquaintances."

Papa guffawed when the man said *acquaintances*, but he didn't turn around. He continued scratching away at the register with the pen.

"*Dobriy den*," Alex replied.

"Ah! A Turk, are you? I'm a dab-hand with languages, but it's been a long while since I visited old Constantinople. Speak English, if you can."

"I'm Russian," Alex said, eyeing the man warily. "And yes, I can speak English."

"I'm reporting on the aftermath of the China Wars and the burning of the Summer Palace."

When the man mentioned the Summer Palace, I looked at Papa. He set his jaw and stabbed the pen against the book so hard the nib broke through the paper. I glared at the man, wishing he would go away.

"I'm a war correspondent, you see." He leaned his skinny frame against the reception desk and tapped his leg with his walking stick. "Wounded in India covering the rebellion of fifty-seven. Left me with a permanent limp."

"You slid from an elephant," Papa said, not lifting his head from the book. "While you were inebriated. I'd hardly call that a war wound."

Mr. Howell smiled a tight smile. "A broken leg is a broken leg," he said. "Dashed painful bloody business, especially in that godforsaken country where the damnable heat alone is enough to cook a man's brain like a soft-boiled egg."

"You've forgotten your manners, sir," Papa said. "I'll thank you to watch your language in front of the girl."

Mr. Howell pulled his head back with a start, as though I'd just appeared in front of him like a fairy—albeit a shabby one dressed in a soiled gown fit only for the rag and bone barrel. "And who is this?"

"You needn't know who she is," Papa said before I could speak.

"I heard you ask old Briarwood here for two rooms." He pointed at each one of us in turn and counted: "One, two, three of you. Who is the lucky owner of this fine filly?"

I didn't like the way the man's gaze raked me from head to toe, as though I were a curio that he could examine in a shop and then dismiss—a thing bereft of feelings that didn't warrant a thought.

"She's nothing to do with you," Papa snapped, his eyes glowing a warning.

Mr. Howell raised his eyebrows. "Suit yourself, then." He propped himself against the counter on his elbows and crossed one ankle over the other as though he planned to stay and chat for a good long while. "Swiftly changing the subject. You'll be interested to hear this bit of news, McGregor. An edict has come out recently that may bring you some comfort. You'll have no trouble moving about the countryside now. The Chinese must provide soldiers for protection to those going into the interior. And you'll need them. Many brigands about now haven't found Westerners very lovable."

Father's pen stilled. "Soldiers?" I saw his throat bob as he swallowed.

"Yes, and if they fail to protect a Westerner, the emperor must compensate the person for any loss. I'll have a little chat with the mandarin here, if you like—he's in my pocket, you see—and make sure he communicates with his fine fellows in the villages along the way to wherever it is you're going. You'll be safe as houses traveling. None of that bad business like last time." He narrowed his eyes, looking at Papa sideways. "How goes your recovery? Would love to sit down with you and chew it over, hey? Make for a good story."

Father set the pen down and turned. "Could you possibly do me a favor, Howell? Could you possibly close that hole of yours you call a mouth and remove yourself from my presence?"

The little innkeeper pressed his lips together, looking for all the world like he might burst out laughing. I suspected that Mr. Howell had not made himself very lovable, if his boorish behavior was anything to go by.

"Can you blame a man looking for a story?" Mr. Howell said with wounded air. "I'm trying to do my job same as you. We're more alike than not, you know. You tromp the country looking for flowers, and I tromp the country looking for stories."

Papa snorted. "We are not alike. I've been in that rag of yours under your byline many a time, I daresay, without my permission, and I don't wish to repeat the exercise. You'll get nothing from me, so don't waste your breath asking."

"Yes, well, we'll see about that. I'm sure you wish old Bowlby were here. You were able to manipulate him, but you can't me."

I stepped forward at the mention of the name Bowlby. T. W. Bowlby was the *Times* journalist who had been swept up with Papa. The one who had died of his wounds in prison.

"That is very disrespectful of you to say, sir," I told him. "You shouldn't speak ill of the dead."

He ignored me.

Papa clenched his fist so hard his knuckles turned white.

"You, sir, are nothing compared to Thomas Bowlby. He didn't hang about in inns waiting for the story to come to him. He went into the theater of war. He was a brave man, and he died a brave man. And if you're covering the burning of the Summer Palace, you are miles away. You should be in Peking. Why not take yourself there? This minute, preferably."

Mr. Howell had the wherewithal to look humiliated. The bravado dropped a little bit. "I think you'd better return to your reading, Mr. Howell," I said before he could make a further dolt of himself. Deacon Wainwright and he would get along smashingly.

"No. I'll go," Papa said, and then turned on his heel and quit the room.

"Well now. Always reverting to type, old McGregor," Mr. Howell said. He tossed his walking stick in the air and caught it in his hand. "Welcome to China, Miss whoever-you-are. I hope we'll see each other again."

"If we do, I hope you'll have found your manners, sir," I said.

"Well, I've been told, haven't I?" He pushed away from the desk, winked at me, nodded at Alex, and returned to the parlor.

The innkeeper held out the room keys to Alex, and he took them. "I'll see to the rooms. Why don't you go after your father, *myshka*?"

❦❦❦❦

I FOUND PAPA AT THE BACK OF THE HOUSE IN A SMALL COURTYARD, sitting on a bench in the cool shade of an exotic tree. Its trunk was gnarled and ancient-looking, and its delicate fan-shaped leaves fluttering in the breeze were green touched with yellow.

"I've never seen a tree like this one." I touched the bark. "It's extraordinary."

"A maidenhair tree," he said. "*Ginkgo biloba.* It's only native to China." He plucked a leaf and held it on his palm. "Kew has one. The Old Lion, planted a hundred years ago. Perhaps you've seen it growing next to the great stove."

"I don't think I have. Will you show it to me when we return?"

"Perhaps," he said. He tossed the leaf down and gently placed his boot over the top of it. "China is a country of contradictions— so much to discover, yet so much to forget. Sometimes I think it would have been best if we'd left China and all her secrets well enough alone. We've only brought strife and sorrow to this land and grabbed the best bits for ourselves."

I sank down onto the bench next to him and stared down at his boot, a bit of the maidenhair tree leaf poked out from under his toe. "I'm sorry about that odious man."

"Stay away from him, Elodie. You must promise me this."

"He seems quite harmless, Papa. Obnoxious, yes, but—"

"Hell's teeth, Elodie! For once simply do as I say. Keep away from that man. If he approaches you, walk away from him. He'll be on the lookout for any sort of story."

"Can we not stay elsewhere?"

Papa lifted an eyebrow. "This is not England, my dear. There's nowhere else for a Westerner to stay in Foochow that's safe enough. We'd be robbed blind within minutes of arrival."

We sat on that bench, in the shade of the tree, for a long while before I gathered up my courage to speak again. "You seemed concerned when Mr. Howell mentioned the soldiers, Papa. I don't blame you. They must bring back terrible memories."

He plucked another leaf and examined it carefully, holding it up to the sunlight and twirling the stem in his fingers.

"But I'm sure these will be different. I'm sure they will be useful to you." I fiddled with the ties of my bonnet nervously, pulling the silken ribbons loose and re-tying them. "To us, I mean."

"Us? What do you mean?"

"I'm not going back to Kent. Alex isn't going back on the *Osprey* after we're married."

"I know this. The captain told me he planned to find him a temporary position on another clipper ship."

"Yes . . . he did say that. But Alex has chosen not to take it." The leaf stilled in his hand.

"Alex and I have decided to go with you."

"You're not. You're going back to England on a steamship, just as soon as I can find passage and a traveling companion for you."

"We will simply follow behind you. Alex will be my husband in a manner of hours and he has decided to go with you. He wishes me to go, too. You cannot oppose him."

I'd never stood directly into the teeth of a storm before and felt the wind and water lash at my face, but given the choice, I would have gladly done so rather than submit myself to Papa's reaction.

Papa stood up. His face was a mask of fury. It was as though I had provoked a dangerous animal. "I should have sent you home with your sister and the abominable deacon that day back at Kew," he shouted. "This expedition has nothing whatsoever to do with you. I could take you by the shoulders and shake you!"

"Well, you may try it!" I said, my voice matching his. "It

won't change anything. We're going with you to find the Queen's Fancy. You have no ability to travel by yourself. I thought it was a ridiculous notion then, and I think it's a ridiculous notion now!"

"A ridiculous notion? Well, because of *your* folly, I have Cleghorn's man nipping at my heels. He's probably taken a steamship, beat us to China by weeks, and is halfway to the Queen's Fancy as we speak! You are a young naïve girl who, it seems, is more lacking in intelligence than I thought!"

I blinked. Papa's voice chilled me. There was not a shred of affection in it. "Please do not shout at me. Please do not say such things. I didn't mean to tell Cleghorn's man! He deceived me. Have you never made a mistake? Never made the wrong decision? Are you so perfect?"

I knew then I had said the wrong thing. He paled and drew his head back as though I had slapped him. I felt instant remorse. Of course he'd made mistakes. His had nearly cost his life.

"Do you think I want you to experience pain and fear? My life is about taking care of you, protecting you, your mother, and your sisters!"

"But by keeping me shuttered away, keeping all of us shuttered away? Like flowers in one of your glasshouses? If I were your son, you'd welcome me, encourage me. Not push me to the side!"

"But you are not my son, Elodie."

"And you regret that most heartily, don't you?"

He drew his head back. "Of course I don't! That's ridiculous."

"You think because I am a girl, I can't want to protect my

family? That I have no longing for adventure? Only a male can have those feelings?"

"Enough, Elodie." He flung his arms out. "You are not going with me. You'll go home on the first steamship. The devil take Alex, for all I care."

"Tell me why I can't go? If you can give me a good reason why, then I'll consider it."

Papa said nothing. He looked away.

"Well then. We're going, Papa. And nothing you can say will change that." I had to stand up to him. Despite mistakes I had made, I knew that my opinions had merit, as I had seen the proof. I shouldn't have backed down to Dr. Thumpston and Deacon Wainwright, but I'd done so because I was frightened of their disapproval. I wouldn't make that same mistake again. Papa was already angry with me for stowing away, and he could continue to be angry. I would rather see him and my family safe, even if that meant he'd never forgive me.

He screwed the leaf up into his hand and punched the tree so hard the trunk shook and the leaves rained down around us.

AN HOUR LATER, ALEX AND I FOUND OURSELVES PLEDGING OUR lives to one another at the mission of the Methodist Episcopal Church, in what was known as the southern suburbs. I stood at the altar in my soiled tartan, Alex in his workmanlike sailor's jacket and trousers, and Papa in his canvas expedition suit. Alex looked dazed and slightly startled, and I'm sure my expression matched his.

The vicar was a large bear-like man with long Dundreary whiskers who looked as though he would be more comfortable on an expedition to the Arctic than as a minister at a humble missionary church in China.

I held Alex's hands tightly as the vicar read out the wedding sermon. We repeated our vows to one another, and when it came time for the wedding ring, I fully expected Alex to say he didn't have one, but instead he reached into his coat pocket and pulled out a ring, and not just an ordinary band of silver. The piece was striking, with three gold bands of varying shades joined together in an interlinking pattern. Alex reached down and took my right hand and slid the ring on.

The vicar beamed down at us. "Well then, you may kiss your bride, Mr. Balashov."

Alex touched his lips briefly to mine, more like a brother to a sister than a husband to a wife. And I wondered if the intimacy I'd felt those days on the ship had been real or if they were a figment of my own imagination.

⁂

I COULDN'T BEAR TO WEAR MY TARTAN GOWN ANY LONGER, SO AT MY insistence Papa directed the coolies to a shop in Foochow where I could purchase some new clothing. I was most surprised by the goods available there, even Western things, and the money Papa gave me went a very long way. I went into a perfumer's shop so that I could purchase some soap. They sold pearl powder in little paper packages along with rouges in colorful cardboard boxes. There were lotions, dyes for the hair, and even Rowland's Macassar Oil hair pomade, sold in the same

British packaging I knew so well. It was funny to find that an English fashion had made it all the way to China. There was a curio stall that sold ordinary China and some with Swiss scenes painted on. A linen drapers shop offered blue stuff for the common tunic and trousers I saw bedecking the Chinese men, as well as calicos, printed cottons, and Russian cloth in red and blue. I purchased two wool skirts and a few blouses as well as several pairs of pantaloons and three chemises.

The sun was setting and Papa was anxious to return to the foreign settlement before it grew dark. When we arrived, the short-statured innkeeper had a hot meal waiting for us—a steamed chicken pie and a trifle for dessert.

It was a somber dinner, a far cry from a joyful wedding breakfast. Alex had grown quiet again, saying nothing after the ceremony and even less at dinner. I was silent as well, apprehensive over our wedding night, and what Alex expected of it. Papa finished his meal quickly and excused himself, saying nothing more than good night, leaving Alex and me alone in the empty dining room.

I wished myself anywhere but here. I wanted to go home, home to my sister, and lie in the dark giggling and telling each other tales. I knew who I was there, I knew who Elodie Buchanan was. She collected ferns and looked after her sisters and mother and went to church. I had no idea who this new girl was, this Elodie Balashov, despite my declaration on the boat when I had thrown my braid into the ocean. Now I wasn't sure I wanted to be her. Not with *my friend* Mr. Balashov sitting there, looking handsome—too handsome with his dark eyes and pale skin and unkempt hair that looked dashing on no one but him.

Finally, after another round of awkward silence, the innkeeper poked his head around the door and said the dining room would be closing.

We couldn't dither any longer, so we rose and went upstairs.

Our room held a small Western-style bed with a wrought iron bedframe covered in pillows and a patchwork quilt. It looked massive compared to the tiny bunk Alex and I had shared on the *Osprey*. A bamboo washstand holding a blue patterned basin and ewer depicting a pagoda and willow tree stood in the corner, a linen towel threaded through a wooden ring on its side. A little beveled mirror hung above it, lined with a shelf that contained a cake of yellow soap.

"Elodie Balashov," I said, sitting on the end of the bed. Alex remained by the door, leaning against the wall with his arms crossed. "The name sounds so exotic. I suppose I should learn some Russian to go along with it." I was trying to jest, but Alex didn't laugh. The smile faded from my lips.

"I don't think it's necessary for you to hold up that wall," I finally said, feeling peevish. I rubbed my temple where a headache was forming, and all I wanted was for this impossible day to be over. I just wished Alex would say something, anything. When I told Violetta that Alex was handsome like Heathcliff, I never meant his personality was similar. But now with him standing against the wall, that shuttered look on his face, I could imagine him as Heathcliff, brooding.

"Are you coming to bed or not?"

"I'm thinking."

"Thinking what?" I snapped.

"That you look very pretty."

"Oh," I said, the anger fading away. Alex left his wall and came to my side. "I'm sorry. I didn't mean to quarrel with you." I rubbed the bridge of my nose again. "It's just . . . the day has been very long."

"Are you feeling unwell? You've gone pale."

"I have a headache. It's silly, really. I felt quite well on the ship, and now we're on dry land and on a bed that doesn't pitch back and forth and I have a headache. My ears are ringing, too." I could feel tears welling up, which sometimes happened to me when I got ill like this. Headaches made me feel wretched and despairing and not a little pathetic.

"It's the climate. It takes people that way sometimes, especially those who are new to it. Here, lie down." Alex slid down the bed a bit to give me some room. And after hesitating for a moment, I stretched out and lay my head on his lap.

Alex removed the pins from my hair one by one. I heard them clink as he dropped each one in a dish on the nightstand. He searched through my hair for the last remaining pin, then smoothed my hair out and began to rub my forehead. I could feel my muscles relaxing under his touch.

"I miss Kukla. Don't you?"

His hands slowed. "Very much. It feels odd without her."

"My sisters will care for her. I wish I were there to see their faces when Robin brings her to my home. They will be so happy."

"Hmmm," Alex said.

"Will you miss the ship?"

"I'll miss the captain and the routine of it. The knowing what was coming next."

"I know what you mean. I felt like that at home." I slid my hand under my face and felt the ring press against my cheek.

"The ring is beautiful. I was surprised that you had one. Where did you find it?"

"It was my mother's," he said. "The three bands represent the holy trinity. In Russia brides wear their rings on the right hand. You can put it on the left if it means more to you like that."

I looked at the ring, turning it round on my finger. "No, I like it there." It made my heart crack a little to think of Alex cherishing the ring and keeping it safe even when he was a penniless orphan. He could have sold it many years ago and made his life better, at least for a little while.

But he didn't, and now he had given it to me. I thought about his father choosing the ring for his mother, about her wearing it when they made Alex, and when she gave birth to him.

"What were your parents' names?" I asked.

"My mother's name was Anna and my father's, Pyotr," he said.

"You don't have any sisters or brothers? I never thought to ask you."

"I had an older brother, Maxim. He was a soldier at sixteen, but he went missing. Several people who knew him said he was killed." Alex explained this to me in a matter-of-fact tone, as though he had said the words many times, getting used to the sound of them. "You mentioned your sister before. Do you have others?"

"I have eight sisters," I said.

A little snort of laughter escaped him. "Well . . . that's quite a lot of family."

"There should have been ten of us," I said. "My mother's firstborn was a boy, but he died as a baby. My parents keep trying for a boy." I shrugged. "But all they have are girls. I know my mother will love you. When she meets you, I mean. She'll like having a son-in-law."

Alex made no comment, and I squeezed my eyes shut. I didn't know if Alex planned to come back to England to meet my mother and sisters. Perhaps I would never see Alex again after this. Suddenly a lump rose to my throat.

"How is your headache now?" he said.

"It's easing, thank you."

Alex's fingers left my hair and his lips fell upon my brow. "There," he said.

I opened my eyes and found Alex looking back at me—his eyes dark and smoky as peat. His mouth curved into a smile.

I could raise my chin and our lips would touch. Only an inch, only a breath lay between us. I never wanted anything more in the whole of my life than to kiss Alex then, to feel the warmth of his mouth on mine. To lay my palm on the nape of his neck where his hair met the coarse linen of his neck hand-kerchief, to tangle my fingertips through his hair and touch the skin underneath. What would he do? What would he say if I were that bold?

I lifted my chin, but Alex was already there. His mouth brushed against mine, a whisper of a kiss.

I slid my hand up to his neck and cupped the back of his head, drawing him into the kiss, hoping he wouldn't pull away.

He didn't.

I was so taken aback that my mind couldn't grasp the truth—I was kissing Alex, and he was kissing me. My worries, my fears, my hurt slid from me and into a puddle on the floor. I knew only Alex and that moment. At first we started shyly, touching our lips together again and again. But then we grew a little bolder and the kisses deepened. We kissed each other for a long time.

And then, just like that, it was over.

Alex lifted his head. He cleared his throat. "Elodie, please forgive me. I forgot myself."

I sat up. My gaze skipped over the contents of the room; desperate to alight on anything but the one thing I wanted most to look upon—Alex. "Don't apologize," I said.

He touched my shoulder. "You're not angry with me?"

"No," I said. I pasted a smile on my face. "What are a few kisses between friends?" I laughed at my stupid joke, but I was dying inside of embarrassment. I had kissed him as much as he had kissed me. Surely he must have known that?

What did I expect anyway? That at the completion of our vows Alex would immediately fall in love with me? How absurd to assume that someone so dashing as Alex could love me.

That night, Alex and I lay in bed like two logs, no longer lighthearted; no longer laughing and whispering long into the night. Instead we held ourselves tightly, not touching, saying nothing. Tentatively I leaned my head on his chest, but Alex did not rest his hand on my shoulder, as he usually did. I turned away from him and wrapped my arms around myself, wishing that were enough to build a wall around my heart.

TWENTY-ONE

lex had already gone down to breakfast when I woke the next morning. I was heading down the stairs when I saw Mr. Howell standing below on the landing leaning on his walking stick, one ankle crossed over the other. I paused, two steps above him, one foot hovering. "Good morning, Mr. Howell," I said slowly. He gazed up at me, his face fixed with a determined expression.

"Ah, just the girl I wanted to see. So . . . I hear from our innkeeper, old Briarwood, that you and the handsome Russian are newlyweds." He put one hand on his chest and bowed. "My congratulations to you." He squinted. "However, Briarwood couldn't, or *wouldn't*, tell me why you're trailing along behind old McGregor. Perhaps I can winkle it out of you, especially since McGregor isn't around to stop you from speaking, hey?"

I took up my skirt in my hand. "Let me pass, Mr. Howell. I wish to go to breakfast." I had no plans to answer a single question he asked. I wasn't going to get tricked into giving information away ever again.

He lifted his stick and stubbed it against the bannister's railing, blocking my way. "Secrets, secrets. Seems everyone has a secret," he said. "Would you like to know Hugh McGregor's secret?"

"Not particularly, no," I said, raising my chin. Any truth that came out of that man was bound to be tainted by yellow journalism.

"He used to be in Jardine, Matheson and Company's employ."

"So what if he did?" I had heard of the company before, as it was well known in England, but never in connection with Papa. Jardine, Matheson & Company exported tea, cotton, and silk from China. Papa had nothing to do with those manufactures. He was a plant hunter, not a tea merchant.

Mr. Howell scrunched up his narrow face, thinking. "I should rephrase. McGregor smuggled opium for them. 'Work' implies he toiled in an honest occupation, when of course that can't be true." He smiled, waiting for my reaction.

"What do you mean?"

"For years he's carried opium to the villagers between here and Wuyishan. Opium." He twiddled his fingers in front of him. "In little cakes wrapped in newspaper. McGregor carried it in those glasshouses. The ones he stows his plants in. What does he call them?" He snapped his finger. "Wardian cases."

That Christmas, when Papa had given the girls the dollhouse. I remembered what he'd said: *Wardian cases are the very reason why your papa is the success he is.* Of course at the time I thought he meant because it had allowed him to ship plants home protected. Had the one he'd given the girls housed opium? Papa had told me if I knew the whole truth, I'd be horrified. Did Mamma know? *Of course she knew.* And that was the reason why they fought all the time.

No. It couldn't be true. "You're telling tales, Mr. Howell. I don't appreciate it one bit! Jardine, Matheson is an important firm. Why would they want to hurt the Chinese people?"

"Open your eyes, young lady! Do you think the world is nothing but a benevolent society?" He rubbed his fingers together. "Anything for money, even if that means making money on the backs of the poor and the ignorant. A young lady like yourself probably has no idea what caused the fracas here in China, hey?"

"The capturing of a British ship."

"That was just a handy excuse. No. It was over the very thing McGregor smuggled in," he whispered. "Opium. *Yang-yao*, the foreign drug, the Chinese call it. They didn't want it, but the Westerners forced it in so that they could afford to buy what the Chinese prized—tea. And now, millions of people in China can't go without their opium—such captive and docile customers they are, too."

He leaned toward me. He was so close I could see the toast crumbs in his moustache, smell the smoked kippers on his breath. I wanted to clap my hands over my ears so I couldn't hear this vitriol he spouted, but God help me, I could not. I stood riveted, unable to move, waiting to hear what he had to say next.

"Soldiers cannot leave an opium den to fight, and a man will sell his wife and children to buy more opium. A wealthy man will pawn the last brick in his house and live in a ditch before he'll give up the habit. A neat and tidy little venture, what?"

He laughed. "He's so sanctimonious, old McGregor, acting as though my newspaper is not fit for him to wipe his boots on. Yet he was happy to visit misery on a people so that he'd have the funds to search for his little plants."

I found my feet and barged past Mr. Howell, not caring if I pushed him down the stairs.

"It's unlucky to cross on the stairs," he called after me. "You'll want all the luck you can get where you're headed."

I turned and stared up at him. "What do you mean?"

"There's a reason I remain in the safety of this inn, miss, and don't head out into the *theater of war*. If I wait long enough, the stories come to me. You see, every Westerner heading out into the interior of China stops here first. Including a plant hunter named Luther Duffey."

"What was he after? Did he tell you?"

He shrugged. "I didn't converse with him. I treasure my limbs too much for that. I don't need a matching set of broken legs. He was here about two days ago." He looked at me carefully, almost hesitantly. And then he spoke. "I see that you judge me. But we all need a story, Mrs. Balashov. For a story is the best defense. Its cut is much sharper than a knife's blade." He touched his forehead with the handle of his cane. "I bid you good day."

❧❦❧❦

I COULDN'T WAIT TO LEAVE THE INN, MR. HOWELL, AND THE HUMIL-iation of my wedding night behind. I felt numb and uncertain about Papa. I didn't know what was true anymore. I had built my father up into a hero, a dashing adventurer. Perhaps Violetta was correct when she said Papa was a figment of my imagination. Maybe everything I had thought about him was untrue. I had defended him, and now I looked the fool.

But then I felt ashamed for believing Mr. Howell over Papa. I had no proof that he was telling the truth about him. I had no one to ask to corroborate his story. Perhaps Mr. Howell wanted to get back at Papa for embarrassing him. That was all.

Reluctantly, Papa had agreed that Alex and I could go along. Two days after we left the *Osprey*, we set off on a path that snaked alongside the Min, traveling in sedan chairs, each of us carried aloft by four coolies. I hated being carried about like that, so much so that every step the men took made me feel as though I was losing a part of my soul. People were not meant to be beasts of burdens, and the guilt lay heavily on me. Each coolie looked so slight and so thin that I couldn't imagine how he lifted anything. To make matters worse, the men didn't walk; they jogged. Up and down hills and through ravines without breaking stride or complaining. Porters behind them bore our goods on poles over their shoulders, and they moved just as quickly. I understood the men earned their living this way, and indeed my father planned to pay them well, but I felt as though my status meant my life was greater than theirs. We were all God's creatures; none of us better than the others, no matter how we came into the world. I wanted nothing more than to get out and walk. I couldn't wait until this part of the journey ended. Thankfully, it only lasted two days and nights.

Whenever we rested, I tried to offer the coolies water to drink, but they huddled in a group, staring at me suspiciously when I approached holding out a tin canteen that contained our boiled water. Alex finally explained that Chinese only drink tea, never water, especially not cold water, and would go thirsty if tea was not available. So the next time we stopped, I made sure they had time to make a fire to brew their tea, and I was rewarded for this kindness with smiles. Alex told me that I had made them rise in status because I had dared to notice them.

Papa grew ever more agitated when the soldiers joined us, leaning away from them and flinching whenever they addressed him. The soldiers seem to find this behavior funny, and began to pull jokes on him, like throwing lit matches at him and hiding his bags.

The soldiers also quarreled with the chair bearers. When we stopped for lunch, Alex told me he'd overheard them trying to "squeeze" the coolies, forcing them to give them a share of their wages. When Alex found this out, he forbade the soldiers to talk to the coolies. I don't think the soldiers realized that Papa and Alex understood Mandarin as well as they did. They left off their harassment after that but turned sullen and taciturn, refusing to respond to Alex or Papa when they asked questions.

I'd wanted adventure, but those two days were anything but—I was afraid of the orchid thief, upset about Papa, and embarrassed over my wedding night. So much so that I couldn't get past my emotions to see the beauty of the land. Everywhere I looked I expected to see the orchid thief's jack-o'-lantern grin. Whenever I brushed against Alex, I felt him pulling away from the kiss. And each time I glanced at Papa I saw him as a villain.

Papa spent those two days away from us, writing in his journal or packing and repacking the supplies. I tried to talk to Papa, but whenever I started to speak he would stand up and move away from me. Despite his attitude toward me, I tried to be as useful as I could. I attempted to help as I had at Kew, but Papa refused to let me. I tidied up the camp, but he took everything apart and redid it. He cut his hand on a tinned lid, and I rushed for the medical kit, but he stood up and walked away from me when I tried to take his hand to bandage it. I watched him for any sign of a fit starting, but he knew I was studying him, and when he caught me at it, he grew angry. I started to feel more resentful than hurt. In a way I wanted nothing other than to find the orchid and head home. The devil take my father.

Alex was equally in his bad books. Every time Alex tried to help, Papa would refuse him. Especially when it came to building the fire. Papa kept the matches in his pocket and declined to relinquish them to Alex. I could see Alex was frustrated, but he backed away and let Papa carry on.

I'd never slept outside before, and the first night I slept very badly. The ground was stony underneath my thin pallet, and every little sound frightened me into wakefulness.

We reached the first village, Cui-Kau, late on the second day. Here we would travel on the river for eight days to the city of Yen-Ping, where we would then swap the boats for horses and mules and head out into the mountain forest. While the coolies loaded our goods onto the hired boats, Papa went off to the *yamen* to pay his respect to the local mandarin. The mandarins were the government officials who ruled the villages throughout China. We were required to announce ourselves to each one, who would then assign us fresh soldiers and send messages telling of our presence to the next mandarin.

We slept on the decks of the boats that night and arose early in the morning to find ourselves floating on the Min, accompanied by other sampans filled with bamboo rods and fishermen and junks with square sails held aloft with bamboo masts.

I thought of Mamma and my sisters constantly, and each time I grew more anxious to find the orchids. I'd stare at hillsides, hoping to see a flash of dark purple, the orchids appearing suddenly, but of course that was ridiculous. We had at least twenty more days to travel until we reached the orchid, and the time on the boat was interminable. It was not possible to make the craft travel any faster, as we were moving upstream and battling rapids and strong currents.

My thoughts began to race, and I found myself sitting with balled-up fists most of the time. I had no control over the boats, so I fidgeted, darting from one task to the next, undoing things I'd already done and finding new ways to pack them. It was all I could do to keep myself from screaming out loud.

I knew Papa was as anxious as I. He scanned the scenery constantly, looking for any signs of the orchid thief and perhaps something or someone else. Alex was the only one who appeared calm.

The Thames and the Medway in Kent were the only rivers I had ever seen. But the Medway and the Thames were tamed by locks and weirs, whereas the Min had never been conquered. It felt larger, wilder. The banks of the river shot straight up into grand hills, reminiscent of pictures I'd seen of the Swiss Alps. The only sign of civilization marked the smaller hills, which were terraced and cultivated with crops. The beauty of the land almost made me forget that a war had raged here recently, and that scars had been left. The air was clear and sweet, filled with the scent of honeysuckle, which set off a pang of homesickness in me. Honeysuckle was Mamma's favorite perfume, and her bedroom always smelled of it. Edencroft seemed so distant to me now, as though it were slumbering and would only awaken upon my return, like a village in a fairy tale.

We stopped to camp on the riverbanks each night, where we were met by new soldiers. Here, there was a very real threat of bandits and tigers. The tigers could be warned away by flinging green bamboo into the flames. The burning bamboo made a sound like a rifle shot. The bandits were another story. These were hopeless deserters from the Imperial Army with no chance of making a living. They were desperate for food and money, and the soldiers' presence was the only thing keeping them from coming closer. We saw them lurking at the edges of our camp every night, their faces wan, their eyes hungry as they surveyed our goods.

The hilly landscape gave way to rice paddies filled with green plants and flanked by mountains terraced with more paddies. Ancient temples with ornate roofs that curled up at each corner dotted the hills and mountains, and knots of small huts, most likely the homes of the rice farmers, lined the riverside.

At first, Papa didn't seem to care about the scenery. But as the days drew on, I saw him repeatedly crane his neck to stare intently onto the riverbanks or off into the forest, as though his vision alone could draw the plants closer to him. When we stopped for the night, the first thing he did was take out his sketchbook to draw the plants he had sighted, his hands moving quickly, his pencil flying over the page, as though desperate to get the vision of the flowers out of his head and down onto paper. I was learning that Papa was a gifted artist; his simple sketches were so exact one could almost smell the perfume of the plant.

The summer heat in Fukien Province was nightmarish. The sun blazed down as we floated on the river, and the humid air lay on a body, never ceasing. What was more, the mosquitos feasted on everyone's blood as though it were champagne. The insects had a way of buzzing in one's ears at nighttime, and I woke myself up more than once from slapping myself in the ear.

I was ashamed to admit that I kept a running list of all my miseries in my head: fear of tigers and the orchid thief, worry over my mother and little sisters, unbearable itching from mosquitos, perishing heat, a chronic thirst that could not be slaked no matter how much boiled water I drank, and worst of all, a dread that Papa would realize how weak I truly was.

It was because of this that I didn't tell anyone I was feeling unwell from the heat. My little straw bonnet was meant for a gentle English summer and could not cope with the fierce rays of a roaring Chinese sun. At dinner one night, Papa remarked upon my red cheeks, and I pretended not to hear him. But after dinner, as I carried our plates to the river to scour them clean, little black spots flitted over my vision. The world tilted as though I were back on the ship. I dropped the plates, heard them rattle against the shingle on the riverside, and felt the ground screaming up to meet me. The next moment I woke with my head in Alex's lap. He was leaning over me, dribbling cold water on my forehead with his neck handkerchief, his face white with fear.

"Don't tell my father," I whispered.

"Elodie, you're not a mule. You can't flog yourself along. The sun can be very draining, and you must say if you need a rest or shade or water. You could die if you don't look after yourself."

I tried to get up, but Alex held my shoulders. "I don't think you're ready to sit up yet."

He was right. That little struggle was enough to make my head spin round. I lay in his lap, letting him bathe my face with cold water from the river, embarrassed that he had seen me faint. But after a few moments that feeling wore away and I felt, for the first time in a long time, grateful that someone was caring for me.

A WEEK LATER WE REACHED YEN-PING AND LEFT BEHIND THE BOATS at last. It was a beautiful city, very old, with high stone walls, and nestled on the top of a hill at the fork of the river. It was a thriving market town, as well, so we went to purchase food and other sundries there. Unlike in Foochow, there were few Westerners about. This was truly a Chinese city. There were fewer beggars and less squalor in the streets. I supposed that the war and Western influences had not come up this far.

The sun's fire was keener than yesterday, and there were so many people about, buffeting against me, that it made the heat worse. My petticoats clung to my legs, and my corset felt three times too small. All the trees had long been chopped down for firewood, so there was little to no shade to be had.

We had tea at a ramshackle shop whose proprietor bustled about pouring boiling water from a large brass kettle, its spout ornamented with a brass butterfly. Next to the shop were stalls offering stews made from chopped pork, seaweed, onions, and eggs, and meat pies kept warm on small charcoal braziers. Another stall sold boiled sliced turnips, onions, yams, and pumpkins served in their own juices. There were pastries and grapes, peaches, watermelons, apples, and pears. There were open cook shops that prepared meals to order. Fish swam in shallow water in round wooden bowls awaiting their demise. I watched as the stall's cook scooped a fish out of the bowl, bashed it on the head with a stick, divested it of its entrails and deep-fried it, laying it before the hungry diner within minutes.

I loved fish, but the smell of the creature's entrails and the cooking oil made my stomach cramp in so much pain I nearly doubled over.

Next to all this industry was the pawnbroker's shop, where Papa said that items could be pawned for as long as thirty moons—Chinese for two and a half years—before they were sold on. I saw thin, sallow-faced men going in holding all manner of goods—china pottery, a painting, and sadly, a child's top, and coming out with their purses bulging.

"Off to buy opium," Papa said. "The poor sots." He stood looking at them quietly for a moment, his face guarded. I wondered if he looked that way because he felt genuinely sad, or guilty. Anger toward my father rose in me and I turned away. I couldn't help it. I saw him in a different light now, and this made me disgusted with myself. Mr. Howell had gotten inside my mind and painted a picture that would not leave. I saw an image of my father, Wardian cases at his side, overflowing with orchids and opium, surrounded by emaciated Chinese men and women.

"I'm going off to report to the mandarin," Papa said. "I suppose we'll have to have new soldiers. Perhaps he'll have news of Luther Duffey. He'll had to have checked in with him as well. Damnable man will most likely want something for the information."

"Hurry, Papa. We've no time to waste."

He pointed to the tea shop. "I will meet you there in an hour." He went off up the hill.

From the moment we'd set foot in the market, Alex had been tense and watchful, searching the crowds. Finally, his gaze lit on a shop hung with bundled herbs, bins full of nuts, and barrels and barrels of dried specimens whose identities I could only guess at. A young woman stood outside, scooping some of the dried objects into a basket for a waiting customer. It was odd to see a woman out in public unaccompanied by a man. Or one that did not teeter along on tiny bound feet. This girl moved with the grace of a dancer, her feet shod not in tiny little shoes but in flat canvas slippers. She looked to be around my age, small and dainty, almost doll-like.

She turned, saw Alex, and her eyes widened, the scoop stilling in her hand.

"Ching Lan!" Alex shouted, his voice joyful. He left my side and dashed across the road to meet her.

I hadn't seen Alex smile so much since the day I brought Kukla back to him. The girl seemed equally pleased to see him, bouncing in her slippers, talking to him in Chinese, waving her scoop in the air. The waiting customer scowled and said something. The girl, without even looking at the man, tugged the basket out of his hands and upturned it, dumping its contents back into the barrel. He gesticulated and shouted, but still she ignored him and continued her conversation with Alex. It was as though the man's bad manners had made him invisible to her. Finally, dashing the basket to the ground, the customer gave up and stomped away.

An old man with a pigtail wound round his head leaned out of the shop's window. He looked in the direction of the man and then at the girl. Letting out an audible sigh, he pulled his head back inside the shop.

I followed Alex across the street. It took him a few moments before he realized I was there. I stood awkwardly, waiting for him to notice me. The girl was beautiful. Her dark brown cat-like eyes tilted up at the corners, and her mouth was shaped like a cupid's bow. Her straight dark hair hung to her waist, free of any ornament or binding. She glanced at me and said something to Alex in Chinese, gesturing to me.

"Elodie, this is Ching Lan. I know her from when I lived in Foochow." He smiled at the girl, that generous kind smile. "Elodie is my wife."

She stared at me, her brow furrowed. "Your wife?"

I was astonished to hear her speak English, and with very little Chinese accent. "She speaks English!" I said, and then quickly tried to take it back. "I'm sorry . . . I mean you . . . you speak English." I was embarrassed at my gaff, as though she were a thing and not a person of her own.

"She does speak English," Ching Lan said. "It's a marvel."

"Ching Lan," Alex said, a little note of exasperation in his voice. She glanced at me sideways, scowling.

"I apologize for my bad manners," I said.

She shrugged and said something to Alex in Chinese.

"In English, Ching Lan. Say it in English so Elodie can understand," Alex said.

She refused to look at me. Instead she stooped and picked up the scoop, letting a long fall of her hair obscure her face.

"You're the first I've seen in China without bound feet," I asked. "Do your parents not believe in such a custom?"

"I'm Manchu," she said, addressing her answer to the barrels. "Foot binding is not our culture." The way she said it, final and firm, put paid to any further conversation from me.

"I didn't expect to see you here," Alex said. "Didn't you go to the Forbidden City?"

She shook her head. "The imperial selection was put off because the war was ongoing. The mandarin says we must go to Peking in the autumn when Emperor Xianfeng returns from the royal Hunting Lodge."

"Oh," Alex said, his expression regretful. "I'm sorry."

Ching Lan shrugged, a nonchalant gesture that did not match the emotion on her face. She looked as though she had resigned herself to something unspeakably awful. "It's the law. I must go."

He touched her shoulder. "I know it worries you, but perhaps you won't be chosen."

She laughed a little. "Everyone says I will. If not a concubine, then a palace servant."

"What is a concubine?" I asked.

Ching Lan scoffed. "*Ai yah*! You don't know what a concubine is?"

I looked at Alex.

"It's a mistress," he said. "The emperor and his brothers have many, hundreds even—it's a way for them to have numerous children. The concubines live in a section of the Forbidden City called the *hou-gong*. They can never leave it. Manchu girls

269

are required to present themselves between the ages of thirteen and sixteen to the Forbidden City in Peking, where they may be chosen as concubine or servant for the royal household. If chosen as concubine, they remain and are never allowed to see their families again."

I was horrified. "You're made to do this? Why don't your parents refuse?"

Ching Lan merely looked at me as though I had a tree growing out of my head.

"If they refused to send her to the Forbidden City for selection, they would be punished and heavily fined," Alex said. "Her parents are humble people, and such a fine would devastate them and cause them to lose face."

"It's considered an honor for a family's daughter to be an imperial concubine," Ching Lan said, making it sound like an insult instead of an honor. "Surely you have concubines in England?"

Embarrassed with where the conversation was going, I pretended to be interested in a barrel of dried mushrooms. Next to it was a basket of dried scorpions. The smell was overpowering. My stomach turned over.

"Do you know where Pru went when she left Foochow?" Alex asked.

"She's here," Ching Lan said, her face brightening. "She's the medical missionary. Up the hill. I bring her things from the apothecary shop, and I go out with her now on her rounds. I'm learning so much from her, Alex. I wish . . ." She bit her lip and Alex reached out and took her hand.

"I'm sorry, Ching Lan."

I looked toward the tea shop, hoping Papa had returned

early. The sun was so hot, but, oddly, I wasn't sweating. In fact, I felt cold; goose bumps rose on my skin, and I began to shiver. Suddenly possessed of a fearsome thirst, I tried to swallow, but my mouth was dry, my tongue wooden against the roof of my mouth.

Alex glanced at me. "Are you feeling unwell again, *myshka*?"

"No. Why?"

"You're swaying on your feet. And you've gone pale."

"Perhaps we should take her to see Pru," Ching Lan said.

Alex was saying something again, but the words weren't making any sense to me. I blinked. A cold sweat came over me, soaking my blouse. A high-pitched noise filled my ears, and my face grew incredibly cold, so cold I felt as though my skin was freezing. A strange haze had come to claim me. I tried to speak, but I could barely muster the strength to breathe. I tried to fight it, but it was as though I were sinking into a black void.

And that was all I knew.

<hr />

I SHIFTED IN AND OUT OF CONSCIOUSNESS, FOR HOW LONG I DID NOT know.

Each time I managed to struggle free, another wave of weariness sent me spinning into the void again, pinning me into place like a butterfly on a specimen board.

And then, slowly, so slowly, I came to myself. I was lying on something soft, a pillow under my head.

"How stupid can you be, Mr. McGregor?" I heard a woman say. "How could you let your daughter head out on a journey so ill-equipped to deal with the China heat?"

"I—" my father said.

"A wool skirt and heavy petticoats are one thing, but that tiny bonnet is quite another," she interrupted. "It's obvious to anyone with eyes how unsuitable that is. You as well, Alex. You both should have known better."

"Is it a putrid fever? Or . . . perhaps malaria?" Papa sounded panicked.

"No, I don't think so."

I opened my eyes.

"There now, she's back with us." The woman leaned over me. She smiled and her eyes tilted up just a little in the corners, a smattering of freckles decorated her cheeks. She had the delicate appearance of a newborn fawn. She wore the most peculiar outfit, an odd looking all-in-one garment, which looked like a combination pantaloons and skirt. The skirt portion fell to below the knees, and underneath this was a pair of pantaloons gathered at the ankle. On her head was a Chinese straw hat, the same as the coolies wore; an upside-down cone that tied under her chin with a bit of string. Her curly dark brown hair was wound up into an untidy bun at the base of her neck.

"How are you feeling?"

"I'm quite well," I said. "Only a dizzy spell."

"Tosh," she said. "Alex told me you'd had a turn like this yesterday."

My eyes shifted to the other side of the bed, where Papa and Alex stood. Papa held his hat, turning it round and round in his hands, looking at me anxiously. Alex had his arms crossed. I narrowed my eyes at him. *Turncoat!* He shrugged, not looking guilty in the least. "I did say you shouldn't flog yourself along, *myshka*," he said. "You should have told me you were feeling unwell again."

The woman laid her hand on my forehead. "You're not as cold as you were when Alex carried you in."

Alex carried me in? I wanted to bury my head under the pillows. How humiliating. I could picture it: Alex panting under my weight, my arms dangling awkwardly, my mouth open, perhaps drooling.

"My name's Prunella Winslow, and I'm the medical missionary here." Miss Winslow removed her hat and flung it in the direction of a table, which it sailed past and landed on the floor. She stepped back and cocked her head, considering. "Tell me, Elodie, are you pregnant?"

I nearly groaned out loud. This was the second time in the space of a few weeks that someone had asked if I carried a child. My gaze shot to Alex again. His face went pink. "We . . . we were married only a few days ago, Pru," he said.

"Marriage has nothing to do with it, my dear boy," she remarked. "You're old enough to know that." She leaned over me again, pulling the corners of my eyes down and bidding me to poke out my tongue, all of which I did, my skin crawling with mortification. I wished with all my heart that Alex and Papa would leave the room and let me die of embarrassment in peace.

Miss Winslow had an unflinching way of speaking, darting from one direct comment to the next, like a bee gathering nectar from one flower to another. Despite her odd appearance, I could almost picture her in a social setting, a ball perhaps, a string of men following behind her. But I could also picture her breezing into a hut, medical case in hand, undaunted at the sight of blood.

"Well, if you're not in the family way, then my next diagnosis is heat and sun exposure," she said. "That's all. No lasting damage."

"Can I continue on the journey?"

"No," Papa said, shifting from foot to foot. "Of course you cannot. May my daughter remain here, Miss Winslow, until I return?"

"Call me Pru. Your daughter will be right as rain by morning." Pru frowned at Papa. "We just have to outfit her in some more appropriate clothing. I see no reason why she mayn't travel with you. She's fit as a fiddle otherwise."

Ching Lan entered the room carrying a pottery mug. "I brought the tea, Pru."

"Ah, just the thing," Miss Winslow said.

I pushed up on one elbow and took the proffered cup from Ching Lan, who studied me carefully as she handed it to me. She must have thought I was the most ridiculous miss she'd ever laid eyes upon. I hid my face in the flower-scented steam that rose from the mug. Ching Lan already thought me a dolt for making that awkward remark about her speaking English. And then to go and faint in front of her like some cossetted lady overcome by vapors. And what was more, I didn't like all this attention; everyone staring at me as though I was a creature to be pitied.

"Thank you," I said, taking a sip of the tea. The floral taste was surprisingly sweet and very comforting. "What is it?"

"It's called *gòngjú*," Ching Lan said. "Chrysanthemum tea. It will help with your dizziness and your anger."

I jerked my head up. "Anger? Who is angry?"

Ching Lan pointed at me. "You, you are angry."

"Wherever did you get that idea?"

Ching Lan lifted her hands palms up. "*Wah!* From your angry face." She pulled a face, her mouth turning down and her eyes widening. "Like that."

"She's got the look of you, Elodie," Alex said. I could hear the laughter in his voice.

So now I was a figure of fun. It was on the tip of my tongue to tell them all to go to the devil when Miss Winslow waved her hands. "Everyone out. Let her rest."

Papa paused at my bedside for a moment and squeezed my hand. "Elodie, I think you should remain here. There's still a week's journey before we reach the area where the Queen's Fancy is, and no more medical missionaries on the way. Should you take ill again, I wouldn't know what to do with you. Miss Winslow will look after you."

"No, Papa. Wait for me. I'm sure I'll be well enough to go."

"We'll see."

I tried to get out of the bed to follow him, to prove that I could, but my limbs would not obey me. They felt sluggish, as though I had not used them for a very long while. I had no time for this. "Alex!"

"Rest, Elodie," he said, and then he and Ching Lan left.

"Stay put," Miss Winslow said.

"Please," I said, desperately hoping that Miss Winslow would take my side over my father. "Don't let them leave without me."

"Don't worry. I won't." She sat on the bed next to me. "Now that they are gone, may I beg a favor of you, Elodie?"

"Of course."

"I need you to ask your father something in front of Ching Lan. You see, Chinese men expect women to remain silent, and

I want her to see that doesn't need to be the case. The best way I've found to bring about change for women without rocking boats is to show them there is another way. Would you do that for me?"

Ching Lan didn't seem unhappy to remain quiet in front of men. There was the man she refused to serve, but then I realized she'd never actually spoken to him. "Is there something specific you want me to ask him?"

"Ask if Ching Lan can go with you on your journey to find your plants. Her parents would let her go, I'm sure, because she could collect medicinal herbs for the shop, but they wouldn't agree unless your father gives his permission."

My heart sank. Ching Lan's presence would only serve to make a fraught journey worse. But I didn't want to refuse Pru. She'd been so kind to help me and speak up for me. "I'll ask my father," I said reluctantly, "but I don't think Ching Lan wants anything to do with me."

"You mustn't let her manner put you off. She's facing a nightmare of change right now, and it's made her ill-mannered."

"You mean that barbarous inspection?"

"Chances are she will never see the outside of the Forbidden Palace for the rest of her life. If chosen, she'll be shut away in the harem, amongst other concubines. Doing nothing. Simply sitting and waiting for the emperor or one of his brothers to mark her name on a slate as his choice for the evening. Ching Lan is very important to me, almost a sister, you understand? She has only a handful of weeks left before she must leave for Peking. She loves the natural world. I can't imagine her away from it."

"Can't anyone do anything?" I asked.

"I intervened when she was thirteen—but that only raised the ire of the mandarins. In Foochow I made a nuisance of myself about these sorts of things concerning the rights of girls, and the mission society asked me to leave. The war had left many Chinese suspicious of Westerners, and I'm afraid I was making it worse. I had to shut my little school down. I have to tread very lightly now. My medical work is important to me, and so I must close my mouth when it comes to political matters. There are certain things that are not for me to change, and I'm learning that."

No matter how hard I tried I couldn't see Ching Lan in that life. I knew what it felt like to be discounted and shut away, to be someone who longed for adventure.

"If she could have an adventure to remember, I think her life in the palace would be bearable," Miss Winslow said.

I nodded. "I'll ask Papa if she may come."

"Good. That's settled."

She noticed me looking at her outfit. "Odd little number, isn't it? It's called a bloomer suit. It helps me get about in these Chinese saddles."

"I like it," I said. "I don't have anything suitable for riding, and it looks just the thing."

"I have them made for me in Foochow. I can let you have one. Consider it a wedding present."

"Thank you!" I said. "You're very kind." In actual fact, Miss Winslow was immensely generous. I'd known her only a few minutes and she was nearly giving me the clothes off her back. I admired her. She looked as though she lived her life exactly as she wanted to; even though she'd been pushed out of her school, she'd found another place to thrive. I wondered what sort of confidence a person had to have to be able to do such a thing.

She knelt on the floor and undid the clasps of a heavy wooden trunk. "I have some skirts and blouses I don't wear anymore. They aren't much in the way of fashion, I'm afraid, but I do believe they will hold you in good stead. You're taller than I, but I think a shorter hem would do you better in the forest and hills." She lifted several blouses out and set them on the floor. Next to them she added two cotton skirts.

"Are there other Westerners here in town, Miss Winslow?" I asked.

"Oh, please, call me Pru, do," she said. "Miss Winslow makes me sound like a governess. And in actual fact it's Mrs. Winslow, which is even worse because I haven't seen my husband in years. Still in London, I suppose."

"Do you miss your husband?"

She put her finger to her cheek pretending to consider. "No. Absolutely not," she replied. "He was a brute and a scoundrel, and I couldn't get far enough away from him. I left when Miss Nightingale called for nurses to join her in the Crimea, you see. And then I never went home. Now, to answer your question, I'm the only Westerner for miles and miles. It's been . . ." She thought, her pretty nose scrunched up. "Oh, two years since I've seen another white woman. Other missionaries come through here every so often, but zealots, mostly. Absolutely dreary company. The Americans are the worst of the lot."

"Miss Winslow . . . Pru. Do you know about Collis Brown's Chlorodyne?"

"Of course. I carry it with me everywhere. It's very good for treating pain. Why?"

"A doctor back home made us give it to our mother after she had our little sister. She was very sad afterward and couldn't rise, so he said it would soothe her nerves. But he made her take it for months and I thought it was harming her, so I poured it out. The doctor wasn't happy about it. I wondered what you thought. Did I do the right thing?"

Pru's face buckled with anger. "Clever girl! You were quite right to pour it out. Chlorodyne's main ingredient, morphine, is an opium derivative and far more addictive. It is truly a wonderful painkiller, but sometimes it kills pain, physical and emotional, *too* well. And therein lies the problem. It must be administered carefully and for short amounts of time, otherwise a person can become habituated."

I knew it. I knew that Chlorodyne would hurt Mamma. I hoped that Violetta continued to dump the medicine out and didn't fold under the steely gaze of Dr. Thumpston.

Pru went over to a cupboard and took out a bundle of cloth and a linen drawstring pouch. "Now, I wouldn't be doing you any service as a doctor whatsoever if I let you light out into the wilderness unprepared." She handed me the cloth. "For your monthlies. And don't try to wash them. Throw them on the fire. You don't want animals slinking round." She handed me the pouch. Inside was an assortment of small sponges with ribbons attached.

"Not for washing," she said. "I'm assuming you know how babies are made?"

I nodded, feeling ridiculously self-conscious once again.

"Now, don't look that way. It's best to know what lies ahead and what you can do about it. When Alex lived with me, I made sure in no uncertain terms that he knew what part he played, too.

"Those sponges stop babies getting made. I don't think you and Alex are in any position at the moment to bring a baby into the world. Later when you have a home of your own and when Alex has found work, when life is calmer for you, a baby will be a wonderful thing. I know this doesn't make me a very popular person in most people's eyes, but I have seen for myself how a birth at the wrong time can be devastating."

Pru went on to explain how to use them. But I felt like a fraud as I listened to her. There was little chance of me ever needing to use them with Alex.

She paused in her explanation. "What is it? Have I overstepped the mark?"

"No, of course not. I very much appreciate this. It's just . . . Alex and I haven't . . ."

Understanding dawned on her face. "You haven't lain together yet? Well, I'm sure it's simply a logistics thing. I'm not sure I would have liked to spend my wedding night in the Chinese wilderness, either."

I shook my head. "It's not because of that. Our marriage is in name only."

Pru listened carefully as I explained how our marriage occurred. Her friendly expression faded.

"What is it?" I asked.

She put the sponges back into the pouch and pulled the string taught. "Has Alex said anything to you of his past?"

"Only that he was an orphan."

She nodded, thinking. "Yes, well. Ching Lan and I found him in the streets. He was very unwell—near death, in fact. The little dog snarled at anyone who came near him except Ching Lan. We brought him back to the school and nursed him to health. Ching Lan wouldn't leave his side. The two are like brother and sister to one another." She hesitated. "Alex has had a very hard time of it through his childhood."

"Can you tell me what? One of the sailors on the ship said something awful about him before we left. He said he's made of terrible things, but this sailor is an unkind man, and I'm sure he means Alex harm. Was there a reason he had to stow away on the *Osprey*?"

Pru's hands paused in her task. "Stowed away? Alex stowed away? I found Alex a job at another mission, a good job, before I left Foochow, three years ago. What was he doing on a ship?"

"I don't know. He only told me he was desperate to leave China. I don't understand why that would be. He seemed so happy to see Ching Lan and then you." I'd only known Miss Winslow for a handful of moments, but if I had to live in China, I would be happy to share a home with her.

"What sort of ship is the *Osprey*?" she asked.

"A tea clipper."

She nodded absentmindedly, thinking. "That's a kind of ship always in motion, always on the sea, very few ports of call."

"The captain adopted him as his son, but because of the circumstances of our marriage, Alex had to leave the ship. His father seemed very upset about it."

From out the open window I heard Alex and Ching Lan speaking to one another in Chinese, their conversation peppered with laughter. Miss Winslow rose and went over to the window to watch them. Her shoulders were tense; the pouch hung loosely from the tips of her fingers. When she turned back to me, her eyes were filled with sorrow.

"Pru, please tell me what is wrong with Alex?"

She sighed. "I cannot. I'm sure Alex will come to tell you in his own time." She tucked the pouch in amongst my things and took my hand. Her hands were tan and rough-looking, the nails bitten to the quick, the kind of hands used to manual labor. "I can tell you this: I've never known Alex to be anything but honorable and kind. His situation in his prior life gives him the rare ability to understand and empathize with people, but it also makes him vulnerable to those who might not have his best interests at heart. Be patient with him. I'm sure all will turn out well."

Miss Winslow left me to rest, but I couldn't. I lay staring up at the beamed ceiling. *Secrets, secrets. Seems everyone has a secret,* Mr. Howell had said. I had always assumed that men went merrily about their lives, able to choose their own destinies. But when I had chosen to stow away, I had no understanding that the world could be like that storm I'd experienced on the sea—death lying just under the surface, biding its time until it built into a wave and sank the boat.

I FELT WELL ENOUGH TO RISE LATER THAT AFTERNOON. I FOLLOWED voices from the front of the house and found everyone in a little sitting room. Alex smiled and stood up when I came in, and I went over and sat next to him.

The room was lovely, with Oriental hangings on the wall and furniture fashioned from bamboo and upholstered with colorful cushions. Papa was inspecting Pru's books overflowing on a single shelf. I saw some of Violetta's favorites, *Wuthering*

Heights and *Northanger Abbey*, and the sight of them filled me with homesickness.

"Would you like some tea, Elodie?" Pru offered. "I'm afraid I don't have much to offer in the way of libation. I've had all the whiskey ages ago, and it takes ever so long to get supplies from Foochow. I feel quite guilty taking up space with bottles and silly whatnots when medicine is more important."

But before I had the chance to reply, the manservant came into the room and said the mandarin was in his sedan chair out front of Pru's house, waiting to speak to her. She exchanged a curious look with my father. "Whatever could he want? He never comes to see me." She dropped her boots to the floor and stood up. She looked visibly shaken, and I thought of how she said she had to step lightly where the women of the village were concerned. Perhaps she had trodden on someone's toes.

Papa stood. "I'll go along with you. He's probably looking for me. He wasn't at the *yamen* earlier, and I'd left before he returned to come to Elodie. I left word that I'd be at the medical missionary's."

What if what Mr. Howell said was true, and the mandarin had heard of Papa's smuggling? What if he wanted him arrested? But no. Opium was legal now, Mr. Howell had said so.

I crossed to the window to watch, followed swiftly by Ching Lan and Alex.

"Do you know this man?" I asked Ching Lan.

"Of course. He only comes to visit when he has something important to say," Ching Lan said, peering out from behind the curtain. "Otherwise people must go to him."

"Pru does not look happy," Alex said.

By the looks of his conveyance, the mandarin was an important figure. He sat inside a red silk–covered sedan chair, the arms of which were carved with ornate figures and made not of bamboo but of a very dark wood, perhaps ebony. The mandarin's head was covered with a black, dish-like hat that rose to a point and was topped with a red bead. A long black pigtail ran down his back. When he lifted his arm to gesture, the sleeves of his robe were so long that they obscured his hands completely. He addressed Papa through the window. Papa replied and then stepped back from the sedan. I saw Pru speak with him briefly and then the two returned to the house.

We turned from the window. "What did he say, Papa?" I asked.

"The mandarin came to warn us. He said there was a Westerner that came through a few days ago who made threats against him and laid hands on him. This is very bad business. Very bad indeed because not every mandarin is so forgiving. Such behavior can tar us all with the same brush."

"Why did he threaten him?" Alex asked.

"Apparently, the Westerner wanted the mandarin to delay our soldiers and keep us here for several days so the man could get a jump on the orchid. The mandarin isn't one to be threatened or bought off, and when the Westerner tried to do so, he told him to leave." Papa hesitated. "The man had a hook for a hand. Luther Duffey is this Westerner, and he's well ahead of us. He's trying to blaze a path of terror in front of us to prevent us from traveling."

"I know this man as well," Pru said. "He came to me a few days back, said he was a missionary. He wanted me to treat him for syphilis. I don't have that kind of medicine on hand; it requires arsenic or mercury, and I can't get them easily. He got very angry with me and I had to ask him to leave."

"Did he have a scar, Pru?" I asked. "Across his cheek?"

"Yes. A bad one, too. I'm not sure it healed very well."

In some ways I was happy that the scar hadn't healed, because maybe it would make him think twice about harming someone, but then I felt guilty again. What right did I have to scar another person?

"We must leave as soon as dawn breaks," Papa said. "Do you happen to know if someone is trading mules and horses? The last time I came through here it was a man called Yan Sing."

She nodded. "He is. How many do you need?"

"Two horses and three mules," Papa replied. "For tomorrow at sunrise."

"Can't we leave now?" I asked.

"We daren't. It's too dangerous," Papa said. "Tigers hunt at night, and the horses will attract them to us."

Pru called out, and the manservant reappeared. She spoke to him for a moment, and then he nodded, bowed, and left. "My man will sort the horses and mules out for you. He'll make sure you get quality mounts. Yan Sing has a string of dreadful ponies he rents to people he doesn't like, and they won't go forward for love nor money. They huddle up in a knot if you try to take them away from the lead horse. Impossible."

"Papa, we'll need more horses. I'm going with you. I'm well enough. Pru said so," I said. If Papa said no, I would hire a horse myself and go. I would not let him leave me behind.

"Out of the question. Especially with Duffey out there threatening people." He shook his head. "No."

Alex piped up. "We won't leave Elodie, sir."

Papa glared at Alex. "If you would have taken care of her in the first place, Alex, then maybe we wouldn't be having this conversation," he said. "You assured me you'd look after Elodie, and look how well you've taken care of her so far."

Ching Lan stared at the floor, her long hair obscuring her face. I couldn't tell what she was thinking, and I wondered if she hid her emotions behind that long waterfall of hair.

"In actual fact, I think Ching Lan should come with us," I said. "So we'll need four horses."

Ching Lan lifted her head. Excitement snapped in her eyes, only to be extinguished a second later. Perhaps she didn't dare to hope.

"Ching Lan?" Papa asked. "Why would she want to come along with us?"

"I don't," Ching Lan said.

Pru looked anxious. She stood up for a moment and then sat back down.

"Pru said she knows a lot about medicinal herbs, and I thought I could learn a bit from her," I said quickly, thinking on my feet. "Maybe collect some things for myself."

"Elodie, we don't have time to go chasing round the countryside after this and that," Papa said. "We have one thing to accomplish. You can see your friend when we come back through. One female on a journey is enough."

Ching Lan and I glanced at each other at the same time. I'm sure my expression mirrored hers. *One female on a journey is enough.*

I tried again. "I think—"

"I have enough to do with looking after you, Elodie. My goodness, you've fainted twice already. You have no idea how to shoot a gun, and I doubt Ching Lan does, either. You'd have to be able to defend yourself—"

"I *can* defend myself! I did it once with Luther Duffey. That's how he got the scar on his face. And I can do it again." My hands were suddenly damp. I wasn't sure at all that I could do it again, but I was desperate for Papa to believe that was true.

"What are you talking about?" Papa asked.

"Mr. Duffey tried to stop me from going to you, and I slashed his face with my billhook. It's how I got away from him."

"I'm sure you caught him by surprise," Papa said, dismissing me with a wave of his hand. "Believe me, he won't let it happen again."

"Oh, I see!" I said. "It was luck, pure and simple." It irritated me in the extreme that Papa refused to believe that I was capable of doing anything of worth and value aside from staying at home and looking after my sisters. "I don't know why you bothered educating me at all, Papa, if you truly feel that I'm incapable of doing anything."

"Don't be ridiculous, Elodie," he said. "Education has nothing to do with using a weapon."

Ching Lan watched our argument unfold, fascinated. As though she'd never seen a father and daughter quarrel before.

"Do you think a female incapable of shooting a gun?" I said. "Must a person wear trousers to do so?"

His answer was evident in his silence.

"Do you think me so feeble that I haven't the wherewithal to pull a trigger?" I asked.

"I'm sure you do," he said in a soothing tone, the kind you'd use on a four-year-old who wanted to play with the older children. "However, in answer to your question, guns are not for females. I would be concerned that you'd lose control of the weapon and it would be used against you."

"I don't agree, Mr. McGregor, if you don't mind my saying so," Pru said. "You seem hell-bent on allowing your daughter to remain ignorant." She *tsk*ed. "I don't think that's good for her at all. How else will she learn to look after herself if you don't teach her? Why, my own father had me shooting pigeons when I was six."

I held my breath, fully expected Papa to tell Pru to go to the devil, but instead he looked as though he was considering her suggestion.

"It wouldn't do any harm for her to understand how the weapon works," Alex said. "I'm happy to teach her."

"So if Ching Lan and I can shoot a gun, you'll let us go?" I asked.

Ching Lan sat up straight in her chair, that light of hope back in her eyes.

"Well . . . I . . . ." Papa looked cornered.

"That's settled, then," Pru said, smiling. She stood up and went to the bookshelf, pulling out the copy of *Northanger Abbey* and taking out a small bottle from behind it. "I do have some whiskey stashed away after all. This calls for a celebration."

࿓ ❀ ࿒ ❁

BEFORE SUNSET EVERYONE EXCEPT PRU, WHO WAS CALLED AWAY to tend a sick child, went to the outskirts of the village to an area of the forest where no one was about. Alex showed Ching Lan and me how the revolver worked, pointing out all the pieces, and how to insert the bullet. He shot the gun himself a couple of times so we could grow used to the sound of it.

I hated it.

The birds immediately stopped chattering after Alex fired the gun. The report was so loud that I wanted to run from it. I clapped my hands over my ears, but that was useless; the blast was impossible to blot out. The acrid smell of cordite burned my eyes.

Ching Lan took the gun next. She was so tiny that the first time the gun went off her head snapped back with the recoil. She blinked and stared at the gun in her hand, fascinated. She shot a few more bullets, hitting the target once or twice. As I watched her, the panic in me grew and grew. I didn't want to shoot the gun, but I'd made the bargain. Now I would be left behind, and Ching Lan would take my place. My heart started to pound as I made myself stand still, arranging my face into an expression of eagerness that I hoped matched Ching Lan's.

"Here, *myshka*. Now you try." Alex handed me the revolver and stepped back.

I took the gun. It was heavier than I had imagined it to be, the handle warm from Ching Lan's palm. I held it out, as Alex showed me. But then the image of the orchid thief appeared in my mind's eye. He cowered in front of me, his eyes widening in fear. I saw him crumpling to the ground as the bullet pierced his body and extinguished his life.

I felt as though I held death in my hand.

I handed the gun back to Alex, unfired. "Take it away from me. I don't want any part of it."

"What's this?" Papa said. "You claim you're not feeble. And now you're trembling, afraid of a gun?"

"I'm not afraid of the gun," I said. *I'm afraid that I'll use it*, I wanted to tell him. *And I'm afraid of who I'll become if I do.* "I don't like it."

Ching Lan took the gun. "She's too scared. Let her be. I'll try it again." Ching Lan shot the gun again and again until Papa stepped in and told her to stop wasting bullets.

I felt a fool. Where had my courage gone? I had stood up to Dr. Thumpston and defended myself from the orchid thief. But now, when I needed it, my bravery had abandoned me. Perhaps Papa was right. I should stay with Pru. Ching Lan and Alex could look after Papa.

"She needs something she's more comfortable with," Alex said. "Something that's less lethal. How about a rock sling?"

Papa thought. "Hmm, excellent notion, Alex. It would be nothing for her to keep a sling and some rocks in her pocket."

"A sling? You mean like how David slew Goliath?" I asked, intrigued.

"Exactly," Alex said. "I can make you one from a bit of string; it's easily done. My brother taught me how when I was ten. We used to sling rocks at wood pigeons and bring them home for our mother to turn into pies."

Alex went off and returned with a long length of string and a handful of small round rocks. He made two loops in the middle of the string and wove the ends over and under the loops, like pie lattice, until he'd created a little pouch about four inches wide. He tied a loop at one end of the string to form a little tether.

"Here's how it works," he said. "The rock goes in this pouch here and you put the tether over your finger so you don't lose the sling when you throw it. Stand back a bit, and I'll show you." Alex held the sling in his right hand and held the pouch in his left. "Swing your arm up and release the rock across your body." Alex's arm whipped around, and the sling made a primal buzzing sound as he let the rock fly. It smashed into the very tree he'd aimed for; the sound of it echoed through the forest.

"*Ai yah!*" Ching Lan shouted.

Papa applauded. "Well done, my boy. A true shot!"

"You're very good at this!" I said.

Alex grinned, reloading the sling. "I haven't done it since I was a child. Maxim and I used to get up to all sorts of mischief with our slings." He flung the weapon, and the rock once again hit the tree. I loved watching Alex. His face shone with joy, and I could almost see him as a ten-year-old boy, him and his brother playing with carefree abandon.

"Now you," Alex said. He stood behind me and directed me through the motions.

"Stand well back, Papa," I said.

"If I could stand in the next village, I would," he replied. He tried to sound stern, but his grin gave away his merriment. He crossed his arms and sat down on a tree stump a few yards back. "Come along now. Impress me."

It wasn't as easy as it looked. I fumbled the first try, and the rock dropped out of the little pouch before I had a chance to throw it. And then I smacked Alex in the shoulder with the sling as I whipped it back. Alex was a patient teacher, and he corrected me gently each time. Papa tossed in a few suggestions, and Ching Lan called out encouragement. And finally, a miracle—I threw the stone. It whizzed off into the forest, striking nothing, but it went in the right direction. I kept trying until it was too dark to see. I never hit the tree, but I grew closer each time. I felt as exhilarated as I had when I climbed to the masthead on the *Osprey*, and I wanted to keep practicing. My shoulder ached from spinning my arm, and a little blister had formed on my ring finger where the tether had rubbed, but truly I hadn't had so much fun in my life.

"It's not the easiest thing in the world to master, but if you practice, you'll be quite good at it," Alex said, rolling up the sling. He stuffed it into my skirt pocket. "Keep this and a few stones with you all the time, *myshka*."

"Thank you, Alex," I said, glancing toward Papa. "For everything."

He kissed me on the forehead. "Happy to help, *myshka*."

"I suppose we'll need four horses now," Papa said.

꙰ ✤ ꙮ ꕥ

PRU'S MAN HAD DONE HIS JOB. TWO MULES AND FOUR HORSES WERE waiting for us at sunset, as well as our soldiers—three of them, who sat atop small Chinese horses. The man renting our horses looked at Ching Lan blankly when she enquired about their names for me. So we called the mules Ink and Nod, and the horses Tinker, Beau, Blossom, and Piggy.

We stuck to the tea road for most of our ten-day journey, which meandered through mountainous bamboo forests. We rode along hillsides that sheared off into ravines, where waterfalls cascaded, feeding the streams below. The shade of the bamboo forest was welcoming because the days had grown unbearably hot and humid. We'd leave our camp each morning before the sun rose and keep our animals to a walk to preserve their energy. The landscape was alive with sounds I'd never heard before. The noise that intrigued me most of all was a loud bark, almost like a dog's, that echoed repeatedly through the canyons. Ching Lan said the noise was made by a tiny deer called a muntjac, which lived in the forest.

Pru's bloomer suit fit me perfectly. She had even given me a straw hat like hers, and my new outfit made all the difference in the world. The hat protected me against the worst of the sun, and the lightweight bloomer suit was a relief after carrying about a long wool skirt and clinging petticoats.

I found I looked forward to riding. I didn't have much chance to ride in Edencroft as we didn't own horses, and I discovered I loved the feeling of freedom the horse gave me. And I loved sweet little Blossom. She greeted me with a whicker every morning, her velvety mouth nipping the bit of turnip that I always saved her from my breakfast bowl from my palm. But still, my muscles were not used to riding. I dismounted at the end of the first few days aching in every bone, wincing whenever I sat down, until finally my muscles adjusted.

Ching Lan's reticence about speaking to Chinese men apparently did not extend to Western men, as she prattled away to Papa, ignoring his stony silence and pointing out plants that she knew. After a time, he began to take an interest in what she said, his posture relaxing. I heard him laugh, a single chuckle, barely qualifying as such, but a laugh all the same. I should have been glad to see this, but instead I felt jealous that she had a way of drawing Papa out when I could not. I was beginning to regret inviting her along. She talked to Papa and Alex in Chinese, deliberately leaving me out of the conversation. I often saw her whispering with Alex. Worse, she and Alex would venture off the trail, returning with plants. Medicinal plants that Alex helped Ching Lan sort and bundle.

I felt an outsider with my own father and husband.

As that day with the revolver had shown, Ching Lan and I were as different as chalk and cheese. Making camp and sleeping on stony ground did not bother her. When I handed her a morning cup of tea mixed with powdered milk, she refused to drink it. She dumped it on the ground and remade a cup of her own, using an elaborate ritual. She chipped leaves from a black brick of pressed tea she kept in her bag. This she poured hot water over, steeping the leaves in a small clay pot, and finally drinking the resulting brew from a tiny little cup that looked like it belonged in a child's tea set. Papa and Alex joined Ching Lan in this preparation until only I was left drinking tea with milk and sugar. I tried a sip of Alex's tea when Ching Lan wasn't looking, and I found I liked it. It was smoky and earthy. If mountains and clouds had flavors, they would taste of that tea.

Ching Lan took over my position as cook after sniffing at the contents of our tinned goods and scrunching up her nose in distaste. Each time we made camp, she'd head off to a nearby village and return with a slew of vegetables in a sack and a newly killed rooster, still dressed in its feathers and dripping blood from the hole where its head used to be. I asked her if she'd killed the rooster herself, and she stared at me in that incredulous way I'd grown to know as typically Ching Lan.

All the vegetables and meat were mixed together and flavored with exotic spices, the likes of which I'd never tasted. They were salty and sweet at the same time. And some were fiery hot, causing my mouth to burn and my eyes to water. When I tried to separate the ingredients out, Ching Lan chided me and said it was bad manners to go searching for the best bits.

Ching Lan, Papa, and Alex ate their meal with two slender sticks, which they called *kuaizi*, held between their fingers and employed like tongs. Ching Lan handed me a pair of *kuaizi*, and I fumbled with them, unable to make headway. I watched how the others used them, and it seemed simple enough, but I could not make them work. Alex showed me how to hold them between my fingers, securing the bottom one with my thumb. But morsel after morsel slipped from my sticks.

"Use a spoon," Papa said.

"I can do it," I said, stubbornly refusing to give in.

"She'll starve, Alex, if you don't help her," Ching Lan said, erupting into giggles.

Alex plucked a slice of chicken from my bowl and held it out for me. "I shall feed you, *myshka*."

Ching Lan laughed again. "In China only old men and babies are fed. Are you a baby now, Elodie?"

That was it. I'd had enough of Ching Lan making mirth. I flung the sticks down and stood up. "I hope you've had a good laugh at my expense."

"*Wah!* It's bad luck to throw *kuaizi* on the ground!"

I wanted to shake her, and I was afraid I would, so I stormed off instead.

I heard Alex say something and then get up to follow me.

"You don't have to come after me, Alex," I said. "Finish your supper. Enjoy your friend, why don't you?" I was so angry I could have spat feathers. I had enough on my plate at the moment, and now I had *her* to deal with. And after I'd been so kind as to ask her along. Well, see what kindness gave a person. . . .

"Why does she hate me so much?" I blurted out. "She won't speak to me, and when she does, she laughs at me."

"You mustn't be so sensitive. Chinese people are very direct. I know it takes a bit of getting used to."

"I don't think I'm being sensitive."

Alex looked uncomfortable, and indeed I felt bad about putting him in the middle of our quarrel. "You never speak to her, either, Elodie. The two of you are worlds away from each other. Perhaps you can find a way to stand on common ground." He took my hand in his. His fingers were warm over mine, and his touch soothed me, as it always did.

"I'll be fine," I said. "Go back to the campsite. I'll be along directly."

"Don't stay out here after the sun sets," Alex said, looking unsure. "There are tigers about."

I went to the shore to splash water on my face and then sat down cross-legged on the shore, looking out at the water.

I heard steps on the gravel behind me.

"I said I'd be along directly, Alex."

"It's not Alex."

I turned. Ching Lan stood, shifting from foot to foot, biting her lip.

"Oh, it's you. What do you want? Come to poke fun at me again?"

She hesitated, and looked around, her hands on her hips. She walked to the riverbank and knelt down next to a weedy-looking plant growing in the shingle. She tore a bit of it off and came over, sitting cross-legged next to me. "Now listen," she said. "This is an herb my father taught me about, an ancient one from the Jin dynasty called *ching-hao*. Westerners call it wormwood. It's known as an emergency prescription to keep up one's sleeve. You can always find it growing by a river like this." She handed me a sprig. A sweet aroma wafted from the yellow flowers and leaves. "A heat-clearing herb," Ching Lan went on. "Good for ridding a body of fever. Take one bunch, soak in two *sheng* of water, squeeze the plant to get the juice, and then drink it."

"Why are you telling me this?"

"You said to your father you wanted to learn about herbal medicine from me, so I'm teaching you about herbal medicine." She pulled some leaves from the branch she was holding and crushed them in her hands, releasing more of the sweet odor. She muttered something in Chinese under her breath and then tossed the plant into the water.

"And *I'm* the one with an angry face?" I said.

"*Ai yah*," she said, scowling.

"There it is. The angry face."

She smiled then, a tiny little quirk at the corner of her mouth, but it counted as a smile. "I've never met anyone like you," she said. "I don't know what to say to you. I'm afraid you'll shout at me like you shout at your father."

"I don't shout at my father. How absurd!"

She drew up her legs and rested her chin on her knees. "In China if you aren't filial, the mandarin will have you whipped and a *cangue* put around your neck so you can't feed yourself. On the *cangue* are written the characters for *not filial* so everyone knows what you've done."

"So you think I should be put in this *cangue* thing now? How happy that would make you."

"Not my place to say if you should wear a *cangue*. I'm not your father. Or the mandarin."

"My father isn't always right," I insisted, wishing she would go away, and indeed it was on the tip of my tongue to say so. "I have to stand up for myself with him or he doesn't hear what I have to say. He needs my help for reasons you don't know about."

"Doesn't this humiliate your father? Cause him to lose face?"

"I . . ." I had nothing to say to that. A cold rush of shame washed over me. In helping my father, had I diminished him in some way? But helping people was the only way I knew. It was who I was. Did Alex feel that way, too? Did I fuss over him like I fussed over Papa? "I don't know." I looked at Ching Lan, who was studying me carefully. "Maybe. Do you think so?"

She lifted her hands. "Maybe you should ask him. I know my own father wouldn't take kindly to this *standing up.*"

"If I hadn't argued with my father, neither of us would be on this journey right now," I pointed out.

Ching Lan didn't look convinced. "Perhaps not. But perhaps you could have spoken in a more respectful way."

The Chinese were very direct, Alex had said. And he was right, at least when it came to Ching Lan. At least I knew what to expect with Ching Lan. If I didn't know, all I had to do was to ask her.

"But I did the same thing to you, and I'm sorry for my behavior," Ching Lan said. "I'm a devil sometimes, and I can't stop myself." She looked so remorseful, like Violetta did when she hurt me, that I couldn't stay angry with her. "I embarrassed you in front of your husband and father, caused *you* to lose face, and I'm awful."

"You aren't awful." I looked down at the wormwood plant

and plucked one of the flowers, twirling it in my fingers. "And I didn't lose face. Don't speak of it further. It's behind us."

"I was mean to you because I'm jealous," she blurted out.

I turned to look at her, astonished. "Of me? Why?"

She lifted one shoulder and let it drop. "Because you have a life of your own. You can have adventures and marry whomever you like. I must spend my life as a concubine, a plaything for a man, unable to shape my own destiny."

"In England it's not much different," I said. "Women who make mistakes wear an invisible *cangue* that only people who judge can see. That's why Alex married me, because otherwise I would have been ruined. I stowed away to come to China, you see. Because Alex helped me, he had to leave the ship. You've nothing to be jealous of. It wasn't easy for me at all."

Tears gathered in her eyes. "Elodie, I won't be able to live in the Forbidden Palace. I'll die inside." She looked away toward the river. "Sometimes I think about killing myself. Other girls have done it to avoid the selection, but if you kill yourself, it's considered a form of protest, and your family is blamed. I wouldn't do that to them. I'd rather be unhappy for the whole of my life than hurt them."

If Ching Lan and I needed to find common ground to stand on, then this was where we'd found it. That's why I was here in the first place, after all: to help my family survive.

"I'm sorry, Ching Lan. I feel badly for reacting as I did at supper. It was childish and stupid."

"It really was," she said, wiping her tears away with the sleeve of her jacket. "What a tantrum. Throwing *kuaizi* on the ground like that."

I sighed. "Can you show me some more medicinal plants?"

We took our shoes and stockings off and walked the edge of the riverbank for the next hour. Tiny fish darted around our ankles and the water felt cool and welcome on such a hot evening. The Chinese wilderness was a veritable chemist shop. Ching Lan pointed out plants for rheumatism and consumption, sleeplessness and fatigue. She looked so happy. She paused in the river for a moment, letting the water stream around her calves, her arms crossed over her body and her eyes closed. The breeze blew her long hair over her shoulders and I thought she looked like a water nymph come to life. I wished with all my heart that she were a water nymph; she could dive into the river and swim away to live her life as she wished. Then I pictured her living in the Forbidden Palace, sitting amongst the other concubines, waiting for the emperor to choose her for his evening's entertainment, and then sending her back, discarded, until he remembered her again. It made my heart ache.

We were turning back, reluctant to return to the camp, when Ching Lan let out a cry and knelt down in the water to examine a plant growing in the mud on the river bank. She tugged and pulled at it, but it remained rooted into the ground.

I opened my billhook and handed it to her. She took the knife and touched the curve with her finger.

"Careful," I said. "It's sharp. That's a billhook for collecting plants. Or at least it was for collecting plants."

"Did you use this to cut that man's face?"

I nodded.

She examined the knife again. "You were very brave to do that." She sliced a bit of the plant off.

"Yes, well, I didn't want to."

"Sometimes we have to do things we don't want so we can

make things better." She touched the knife again and then handed it back to me. She stood and looked up into the cliffs overhead. "See there?" She pointed to a group of rectangular shaped boxes pegged onto the top of the sheer cliffs. "Those are the hanging coffins of the Guyue people. No one knows how they put them there. It's impossible, people say. But how can it be impossible if the coffins are there?"

I shaded my eyes against the evening sun and looked at the coffins. "Extraordinary."

"Do you ever wonder about how you fit into the world, Elodie?" Ching Lan asked. "If there's a place for you? A place you can choose for yourself, no matter how impossible?"

"Always," I said. "Every single day."

She picked up two rocks and handed me one, tossing the other in her hand. "Let's pretend these rocks are our troubles and we can throw them into the river. Maybe the river goddess, Mazu, will hear us and carry our sadness away."

We threw the rocks in the river as far as we could pitch them and watched as the ripples faded away.

"Do you think it worked?" I asked.

She thought for a moment. "Well, only time will tell us."

I put my hand on Ching Lan's shoulder. "Pru wanted you to come on the trip so that you might have happy memories to hold you in good stead while you are in the palace. I think you should try very hard not to dwell on the selection. There will be time enough when we return."

We waded back to where we started and stepped out of the river. We sat and stretched our feet out, letting the evening sun dry our legs.

"Thank you for forgiving me, Elodie," she said, drawing out

my name: *El-oh-dee.* "Your name sounds like the jingle of wind bells. What does it mean?"

"It's a common name for a kind of wildflower," I said. "All of my sisters are named for flowers."

"My name is also a flower. It means beautiful orchid. I think it's fated that we should meet—one flower to another. Come along, wildflower. We'll get you a spoon, and you can finish your supper."

"No, I'm going to master those sticks, Beautiful Orchid." I pulled on my boots and brushed the twigs and dirt from my skirt. "No matter what. I'm not going to let you have the last laugh."

"I have no doubt you will." She threw a smile at me. "If you don't starve first!"

Just then, one of the mules brayed and we heard someone shout. A few seconds later the clop of hooves echoed through the ravine as a horse galloped up the trail. Piggy came into view, his broken rope lead flying behind him, his eyes wide with terror. We dashed to the path, waving our arms until Piggy stopped short in front of us, his sides heaving and dripping with sweat. Ching Lan gathered up his lead.

"He didn't just escape," I said. "Something terrified him enough to break loose." Round little Piggy was the calmest horse we had, usually content to fall asleep at the picket line, his eyes half closed, one leg cocked and tail swishing gently.

"Something at the camp? A tiger?" Ching Lan said.

We ran.

TWENTY-TWO

e had nearly made it back to the campsite when we heard male voices speaking in Chinese. I heard Alex answer them, his voice sounding desperate, pleading.

Ching Lan slowed her step, listening.

My heart began to thrum. "Bandits?" I whispered.

Ching Lan nodded.

We hid behind one of the large pines bordering our pitch and saw three men standing in a tight knot around Alex, one holding his arms behind his back. Another man searched Papa's clothing as he lay, unmoving, on the ground, while another rifled through our packs near the mules. Ink, unsettled by the unfamiliar person near his hind legs, snorted and shied away.

Fear spiked through me. *Where were our soldiers?* Ching Lan and I exchanged looks of fear.

I reached in my pocket and felt my billhook and the sling next to it. I didn't think I was good enough to hit someone, but perhaps I could do enough to scare them away. I gathered up a handful of stones, filling my pockets with them.

"Here," Ching Lan whispered, holding out her cupped hands. "Give me some pebbles. I can climb the tree and throw rocks at them. Maybe they will leave us."

The tree we'd sheltered behind looked perfect for climbing, with low branches and a strong fork high enough for her to perch. She filled her pockets with stones and began to climb. A sturdy limb stretched over the campsite, and I watched Ching Lan hold on to it with one hand and reach into her pocket for the first rock with the other.

The first rock landed clear of the men, and bounced into a pile of leaf litter.

I loaded my sling and let it fly. The stone hit poor Ink in the side. Already agitated, he brayed in protest and bucked. The man turned his head just as Ink's hind legs kicked out, and I heard a loud *clonk* as one of his hooves struck the side of his face. The man dropped to the ground, a pool of blood blooming under his head. I flung another rock and hit one of the bandits square in the chest. He dropped to the ground, clutching his chest and crying out.

One of the thieves at the edge of the camp shouted to his comrades. He picked up a thick branch from our pile of firewood and stood over Papa, holding it over his head, and shouted.

"Stop firing rocks, Elodie," Ching Lan said from her place in the tree. Her eyes were wide with fright. "They say they will kill your father if you don't."

Papa. Kill Papa.

Those words echoed round and round my head, and I don't remember pulling my billhook from my pocket. I don't remember how I moved across the camp. In a haze, in a blur I saw the other men's astonished faces as I swept past them. I felt the breath leave my body as I threw myself on top of Papa's attacker. I saw the branch whirl out of his hand and heard the *womp* his head made as it hit the ground.

I screamed into the man's face, a savage, primitive shriek that came from the deepest part of me. I pressed the knife to his throat. The skin was so thin there that I could see the vein pulsing against the blade. My hands were steady and true on the handle. I was prepared to slice his neck to the bone if I had to. My hat had fallen back and dangled by its string, and the leather strap that held my hair back had broken, so my hair hung in a tangle to my shoulders. I must have looked a wild thing.

Alex shouted something at the men, and they ran. He grabbed the rifle and chased them down the path, screaming in Chinese. I removed my knife from the man's throat and stood up. He threw his hands over his head, cowering, and fled, grabbing his wounded comrade by the arms and dragging him along with him into the forest.

I felt not one moment's remorse. I knew I had it in me to defend Alex, my father, or anyone I loved. I could have taken someone's life. I could have made that decision. And I would have lived with it.

THE SOLDIERS MYSTERIOUSLY RETURNED TO CAMP AFTER THE BANdits left, their faces innocent. The leader said they had heard a noise and gone off to investigate. Alex and Ching Lan screamed at them, but they didn't seem to care. Papa vowed to tell the mandarin at the next village to report their negligence. But nothing was taken and no one was badly hurt, so the soldiers said Papa had no right to report them.

"I was nearly back to the camp when I saw the bandits hit your father," Alex said. "Well done, you, with the rock sling. There's no doubt now that you and Ching Lan can defend yourselves . . . and us."

"It seems too much of a coincidence," I said, thinking aloud, "that those bandits should strike when all three of us are away from camp as well as the soldiers."

"Do you think this is the doing of the orchid thief? That he paid these men to terrorize your father?"

"I do," I said.

We should have turned right around and taken Papa back to Pru's. He wouldn't hear of it, but he let me see to the bruise on his cheek. Afterward, he squeezed my fingers, a simple touch, but the first we'd shared in months.

The attack had left Papa anxious. He would not lie down on his cot that night. He sat by the fire, the rifle within reaching distance, feeding stick after stick of bamboo to the flames. Every time he heard a noise from the forest he stood and cocked the rifle, pointing it toward the noise. Between the bangs of the green bamboo exploding in the fire and Papa's cocking the rifle, no one slept.

We had been riding for a week when things started to get worse. The mountain villagers were wary of us. The monks at the temples either didn't want us to stay, refusing to come out when we appeared, or showed us to our sleeping area and left, moving as fast as they could, as though they were afraid. In the morning, they were nowhere to be found. It was the same situation at each temple or inn ahead of us. Even the mandarins watched us with fear and suspicion.

Our new soldiers the mandarin in the next village assigned us were ridiculous. There was no other word for them. Their uniforms looked cobbled together as though they had thrown together fancy dress for a masquerade party five minutes before they left the house. Worse, they looked at us with contempt. The other soldiers had been armed, albeit with dubious-looking ancient matchlock rifles, more show than anything else, as none of them looked as though they could fire, but these soldiers each held a furled umbrella and made a great show of pretending to fire them, and then laughing. Papa complained to the mandarin in the village, but he was not like the kind official in Yen-Ping, and the man only pretended that he didn't understand what Papa was telling him.

"He's in Duffey's employ," Papa said to us. "I'm sure of it. He's given us these soldiers to slow us down."

Ching Lan took Alex and me aside. "Your father is telling you true, Elodie. No soldier would behave in such a way unless he's had a reason to rise in the world and gain face. Something or someone has done that for him."

This group of soldiers were to stay with us for four days. They couldn't ride, or wouldn't ride, and insisted on remaining on foot, which meant that we couldn't move faster than a walk or else we'd leave the men behind. Papa grumbled that he'd be happy to do so. Each time we stopped, the men lit a fire to make their tea, and then one would either disappear into the forest, not reappearing for hours, or they would all lie down and take a nap. We made to leave them, but they seemed prepared for this and jumped up from their naps to block our path. The leader shouted, and the men behind us grabbed the bridles of our mules. Next to me, Papa's eyes widened and I could hear his breathing grow rougher.

"It will be all right, Papa," I said, my fingers clenching on Blossom's reins. "They won't hurt us." But I wasn't at all sure that was true. If only it weren't so dangerous to travel at nighttime, we might have a better chance to leave the soldiers behind while they were sleeping. I was growing ever more anxious and fretful. In my mind I saw the bailiffs turning up at the house, this time with a Pantechnicon van drawn by two strong dray horses. My little sisters standing in a row watching as the men removed all of our goods and furniture from the house, leaving not so much as a rug to sit on. And where was Mamma in this scenario? Was she still lying abed or had she thrown off her melancholy along with Dr. Thumpston's treatment? I wished I possessed some sort of magical looking glass where I could peer in and see them, talk to them, and know they were safe.

At dusk, we had been moving so slowly that we were still hours away from the next temple, so the soldiers directed us to a shabby, ramshackle place at the side of the road, insisting it was a guesthouse. Foul-smelling and ill-tempered, the innkeeper shambled forward and refused to show us to rooms unless Papa paid him first, and not in Chinese coins but in the more sought-after Mexican silver dollars. The man insisted on being paid at triple the usual rate of most wayside inns. Papa didn't even try to haggle with the man. He gave him what he wanted. The man palmed the money, flashing a gap-toothed grin, and then let us into the inn.

Several men turned from their stools and stared at us, watching as we walked through. The place was bare of any furnishings apart from a few benches against one wall and some tables in the middle of the room. Several men crouched in front of one, playing a dice game. Our soldiers joined them, mixing in with the tavern patrons as though they were long-lost friends.

The innkeeper shouted at an old woman squatting by the fire. She cringed and cowered under the man's raised fists and then shuffled toward us, arms waving at her side, in the telltale gait of bound feet. She gestured for us to sit at one of the tables and then served us a meal of rice with some sort of gravy over it, eggs boiled in tea, and pickled vegetables. We were so hungry from our long ride that the meal was welcome and delicious. I told the woman so in what Chinese I knew, and when she beamed, I saw there was not a single tooth in her head.

After dinner, she showed Ching Lan and Papa to their rooms, tiny stall-like cupboards devoid of any decoration or luxury, only a stub of candle next to a bamboo mat. Papa tried to hand her some coins but she ducked her head and handed them back to him. As Alex and I were shown to a long ladder that led to a loft upstairs, I could hear feminine laughter coming from behind the doors of the stalls we passed. This was a very strange inn, indeed.

Our room was decorated as sparsely as the ones below, but we had a window covered by a stained paper covering. The heat from the kitchen fire had risen into the room, so Alex threw open the shutter. The air was so oppressive in that mean room that we both hung out of the window for a moment gulping in the fresh air. Shouting broke out from downstairs, sounding as though more men had come to the tavern and a raucous game had commenced.

We ignored the bamboo mat and laid out our own bedding, settling down in our traveling clothes, and trying to get some rest despite the din from downstairs. I was so exhausted I fell asleep almost immediately.

I don't know how long I had been sleeping when I began dreaming I was in a bakeshop. I could smell the scent of something sweet, but the scent in my dream was sickly, cloying, and very like the aroma of burnt sugar. The air was fuggy with it, sticky and smoky at the same time. When my nose began to burn from the acrid smell, I realized I wasn't dreaming.

I opened my eyes and saw that the smoke was real; I could see it wafting through the cracks of the bamboo floorboards.

"Alex!" I shook him. "I think something is burning. Something is on fire."

Alex stirred. "What? What is it? What's happening?" He sat up, the blanket falling away from his chest. His hair was rucked up in the back and he blinked and rubbed his eyes with the palms of his hands.

"Look!" I pointed at the floorboards.

He dropped his hands and peered down at the floor, growing very still as the enormity of the situation sank in.

I felt the floorboards; they were cool, so there was no fire underneath us, but the smoke was quite real. "Do you smell it? It's an odd smell."

"It's opium smoke," he said flatly. "This is no traveler's inn. We're in a *huayan guan*."

"A what?"

"A flower smoke den. It's . . . it's a place where men go for opium and women. Those damned soldiers led us here." He flung off the covers and stood up, searching around in the darkened room. He grabbed his boots from the corner and sat on the bench, pulling them on.

"Where are you going?"

"I can't stay in here. Forgive me, Elodie, but I can't. I'll have to sleep outside."

"I know the smoke is unpleasant, but it's safer in here than out there with all those strange men about." I got up and went over to the open window. A few men had gone outside, and they were milling around a person lying on the ground. From his clothing I recognized him as one of our soldiers. The men were jeering at him, poking at him with the toes of their slippers. The prostrate man laughed, swiping at their feet with his hands, trying to grab them, as though it were some sort of parlor game. I backed away from the window. "One of our soldiers is out there, and he looks beyond useless. Come back to bed. I'm sure the smoke will clear soon."

"You don't understand," he said, his face frantic. "I *can't* stay in here."

I didn't like the way he looked, trapped and desperate, as though his life depended on getting away from the smoke. "Why wouldn't I understand? Alex, what is it? You're frightening me!"

He muttered something under his breath in Russian and then looked at me, his face pained. "I must tell you something. And I worry that . . . that you'll hate me when I tell you."

A shot of dread leapt up from my stomach, gripping me hard.

What could Alex have done that would make me hate him? Did it have to do with what Holst and Pru had said? Sometimes I forgot that I knew very little of Alex, despite the closeness that we'd developed in the past few months. It was as though he'd had no life before I met him, as though I'd imagined him into being, fully formed, with only the faults and foibles that I chose to give him, ignoring what I didn't want to see. "Tell me," I whispered, suddenly wary of him.

"Do you remember in London, when the captain scolded me for being away from the ship?"

"Yes."

"The captain never wanted me to leave the ship on my own because he thought I'd go looking for an opium den," Alex said, his voice so low that I could barely hear him, and indeed I thought I'd misheard him at first.

"Did you say an opium den? You? What a great nonsense!"

Alex leaned forward and rested his forearms on his legs. He wouldn't look at me. "I'm telling you true, *myshka*. It's one of the reasons why Holst hates me so much. He despises opium addicts and has always been suspicious of me."

"But you were a child. You were, what? Fourteen or so when you left China?"

"Opium sots come in all ages, men, women, and children." He stood up and crossed over to the window, gazing down at the men below. "For a long time the *Osprey* was the only safe place for me, because as soon as we docked I tried to run off to find opium. The captain had Holst lock me in my cabin and bar the windows. I craved smoking; it was like an itch that demanded to be scratched. I didn't want to feel that way, but once opium takes you it's difficult to turn yourself loose from it. It's painful to do so, excruciating, sometimes even deadly to try to stop." He started pacing the room, cracking his knuckles. The splintered floorboards creaked under his boots.

"But how did such a thing happen to you?"

"The ship I'd worked on after I left the Crimea sank in the Pearl River outside of Canton. I thought about going back to Russia, but I couldn't get on another ship, so I found a job in a flower smoke den in Canton, fetching things for the women who worked there and doing odd jobs of the sort. Mostly my task was to prepare the *chandu* for the men who came in to smoke."

"I'm sorry, Alex. I don't understand—"

"The *chandu*." He repeated the word, sounding frustrated. "It's . . . I don't know the word in English. It's a little portion of opium that goes into the pipe, and it's a tradition for a boy to prepare it for the patrons. The man who owned the den liked that I wasn't Chinese. He said it made his place different. Exotic."

Alex stopped talking for a moment, gathering his wits to tell me the rest of the story. He returned to the window, watching the men below, tapping his hand against the windowsill.

"You smoked opium, then? At this tavern, or whatever it's called?"

"No. Not then. I'd been working maybe a month or so at the place, and I had no idea there was another duty to fulfill. I was so stupid, so green. I had the barest of Chinese, and I was so desperate to find a place to live that I just agreed to whatever was asked of me, even though I didn't know what they were asking. One morning the owner came to me and said something. I nodded and said yes. And then . . . one of the girls who spoke a little English came and told me he'd sold me to one of the patrons. That's what the owner was telling me."

"Sold you? Do you mean for his slave?"

Alex lifted his fingers. "For the night."

"The night?" I asked. The meaning of the situation was dawning on me, and I felt a creeping horror rise. "He wanted you to . . ." My lips felt frozen. I didn't want to say the words because saying them would make it real.

"The owner expected me to be a . . . a catamite." Alex turned from the window and sank down on the floor, as though his story was too much for him to deal with standing up. He was holding his shoulders tightly, his arms rigid at his sides and his hands in fists.

"He wanted to lie with you?"

He nodded, a small little nod, as though he couldn't bear to acknowledge the truth of it. "That's what a catamite is—a boy who is used by a man. The patron had offered a lot of money, and as it turned out I owed for my upkeep that I hadn't earned, or so the owner claimed. I went to him and begged him to reconsider. I couldn't help it, but I cried. He was so angry with me for making a fuss, and he hit me. He said I had no right to refuse and that I didn't own my body, he did."

"Alex." I crossed the room and sank down next to him. I tried to touch him to comfort him, but he flinched, leaning away from me.

"I didn't want to leave because I had no other place to go. So I agreed I would go with the man. But I was afraid. I was really afraid. One of the women who worked there told me to smoke opium on the night and that I wouldn't mind it so much." Alex's voice had become dull, almost monotonous, his accent heavier, and I had to listen close to understand him. "So I smoked it. Most people become tired when they smoke opium, but I felt invincible. I felt strong, like I could do anything. When the man came in the room, I . . ."

I took his hand. This time he didn't pull away from me, but his hand lay unmoving in mine. "Don't say another word, Alex, if you don't want to. If it's too painful."

"I want to tell you the truth of it. I've never told anyone before. Ever."

"Surely the captain knows?"

He swallowed. "He only knows I was an orphan, and about the opium. But that's all he knows, I never told him about the flower smoke den."

The room was steadily filling up with the sweet smoke, making me feel light-headed. Outside, the wind picked up, sending the paper-latticework shutter swinging back and forth, clacking against the windowsill. "I was waiting for the man," he said. "I had a knife from the kitchen, and when he came in . . . I stabbed him." Alex was trembling, shaking so hard I could feel his shoulder juddering against mine. "But it wasn't him; it wasn't the man who'd bought me."

"Was it the owner of the den?"

"No!" The word burst out of Alex in a sob. He pressed his face into the crook of his elbow, his voice muffled when he spoke again. "It was one of the servants, a man I knew."

"Did . . . did you kill him?"

"Maybe. I don't know. I didn't wait around to find out. I ran away. I climbed out the window and made my way to Foochow. It took me a month to reach the city, and I started begging in the streets. I remembered how the opium made me feel. I wanted all that pain to end, so I began smoking in earnest. I could only afford the scrapings from inside used opium pipes, but it was enough to make me forget the feeling of the knife piercing the man's body, the sadness I felt from losing my family. And then one day I found Kukla, and then I met Ching Lan, who brought Prunella Winslow to me. Pru took pity on me and helped get me away from the opium. I worked as an errand boy for her school. Before she left, Pru found me a position at another place, but without her guidance I fell back into my old ways again. I'd still be smoking now if it hadn't been for Kukla. Someone stole her away when I was in an opium den one day. I found her later locked in a trunk, and I knew it would happen again if I didn't leave China and its abundance of opium. I knew I wouldn't be able to find opium on board a ship. I thought it the only safe place for Kukla and me. If I hadn't stowed away aboard the *Osprey*, I probably would be dead by now. Maybe I should be."

"Don't say that, Alex. You mustn't blame yourself for stabbing the servant. It was an accident." I could understand why Alex felt himself culpable. I'd felt the same when I'd defended myself against the orchid thief. It's hard to forgive yourself when you've hurt someone, even if it's for the best of reasons. You're never the same after.

"I should have just run away from the flower smoke den, but instead I chose to stay because I was afraid. I chose to attack the man. I . . . I think I even liked it. It didn't horrify me like it should have done. I felt no remorse, only fear that I'd be caught."

"That was the opium that made you feel that way. It wasn't you."

But Alex wasn't listening to me any longer.

I don't know if it was the smoke from the opium pipes below or the demon gnawing at his soul, but whatever it was, at that moment, Alex was lost to me, and nothing I could do or say could retrieve him. I wanted to hold him so badly, to make the hurt go away. But I knew I couldn't. No more than I could make my father's hurt go away or Ching Lan's.

"I'm not a good person, Elodie."

I could almost feel Alex's despair, and it terrified me. It reminded me of Papa's that day at the train station. Their anguish was almost tangible, an evil miasma that one could taste and feel. I could sense it stealing Alex away, as sure as the opium's blue smoke curled around him, kidnapping him.

"Forgive me," he said. And then, shaking off my hand, he left.

TWENTY-THREE

I wanted to believe that Alex wouldn't smoke the opium, and that he'd left the room to gather his thoughts, but I was naïve.

I fell asleep. Sometime in the night I turned over and reached out for him, finding nothing but an empty blanket where he should have been. I got up and looked out the window. No one was outside, and there were no sounds from below. I sat back on the pallet and waited. Fear for Alex increased as time went by until desperation had become a live thing clawing at me. I couldn't wait there any longer. I wanted to find Alex; make him see sense. I dressed quickly and descended the ladder.

It was deathly quiet in the tavern. The raucous activity of the evening had given way to a quieter kind of vice. Several men lay unmoving on bamboo mats and benches around the floor, tiny oil lamps flickering next to them.

I saw Alex lying on a bench in the corner, his legs splayed out, his arms stretched overhead. An opium pipe lay next to him, its ashy contents spilling out onto the bamboo mat below.

I imagined him climbing down the ladder after he left me, joining the men in their vice, buying a little bit of opium, and then lying back to smoke it, floating away, forgetting all about the horror of his past, paying for one more moment of nothingness.

I crossed the room and picked up the pipe. I held it gingerly, as though it were a snake about to strike.

The pipe was almost a thing of beauty, a long flutelike object, painted along its length with blue and red flowers. A silver bowl attached by a filigreed plate held the opium. I wondered how something so lovely could deliver such torment. The burnt sugar smell wafted from the pipe. The scent reminded me of Collis Browne's Chlorodyne.

Perhaps the only difference lay in the method of execution— one dispensed from a pretty cobalt blue bottle; the other delivered from a decorative pipe. Thanks to Pru's explanation, I knew the truth of it now. Opium and morphine were the same. And indeed Alex had the look of my mother when she was under the Chlorodyne's spell: he was in a place where no one could reach.

I remembered how the medicine had made me feel—happy, all my sorrows diluted, drop by drop. If I had felt a fraction of the pain that had been visited upon Alex, I might well have been driven to opium, too. But I knew from my own brief experience that what lay beyond that heaven of oblivion was a kind of hell on earth. I couldn't lose Alex to opium any more than I could Mamma to the Chlorodyne. What was more, I knew Alex didn't want that for himself.

I looked up from the pipe and saw that Alex was awake and

watching me. His skin was sallow; dark circles marked the skin under his eyes, his beard rough and patchy. He looked years older than eighteen.

I ran out of the tavern and into the forest. I flung the pipe into the ravine as far as I could. I watched it tumble in the rays of the rising sun, end over end, and landing with a splash into the stream below.

I knew what I'd done was fruitless. I couldn't pour Alex's opium away as I'd poured away Mamma's medicine. There would always be more. People would always make more. And smuggle more. People who needed money and knew how to get it easily. Perhaps like Papa did.

Had Papa supplied people here with opium? Perhaps he'd sold the men opium last night. He might still be smuggling, for all I knew. Were the clothes my sister and I wore purchased with opium? Were my sister's dollies? Was our house?

I wanted to run and keep running, through the forest and up the mountain, past every orchid there ever was, wade through the streams until I reached the very tip of the far mountain, because it was probably the only place on earth this horrible thing, this opium, had never been. But instead of running I returned to the inn, having no idea of what to do. How to help anyone.

I saw my father coming from across the yard from the direction of the animal enclosure, and anger rose inside of me. From the way he was walking I could tell he was angry, too. He kicked at the ground as he strode, muttering under his breath and whacking his hat against his leg.

"Good morning, Papa," I called out. "May I speak a word?"

"Nothing good about it," he replied. "Those soldiers have

decamped, thank goodness, but they took one of our mules with them!" He stood, looking around, his jaw working, hands clenching and unclenching. "Where is Alex?"

"I'm here, sir," Alex called from the door.

"What's the matter with you? You don't look the thing at all. You're not ailing, are you? That's the last thing we need."

Alex didn't look at me, didn't even glance in my direction. "I'm quite well, thank you. Only a bit tired. I'll be ready in a moment, and then we'll see what we can do to make up for the missing mules." He disappeared into the inn.

Papa, looking very much like a bull about to charge, made a noise under his breath. "Well then, we'll have to carry on. These things happen, and we have to make the best of it."

My anger grew. Papa would have had to walk right by Alex this morning when he'd left the inn. He had to have seen him lying there amongst the other opium users.

"You know why Alex looks like he does," I said. "You must have seen him amongst the opium users. You know he's not ill."

Papa thumped his hat against his leg for a moment. "Speak plain, Elodie. I don't have time for this. Are you claiming that your husband is an opium sot?"

"Are you smuggling opium? Is that plain enough?"

"Smuggling?" Realization dawned on his face. "So Howell got to you, then?"

"Is it true?"

"Yes." He didn't even try to deny it, or explain himself. He didn't care. I felt my heart shatter into a million pieces. Violetta had already known what I refused to believe. My father was not what I thought he was. He was a blaggard and a criminal, and everything he gave us was tainted by his terrible deeds. Even Alex.

"You must have recognized this as an opium den. You should have fashioned a noose and placed it around Alex's neck, it would have been kinder!"

"Now wait a minute. I didn't know this was an opium den until late in the night when it was too late to leave. I had no idea Alex was an opium sot. I didn't shove the pipe in Alex's mouth and light it. He did that all on his own. Not I."

"Nothing is ever your fault, is it? You make baby after baby with Mamma and leave. You sell opium to these poor people and leave. You never have to face up to what you do. I smooth things over with Mamma, take care of the children so you aren't bothered. I've protected them and Mamma against people like Dr. Thumpston and Deacon Wainwright." There was no stopping me in my accusations. It all came out in a burst. "And how could you have turned the Wardian cases into a conveyance of evil? They are meant to hold life, not death, Papa!"

"Well then, you have it all sorted out." We were standing toe-to-toe now, our grief and anger matching one for one. "How perceptive you are! And now you know why I didn't want you to come." Papa turned away, his shoulders stiff. For once I didn't care how he was feeling or if he needed soothing. For once I let him be.

"When we find the orchids and sail to England, you can return to your life at Kew," I said. "Mamma doesn't want you home, nor do I. You have blood on your hands, and only God can forgive you. Violetta once said she hoped she'd never see you again, and I told her she shouldn't say such things, but now I agree with her."

He turned back, his face a mask of pain. "You think people

are either one way or the other—evil or good. You stand in judgment, don't you? The almighty Elodie, who is perfect. Think on this, my daughter. Why would I be chasing after a flower to save my family when all I need do is write to Jardine Matheson and offer to bring in opium to the people here? It's legal now; no one can harm me, I can sell with impunity. One Wardian case full of opium bricks is all I need to discharge Mr. Pringle's debt. But I choose not to, because I refuse to take part in this horror one more minute. I can't put the lid back on this Pandora's box we English let loose, and I don't know if anyone ever can. But I won't be a part of it ever again. I won't save my family to ruin someone else's.

"Now you know why your mother despises me. I don't wish that you were a boy. That's not why I didn't want you with me. It's because I wished to protect you from all of this. Don't you see, Elodie? You and your sisters are the only thing left to me that hasn't been sullied by what I've done."

Ching Lan came out then. "I heard shouting," she said. "Is everything all right?"

"The soldiers have stolen one of the mules," he told her. He looked away from me, and if Ching Lan suspected any other reasons for our loud voices, she said nothing.

Papa returned to the inn with Ching Lan, but I couldn't go back in there. I sat on a boulder next to the path. My stomach roiled and pitched, my pulse would not settle. *Not filial.* I felt those words around my shoulders, heavy as one of those *cangues*. What if Papa was right? What if I was judging people, naming them good or bad? Pru and Alex were perfect, Mamma was a saint, Papa adventurous and dashing, Holst and Deacon

Wainwright were villains. I never thought good and bad could exist in one person because I had never let myself be anything less than perfect.

I RETURNED TO THE INN TO FIND CHING LAN EATING BREAKFAST alone. The old Chinese lady served me rice, tea, and pickled vegetables for breakfast. The inn was quiet. Either all the men had returned home or they were sleeping behind the closed doors.

"What is wrong, Elodie?" Ching Lan asked. "You're sad. Everyone is sad."

The rice stuck in my throat along with the words I wanted to say. "Papa and I argued," I finally said. "I said some terrible things to him."

Ching Lan looked sympathetic.

"I deserve the *cangue*."

"Oh," she said, nodding. She took another bite of vegetables. "Can you say sorry? Would that work?"

"I don't know." I pushed the dish away. I wanted nothing more than to lay my head on the table and sleep for a year.

When I saw Papa after breakfast, he refused to speak to me, walking away whenever I tried to approach him. Alex was equally quiet, busying himself with transferring our goods to Ink and Tinker, as he was the biggest horse we had who could carry a pack and a rider. I didn't know what to say to Alex. How could he have so easily returned to smoking opium after all he had told me? I didn't understand. We finally left at noon.

We had been riding in silence for a few hours when the

weather began to change. The sky grew heavy and dark, the temperature cooling as we rode higher into the mountains. An ominous fog rolled in, wrapping around the trees and gathering into the valleys. The tops of the hills floated on top of the fog, making them look as though they wore collars of white gossamer. As we wound around the mountain, the mist grew so dense I could only just see Ink's tail in front of me.

My memory kept casting back to last night and my discussion with Alex and that awful word *catamite*. Alex as a young boy, with no one to care for him or tend to him. The only affection came from a prostitute who gave him drugs in order to help him tolerate the intolerable. I hadn't believed Mr. Howell before, so I hadn't let myself understand the consequences of opium, but now I could not stop seeing Papa passing the opium bricks out, like sweeties from Father Christmas. I was suddenly glad of the fog, because no one would see me crying.

An hour later it began to rain, a searing, downward torrent that fell so hard it threatened to knock us out of our saddles. We scanned the hills for a temple or another wayside inn where we could shelter, but nothing was in sight. We were in a remote area in between villages. I suggested we camp, but Papa refused. We kept moving, hoping to reach some sort of civilization by nightfall.

Beau, with Alex riding him, lead the way, gamely trudging on, his head down and his ears tilting sideways to keep the rain out, followed by Ink, and then me on Blossom. Behind me, I could hear Piggy snorting in alarm, his hooves rattling on the stone path as he jigged along, and Ching Lan's exclamations in Chinese.

I swear the rain came down stronger, barreling against us so hard that the droplets stung when they hit my skin. The paths ran with water, making a difficult going that much harder. Ink's hooves slipped on the path, scrambling for purchase. A snap sounded from overhead; a tree branch broke off and slithered down the hillside and behind the mule. Startled, Ink jumped to the side, his hooves slipping out from under him, and he fell to his knees, his muzzle striking the ground.

As he struggled to stand up, one of his packs containing our precious supplies tumbled from his back and hurtled down the hill. Piggy stopped, refusing to go on, refusing to follow Blossom as he had been trained to do.

"Piggy," I twisted in my saddle. "Go!"

Ching Lan shouted at him in Chinese, but he ignored both of us. He stood there, trembling, his ears flattened against his head.

But Piggy knew something we did not.

Another snap sounded, and stones began to rain down from the slope of the hill. At first only gentle, the slew of gravel picked up speed as it went, and soon it was tumbling, sliding in a wedge of dirt and rocks. It was as though the entire hillside had broken loose from its moorings. I watched, horrified, as debris, trees, plants, rocks, dirt slid in a loud jumble of chaos. Ink brayed in fear, leaping ahead and bumping into Alex.

Alex shouted, and I kicked Blossom forward, just in time to avoid being swept over the gorge in that river of debris.

The landslide blocked the path behind Ink, separating us from Papa and Ching Lan. I didn't know if we were only divided or if the rocks had swept them over.

Alex and I leapt from our horses and ran to the rubble. The rocks had blocked the path entirely. The path sheered off into a deep ravine that dropped hundreds of feet to the river below. The only way out was forward.

"Papa! Ching Lan!" I shouted, my voice sounding high and not at all like myself. Panic grabbed me thick and hot, and I began to scramble through the debris, desperate to reach Papa and Ching Lan. Alex pulled me back.

"Careful, Elodie," he said, gripping my shoulders. "The ground may still be unstable."

"I don't care!" I said. "My father!" What if the last words I'd said to him were those awful things? If he died believing I hated him.

"You're not going to help either of them if you cause another landslide."

The rain was stopping, clouds scuttling away, leaving blue sky in their wake. A cool breeze began to sweep through the ravine.

And then, from behind the mound of rubble, we heard Ching Lan and Papa call out.

"Are you all right?" I answered. I wanted to sob with relief.

"We are," Ching Lan said. "Thanks to Piggy."

"Are you harmed, my dear?" Papa called. The concern in his voice broke my heart. I wanted to push my way through the rubble and hug him, tell him how sorry I was for the terrible things I had said to him. "You and Alex have to go now in case another landslide occurs. Ching Lan and I will return to the base of this hill and go around," Papa said. "But it will take a day or so."

"We'll wait for you at a temple," I said.

"You'll have to go on without us. Ching Lan and I will meet you at the orchid's location."

"We can't go on without you. I don't know where it is!" It was impossible. My plant hunting in England was all make-believe. I ventured into the woods only a few yards from the path. I knew my way around Edencroft perfectly. If I were lost here, I would never find my way back.

"My sketchbook is in one of Ink's packs. Go and find it."

The packs. I looked down into the ravine to see the one that had fallen from Ink's back snagged on a boulder, impossible to retrieve.

"I'll look through the others," Alex said, putting a comforting hand on my shoulder.

Thankfully, Alex found the sketchbook in one of Ink's remaining packs. I opened it to the map Papa had redrawn. "I have it."

"Do you see where we are? There's a temple just ahead. There's a bamboo forest around it."

I ran my finger up the trail to the drawing of the temple. "Yes, I see it."

"Now, the orchids are a day's ride from there. It's growing dark, so Ching Lan and I must turn back and make a shelter. Go on ahead and stay at the temple for the night."

"But—"

"Elodie! There's no other choice." Papa sounded so desperate, so much like the broken man I had seen at that little cottage in Kew, that I remembered why I had come on the expedition in the first place. I shook myself out of my fear—it was up to me to find the orchid, and I would prove to Papa and to myself that I could. "Follow the map."

"Are you sure it's correct?"

"Make sure to look for a thin rock standing on its own. It's quite unusual. You'll know you're in the right place. Alex, stay vigilant for Luther Duffey, and keep the rifle with you."

"Go, Elodie," Ching Lan said. "You can find the wildflower. I know you can."

I stood, waiting until the din of their horses' hooves faded away. Only then did Alex and I mount our horses and leave.

WE FOUND SHELTER AT THE TEMPLE ON PAPA'S MAP, THE MONKS AL-lowing us room in the shabby pavilion and a spot to hobble our animals and let them graze. Alex and I set about arranging camp, building a little fire in the forecourt of the temple and laying out the mats for the night. We took stock of what we had left. Two of the four Wardian cases had been lost when the pack fell from Ink's back, along with our medical kit and tents.

I set to making supper, searching for a pack with food supplies. Most of our food was in Tinker's pack, with Papa and Ching Lan, but I knew we had a few sacks of dried beef and peas, tea, and powdered milk in each pack for emergencies. I was aware of Alex next to me, his shoulders as stiff as mine. He looked at me sideways a few times, but I pretended not to notice.

I found my hands shaking as I sorted through the packs. I felt as though the opium had stolen Alex's life, as surely as it had stolen Mamma and Papa's. What was more, Alex still looked unwell, stopping in his task several times to rub his forehead. His eyes looked pinched and strained.

"I'm sorry for last night," Alex said, finally breaking our awkward silence. "I'm sorry for what I did, for what I said."

"You don't owe me an apology, Alex," I said, keeping my back to him.

"Why do you say that?"

Finally I saw the sack I wanted, wedged underneath a Wardian case. I struggled to lift it.

"Here, let me," Alex said, and I moved out of the way. He retrieved the sack and handed it to me.

"Because you don't owe me an explanation," I said. "Your life is yours to live, as is mine. We are friends, and that's all. What you do is not my business." My words came out harsher than I meant them to, and Alex looked hurt. I'd never felt more alone in the whole of my life.

The monks began their evening service, raising their voices together in a tuneless chant both beautiful and heartbreaking.

Alex nodded slowly. "Yes, of course." He looked as though he were going to say something else. "I'll see to the horses, then."

I went to the edge of the temple's courtyard and looked out into the wilderness. Mountains, pine, and bamboo forests stretched before me mile after mile, the Queen's Fancy nestled somewhere inside it.

My family's safety and future lay upon that tiny orchid's petals.

TWENTY-FOUR

lex and I left before daybreak the next day. We followed Papa's map along the mountain trail, which here was little more than a thin line of cobblestones worn smooth from the feet of coolies traveling over them for hundreds of years. We were forced to keep the horses to a walk for most of the way, but when it was safe to do so, we pushed them into a canter, Ink ambling gamely behind. We skirted the village, disappearing into the forest, to avoid being seen by anyone, should the orchid thief be about.

Several hours later we reached the turning. Papa had marked its presence with a drawing of a tall cracked boulder, and it was simple enough to find. The undergrowth had swallowed up the trail from there, so we had to hobble the horses and go on foot, pushing our way through. I was so desperate to see the Queen's Fancies and collect them that my entire body was humming with tension.

There was a little path, most likely made by a serow or

muntjac, that we walked along. Wild goats and deer may have had an easy way of traveling along the trail, but there was no easy way for us. The path was often overhung with heavy grass and brambles, and at times we had to drop to all fours and squeeze our way through. Alex, rifle in hand, kept a keen eye out for tigers (and orchid thieves) that might have been lurking in the brush, waiting for a chance to pounce. The brambles and sword grass were like live things, scratching and cutting into our skin, grabbing at our hair and clothing, pulling us back so that each movement was an ordeal. It seemed as though every step we took forward, we took three backward.

It soon became evident that we had taken the wrong turning. The needlelike rock Papa had drawn on the map to mark the orchids' presence never appeared. Frustrated behind measure, we pushed our way back and rode ahead another mile where we saw a second boulder that better resembled the picture. But there was no undergrowth here. The vegetation had been trampled down, and the branches that overhung the path slashed away with machetes.

"Are you sure this is correct?" Alex asked.

"It must be," I said. "There's the cracked boulder. Someone's been this way."

"It might not be the orchid thief," Alex said. "Villagers may have come down to forage for food or to hunt muntjacs." All the same, he returned to his horse and took the rifle from his saddle.

The path wound down the mountain and then up again. As Alex and I traveled farther into the wilderness, the woodsy scent of the forest became covered over by something else, something acrid and bitter.

It was the stench of burning.

The trees abruptly ended, and the beauty of the forest swiftly changed into a nightmare of destruction. Everywhere we looked the land had been scorched; nothing was left. An entire swathe of jungle had been destroyed, and quite recently. Smoke rose from blackened branches, and the ground was dotted with the scorched carcasses of animals that hadn't been swift enough to escape the fire. There was not a single Queen's Fancy to be found.

Alex searched around, kicking the brush over. "This is where your father said the orchid was?"

"There's the rock shaped like a needle," I said. "Would there be a reason for the mountain villagers to burn the forest?"

"No."

I looked around, speechless, horrified, not only by the needless destruction of such beautiful land, but by the realization that I had failed. Luther Duffey had been before me, had taken every orchid, and then torched what he couldn't carry.

The beauty and fecundity of the land that surrounded the devastation gave some sense of hope that nature might someday creep in over the edges and reclaim its former glory. But would the orchid return to the wild? Would it ever be seen here again?

We returned to the horses and found a place to make our camp in a clearing to wait for Papa and Ching Lan. The mordant smell of smoke followed us, clinging to our clothing and hair, a macabre reminder of what had been lost.

I scrubbed my face and hands over and over in a nearby stream, trying to wash away the smell of smoke and failure.

It couldn't be over. There had to be another way. Perhaps I

could write to Mr. Pringle and throw myself on his mercy. It wasn't as though we hadn't *tried* to find it.

But then I thought of Mr. Pringle that day he came to Edencroft, how he had ruthlessly knocked my plants to the ground. How he had sent bailiffs to our house to sort through our things. A man willing to compromise would not behave in such a way.

What if . . . what if Papa decided to sell opium again to save us? That horrible thought cut through me like a blade. Papa had said he wouldn't save our family only to hurt another. But faced with desperation and penury, would he turn back to transporting opium? If he had to, I knew he would never forgive himself, nor would Mamma.

And I would never forgive myself for failing.

I felt a hand on my shoulder. "I'm so sorry, *myshka*."

It took the remaining strength I had to stand tall and not crumple, to fight back the tears that waited to burst forth, to swallow the sobs that threatened. I lifted my head and saw Alex watching me, pity in his eyes.

I shrugged his hand off and pressed my palms into my eyes so hard I saw stars. I couldn't bear it. I stumbled off into the forest and sank down on a rock. For one moment I thought I smelled burnt raspberries and cream, like a fruit crumble that had been left too long in the oven. I kept picturing the Queen's Fancy orchids curling up in the heat, succumbing to the flames, the petals and leaves reduced to ashes in moments, my family's lives reduced to ashes along with them. I cried until I couldn't cry anymore, until my throat burned and my eyes ached. Everything I had done to protect my family had failed.

Alex left me alone, saying nothing, and we set the camp up

together silently, moving around each other as though we were strangers. I was numb.

Alex looked pale and drawn, pinching the bridge of his nose every so often. It took him twice as long to light the fire as it usually did, his fingers fumbling with the matches and kindling. Then he sat back on his heels, blinking, staring into the fire as though it had taken his last ounce of strength.

That night, I woke somewhere around midnight, unable to work out what had awakened me so suddenly. The blankets were damp, but it hadn't rained nor was the ground wet with dew. As usual we had placed a canvas on the ground to protect what bedding we had left from the forest floor. It was very dark, the clouds had scuttled across the moon, and the stars, usually so bright and plentiful, had been blotted out. Alex turned away from me, and I reached out to touch him for reassurance. That's when I discovered the reason for the wet bedclothes—Alex was soaked. And he was shivering, trembling so hard that I could hear his teeth clattering together.

Quickly I patted around the ground for the lantern, found it, and lit it with the matches in my skirt pocket. I twisted the little brass knob, coaxing the lamp to its highest flame, not caring if I wasted the oil. When I held the lantern up I saw that Alex lay hunched over in the pool of light, his legs drawn up and his arms wrapped around his body.

Thinking he was in the throes of a nightmare, I shook him. "Alex! Alex, wake up!" But this did not rouse him. Instead, he shrank away from my touch and shivered all the more. I felt his forehead.

Not a nightmare. A fever. And a bad one at that. His skin was hot to the touch; so hot I could barely stand to keep my hand against it. I laid my hand on his shoulder, and I could feel the heat seeping through his shirt.

Alex shuddered and jerked his shoulder away. "Don't touch me."

"I'm sorry!" I sat back on my heels. "I didn't mean to hurt you."

"Get out!" he shouted. "Get away from me. I don't want it!"

I dared to touch him again, and he sat up, his face slick with sweat, his eyes darting around in their sockets. Despite the fever, his face was white, and he glared at something in front of him, an apparition that only he could see. Whatever illness had taken him, he was deep in its grip. He shot out his fist, punching the air.

I grabbed the lantern and stood up well out of his reach. The fit had taken his last bit of strength, and he fell back onto the ground.

Water. Where had we left the pan of boiled water? I swung the lantern to orient myself. The horses snorted and stamped, upset by Alex's shouting and the sudden appearance of light. Beau jumped forward, testing the limits of his hobbles. As I spoke softly to them to calm them, I spied the covered pan sitting on the other side of the campfire, ready for morning. I fetched it, along with a bundle of cloth, and brought it back to Alex.

He lay on his back, half on, half off, our pallet. I swished the rags into the water, wrung them out, and pressed the cloths against his forehead. He grabbed my wrist, squeezing hard.

"No!" he said. "I told you." This was followed by a string of Russian.

"Alex!" I pried at his fingers. "Let go of me. I'm trying to help you!"

Alex's eyes popped open. He lifted his head a little, his eyes squinting against the lantern's light. He moaned and let his head fall back. "Oh no. It's not happening again," he muttered. "Not again, not now."

I leaned closer to him. "What is happening again?" I shook his shoulder a little when he failed to respond. "Alex! Tell me."

"I can't stop shaking," he said, his teeth clattering. "I can't. I'm so cold."

"Do you know what this illness is?" I pulled the blanket from the pallet and draped it over him. "Is this an effect of the opium?"

"No . . . it's ague," he said. "Malaria."

"Are you sure? Have you had it before?"

"Yes. But not for years. I don't know. I don't remember. I'm cold." He reached out, his fingers grasping at my clothing. I tucked the blanket tight around his sides, but still he shivered. His body shook so violently that he threw the blanket off. I tucked it under again, and yet he tossed it off once more. Desperate, I replaced the blanket and lay on top of him, hoping that some of my own warmth would transfer to him. I could feel his muscles jerking and twisting under my body.

I felt utterly helpless, unable to help him in any real way. I'd heard of malaria before, of course I had. And I knew that once a person had it, the illness could attack again whenever and however it pleased. I'd read of men struck down, reduced to shadows of themselves, wracked by fever, convulsions, and sweating. And even killed by the disease outright. Quinine was the treatment, and there was another medicine that was sworn by. I tried to remember its name. Warburg's tincture, that was it. But knowing the name was useless to me because where in the wilderness could I find a shop that sold it? Ridiculous. Nowhere. I touched Alex's forehead again. Still blazing hot.

"What can I do, Alex? I don't know what to do." What I wanted to do was cry, but I needed to get hold of myself. Crying and whimpering would do nothing to help him.

"Get off!" Alex pushed at me. "I'm hot!"

It was insane how fast he was swinging from one temperature to the next. I dipped the cloth into the pot of cool water and laid it on his forehead.

"Will Ching Lan know what to do, Alex? Alex, listen to me." I leaned close to him so he could hear me. "Will Ching Lan know?"

Alex opened his eyes. "*Myshka*?" he said. "What are you doing here? Where's Kukla?"

"Kukla's back on the *Osprey*, Alex."

"Why?"

"Robin is looking after her for you. Remember? We decided she was safer on the ship than here."

"That's all wrong." His brow knit together. "Elodie is looking after her."

Oh dear lord, please don't let him be losing his senses. A strong fever could do that, the heat baking the brain until very little memory remained. I had to get his fever to break. The cloth was growing hot under my hand, and I swished it around in the water again, returning it to his forehead.

"My head aches."

"I know. I know it must. What can I do? What did you do before when the malaria struck?"

He kicked at the blanket. "I want to get up. I have to go. I don't want to be here." I took his hand, but he yanked it away. He sat up again, blinking around him.

"Will you take some water?" I held the tin cup to his mouth, cupping his head in my hand, and mercifully he drank. "I think you should try to sleep, and then in the morning we'll see where we are. I'm sure you'll feel better. Sleep helps everything." I was babbling, saying whatever came into my mind because I didn't know what else to do.

I poured another cup of water and held it up to Alex's lips, and he drank it down willingly. But then he turned his head and vomited it all up, splashing me in the process.

He slumped back to the ground, groaning, his knees pulled up to his chest. I covered him with the blanket and stared at him stupidly. I felt like the weakest, dumbest girl, fluttering my hands and uttering such mewling words. I was good for nothing. In fact, worse than nothing. Alex was in my life at my insistence, and now he was forced to drag me along like an old millstone. If it weren't for me, he'd be back on his ship with his father and Kukla where he belonged, most likely sailing for home, racing another tea clipper and earning fame and fortune. He wouldn't be here, lying on the stony ground shivering and vomiting. He wouldn't have ended up in that opium den. He'd be well and happy. If he died . . . if he died, it would be my fault.

I wished desperately that my father were here, that Ching Lan were here. I wished that I wasn't so useless.

I crossed my arms over my chest, gripping myself hard. I had to stop being afraid and work out what to do on my own. Wishing Alex were safe on the *Osprey* wasn't going to help him. When I nursed Mamma through Dahlia's birth, I sat up with her, doing the best I could. So I would do the same for Alex. Perhaps the herb that Ching Lan had shown me could help, the one that grew along the riverbank. When the sun rose, I would look for it.

The rest of the night passed by in a haze. I bathed Alex's face and chest with cold water from the stream in an effort to bring his temperature down. My fingers grew wrinkled and numb from the water, and my arm ached from holding the wet cloth to his head. Each time he grew cold I would lie on him. Each time he grew hot, I would fan him and bathe him with fresh water from the stream. His fever reached such a pitch that he was babbling in Russian and Chinese. I constantly banked the fire so it wouldn't go out, making sure to throw green bamboo on it to ward off any tigers. I kept the rifle near me, just in case the loud shots from the burning bamboo failed to scare the animals away. I'd have to pull the trigger, no matter how afraid of the gun I was. I was worried a tiger would prey on the animals, so I checked on them often. I went from Alex to the fire to the mules and horses to the stream and back again. Over and over like some kind of never-ending nightmarish task.

Finally, weary beyond measure, I lay down next to Alex, holding the cloth against his brow. I was so tired, my eyes felt so heavy. I would just sleep a moment. Just a moment.

I don't know how much time had passed when I suddenly awoke to find Alex looming over me, his unbuttoned shirt sliding over his shoulder, his dark hair mussed up.

"Elodie, wake up," he said, shaking me. "Wake up, will you! I want to tell you something." His face, illuminated by the firelight, blazed red as though he were lit from within, and his eyes glowed with a mad desperation.

"What is it?" I struggled to sit up, but his hands on my shoulders held me firm to the ground. He said something in

Russian. "I don't know what you're saying, Alex," I said. "Say it in English."

"I love you." He let go of my shoulders and pressed his palms against my face; they were so hot they burned.

"What? What did you say?" The clouds had blown away, and now the night sky was filled with a thousand stars, so many they seemed to join together. From off in the distance I could hear a tiger cry. It all seemed quite dreamlike. For a moment I wondered if I'd gone so long without sleep that I was hallucinating all of this. But Alex felt real enough against me, the ground underneath me as unyielding as ever.

"I love you with all my heart. Do you hear me? Do you understand?"

"I . . . yes." I was stunned, dumbfounded. "But Alex, I think that's just the fever—"

And then he dipped his head and kissed me.

Before my mind could comprehend what was happening, my body responded, arching against him, pulling him closer. I kissed him back, starving for his touch, drinking him in like water. His body was familiar to me as my own bed at home, having spent so much time in repose together. But we occupied a different space now. It was as though a silken cord had been woven around our bodies, holding us together and preventing us from ever breaking apart. I was utterly lost in him.

He leaned away and brushed his thumb over my cheek. "Promise me you won't leave me. Promise me you'll always be with me. You're my family now. You are all I have."

"I promise," I said, knowing that he would remember little about this moment once his fever broke. But I didn't care.

I wanted to pretend, for just that moment, that we could be together, that it could be possible. "Alex, I love you."

But I don't believe he heard me, because seconds later the fever reclaimed him.

THE MORNING BROKE, THE JUNGLE COMING ALIVE WITH BIRDSONG and chattering monkeys. Something crawled across my face and I jolted awake, slapping at my face. And suddenly I remembered.

Alex.

He lay on his back, one hand on his chest, the other stretched over his head. I sat up and felt his forehead. It was cool to my touch, but he didn't waken. He breathed evenly, his chest rising and falling. He'd kicked the blanket off in the night, and so I pulled it back over him, tucking the edges around him.

"Alex, I'm going to get an herb to help you. I shan't be long."

He nodded, but didn't open his eyes.

I got up and went behind a tree to relieve myself and then to the stream to splash water on my face. Groggy and disoriented, my legs feeling as though I wore leaden boots, I checked on the animals and fed them their dried beans, and then went off to search for the herb.

I headed into the nearby ravine, where a stream tumbled through the bottom, and picked my way down the steep bank, following an animal track. There was the wormwood, hanging in a clump over the river. The ravine sheered off above it, and there was no simple way to reach it from the bank. There was nothing else for it but to take my boots and stockings off and slosh along through the water. By the time I reached the plants I was covered in mud and leeches. Although the leeches didn't hurt, they still caused my skin to crawl. I stood on a gravel bank and pulled them off, their slimy bodies already plump from drinking in my blood. There was a lot of wormwood, so I pulled up great armfuls, as much as I could carry, tied it in a bundle, and slung it over my back.

I climbed out of the river farther downstream, hoping to find an easier way out. I put my stockings and boots on over my wet feet and chose what looked like a clear path up the hill. I was nearly to the top of the ravine when I trod on a log, hidden in the leaves. It rolled away, sending me plummeting down the hill.

My boots scrambled for purchase in the leaf litter, my chin skidded along the ground, the tips of my fingers clawing the soft earth. Trees whipped by in a blur, and in desperation I threw my arms out and managed to grab hold of a branch, halting my plummet toward the river.

Panting with exertion, my heart pounding, I lay in the leaf litter for a moment, scratched and bleeding and gripping that branch for all I was worth. I was too terrified to let go, too terrified to stand up. Finally, I pushed myself to my knees, and there, right in front of me, on the tree I had grabbed, I saw an orchid.

TWENTY-FIVE

t was half the size of the Queen's Fancy, and perfect in every way. Like the Queen's Fancy, it was a deep purple with a bulbous sack below and three petals above. But the petals were shot through with stripes of gold so vivid they were almost irides-cent. So brilliant was the bloom that it made the Queen's Fancy look dowdy by comparison. It was scented as well, but the per-fume wasn't so much raspberries and cream as something more exotic, spicy even. It reminded me of the Oriental scent I'd smelled in the perfumer's shop in Foochow.

I glanced up, shading my hand against the sun. The tree was laden with them, so many in bloom that I couldn't count them. It looked as though it had been bedecked with joyful Christmas baubles. It was the same with the tree next to it and five more near that one. I turned in a slow circle and found a bloom on every tree in each direction. They sat cradled in the nooks and crannies of each one, the gold stripes shining in the sun, the scent heady. I inspected the orchid in front of me perched on its own roots, as though placed there, not connected to the tree in any way that I could tell. It was a simple thing to lift it off its perch like a songbird, to untangle the roots from the lichen and bark.

From the edge of my eye, a large bumblebee darted into view, her wings beating so rapidly that I could hear them buzzing. Completely unafraid of me, she hovered in front of the blossom in my hand and climbed into the petals, disappearing into the crevice between the three petals and emerging from the sack, completely covered in pollen. I could see that the bloom was perfectly matched to the insect, its body fitting quite neatly inside of it, like a key in a lock. Here before me was evidence of what Mr. Darwin had written. Here was the flower's pollinator, the one that had evolved alongside it.

Sated, the insect turned, hovering for a moment, regarding me. And I regarded it.

I made my way carefully to the top of the hill, and tied a strip of cloth around a tree limb to note where the orchids were. I had to leave the flowers to help Alex, and hope the orchid thief had left the area already. I would come back to collect the plants as soon as I could.

Flush with triumph, I headed back to the camp. Perhaps Mr. Pringle would accept this orchid in the Queen's Fancy's stead, or perhaps Sir William could help me find a buyer for these, and we could pay Mr. Pringle off. I could still smell the spicy scent of the orchid, and the fragrant bundles of wormwood on my shoulder lifted my spirits even further.

Back at camp, I dipped water into the pan and carried it to the fire, which was still smoldering. I poked it alight and settled the pot over the sputtering flames. Alex still hadn't awoken. Hadn't even shifted on the ground.

I went over and knelt beside him. "Alex?" I shook him a little, and his head lolled to one side. His face had been pale last night, but now it was beginning to take on a yellowish tinge. My mouth went dry; fear nipped at my stomach. I laid my head to his chest, and I could hear his heart beating faintly. I sat up and shook him again. He did not respond. I pressed my hands to my mouth. Why didn't he awaken?

One of the mules brayed, calling out to someone or something coming up the path. I stood. The hatchet was close by, and I picked it up and stepped closer to Alex. The mule brayed again, and I heard the clop of hooves as horses approached.

"Elodie?" I heard Papa's voice call out, and then a moment later Ching Lan and Papa came into view. I dropped the hatchet and ran to them. Papa slid off his horse, and I threw my arms around him.

"My darling girl," he said, hugging me close to him. "I am so happy to see you. I'm surprised to see you camping here. I thought you might be farther up ahead by the orchid site."

But all I could do was shake my head and say *"Alex, Alex,"* over and over.

"Elodie! What is the matter?" He looked around me and saw Alex lying prone on his pallet.

"He told me it was malaria," I said.

Ching Lan cried out and ran to Alex, moving swiftly into action as I relayed his symptoms and what I'd done for him. She felt his forehead and laid her head against his chest as I had, listening to his heart. She straightened. "He sleeps, but it's not a good sleep."

"Have you seen him like this before?" Papa asked.

"When Pru and I first found him in Foochow, he was very unwell from malaria. We treated him with quinine, and he got better in a few days."

"I found that herb in the ravine," I said. "The one you told me about, for clearing heat in the body. Will it work for malaria?"

"Yes, perfectly!"

I fetched the plants for Ching Lan, and she set to work. She took the wormwood and tore a bunch of it from the bundle, plunging it into a pan of hot water. After it had steeped for several minutes, she wrung the wilted plants out over a cup.

Papa sat Alex up, propping his near lifeless body against him.

"Alex, you have to drink this." I held the cup to his mouth, desperately hoping that he would hear me and swallow the medicine. I tipped a little of the liquid into his mouth, and I saw his throat bob as he swallowed it. A little bit more and then a little more, and finally he'd finished the entire cup. I prayed that he'd keep it down and not vomit it up like he had with the water. Minutes went by, we held our breaths, and the medicine stayed down.

"How quickly will the herb work?" Papa asked.

Ching Lan began preparing another bundle. "Three to five days is the treatment. If he doesn't get better during that time, then we'll know the fever damaged his body. If he does respond, I'm afraid he'll remain weak for a long while. When malaria takes people this strongly, it can be weeks or months before they recover."

Papa laid Alex back down, and I took his hand in mine. It felt dry and hot, the fingers lifeless. I chafed them, trying to bring some movement back to them, wishing to feel his fingers gripping mine to reassure me, as he always did. He didn't move, he didn't respond, not even a quiver. It was as though the illness had reduced him to a living corpse.

I left Alex in Ching Lan's care an hour later, and I took Papa to the Queen's Fancy site. The scene was as nightmarish as I'd remembered. It looked like a giant had passed his hand over the top of the forest, snapping off the treetops, shuffled through the undergrowth on his way out, burning what remained.

Papa walked about, searching for any signs of life. "Collecting out, that's what this is. Some hunters take everything, stripping out every orchid, leaving a path of destruction behind them. It's easier to cut down the trees than to climb them to remove the orchids. Then they set fire to the habitat so no one else can find the plants. I'm afraid this sort of behavior is normal with Cleghorn's men. They may as well have signed their name to this." Papa sank down on a tree stump and braced his elbows on his legs. He stared dully out onto the destruction, shaking his head. "And after we came all this way," he whispered.

"I did find another orchid," I offered. "I found it by chance when I was looking for the herbs for Alex. It's similar to the Queen's Fancy, so I was thinking Mr. Pringle would accept this one in its stead. I think it's more beautiful than the Queen's Fancy."

Papa lifted his head. "Another orchid? Where?"

"It's not far. I'll take you there."

We left the forest, and I led Papa along the path toward the ravine. The strip of cloth was still tied to the tree, fluttering in the breeze, marking the way. Papa followed me down the ravine to the new orchid's site.

And there they were; exactly as I had left them. When Papa leaned close to the nearest one, a ray of sun chose to shine down through the forest at that very moment, touching the stripes with light and illuminating them into burnished gold. The flower's exotic scent bust forth, lingered for a moment, and then disappeared as the light shifted.

"Extraordinary," Papa said. He removed it from the tree, holding it with reverence, inspecting the petals carefully. "It's the Queen's Fancy dressed in a ball gown, my dear, perfumed with a Parisian scent. I've never seen one like it, and I don't know anyone who has." He looked delighted, his face more animated than I had ever seen it. The tension and fear I'd held on to for months, since I stowed away on board the *Osprey*, perhaps since the day when Mr. Pringle's men first appeared in my conservatory, began to ebb away.

"Do you think it will be enough? Do you think Mr. Pringle will accept it?"

He touched the petals. "Perhaps. There's nothing more we can do. This is plant collecting. Sometimes you are too late, and sometimes you are bang on time."

"I saw a bumblebee pollinate one. It fit perfectly into this little aperture and came out the bulb below. It was as Darwin said. Each plant has its own pollinator that evolved alongside it." I was eager to tell him all about it because I knew he would share in my excitement, would approve of what I had seen and noted. "I think we should record its natural setting and take a sample of the medium it sits in, because maybe the orchid will live longer if we can duplicate its natural home."

"Hmm, I do agree." He smiled. "What are you going to name it? The plant hunter, or in this case the plant huntress, who discovers the plant has the privilege of naming it."

I thought it very kind that Papa would allow me to name it, but I would feel a fraud if I did so. The expedition was his, not mine. "I'm not a plant huntress. I found this by mistake."

"That's how most of us find our plants," he said. "I would go so far to say that you are better than a plant hunter; you're a collector. You have a reverence for plants that most hunters lack." He examined the plant again in the fading light. "Genus is *Paphiopedilum*, like the Queen's Fancy. But the species and common name are up to you."

Papa and I settled on *Paphiopedilum elodiae*. For its common name I chose "the Sister Orchid," both for its relationship to the Queen's Fancy and in honor of my own sisters.

We returned to camp to fetch the Wardian cases. The sun was high in the sky when we returned, and the orchids' scent was even stronger, the exotic scent spicier. The orchids' pollinators swarmed around the orchids, flitting from one to the other. I couldn't bear to deprive the bees of their food source, so for every two orchids I removed I left one behind. We made sure to leave the habitat intact, even smoothing over the loose bark where the former orchid had stood. To the casual observer, who hadn't seen the plants before, nothing looked amiss.

As we worked, we wrapped each plant in dampened moss, standing them up, side by side, in the Wardian cases draped over Ink, who stood still as a statue.

We removed three hundred orchids in various stages of flowering—some were in bloom, some were in spike, and some were in bud. We took a sampling of the substance they sat in so as to duplicate it as best we could in England. We noted the type of trees they lived on, the disparity of temperature between the forest and the open land, that the plant lived in shade, and that it did not mind being buffeted about by the wind.

"I'm going to remain in China with Alex," I said. Papa looked astonished, as though I was telling him I'd decided to live on the moon. "He'll need looking after . . . and . . . and I promised him I wouldn't leave him. I'll ask Pru if we may stay with her."

"Oh, my dear," Papa said. "We don't even know yet if Alex will live through this."

"Don't say that!" I said. "He will!" Of course I worried that Alex would die, but I didn't dare give voice to that. I had to believe that he would live.

"I think it's best you leave Alex to Pru. She knows him better than you, after all. He'll return to the sea when he's well, and then where will you be? Your marriage is in name only, isn't that right? Isn't that what you both told me?" Papa didn't wait for my reply, he continued on: "The captain assured me he'd have a place on the *Osprey* in December. It's your sisters and your mother who need you. It's time to go home now."

"Oh, I . . ." The confidence I had gained by finding the orchid slipped away from me. I'd forgotten that Mamma and my sisters needed me. Papa would return to his life at Kew, and I must return to mine. This world I had stepped into and grown to love was not mine for the taking. My life was back in England. Back in Edencroft. For the rest of my life I would remain a kind of widow, unable to re-marry as long as Alex remained alive. Should he decide to divorce me or annul our marriage, I'd never be able to wed anyway because no one would marry a discarded woman.

But Alex had said he loved me. Perhaps when he was well, he would come to Kent with me? But I couldn't see Alex living in Edencroft. There was nothing for him there. What would he do? Go on my little plant hunting expeditions with me? What a fabulous idea. Lock Alex in the glasshouse alongside me. My stomach twisted. Alex was made for adventure, not for a staid existence. I had to let him go.

"Of course, Papa," I said. "What was I thinking?"

He brushed my cheek with his fingers. "There's my good girl. My steady Elodie." He looked at my hand. "Easy there, watch what you're doing."

Startled, I opened my hand; my palm was stained green. I had squeezed the orchid in my hand so tightly that I had crushed it.

❋ ❋ ❋ ❋

ON THE FOURTH DAY OF HIS ILLNESS, ALEX AWOKE. I WAS SITTING with his head in my lap, my hand resting on his shoulder and my eyes closed when I felt his hand on mine. Startled, I looked down to see his eyes open. Apart from the dark circles smudging the skin under them, his eyes were clear and alert.

I wanted to kiss him. I wanted to tell him that I loved him and I would never leave him, but I couldn't. It hurt too much to say those words. So instead, like a coward, I hardened my heart toward him.

I called to Ching Lan and left him in her care.

Within a few more days, Alex was able to sit up on his own, eat a little rice, and hold down a few cups of weak tea. It was time to take him back to Pru's, where he could recover fully.

Alex was not strong enough to manage a horse by himself, even for short distances, so Papa hired chair bearers from the nearest village. I nearly cried watching the coolies help Alex into the sedan chair. He looked so gaunt and weak, and I was terrified he wouldn't survive the long journey back.

I worried about Ching Lan, too. The closer we drew to Yen-Ping, the more subdued she became. She only had a handful of days before she was to depart with her parents for Peking. She stopped talking, stopped collecting plants, stopped noticing anything. She replied to my questions with short answers. Her time of freedom was growing short.

We were one day out from Pru's when I woke to the sound of someone crying. In the moonlight I saw Ching Lan kneeling on the ground, her long hair falling all around her, keening. It was the sound of utter heartbreak. The kind of weeping that is uncontrollable, where one can only wait until the grief completely passes. She was trying in vain to make it stop, the back of her hands dashing over and over at her eyes.

I went to her and put my arms around her, just as I would any of my sisters. She resisted at first, her body stiffening, but then she laid her head on my shoulder and let herself cry.

"I can't go to the Forbidden City," she said. "I won't go."

I didn't know what to do to help her. "Come with me to England," I said, grasping at straws. "You can live with me and my sisters. You'll be welcome there. And safe."

She shook her head. "Chinese women cannot travel. It's illegal."

I couldn't think of anything to say to her to comfort her. She had every right to her tears, and nothing I could do would help her.

"Lend me your knife," she said.

I pulled it out of my pocket and handed it to her. "Searching for plants at night?"

She flipped open the knife and touched the blade again and again with the tip of her finger, almost as though she were testing herself. She kept on until the blade sliced through and a bead of blood appeared.

"I told you to be careful with that, Ching Lan. It's sharp."

I put out my hand to get the knife back, and she held it out of my reach, her expression defiant.

A cold dread washed over me. I was stupid to give her the knife. "What are you doing, Ching Lan? If you think I'm going to let you kill yourself, you're wrong!"

"I'm not going to kill myself," she said. "I'm going to cut my face, like you did the orchid thief's. I'll say it was a tiger that bit me."

"Give me the knife back. You're mad!"

"Girls who are ill or deformed aren't accepted. Don't you see? This is what I need to do to make things better. I should have done it when I was thirteen, and then maybe Pru wouldn't have been sent away. Maybe Alex wouldn't have turned to opium again if we were there to be his family. I should have done it then, but I was too scared."

"None of that is your fault." But I understood how Ching Lan felt because I held myself to the same standards. Perhaps we were both wrong. Perhaps fault wasn't as simple as blaming ourselves.

"Elodie, this is my decision, not yours! If I become a concubine, I'll a die a new death every day."

"There has to be something else we can do. I'll ask Papa—"

"You can't fix everything! What else do you think you control? The ocean tides? The moon's beams? You Westerners think you can change China, that it needs fixing. We are not yours to fix or to change."

"What about Pru? She's a Westerner, and it seems to me that she taught you another life."

"Pru understands Chinese people. She knows she's the same as us, not above us."

"I don't think I'm above you."

"I know you don't, but you will go home. Pru is not like the missionaries who live on a hill. She lives simply, alongside us. She never thinks she knows best. If you want to really help me, you can leave me be."

I couldn't leave her alone in the wilderness to maim herself. And I couldn't stay to watch her do it, either. She was my friend—no, more than a friend, my sister. My throat constricted, and my fear for Ching Lan nearly knocked the breath from my chest. "Here, give me the knife." I held out my hand. She hesitated a moment and handed me the billhook.

I swallowed and lifted the knife to her cheekbone; she tilted her face up and closed her eyes. I set the hook on the edge of her cheek; the tip bit into her skin until blood began to flow around the wound. My heart roared in my ears, and I thought I might be sick. And then I saw tears trickle out from under her eyelids. "I can't," I said. "I can't do this."

And then, quick as a flash, Ching Lan wrapped her fingers around mine and tugged, slashing the knife through her skin. I didn't have a second to react. Blood spilled from her face, and a jagged open wound stretched in a horrific gash from her cheekbone through the edge of her lip.

I dropped the knife. In a panic I reached into my pocket for a clean handkerchief and pressed it to the wound.

She gritted her teeth in pain and grabbed my wrist. "Leave it."

"Ching Lan, please! You could die if it gets infected. Let me take you back to camp."

She pushed me so hard that I fell backward into the leaves. "*Wah!* You aren't listening to me. You don't listen to anyone. I *want* to have a scar; I *want* to be ugly so that that emperor doesn't desire me, that no man desires me. It's the only way I can be free."

"I'm sorry," I said.

"Don't be sorry, Elodie," she said. Her face looked ghoulish in the moonlight, but there was a peace about her now. The fear and apprehension had left her. "Just be happy for me."

Ching Lan left on Piggy the next morning. She didn't want to answer Papa's or Alex's questions. She would go straight to Pru, then to her parents and the mandarin and tell them what had happened. The mandarin would have to speak for her, to remove her from the selection list.

As we rode those last few miles to Yen-Ping, I memorized every detail of the wilderness, impressed upon my memory the sights, scents, and sounds so that I might remember them when I returned to Kent. I'd been right: Edencroft was my life, and once again, it always would be.

While Pru's manservant helped Alex inside the house, Papa and I took the animals back to their owner and paid him for the lost mule. I stroked Blossom's neck and made my good-byes. I would miss the little mare.

On our way back, Papa chatted. "I'll head down to the river to see about a sampan for tomorrow," he said. "We should leave as soon as possible to arrange for a steamship home. Many of those orchids in spike will be coming into bud in a month and then into bloom a month or so after that. If we look after them carefully on the journey, the flowers will be in prime condition when we arrive in London, and so they will fetch the best price."

As Papa strolled alongside me he failed to look my way once. Couldn't he see that I was upset about leaving Alex? Did he think me so uncaring that it wouldn't distress me? But perhaps Papa knew something I did not. Perhaps Alex didn't want me to stay with him anyway. Perhaps his pledge of love was nothing but the result of a fevered haze.

When we returned to Pru's house, I went to see Alex. The door was open, and I paused, unsure of whether to go in or not. Pru sat on the bedside, examining Alex, listening to his heart with a metal tube-shaped instrument. Alex, his shirt open, lay on his back, staring up at the ceiling. Ching Lan sat next to him. Her wound had been closed in a neat line of stitches.

Pru sat up and began buttoning Alex's shirt. She saw me standing in the doorway. "Come in, Elodie."

"I've come to see how Alex is faring. I'm happy to see Ching Lan, as well."

Pru replaced the instrument in her medical bag and snapped it closed. "I think he's on the mend. A few weeks' rest will see him back on his feet. You and Ching Lan looked after him very well." She set her hand on Alex's shoulder. She hesitated for a moment at the doorway, as though she wanted to say something, but then she squeezed my hand and pulled the door shut behind her.

I sat next to him. "I'm leaving tomorrow with Papa to take

the orchids back to England. I expect you'll rejoin the *Osprey* in December? I'll bring Kukla to you." I babbled on, talking about how happy she'd be to see him and how if he had time I'd love for him to come to Kent to see my sisters and Mamma. "I know they'd want to meet you."

Ching Lan opened her mouth to say something, but Alex interrupted her. "Can I speak to Elodie alone?"

She nodded and left.

Alex struggled to sit up, and when I stepped up to help him, he lifted a hand. "Don't help," he said. "I can do it."

I bit my lip, watching him fumble to pull himself upright. Sweat sheened his brow, and his arms trembled under his own weight. Exhausted by the effort, he sank back against the pillows. His cheeks were hollow, and his skin looked paper-thin.

"Can I fetch you anything? Water or tea—"

He shook his head.

There was a window at the side of the bed, and this looked over a bare patch of ground where a few plants struggled to grow. Alex turned away from me and looked out at the window. "I didn't smoke the opium," he said.

"What?"

"I didn't smoke it. You thought I did, though. You didn't give me a chance to explain. At all. How do you think that made me feel?"

"But I saw—"

"I know what you think you saw."

"But I thought . . . the pipe?"

"The pipe you saw was from another man who left it behind. I was worried someone would try to go into your room, so I sat by the ladder, keeping watch. I was too much of a coward to return to you after what I said. So I know that's why you're leaving me, why you left my care to Ching Lan when I awoke. Why you don't want to be near me anymore. Because of who I am, and what I've done. I understand. You could be honest with me."

He looked at me then, but his eyes were so blank and expressionless that it scared me. Where was the friendliness and kindness that always shone forth from them? It was as though the fever had extinguished it.

"That's not why, Alex. If that were true, then I wouldn't have made that promise to you."

"What promise?" he asked. From the look on his face I knew he remembered what had come between us the night he fell ill. But he glared at me, as though daring me to say it out loud.

"You know what I'm speaking of, Alex. You woke me and said you loved me."

"I remember nothing. It was *fignya*, gibberish, I'm sure."

"It wasn't. Not to me it wasn't."

He returned his gaze to the window. "Well, I'm sorry for you, then."

Those words, coming from Alex, struck me so hard I was nearly breathless. I wanted to double over with the pain of it.

"Alex, please . . ."

"Go away, Elodie," he said, his voice hitching. "Just go away."

I knew then that I was making the right choice. Alex didn't want me. He was better off here with Ching Lan and Pru, as Papa had said.

I was glad, I told myself. I was relieved.

Perhaps someday I might believe it.

I left the room silently and headed outside to find

Papa. I had just reached the door when I felt a hand on my shoulder.

Ching Lan spun me around. She reached out as though to slap me, and I caught her hand. "What are you doing?"

Her cheeks were red with fury, and tears pooled in her eyes. "For the first time in three years I am not afraid anymore. I know now that I can find a way to live my life the way I want to, no matter how hard or how painful. And here you are, going back to England and leaving Alex behind. How can you do that? He loves you!"

"You don't know everything!" I said. "Our marriage is a farce, Ching Lan."

"It's not a farce! When we were searching for plants together, he wouldn't stop talking about you. He dared to love you, and now you're leaving him."

"He doesn't love me!" I said. "He said as much just now."

Ching Lan lunged at me, her hands outstretched as though she wanted to scratch my eyes out.

I caught her hands and pushed her away. "My family needs me. My father needs me at home to look after my sisters. Can you tell me you don't understand that? You are the one who told me about being filial, and that's what I'm doing."

"Not before your husband. Husband comes first." Ching Lan pulled away from me and crossed her arms.

Papa came around the house just then, carrying a pack in each hand. "Elodie," Papa said. "Can you help me go through these? We need to make sure everything is dry before we leave or it will be rotted through by the time we reach England."

Ching Lan turned and stared at Papa, defiant. Papa sucked

in his breath when he saw her face. "Your face, my dear. What happened?"

"I did it myself, and I'm not ashamed for anyone to see."

"Because of the emperor's selection?"

She nodded once.

"Well then." He dropped the packs and slid the sleeves of his jacket up. He held his wrists out to show her. "If you are not ashamed, then I suppose I should not be, either." They were exactly as I remembered them, the skin dented and thick with scars.

Ching Lan gasped. "*Kao-niu?*" she said.

"Yes. So I know a little bit about scars the emperor inflicts," Papa said. "Some are more noble than others, and we have to bear it the best we can."

She took Papa's wrists in her hands, holding them gently, meeting his eyes for a moment before she released them. Papa nodded to her, picked up the bags, and left.

"I'm sorry, Elodie," Ching Lan said. "If you have to go, I suppose you should go."

"Promise me you'll look after Alex," I said.

Ching Lan began to cry, and her tears set me crying, too. "In China we have a custom," she said. "If we love someone, we try to make them part of our family. Would you be my sister?"

I looked at her sweet face and said yes, but only if she would be mine. I found I had come to love Ching Lan like a sister, and I wished with all my heart that I could take her home with me and keep her safe there. But her life was not mine to govern, and she had a life of her own in China. I wished we could meet again someday.

WHEN DAWN CAME, PAPA AND I SAID GOOD-BYE TO CHING LAN AND
Pru. They stood in the doorway and watched us go, waving us
good-bye.

Although it had taken many days to travel up the Min, it
took only two to travel back, as the currents swept the boat
down the river.

I sat, cross-legged, watching the scenery go by. As the miles
built up behind me, I mourned the loss of my friends and of
Alex and the months of freedom gone by, possibly never to be
repeated again. Somehow I had to return home and carve out
a new life, but I was leaving my heart with Alex and my soul in
the mountains and rivers of the Chinese landscape. "I wanted
to ask you, Papa," I said. "That word Ching Lan used when she
saw your scars. *Kao-niu*. What does that mean?"

"It's the name of the punishment, this cuffing of the wrists
with soaked ties. Most people don't live through it. One of the
jailers knew me and released me of my bonds in time."

"I think it's cruel that Mr. Pringle forced you to come back
to get the orchids. Especially since he knows what happened to
you."

"He was perfectly in his right to do so. It was my fault that
I lost his plants. I wasn't meant to be where I was. I had the
Queen's Fancy orchids crated up in their Wardian cases and
ready to go, but the ship had been delayed, and so I decided to
travel north, to look for plants for Kew. I saw Bowlby before he
set out on his mission, so I went along with him. I have always
had a taste for adventure and an eagerness to search for new
things. Sometimes this feeling is so great that it quite undoes

me, and I act without thinking." Papa's voice trailed off, and he looked out at the river for a long time.

Before I fell in love with the Queen's Fancy, I wouldn't have understood Papa's yearning, but now I did. I wanted to know what lay farther beyond the mountains; I wanted to find more orchids. Despite all of the danger and heartbreak I'd experienced, China called to me still.

TWENTY-SIX

That first night, in the inn at Foochow, the bed felt too soft, the pillow under my neck an odd sensation. It was too quiet. I missed the sounds of the forest and the dew on my face in the early morning. I felt restless; the blankets lay heavy on my legs, trapping me in place. The nightgown felt too tight around my neck, the lace scratching, the skirt twisting around my legs. I was plagued by worry about the Sister Orchid. What if it wasn't enough for Mr. Pringle? What if we were leaving too soon? Perhaps I should have explored the forest more, seeking other plants that might do for him.

Papa arranged our transport on a steamship that was returning to England at the end of the week. He telegrammed Mr. Pringle, Kew, and my mother. The telegrams would be sent on the mail ship from Alexandria and arrive before we did. I felt myself sinking deeper and deeper into despair as we grew closer to departing. I thought about what I would do when I returned. I would go back to my usual tasks, looking after the children and Mamma. Working in my glasshouse.

At breakfast the following morning, Papa sat writing in his notebook. "I'm very interested in researching the medium we collected to see if I can duplicate it at Kew. I plan to create a miniature Chinese environment for the plants. Also, can you remind me about the pollinator? What the bee looked like? I'm going to write to Mr. Darwin and tell him about it. He's very interested in orchids and their pollinators."

"You're returning to Kew, then?" I pushed my porridge about in the bowl.

"Yes. I wish to do some research on the new orchid," he went on. "I trust you'll be my eyes and ears at home again." It wasn't a question, rather a statement. *You'll be my eyes and ears.*

I started to say yes, but every fiber in my being began to resist. I saw my life in front of me again. Steady Elodie, whom everyone depended on.

I didn't want to be that girl anymore. I'd made up my mind not to when I tossed my braid in the ocean. I couldn't remain in Edencroft, my life unlived. I could not live a life bereft of adventure. I longed to see more of the world. I longed to break out of the glasshouse for good. I couldn't stop my parents from arguing: they would fight whether I was there or not. I couldn't continue to prop them up. Ching Lan was right when she said I couldn't fix everything.

Like a dress I had outgrown, perhaps my old life no longer fit me.

I loved my family, but I wanted to take my place in the world. My father had named me after a wildflower, and I knew now that wildflowers could not thrive inside of greenhouses.

Papa's mention of Mr. Darwin reminded me of the final line in his book: *from so simple a beginning, endless forms most beautiful and most wonderful have been, and are being evolved.*

I had to continue evolving too.

When we first set foot in Foochow, the relief in Papa was almost tangible. I doubted he would ever travel again. His life was no longer as an adventurer. But I set foot in Foochow feeling nothing but dread.

His passion for plant hunting had abandoned him and found a new home in me.

I pushed my bowl away. "No, Papa. I don't want you to depend upon me anymore. Mamma and the girls . . . that is your life, your responsibilities. It's not fair to ask it of me. You must go home and stay home."

"Elodie, my work is at Kew," he said firmly, not raising his head from his book. "I couldn't possibly—"

"My conservatory is perfect for your work. We already know Chinese orchids thrive in it. You can do your work very well at home and look after Mamma and the children."

Finally he looked at me. "The children? What about you?"

"I don't belong there anymore, Papa," I said.

"Where do you belong?" he asked carefully.

"Here, in China. I want to search for more orchids just in case the Sister Orchid isn't enough. I want to explore the area where I found it. I want to see what else is out there for me. And I want to be with Alex." I wanted to be with Alex because I loved him, not because I felt obligated. Ching Lan wasn't right when she said that a husband came before family. It was the responsibility to myself that came first. That was the most important thing. Otherwise how could I help anyone if I were an unhappy shell of a being?

"My dear." He closed his book. "I don't know what to say to you about Alex. You must try to move forward with your life. Elodie, his life is as a sailor. "

"Maybe it is, and maybe it isn't. I won't know unless I ask him. But that isn't the entire reason why I wish to stay. I want to be a plant hunter. I don't want that world forbidden to me anymore. I want . . ." I hesitated, searching for the words that would make him understand. "I want what you wanted," I finally said.

"I do believe you've been afflicted with the illness most plant hunters have. After seeking adventure they have a difficult time fitting into civilization. The excitement of newness takes you. You find that you crave it. But you can't think to go collecting by yourself, Elodie. The Chinese wilderness is not a place for a girl . . ." Papa's voice trailed off. He set his pencil down and sat back. "Well now. I apologize. That statement is most certainly not true. You've proven to me that you can look after yourself, and everyone else around you. And you do it with kindness and love." He sighed. "So you're set on staying?"

"I am."

He picked up his pencil and turned to a blank page, and slid them across the table. "Then you'd better write and explain it to your Mamma. I most certainly don't want to be the one to do it."

PAPA HELPED ME ORGANIZE MY TRIP BACK UP THE MIN, BACK TO Pru's. After making enquiries of the vicar who'd married us,

Papa found a group of missionaries that I could travel with, as he still wasn't happy with letting me travel alone. But if he had any more reservations, he kept them to himself. He gathered the supplies I needed, purchasing each one carefully and thoughtfully, testing me on my fire-making skills and making me repeat phrases in Chinese that would be useful. I knew that in his way, this was how he was showing me that he loved me, and that he approved.

He left on the steamship two days before me. I traveled down to the quay with him where he was to take a launch out to the Pagoda Anchorage. We stood on the dock together.

"Take care of Mamma and the girls, and please try not to quarrel. Promise me."

He smiled. "I'll do my best. Make sure to write. You can send letters through the mission, and they will send them on to England."

"I will, Papa." Suddenly I was overcome with a wave of homesickness. I didn't want to say good-bye to Papa. Some part of me wanted to get on that boat with him and go home to where it was safe and I knew what to expect from each day.

Papa must have seen the hesitation in my face. "I'm very glad you're staying here. Now you'll be my eyes and ears in China. We need new plants in England, and I expect you to find them. Be as careful as you can with the buds and flowers; always wrap them in damp moss. And always note your surroundings; don't just ramble about. Make sure you mark your way off the path with strips of cloth so you don't get lost. And keep notes. Lots of notes."

"Of course, Papa," I said, suddenly unable to see him through my tears.

"Hey, now," he said. "No tears, now. Just think, if you had remained at home, you might have married that dunderhead of a deacon or surely someone just as dull and witless."

I smiled. "I don't think that would have happened. Not now."

He grunted. "Well, I can't imagine any other man matching your wit and intelligence besides Alex Balashov."

The captain of the boat called out. Sailors rushed to and fro, and passengers bustled past us to climb into the boat. There wasn't much time left. I picked up Papa's bag and handed it to him. "We must say good-bye, Papa."

He took the bag and set it back down on the deck. "We have a minute, and there's something I want to say to you." Papa shuffled about, taking a goodly while to come to the point, which was making me feel anxious about what he had to say.

"I was afraid I would never be the same man again. I dreaded returning to China, dreaded going out into the world again. After I was captured I began to see only danger where once there was beauty. But now I see the world anew. I see it through your eyes, and I feel a little of my old self returning.

"That day on the ship . . . I was so harsh with you, but I understand now why you made the decision to remain hidden. I would have demanded we turn back, whatever the cost. And you were the one who saved the family, not I. If you hadn't come, I doubt I would have had the strength to leave the inn."

"You were right to want to protect me, Papa. I'm not sure I would want my sisters to see all of this pain," I said. "The people addicted to opium and those poor girls with their bound feet." I shook my head.

"This is the life of the adventurer, my dear. Sometimes you see things you don't want to see, and experience things you'll never forget, both good and bad. But that is life itself, is it not? And I know that whatever comes your way you rise up to greet it and make the best of it."

He slid his hand inside his pocket and drew something out. He took my hand and set the object in it. It was a pearl-handled pocket knife. "Mr. Darwin carried this on the *Beagle* and he gave it to me several years ago. I want you to have it."

I stared at the knife in my hand. "It's too special, Papa, I can't—"

"Don't argue. It belongs with an adventurer now, and that is you." He kissed my cheek then, picked up his bag, and stepped into the launch. I didn't want to see him leave, and so I left the quay. But in the end, I turned back and saw Papa watching me from the bow, holding his hat in his hands.

⚜ ✿ ❧ ⚜

ON MY WAY BACK DOWN THE PIER, I NOTICED A GREAT MANY Wardian cases sitting on the docks. I looked around. No one was near, so I went up to inspect the cases. A hot flush spread over me.

They were filled to bursting with Queen's Fancy orchids.

Some of the orchids were in bud, some in bloom. The plants were crammed into the cases, one on top of the other. It saddened me to see them jumbled up like that, without care, as though they were leeks headed to market to be chopped up into stews. The person who had collected the orchids had no idea how to store them, or maybe he did and simply didn't care. If only a few survived, the rarity would make them all the more sought after.

"Lovely things, ain't they?"

Startled, I jerked my head up. So intent was I on the flowers that I hadn't noticed a man had approached me—none other than Luther Duffey. I took an involuntary step back, flinching.

"Beggin' your pardon, miss. I didn't mean to frighten you." He pulled his hat off his head and bowed low. "Luther Duffey, at your service." He scratched his head with his hook. I saw up close what my knife had done to him. A deep, badly healed scar ran across his cheek. "I know me looks is off-puttin' to some. Don't often see young ladies like yourself in Foochow."

He did not recognize me. I was a different person now, both in my body and my mind. I had always been slender, but now I was leaner and stronger from riding and walking the mountains. My face was tanned from the sun, and my hands were rough from the weather.

"I was just admiring these blooms. Are they yours?" I asked.

"They belong to my employer, but I found them, as it goes. Takin' 'em back to England, where they'll sell for a pretty penny." He considered me, and I looked back, almost daring him to remember me, but not a flicker of recognition crossed his face. "You a missionary?"

"You might say so." I listened, a polite smile pasted to my face, as the orchid thief gabbled on, talking about how he'd beat another hunter to the orchids and how he wished he could have been there to see his face.

"I must take my leave, Mr. Duffey," I said. "I wish you the best of luck with your orchids." I turned to leave but then reached into my pocket. "Oh. A small gift for you. Just in case you need to prune your plants."

"Orchids don't need no pruning, miss," he said, grinning.

"Oh, I don't know about that." I handed him my billhook.

He stared at the tool in his palm, and then looked at me, recognition sparking in his eyes. His smile faded, and his mouth opened.

"I do hope you fetch that pretty penny for your flowers. Good day, Mr. Duffey."

TWENTY-SEVEN

week later, I was at Yen-Ping. As I drew closer to Pru's house, apprehension filled me. I wasn't sure what I was going to find. If Alex would welcome me.

And then I saw him. He sat outside Pru's house, sitting in a chair, sleeping in the sunshine, his arms crossed over his chest. My heart squeezed. His face no longer held that awful yellow pallor. He was a little thin, but in the fortnight I'd been away, he'd regained some of his weight already. I stood in front of him, blocking the sun, and he opened his eyes.

"*Myshka?*" He looked astonished, as though he couldn't believe I was real. He opened his mouth to say something, but I didn't give him a chance. For once in my life I wanted to say how I felt, to embrace my own emotions, no matter what.

"I'm not returning to England, Alex. My place is here. With you. Just as you belong with me. I'm sorry I thought you'd smoked the opium. You're right. I shouldn't have assumed that you had."

Alex was shaking his head. "Even though I didn't smoke it, I wanted to. I'm afraid I'll be an opium sot for the rest of my life, and I don't wish to drag you down with me. The only place I know for sure that I'll be safe is on the *Osprey*. That's the reason why I never leave the ship. I know I'll never be tempted there."

"Listen to me, Alex Balashov! Just because you wanted to return to opium doesn't mean you will. If you want to be on the *Osprey* because you love it, then I want you to go—but not because you're frightened of what will happen if you don't. I know people who've lived a moral life, who think they are doing good work, God's work, even." I thought about Deacon Wainwright, Dr. Thumpston, and the gossiping villagers when I said this. "But their actions hurt people because of the way they judge and condemn. You think a happy life is forbidden to you because of your past? Well then, in that reckoning no one deserves a happy life. I said I loved you and I meant it. I said I wouldn't leave you and I meant that, too. I don't care if you don't remember, but I do."

He stood up then. He was a little wobbly on his feet, so I stepped closer and put my arms about his waist. He was so thin I could feel his hip bones.

"Of course I remember that night," he said. "I remember every word I said, every moment. Everything I did for you was because I loved you, not because I owed you. The only place I want to be is with you." He laughed a little, a soft little murmur that went all the way through my heart. He took my hand away and lifted it, pressing his palm against mine. "We've touched each other before, but now it feels not the same."

I smiled. "No, it feels not the same at all."

And then we were in each other's arms, kissing one another as though we'd die if we tried to part, just as I imagined it.

AT THE BEGINNING OF DECEMBER, ALEX AND I WERE BACK IN Foochow to return to England on the *Osprey*. We had collected several orchids for Kew—one a pure white that smelled of vanilla that we had named "Ching Lan"—and the seedlings of an odd-looking pine. If Mr. Pringle had refused the Sister Orchid, if it wasn't worth a penny and Papa had been sent to the workhouse, then I hoped I'd be able to sell the orchids and pay the fee to release him.

There was a telegram waiting for us at the inn. From Papa.

I held the paper tightly in my hands. The answer to my family's future lay inside that envelope.

PAPHIOPEDILUM ELODIAE "SISTER ORCHID" IS
NEW FIND. PRINGLE'S CONTRACT ASKS FOR THE
QUEEN'S FANCY. KEW TO SELL ORCHID ON OUR
BEHALF. BUYERS INTERESTED AT ONE HUNDRED
GUINEAS EACH.
LOVE, PAPA

One hundred guineas for each orchid. At three hundred

orchids, it added up to a huge sum, well over thirty thousand pounds. So huge that we could pay Mr. Pringle the amount he demanded plus repay him the cost of traveling, and have plenty left over.

My family was finally free. And I was free, too.

EPILOGUE

September 1862
East India Docks, London

"Go on, Robin," Alex said.

Robin Tewkes gripped the tea chest that lay on his shoulder, grinning.

"Roundly, now," Alex said. "On my count as we pass the dock. Throw the tea chest as hard as you can."

Robin nodded, his expression earnest.

Throwing the tea chest was only a formality, because the *Osprey* had left our opponent far behind at the mouth of the Thames. The paddle wheel tug in front of us let loose a peal from its whistle, and the crowd lining the quay sent up a cheer. Captain Everett stood on the quarterdeck, his hands behind his back, seemingly oblivious to the crowd, but I caught him smiling.

Alex and I would spend the autumn and Christmas with our family, but we didn't know where we would go from there. We had heard of beautiful orchids to be found in the Sandwich Islands. But wherever we found ourselves, we would always return to Edencroft once a year. I would make that promise to my mother.

I saw Mamma and Papa coming down the dock, Violetta behind with a string of little girls holding hands and trailing after her. Kukla trotted along at their side, her sweet face turning to look at the children from time to time. My heart nearly burst when I saw Mamma looking well and happy and holding Papa's arm. As Violetta had said that fateful Christmas, perhaps the reunion wouldn't last, but I knew they were trying, and that was enough for now.

"Violetta!" I shouted.

Violetta shaded her eyes against the sun, looking up. "Sister!" She waved her entire arm back and forth like a semaphore.

I leaned over the railing of the tea clipper, watching my family, as the bow of the ship dipped and rose as it carved a path through the Thames. Water rose up to splash against the wooden mermaid who held the *Osprey* in her outstretched hand, and I felt as free as that maiden of the sea.

AUTHOR'S NOTE

Orchids

Orchids (*orchidaceae*) are considered the most highly evolved and adaptable flowering plants on earth and are thought to be over 100 million years old. Most orchids perch in trees (epiphytes); others grow on stones or in stony soil (lithophytes), or in forest or grassland soil (terrestrial). Diverse in appearance, color, scent, and size, the approximately 25,000 known orchid species are found all over the world except Antarctica—from the bogs and roadsides of America's Midwest to the hedgerows of England and the jungles of Madagascar. The tiny, dustlike seeds (the tiniest in the plant kingdom) are borne on the wind to populate areas far from the mother plant. After hurricanes, new species of orchids are found in unlikely places.

Some orchids are self-pollinated, but many rely on specific pollinators, or even one pollinator. The star orchid (*Angraecum sesquipedale*), found in Madagascar, has an eleven and a half inch nectary that hangs behind the flower. Charles Darwin predicted, based on his understanding of evolution, that a moth with an eleven-inch proboscis must have evolved alongside the star orchid. In 1907, more than twenty years after Darwin's death, a subspecies of the Congo moth, *Xanthopan morganii praedicta*, whose name means "predicted moth," was discovered with this lengthy proboscis. In 1992 the moth was observed feeding on the flower, proving Darwin correct 130 years after his prediction.

The name orchid comes from the Latin *orchis*, which means "testicle." In Victorian England, orchid collecting sparked a madness called "orchidelirium." The plants raised such passion that orchid collecting was considered improper for young ladies, although Queen Victoria was an avid collector. Unusual and rare orchids were status symbols, but no one knew how to cultivate tropical orchids, so wealthy men would send orchid hunters on expeditions to dangerous and often uncharted lands. Once the orchids were collected, the hunters would often destroy the area, so no one else would be able to collect the plant. Sometimes plants would be brought back to England and then never found again in the wild. These were called "lost orchids," and became even more collectible. Victorians were notorious for killing their orchids, having no idea how to care for them (their greenhouses, or "stoves," were too hot and humid), so collectors were the only means to new plants.

There are over 1,000 orchid (*lanhua*) species in China. The orchid, considered a symbol of spring, female beauty, and love, is one of China's "Four Noble Plants"; plum, bamboo, and chrysanthemum are the other three. The flowers are also used in tea and Chinese medicine.

Today orchids in the wild are heavily protected and it is illegal to collect and transport them without official CITES (Convention on International Trade in Endangered Species of Wild Fauna and Flora) permits. However, there are over 100,000 cultivated hybrid orchids, created through meristem cloning (using plant tissue made of cells that can grow indefinitely to produce similar cells), at all price points, available to anyone who wants to become a collector.

Plant Hunters

Plants were valuable commodities before people learned how to breed them from a mother plant (a process called propagation). The female pharaoh Hatshepsut (1508-1458 BCE) is the first known plant hunter. She brought incense trees to Egypt from her expedition of 1469 BCE. Through the ages, plant hunters have collected most of the garden plants that are common today, such as the lupine, azalea, and rhododendron. Plant hunting was a dangerous business, fraught with peril, discomfort, and failure. Hunters traveled into unfriendly territories; faced landslides and earthquakes, harassment and kidnapping by natives; contracted exotic diseases with no known cure; and battled rival plant hunters, often to the death.

Many men met a grisly end while hunting, including Scotsman David Douglas (1799-1834), who discovered the Douglas fir (*Pseudotsuga menziesii*) and hundreds of other species. While recovering from an accident in Hawaii he fell into a pit meant to catch wild cattle and was gored to death by a bull. Others drowned, fell to their death, died of tropical illnesses, were murdered by bandits, natives, or fellow plant hunters, were eaten by creatures, or simply vanished, never to be seen or heard from again. But this danger was often what drew the plant hunter to his work. Danger also thrilled his employer, who lived vicariously through the dashing plant hunter. The employers would often pit their hunters against one another, spying on each other to see what plants they were after.

Most of the plant hunters stated they were no longer able to fit into polite society when they returned. No one could understand what they went through, and yet they were expected to step back into the old society roles.

Notable plant hunters include John Tradescant the younger (1608–1662) who collected the tulip tree (*Liriodendron tulipifera*); Thomas Lobb (1818–1894) who collected the moth orchid (*Phalaenopsis amabilis dayana*); Richard Spruce (1817–1893) who collected *Cinchona* tree saplings, which were transplanted in India to fight malaria; Robert Fortune (1812–1880) who smuggled tea out of China to grow in India; and the explorers Meriwether Lewis (1774–1809) and William Clark (1770–1838) who collected flora from the Western half of the United States. The Victorian painter Marianne North (1830–1890) did not collect plants; instead she captured their likenesses. She traveled the world alone and painted plants, most of which were unknown to Europeans, right where they grew, often including their seeds, fruits, and pollinators in the paintings. She was outspoken in pointing out the damages man did to the natural world. Today, her beautiful and valuable paintings hang in an exquisitely beautiful gallery in the Royal Botanic Gardens, Kew, which she designed and paid for.

Plants are often named for, or in honor of, their discoverer—such as *Hosta fortunei* (plantain lily) for Robert Fortune; *Kniphofia northiana* (poker plant) for Marianne North; and *Dendrophylax lindenii* for the orchid hunter Jean Jules Linden.

Opium

Humankind has used opium, derived from the opium poppy (*Papaver somniferum*), for recreation, and for pain and emotional relief for over six thousand years. Considered man's first addiction, opium is both a savior and a curse—it brings relief to those in pain, and hell to those addicted to it. Addiction is not a new phenomenon, but the first widespread substance abuse began over tea.

From 1669, the English East India Company held a monopoly on the right to export tea from China to England. The Chinese would accept payment only in silver. They didn't allow English traders into the country. In 1793, the Chinese emperor Qianlong (reigned 1736–1795) proclaimed that China wanted none of England's "manufactures" and demanded that England continue to pay for tea only with silver. Such was England's appetite for tea that a major trade imbalance between the two countries had developed. That meant that China was earning a great deal of money from England but England was earning very little from China. To right this trade imbalance, England began to export more and more opium into China from India, although opium was illegal in China except for medicinal purposes. By 1799, so many Chinese were becoming addicted to smoking opium, and so much silver was leaving the country, that China outlawed the drug completely.

The East India Company of England also held a monopoly on opium. Ignoring the Chinese law, they grew and sold it in India, after which it was smuggled into China by companies such as Jardine, Matheson & Co. The Chinese destroyed the huge warehouses full of smuggled opium in 1839. England retaliated, and two wars were fought, known as the First Opium War (1839–1842) and the Second Opium War or Arrow War (1856–1860). As a result of England's victory in these wars, opium became legal in China, more Chinese ports were opened, Hong Kong was lost to England, and the interior of the country was opened for the first time to Westerners.

It hadn't taken long for opium to arrive on Western shores. It became popular as a medicine in England around 1680. Although addiction was considered shameful, there was no shame in imbibing it as a medicine. Most people took opium through liquid medicines such as laudanum, Hydrochlorate of Morphia, and chlorodyne. Because it eased the pain of menstrual cramps, child birth, and hysteria and stopped the crying of fretful babies and eased their teething pain, opium was a doctor's remedy of choice for women and babies. In the nineteenth century, unregulated "patent" medicines, purchased easily over the counter or through mail order, such as Dr. J. Collis Browne's Chlorodyne, Mrs. Winslow's Soothing Syrup, Dr. Seth Arnold's Cough Killer, and Jayne's Expectorant, flooded the market.

T. W. Bowlby

The incident that befell Elodie's father was a true event that occurred in mid-September in 1860, near the end of the Second Opium War. After England and France took Tien-Tsin, Thomas Bowlby, a journalist for *The Times*, and several others, traveled with Imperial Commissioners Wade and Parkes to Tungchow to arrange peace proceedings. A detachment of this group was captured by soldiers and taken to the Chinese Board of Punishments. There several of the men, including Bowlby, were tied hand and foot with leather bindings, which were soaked in water. As the bindings dried, they cut into the skin, causing agonizing wounds. Bowlby died on the fifth day of capture. In retaliation, the British sacked and burned the Summer Palace (*Yuanmingyuan*) in Peking, an exquisite estate created during the Qing dynasty (1644–1911).

Clipper Ships

The clipper ship was the racing ship of its day. Fast and sleek, tall and beautiful, a clipper could pay for itself in one trip. The first clippers (which take their name from their ability to "go at a clip" over the water) were developed in the United States in the 1830s to transport goods in a timely manner from China to New York and around Cape Horn to California. The British soon began creating their own design, which was very different from American ships. The British clipper was a long, slim vessel that carried a huge spread of sail on three tall masts. The shape of the ship meant it could cut through the water like a blade.

It used to take large sailing ships, called East Indiamen, up to a year to make a homeward journey, but a tea clipper could do it in around one hundred days, traveling from Fuzhou (Foochow) to London. Clipper ships would race each other home, and from 1861, shipowners offered a premium of ten shillings per ton for the winning ship. But often, clippers raced each other only for the glory of setting a record for fastest passage home.

The clipper ship boom ended in 1869 with the opening of the Suez Canal in Egypt, which connected the Mediterranean Sea to the Red Sea and cut out the journey around Africa for ships on the way to China. Clippers could not sail in the canal's waterway, and modern steamships could cut a journey in half, reaching China before the clippers. The last remaining tea clipper is the *Cutty Sark*, housed at Greenwich, England, by Royal Museums Greenwich.

Royal Botanic Gardens, Kew

Originally a residence of many monarchs, including George III and his family, the Royal Botanic Gardens, Kew, founded on the palace grounds in 1840 in the village of Richmond, became an important collection of botanical species, sending plant hunters out all over the world to retrieve plants that might prove important, financially, medically, or scientifically, for the British empire. The Palm House was built between 1844 and 1848 using 200 tons of iron and 16,000 panes of glass. No one had ever built a glasshouse like it. It was based on a ship's design—an upside-down hull—and was intended to house plants that Victorian explorers brought back from the tropics. Plants were kept in pots in the Palm House during the Victorian era. The oldest potted plant in the world, a Cycad (*Encephalartos altensteinii*), brought to Britain in 1775 by Francis Masson, Kew's first plant hunter, from a voyage with Captain Cook, still lives there today.

Kew remains the world's most important botanical institution, containing 30,000 different kinds of live plants (including orchids), seven million preserved plant specimens, a seed and DNA bank, botanical art, and garden designs of every kind from alpine to desert to rain forest. Kew employs a staff of world-renowned experts in their field. It was made a UNESCO World Heritage Site in 2003.

Tea

Tea is made from an evergreen shrub called *Camellia sinensis*, which originated in China (hence the species name *sinensis*, which means "from China" in Latin).

TEAS THE ENGLISH PREFER:

> Dark tea blends such as English Breakfast, Irish Breakfast, Earl Grey, Lady Grey, Darjeeling, oolong, Lapsang Souchong

TEAS THE CHINESE PREFER:

> Green tea, white tea, oolong (*wu-long*), *pu-erh* (an aged, fermented tea compressed into disks or bricks), gunpowder tea (*zhu cha*, which refers to the pelleted shape as green tea is rolled and dried), and *bu zhi chun* (a type of oolong produced on Mount Wuyi).

How to Make English Tea

YOU WILL NEED:

A teapot
Boiling water
Tea bags or loose tea
Milk
Sugar

Heat the teapot and cups with some of the boiling water and then discard the water. Into the pot, place one teaspoon per person plus one for the pot (if you have a four-cup teapot you'll use five teaspoons) or two teabags. Pour in the boiling water, stir once, and replace the lid. Leave to steep for three to five minutes (longer if you like strong or "builder's" tea). Pour into cups and add milk and a teaspoon of sugar, if desired. Alternatively, make a single cup with one tea bag. Add boiling water to the tea bag in the cup, let it steep for three to five minutes, remove the bag, and add milk and/or sugar.

How to Make Chinese Tea

You will need:

A Yixing teapot (small clay pot) or a *gaiwan*
   (a spoutless pot with a lid)
Chinese teacups
Loose tea
Water just under a boil (boiling water is too hot
   for green tea)

Place a handful of loose tea into the pot and pour
in the hot water. Replace the lid, leave to sit for
around a minute, and then drain off the water.
(This first steeping is to wash the tea leaves.) Add
hot water to the rinsed leaves and leave to sit
for around thirty seconds, then pour into cups.
Refill the pot one to two more times. Each drinking will yield a different taste as the tea becomes
more diluted.

There are a few rituals when drinking Chinese
tea. It's considered bad manners to allow the
spout of the teapot to point at anyone. To thank
the pourer, tap two fingers on the table. When
pouring tea for yourself, make sure you serve
others, too. And don't add anything to your tea;
enjoy the flavors on their own.

Ships Biscuits (Also Called Sea Biscuits)

Ships biscuits were the answer to how to preserve bread on a long voyage, but they often became a home for tiny beetles called weevils. Sailors tapped them on the table before eating to rid the biscuit of pests. Often softened with beer to make them edible, the biscuits were also crushed into crumbs and used as flour.

1 pound of medium to course stone-ground whole
    wheat flour
1 teaspoon of salt
Water
(Weevils optional)

Combine the flour and salt and add enough water to make a stiff dough. Let it stand for 30 minutes to allow the flour to absorb all the water, then roll out into a thick sheet. Use a biscuit cutter or a water glass to make half a dozen biscuits. Bake them at 425 degrees for 30 minutes. Them leave them out to dry and harden.

BIBLIOGRAPHY

Adams, Amanda. *Ladies of the Field: Early Women Archaeologists and Their Search for Adventure.* Vancouver, Canada: Greystone Books, 2010.

Andrews, Roy Chapman, and Yvette Borup Andrews. *Camps and Trails of China: A Narrative of Exploration, Adventure, and Sport in Little-Known China.* New York: D. Appleton and Company, 1918.

Beeton, Isabella Mary. *Beeton's Book of Household Management.* London: S.O. Beeton Publishing, 1861.

Booth, Martin. *Opium: A History.* New York: St. Martin's Griffin, 2013.

Bowlby, Thomas William. *An Account of the Last Mission and Death of Thomas William Bowlby.* Private printing, 1906.

Bradley, James. *The China Mirage: The Hidden History of American Disaster in Asia.* New York: Little, Brown & Company, 2015.

Chang, Jung. *Empress Dowager Cixi*. New York: Knopf, 2013.

Conefrey, Mick. *How to Climb Mont Blanc in a Skirt: A Handbook for the Lady Adventurer*. New York: Palgrave Macmillan, 2011.

Cordingly, David. *Seafaring Women: Adventures of Pirate Queens, Female Stowaways, and Sailors' Wives*. New York: Random House, 2001.

Darwin, Charles. *On The Origin of Species*. London: John Murray, 1859.

Doolittle, Justus. *Social Life of the Chinese*. London: Sampson Low, Son & Marston, 1865.

Elliott, Mark C. *The Manchu Way: The Eight Banners and Ethnic Identity in Late Imperial China*. Stanford, Calif.: Stanford University Press, 2001.

Flanders, Judith. *The Victorian City: Everyday Life in Dickens' London*. New York: Thomas Dunne Books, 2014.

Fry, Carolyn. *The Plant Hunters: The Adventures of the World's Greatest Botanical Explorers*. London: Andre Deutsch, 2009.

Goodman, Ruth. *How to Be a Victorian: A Dawn to Dusk Guide to Victorian Life*. New York: Liveright, 2014.

Gribbin, Mary, and John Gribbin. *Flower Hunters*. Oxford: Oxford University Press, 2008.

Hanes, Travis W. III, and Frank Sanello. *The Opium Wars: The Addiction of One Empire and the Corruption of Another*. Naperville, Ill.: Sourcebooks, 2004.

Hansen, Eric. *Orchid Fever: A Horticultural Tale of Love, Lust, and Lunacy*. New York: Vintage Books, 2000.

Hodgson, Barbara. *In the Arms of Morpheus: The Tragic History of Laudanum, Morphine, and Patent Medicines*. Buffalo, N.Y.: Firefly Books, 2001.

Johnson, Paul. *Darwin: Portrait of a Genius*. New York: Viking, 2012.

Lubbock, Basil. *The China Clippers*. Glasgow: James Brown & Son, 1914.

Macgregor, David. *The Tea Clippers: Their History and Development 1833-1875*. London: Naval Institute Press, 1972.

Merwin, Samuel. *Drugging a Nation: The Story of China and the Opium Curse*. London: Fleming H. Revell Company, 1908.

Middleton, Dorothy. *Victorian Lady Travellers*. Chicago: Academy Chicago Publishers, 1965.

Mitchell, Sally. *Victorian England: An Encyclopedia*. New York: Garland Publishing, 1988.

Murray, Janet Horowitz. *Strong Minded Women and Other Lost Voices from Nineteenth Century England*. New York: Pantheon Books, 1982.

Musgrave, Toby, and Will Musgrave. *An Empire of Plants: People and Plants that Changed the World.* London: Cassell, 2001.

Orlean, Susan. *The Orchid Thief: A True Story of Beauty and Obsession.* New York: Random House, 1998.

Perkins, Dorothy. *Encyclopedia of China: The Essential Reference to China, Its History and Culture.* New York: Checkmark Books, 1999.

Pool, Daniel. *What Jane Austen Ate and Charles Dickens Knew: From Fox Hunting to Whist—the Facts of Daily Life in Nineteenth-Century England.* New York: Simon & Schuster, 1993.

Rose, Sarah. *For All the Tea in China: How England Stole the World's Favorite Drink and Changed History.* London: Hutchinson, 2009.

Shulman, Nicola. *A Rage for Rock Gardening: The Story of Reginald Farrer, Gardener, Writer & Plant Collector.* Boston: David R. Godine, 2002.

Tsao, Lady. *The Chinese Book of Etiquette and Conduct for Women and Girls.* Translated from the Chinese by Mrs. S. L. Baldwin. New York: Eaton & Mains, 1900.

Williams, Tom. *The Complete Illustrated Guide to Chinese Medicine: A Comprehensive System for Health and Fitness.* Shaftsesbury, Dorset: Element Books, 1996.

Acknowledgments

A big thanks goes out to my editor, Leila Sales, for your gentle guidance. You always help me create the story I want to tell. And to my agent, John M. Cusick, for believing in me.

Thanks to my amazing friends who give advice, constructive criticism, and your eagle eyes: the Tale Blazers, Melissa Azarian, Terri King, and Jen Doktorski.

A huge amount of gratitude goes to my friend Jessamyn Huang for beta-reading *Orchid* and for helping me with Chinese history, language, and customs. And to my friend Sofia Del Carmen De León Maisonet for beta-reading *Orchid* and for your support. You both mean so much to me.

To my father for naming the *Osprey*. And to my mother and niece Ashley for catching some pesky mistakes and listening to me complain about story issues.

To my nephew Ethan Biggs for helping me sort out those irksome knots/nautical miles and math questions. And to my husband, Mark Waller, and friends Jeff Vargas and Doug Santiago for helping me see the guy's perspective.

To Stawell Heard, Librarian, Acquisitions and Cataloguing for Royal Museums Greenwich, who answered my queries on the Merchant Navy and clipper ships.

Thanks to my Daisy Mabel, who turned up on my doorstep, days after I wrote Kukla into life, with her exact looks and penchant for stealing food. Sometimes I wonder . . .

And as ever, thanks to my family on both sides of the pond. You are everything to me.